Seryys Chronicles: Death Wish

Joseph Nicholson

CLOCKWORK QUILLS
SCIENCE FICTION TALES

SERYYS CHRONICLES: DEATH WISH
Book One of the Seryys Chronicles

Copyright © 2012 by Joseph Noicholson
Edited by Kristin N. Hamm
Cover Copyright © 2012 by AcidKru
ISBN-13: 978-1623750152

Publisher's Note: This is a work of fiction. All characters, places, businesses, and incidents are from the author's imagination. Any resemblance to actual places, people, or events is purely coincidental. Any trademarks mentioned herein are not authorized by the trademark owners and do not in any way mean the work is sponsored by or associated with the trademark owners. Any trademarks used are specifically in a descriptive capacity.

First Edition

Visit our website: www.mquills.com

NICHOLSON

DEATH WISH

Prologue

Chang-chang-chang-chang, the hydraulic jackhammer shook the muscled arms of its user as it cut through the crete layer of the bottom level of an old skyscraper that had seen its last days well over fifty years ago. The upper levels were easy to break down after the last skirmish with the Vyysarri had demolished most of the building. Fortunately, the population was down since the building had been condemned for a long time. The only people inside were mostly homeless squatters and some local gang members who used the deep, dark innards as a spot for gambling, prostitution and worse.

Khai'Xander Khail grimaced as the he jacked his way through slab after slab of crete. The last attack from the Vyysarri had pounded through the Seryys Naval Forces in a quick and decisive strike that left the planetary navy scratching their heads and still pulling up their pants. Fortunately, before the planet wide Net'Vyyd had gone down during the attack, the navy was at least able send a message to the surface warning them of the imminent attack by Vyysarri ground forces. The anti-aircraft turrets were able to gun down a good portion of the troop-landers before they touched down.

That was until the Vyysarri capital ships punched through the defense perimeter and started their bombardment. Several high-rises crumbled to the ground, killing thousands- *tens* of thousands. Eventually, the Seryys Planetary Defensive Naval Forces, or SPDNF, finally responded and drove the invaders out. The remaining ground forces were rounded up and executed immediately-all before any real damage could be done. The Vyysarri soldiers had only killed a handful of civilians each, tossing them about like ragdolls. Khai was there for the execution. He was leaning against the wall of a dilapidated building that was brought down by Vyysarri cannon fire. Corporal Gor'Sky Gorn stood stoically, casting a long shadow behind himself- facing the setting sun- as the captured Vyysarri were stripped of their protective helmets and were then literally cooked alive. Their pale, albino skin couldn't handle the UV rays emitted by the Seryys sun.

Fucking leaches, Khai thought. *Only cowards target civilians.*

If only Corporal Gorn-a descendant of two very famous, and influential, military leaders-had pressed his troops harder into the landing zone, he could have sprung a trap amongst the rubble from the bombardment that would have stopped the invasion before it happened. It was all Khai had, to not charge in there, knock the Corporal out and take control of the situation. But he was retired, now. And he was sick of fighting-sick to his stomach of it. Still, there was something missing...

"Get back to work, Khail!" the foreman shouted. The portly, multiple-chinned foreman with a slightly upturned nose- which gave him a remarkably pig-faced appearance- stalked over to him. "You're drifting! I swear," he steamed, "the *only* reason you still have a job here is because you're a vet and I can't fire you. You're damn lucky the government compensates me for keeping you here."

Khai shook the reverie from his head and got back to work, saying nothing.

You mean, "You're lucky the government would tax the hell out of me if I fire you," Khai thought, ruefully.

DEATH WISH

Chapter One

Two weeks- and several sleepless nights- after the attack, the excavation was progressing nicely. They had cleared a huge, flat hole six hundred yards in diameter and nearly a hundred yards deep, almost fifty yards deeper than any building ever constructed. In that excavated ground, they were building a giant coliseum-style skyscraper that was also going to have the deepest foundation in history- twenty-five stories underground. It was going to house its own water treatment plant on the lowest five levels; the next five levels were going to house several state-of-the-art cinemas, where they were going to premier the latest movies and bring the hottest stars; the next ten levels were reserved for all of the employees that would work there (the company was advertising free rent for their future employees.) Before demolition even started they had over forty thousand applications to fill the five thousand jobs the skyscraper would create.

Seryys City was a sprawling megalopolis of nearly fifteen million residents and the capital of the whole planet and planetary system. The city spanned over two hundred and twenty square miles and was slightly circular in shape. The southern end, the most prominently circular, banked a large river - the "Great Rush"- named for its dangerously fast currents. The city was broken into three major sectors, Corporate, Residential and Red-Light. The Residential Sector, which housed almost the whole population for the city and the largest concentration of mom-and-pop-type shops, constituted the bulk of the area in Seryys City, from the center to the northeast corner up into Upper Seryys and Seryys Heights. Seryys Heights looked much like a large bubble that protruded northeast from the rest of the circular-shaped city and had a higher elevation than the rest of the city, hence the name. Prime Minister Pual'Kin Puar called the upscale Aurora area home, as well as several of the crème de la crème of Seryysan society. Aurora was located on the northern tip of the "bubble" that was Seryys Heights.

The southern Corporate Sector was the backbone and pumping heart of the city. It occupied a large percentage of the southernmost edge in a crescent-shaped area along the Great Rush. Most of the world's economy rode on the war machine that repelled the hated Vyysarri. Problem was, most of the purchases were coming from the government and were considered tax-free.

Just Northeast and east of the Corporate Sector sat Lower Seryys. These were considered the slums of Seryys City. Mostly gangbangers, drug dealers, and the impoverished lived there. Many of the high-society people in Seryys Heights considered Lower Seryys an "eye sore" for the whole city, and several of them at one time tried to start a petition to have it leveled to the ground and used for waste management. Prime Minister Puar shot the petition down so quickly, it barely had time to reach legislation.

The last Sector was the Red-Light District, the hopeful future of the city. A place designed for people to be able to come and have fun, to forget about the centuries-old war with the Vyysarri, and most importantly, to spend money. The driving force behind renovating the whole Red-Light District was to make some *taxable* money. Not much resided within the bounds of the RLD except for movie theaters, casinos, sports arenas and other recreational buildings; however there were some residential dwellings for people who worked in the northwest protrusion known as the RLD.

However, in the last twenty years, the city had been in a constant state of economic flux, being a main target for nearly every invasion the Vyysarri mounted. In a last-ditch effort, the government funded a huge operation to rebuild the Red-Light District and make it the grandest the planet had ever seen, starting with the mammoth casino on which Khai was currently working. It was the first prong in a multi-pronged operation to bring some revenue back into the economy by promoting some frivolous spending.

Though the initial hole for the deep foundation was nearly ready, there was still more digging to do to get ready for the water works, sewer and electrical. Khai put the chisel on the mark and started the jackhammer up. The rhythmic pounding lulled him into yet another reverie. He tried to shake himself out of it. *Damn! Forgot my pills again,* he admonished himself. It was inevitable, though. His thoughts drifted again.

Chang-chang-chang-chang-tat-tat-tat-tat-tat-tat!

"We've got inbound to my six o'clock!" Khai shouted, discharging his weapon.

"Shit!" another yelled, spinning to bear his ground-mounted, high-caliber weapon on the flanking enemy. He opened fire.

Cham, cham, cham, cham, cham, chunk-chunk-chunk, chunk. Chunk... chunk.

"The hell'd you do this time, Khai? I swear to shit, if you broke that thing, it's comin' right out of..."

His sentence trailed off as Khai pulled his jackhammer out of the six-by-six foot circular hole he had dug in the last two hours, hours that seemed to pass by in a few minutes of reverie. The usually wedge-like attachment at the end of the jackhammer was mangled and twisted beyond recognition-or repair.

"What the f...?" the foreman asked.

"What the hell happened, Khai?" another worker asked him.

"Don't know," Khai said in his gruff voice. "Just... struck something solid."

"Khai, get in there and check it out," the foreman ordered.

"Yes, sir," Khai said with a mock salute.

He climbed into the hole and was whisked back to a day long ago, when he was a pre-teen. He dropped down—no, he was *pushed*—into a hole with a fellow recruit. It was raining hard and mud was filling the hole quickly.

"Try to get out!" a burly drill sergeant shouted.

The fellow recruit in the hole with him called out to Khai for help as the mud levels rose rapidly.

"Khai? Khai? KHAI! Fuck, you're worthless!" the foreman snapped. "You forget your pills again?"

"Huh?" Khai asked in haunted voice. "Oh... yeah."

"Great," the foreman scoffed. "You're a fucking basket case, Khail. You know that?"

"You're a fucking basket case, Recruit Khail!" Drill Sergeant Moon'Sinder Moore screamed into Khai's face. Khai lost it. He charged his superior and tackled him.

"That's more like it, Recruit! Bring it!"

Khai wrapped his left hand around the sergeant's neck and brought the other back to wind up for a bludgeoning blow, when another sergeant grabbed his arm.

"That's enough, Khai!"

"That's enough Khai!" another worker said, both his hands holding back Khai's fist.

He was straddling the foreman with his left hand wrapped firmly around the terrified, wide-eyed man's throat. His green eyes were rolling back into his head. Khai immediately released his boss and stumbled back, staring at one spot on the ground, almost comatose.

"FUCK!" the fat foreman shouted as he stood, rubbing his neck and coughing. "Keep this shit up, and I don't care how much I have to pay in taxes, I'll fire you! Just like your friend, Ralm'Es Ra!"

Ralm'Es Ra was a fellow retired veteran of the military who also suffered from Post-Traumatic Stress Disorder. However, his was far worse than Khai's because an anti-personnel mine went off behind him, vaporizing the medic behind him and blowing his own arms off. He was put back together with bionics, but there was nothing they could do to repair his mind. He ended up hospitalizing a co-worker by nearly pummeling him to death on another construction site in the Corporate Sector where they were about to finish a revolutionary device that emitted an energy field around the city, much like that of a capital ship, that would protect the city from orbital bombardment and ships cutting through from within the atmosphere.

It was completed a few days prior and so far was able to withstand a test bombardment from Seryys ships. Though, the true test would be when the Vyysarri attack inevitably came. If the prototype worked, it would be the greatest invention since Eve'Zon Drive, or, "Event Horizon Drive"- the means by which a ship could travel faster than light. It created a micro black hole in space, by super-colliding atomic particles, through which a ship would fly and come out on the end at their destination.

The research was extremely dangerous and progressed painstakingly slowly at first. Thousands of naval officers and scientist's lives- as well as trillions of credits in ships, equipment, research and lawsuits- were lost in the initial test runs, but once they developed the technology to stabilize the black hole long enough for a ship to pass through, the research progressed relatively quickly. But, even at the current state of technology, controlling the most destructive force in the universe was limited. Only one ship could pass through a singularity at a time and it was still a bumpy, if not exhilarating, ride.

The next set of problems scientists faced were radiation and radiant heat produced by black holes. The initial gamma radiation spike produced at the point of creation caused hundreds of latent radiation poisoning deaths. Then the crew of the first ship to pass through a black hole, and make out the other side, was found dead, cooked to death from the heat generated by the radiant energy. This prompted scientists to develop a force field around the ship that absorbed the particles, and also by simply lining the inner hull with a six-inch layer of lead. However, a desirable effect came from the radiation as well. Scientists had no idea how to close a black hole once the ship had passed through. Radiation is an emission of atomic particles. The black hole would radiate particles until there were none left and then evaporate.

Each ship was equipped with its own Eve'Zon Drive so that multiple ships could jump at one time using their own drives in tandem; which, in the early days of Eve'Zon travel, presented its own set of problems. The gravitational forces produced by each ship's black hole would occasionally draw other ships in the fleet toward it causing ships to collide and get sucked into the same black hole at the same time. Eventually, each ship was outfitted with a gravitational inhibiter that allowed the ship to be piloted through when the crew wanted, rather than *pulled* through as soon as the singularity was created.

In the end, each multi-trillion-credit ship was equipped with an Eve'Zon Drive, a radiation shield and gravitational inhibiter. The resources required to produce, maintain and pass through a black hole, and protect the crew while doing so, were extremely taxing on a ship's power supply. A ship could only jump once every hour without draining both main and emergency power. The distance a ship could travel was limited only by the amount of power the ship generated. Some destinations took multiple jumps with a rest period between to recharge main power.

Also- aside from power consumption, the distance a ship could travel was limited by the area of the galaxy that had been explored. The navigational computer had a fail-safe that prevented a ship from jumping to an uncharted area of space, to help prevent catastrophes such as jumping into an asteroid belt, or worse, jumping into a planet and killing the entire population by creating a black hole at its center.

Exploration of the galaxy began nearly ten thousand years before the war started. Tens of thousands of ships, some were even cryogenic transports called "Sleeper Ships," roamed the galaxy, charting asteroid belts, black holes and sometimes, if a crew was lucky, a whole star system. It was a hazardous business and, sadly, some ships were lost, never to be heard from again. The government funded private organizations and, in some cases, families to take their ships out into the unknown. The government made it sound dashing and exciting to explore space, like it was some space-based Net'Vyyd. In fact, there *was* a series that ran for seven seasons. It followed the adventures of an intrepid crew of explorers aboard a starship and every week, the crew faced a new crisis on their trek across the stars. Unfortunately, the cold reality was that hundreds of ships were lost every year. Entire family lines, to the tune of six generations, were lost when ship convoys, or even one ship, would perish.

Aside from accumulating knowledge of the surrounding galaxy, the exploration initiative had other more useful applications. In one instance, a patched-up, rundown freighter with a ragtag crew of misfits discovered a star in its final stages of life. They sent an emergency subspace transmission back to Seryys with preliminary and very basic scans (as the ship simply didn't have the sensor package necessary to perform a scan with any real detail.) The supergiant star was threatening to go supernova and the shock wave would have shifted the orbit of the entire Seryys Star System which would have resulted in its annihilation. The planet's brightest minds and top researchers pooled their abilities and resources together to find a way to save their planet. As a star matures, it burns helium, which burns during the fusion process. As the helium supply wanes, the fusion goes with it. Once the helium is gone, the outward force decreases and the star's own gravitational pull causes it to collapse in on itself creating a supernova and later, a neutron star or black hole.

It took almost a hundred years, but eventually, they came up with a solution. The theory was easy: inject the dying star with more helium to burn. The application was the hard part. With the extreme temperatures, getting anything close enough to reach the core was nearly impossible. It was only with the discovery of Ti'tan'lium that they were able to develop a delivery method. The precious metal was the key; its ability to absorb massive amounts of energy was the answer to their prayers. Encasing several thousand probes with the armor would get them into the gravitational pull. Once the probes reached the core, the metal would melt and the gas would be released.

It worked.

Not only did it slow down the aging process, it actually *reversed* the process significantly. The star reverted back to a state of stability, saving the planet, the star system and many others.

Once the war started, the civilian ships were grounded for their own safety and the navy started sending out ships to chart new areas of space in an expensive and sometimes dangerous exploration operation.

But, it was a big galaxy and with a majority of the navy committed to the war effort, much of the galaxy was left unexplored. In fact, less than ten percent of the charted galaxy was charted after the war began.

The pig-faced foreman clambered into the hole and inspected the surface Khai had hit with the jackhammer. Pulling out a magnifying glass and crawling on his hands and knees over the surface, he examined it closely.

"Get our geologist over here on the double!" he shouted.

A lengthy hover ride, and forty minutes later, the geologist showed up with all his gear.

"Where the hell were you, Gor'Tsu Gorn Planet?"

"Might as well have been," the geologist scoffed. "Most of the sky lanes are down until the shield has been successfully tested. I had to stick to the surface roads."

"Whatever. Just get in the hole and tell me what that is in my way," the foreman ordered, pointing a chubby finger at the hole.

The geologist climbed down and put on a helmet with built-in microscopes and geological scanners of all kinds. Within seconds, he knew exactly what it was. Using a high-powered, ultra-fine cutting laser and extracting a small piece to be sure, he scrutinized it very closely.

"I don't believe it..." he said.

"Well? What is it?" the foreman asked impatiently. "*Hello*! What *is it*?"

Chapter Two

"Ti'tan'lium," said the Minister of Planetary Affairs, Tran'Ri Trall, a tall, lanky man of sixty-two years, whose sunken-in green eyes and gaunt features gave him a sickly look.

Ti'tan'lium was discovered during the golden age of Seryys history. The metal was discovered by accident during a mining operation that was digging for gold and silver. At first, the metal was discarded as a nuisance, as it was impossible to cut because it absorbed laser energy and was insufferably resilient, so cutting through with jackhammers and chisels simply wasn't an option, and it was ridiculously time consuming. The mere presence of Ti'tan'lium on a site could bankrupt a mining or excavation company. Places where it was discovered were marked as useless wastes of land where nothing could be built or harvested.

Roughly fifty years later, an inventor and registered genius, developed a cutting laser of high-energy that could slowly cut through the metal. He became an overnight billionaire for both developing the technique and using it to make over-priced jewelry. He could charge such high prices because of the extreme difficulty to extract and manipulate the metal. Before long, the crème de la crème were all wearing rings and bracelets of the precious metal.

The Prime Minister at that time had approached the maker of this revolutionary method because his advisors saw another application for the metal... currency. With a value of ten times what gold or platinum was worth, it had very attractive monetary value. Eventually, after several failed attempts at trying to buy the patent from him, the Prime Minister ordered a seizure of all assets and had the inventor thrown in jail to rot. Of course, the general public was told that he sold the patent, bought an island and fell of the grid. Prime Minister Puar was not proud of the things his government had done. But he was determined not to make those kinds of mistakes.

Later on, the government found another more relevant use for the metal. Given its resilience to laser energy and physical damage, it was eventually used as hull plating for warships, as ablative armor for a second line of defense after a ship's shields failed. This made Ti'tan'lium even more valuable. That was when Seryys began really exploring the stars. Being able to move through space and avoid being pulverized by a meteor, or being able to get detailed sensor readings of a sun from within its corona doubled the efficiency of the navy to chart the galaxy.

"What?" Prime Minister Pual'Kin Puar asked. "Are you sure?"

"Yes, Prime Minister. Department of Planetary Agriculture and Geology confirms it."

"The entire city?"

"That's right," Trall said dryly.

"How did something like this go unnoticed for so long?"

"I can tell you that, sir," said a young man, thirty-something years old, with black hair parted on the left side, lean, roughly five and a half feet tall, wearing the clothes of a professional, pressed trousers and a shirt of black with a high collar. It was nothing fancy, nothing like what the Prime Minister wore.

"Prime Minister, may I present Sam'Ule San, Director of D-PAG."

"Pleasure, sir," Prime Minister Puar said, standing to his full height of six and a half feet and extending his muscular hand in greeting. "Please, proceed," he said, his pale green eyes beneath groomed eyebrows met the young man's calm blue eyes.

A holographic image of Seryys City was hanging in the middle of the room. It was an over-head image taken by satellite. With the press of button on a laser pointer, the image rotated ninety degrees on its y-axis to reveal a three-dimensional side view of the city. The image also included points of interest beneath the ground, like watersheds, sewer systems and superstructures. Considerably lower than any watershed or basement was a pulsating blue section. Only one spot on the map showed a point where something reached the depth of the pulsating blue section of the underground map.

"As you can see here, Prime Minister, this slab of Ti'tan'lium is far below any structure in the city and was never touched-"

"Until now," the Prime Minister interrupted.

"Yes, sir." San agreed. "The sheer size of the casino demanded a superstructure bigger and deeper than any building in recorded history."

"Surely, you can't expect me to believe that this whole time we've been sitting on top of the biggest vein of Ti'tan'lium in Seryys history."

Ti'tan'lium was forged much the same way gold was. The only real difference being that the veins developed horizontally rather than vertically, forming "plates" of ore between sections of crust. It was public knowledge that Seryys was mined completely out of Ti'tan'lium; the Naval Corps of Engineers were mining other uninhabited worlds to feed the ever growing military demand for the metal.

"Seryys city has stood for over a millennium, sir. We simply didn't have the technology back then to detect such a large deposit. Hell, we didn't even know what Ti'tan'lium was until a thousand years ago."

He was right. *Smart kid,* Prime Minster Puar thought.

"So, what do we do?" Puar asked the young director.

"Well, nothing," he said very matter-of-factly. "To mine it would be to destroy the whole city."

"I see," Puar said, leaning back in his seat in an almost defeated posture. "There's no way to tunnel to it from the east, here?" Puar clicked a button on his desk and the map zoomed out to reveal a cliff ten miles to the east Seryys City. "Kal'Hoom Karr Canyon could make a very good staging point."

"It's not a matter of how to approach it," San said. "It has everything to do with size of the plate. To excavate that much material from under the city would cause the whole city to collapse into the ground."

"Can we relocate the city?" Trall chimed in.

"Relocate the city? Are you crazy?" the director asked. "You're talking more money to rebuild the city than the worth of what's down there."

"Indeed." Trall said.

"Besides," Puar said, "aside from the physical impossibility of relocation, the council would never go with it. I couldn't even begin to think of all the red tape involved with something like that. I would be buried in paperwork for years—no *decades.*" Puar leaned forward and leaned on his elbows. "That's why I still prefer combat to politics. No committees, no councils, just you and your enemy. No rules. Kill or be killed."

Prime Minister Pual'Kin Puar had been in his position for two terms of a maximum four-term presidency. Each term was five years long. He was hugely popular among the people and was highly regarded, respected and admired by the military as he was the first retired war veteran to serve in office. He was highly decorated in his lifetime career in the SCGF (Seryys Combat Ground Forces). Now, at the age of seventy-eight, he was still an active man—far too busy to ever marry. He was tall, dashing and still muscle-bound after all these years with a graying goatee and military-style haircut. He was less than two-thirds through his life, as most Seryysans lived to be roughly a hundred and twenty-five years old.

Suddenly a klaxon filled the air and red lights started flashing around the Honorifical Office.

"Finally!" Puar barked.

"What?" San asked.

"The Vyysarri are attacking," Trall said.

"We can finally see if our new line of defense works."

"Oh, the new shield!" San said with sudden realization.

From the Honorifical Office, the three watched the battle's progress on a holomonitor in the center of the room where the map of Seryys City had been floating. A Vyysarri capital ship, a fierce-looking battle cruiser which was comprised of two elongated, wedge-shaped hulls with sharp angles, bristled with cannons, mounted side-by-side like wings on top of a larger elongated wedge-shaped hull with a curved stern that housed powerful sub-light engines, a *Fang*-Class destroyer, broke the line and commenced fire on the planet. The cannons unleashed hell, the shield shimmered as the energy was absorbed and shunted to the energy collectors lined around the parameter of the city and stored for future use in powering the shield.

From the streets, people dazzled at the spectacle as if it was a fireworks display. There was cheering and clapping as people flooded the streets to see the marvel at work. To not have to cower in designated bunkers during an attack was a blessing the residents of Seryys City rarely enjoyed. The fireworks were punctuated by blossoms in the sky high above the shield, as giant titans winked out of existence in the blink of an eye.

"Admiral! The drop ships are debarking!" a young tactical officer announced.

Let's hope that shield holds. "Focus the cannons on them!"

"Aye, sir."

The cannons on a Seryys *Dagger*-Class dreadnaught, a standard warship shaped much like the ships of old that used to sail the seas of Seryys, blasted away at the drop ships. The *Dagger*-Class dreadnaught was over a thousand feet long and two hundred feet wide. The belly of the ship was curved with a flatter top and the gunwale of the ship was lined with cannons. Where the mast should have been, the bridge, com tower, sensor array and shield generator sat. The deck of the ship was a runway for smaller dogfighters. The aft of the ship curved inward like a boomerang and housed the ship's propulsion.

The battle was going well. With the shield up and holding, the navy was able to focus on shooting them down, rather than trying to shoot them down all the while maneuvering themselves between the Vyysarri gun boats and Seryys. The same scene was playing out for hundreds of Seryysan ships in orbit over Seryys City.

Once the Vyysarri realized that they couldn't punch through the shield, and all their drop ships were reduced to debris, they cut their losses and retreated in a hurry. Cheering rang through the ship and com channel as the first major victory was won against a hostile, brutally violent adversary.

"I would say that was successful test," Trall said almost casually.

"Yes, I agree!" Puar said very happily. "Not a single civilian was killed."

"Congratulations, Prime Minister." San said with a smile and hearty handshake.

"Thank you." he beamed with pride, like the father of a kid who scored the winning goal at the buzzer. "Thank you very much. Now, would you like to continue our conversation?"

"Uh, no, thank you. Watching that battle wore me out. I think I should retire, but thank you for your audience and I will leave the technical details with Minister Trall for you to review at your earliest convenience."

"Again, Director, you have my thanks. Good evening."

"Prime Minister," San said cordially with a slight dip of the head.

He took one last look upward through the skylights in the office and strolled out to the lift car.

Khai strode through a large alley, his fists balled up ready for a fight... possibly the fight of his life. He could hear footsteps behind him, heavy ones. Suddenly, he realized that he could not win this fight- not by a long shot. So he did the only thing he could... hide. He wriggled in between two giant trash receptacles and tried his best not to breathe. He shook uncontrollably. Whether it was the cool, winter night of the Seryys Slums or the sheer terror he felt, he couldn't tell. What he knew at that point was that he was going to die that night and there was nothing he could do about it.

His father would have saved him, had he still been alive. He was dead, killed by a burglar who was simply looking for money to get his fix a few years ago. Now, without his father, Khai roamed the streets, sifting through garbage for food and discarded clothes; collecting useless trinkets he could use to barter for other things he needed.

So there he was, cowering from a stranger who was most likely going to kill him or worse... The giant boots stalked past, clumping with every step. They paused. Then, they started stalking down the street again. Khai let out a whimpering sigh of relief. He dared not move. Instead, he gathered whatever filth there was around and bundled up to stay warm. His little, watery eyes began to grow heavier and heavier. His eyes were about to close.

A giant hand wrapped around his neck. He yelped in pain and terror as the hand yanked him out from between the bins. Little Khai'Xander Khail kicked and cried as the hand held him by the back of his neck. An evil giggle clucked up from the man's belly as he shook the boy violently.

"Hold still, you little shit, or this is gonna hurt even more," he said with a high-pitched voice.

The man reached for the boy with his other hand to do who-knows-what.

"Hey!" a deep, commanding voice shouted, stopping the man from his dark deeds.

He dropped little Khai. He hit the ground with a thud.

Khai sat up in his soaked sheets, his heart pounding and sweat dripping down his face, chest and back. His chest heaved deep breaths as he swung his feet around and planted them on the cool, hardwood floor beneath his bed. The floor thumped under his feet and he rolled his eyes as an elderly voice shouted at him.

"Hey! Keep it down! I'm trying to sleep, damn it!"

"You and me both, pal," Khai growled.

Rubbing the back of his neck, he zombie-walked to the bathroom. The door hissed open and a dull light turned on, casting a soft glow over the sink. He dipped his hands into the sink and cold water automatically poured into them, cupped together. Khai splashed it on his face; the cool stream crept comfortably down his chest and back and all the way to his feet where it pooled on the floor.

Taking a good look at his doppelganger in the mirror, his cold, gray eyes stared back at him above prominent cheek bones and below an even more prominent brow. He took another dip from the sink and ran the cool water on his fingers over his military-style buzzed head, which was already mostly gray, but had some flecks of brown still left. As the water slowly dripped down, it paused on a large scar that ran horizontally over his left eyebrow, one of many wounds he sustained over his years of service. *Now* there's *the nightmare*, he said silently to himself. Though he was only forty-six years old—not even midlife by Seryysan standards—he looked old and haggard from the hard life he had lived. Sometimes, he was mistaken for someone twice his age.

He was still in top physical shape, though. Muscled from neck to feet, he was the epitome of military physique. On Seryys, it was harder for him to keep his strength up to what it used to be—which is why he chose a job of hard labor. A man of his background was naturally—or *un*naturally, depending on whom you asked—stronger than most people his age, and was a viable threat well into his eighties.

On his left arm just above his bicep, was a tattoo. His entire platoon got the same one. It was a picture of crossing swords behind the roaring face of a Seryysan Panther with "SCGF" in script over the top and "109" beneath it. He was part of the 109th Mobile Infantry Division of the Seryys Combat Ground Forces. After his mandatory five-year term of service, he stayed on for an additional twenty years to fight the hated Vyysarri.

Khai pressed and held his finger on a hidden button next to the mirror. A little chime dinged and then the sound of whirring servos filled the bathroom. The mirror slid back and to the left into the wall, revealing a secret compartment within. He reached in and pulled out his service sidearm, a high-caliber pistol with hundreds of notches in sets of five along the barrel and grip. These notches didn't necessarily denote kills as much as it did kills by headshots from that gun.

That gun held more meaning to him than any trinket or Medal of Honor he had ever been awarded. It was proof that he was good at what he did... what he used to do. Now, he was just a lonely construction worker whose friends were dead, killed in an ongoing, bloody and costly war. After holding the familiar and oddly comforting weight of that weapon for a while, he re-engaged the safety and put it back. The mirror slid back into place and he left the bathroom, completely forgetting that the whole reason he went in there to begin with was to take his pills.

Khai was lying in bed, his hands behind his head, staring at the ceiling. He could remember the day he was saved by the man he would admire for decades to come.

It started that same night.

"Hey!" that same deep voice called out. The impact from being dropped made the alley spin abruptly. He could hear the heavy boots running off further into the darkness of the alley. Before even being picked up, a voice called out to him:

"You okay, son?"

"Yeah, I think so."

"Good. You wait here, I'll be right back."

Khai's savior darted into the darkness. Only seconds later, he heard shouting and what sounded like a man crying. A little more than a minute later, the hero emerged from the darkness with the man that chased him down the alley. His face was bloody and swollen; he was hacking up blood all over the ground as he was tossed at Khai's feet.

"What do you have to say?" the hero asked.

Khai was about to respond, thinking the question was directed at him, when the bloodied man cried out.

"I'm sorry!" he sobbed.

"What?" the hero asked again.

"I'm SORRY!" he wailed. "Please, don't kill me!"

"I'm not going to kill you, you piece of shit," the hero said with a slight hint of amusement in his voice. "You're not a Vyysarri. Now get the fuck out of here, and keep your damned hands off these kids, for Founders help you if I catch you again."

"I will," he cried, as the hero dragged him to his feet by the back of his filthy shirt with one hand. "I swear to the Founders!"

"Good, now get the hell out of here!" he said, tossing the whimpering man back into the dark with the strength of two or three men.

Once he was thoroughly convinced that the cry baby was gone, he turned back to Khai who was still sitting on his bruised backside.

The man was tall, roughly six and half feet tall, wearing a long coat with shiny pins on it. He knelt down to Khai's level.

"Are you all right, son?"

Khai felt no fear, only calm and safety.

"I'm fine," he said quietly.

"So you *do* talk," the huge man chuckled. "I thought for sure you were a mute."

"Actually, I talk a lot. Some people can't get me to shut up. Like the really nice lady in the diner down the street. She gives me free pie whenever I come in and we'll just talk and talk and talk."

"You like pie?"

"Yup," Khai said with a smile.

"Good, me too. Let's go to that diner. Do you know where it is?"

"Well, yeah," Khai said with an over-dramatic roll of his eyes. "Follow me."

It only took a few minutes to walk to the local diner. The lights were on and there were definitely people inside. The hero didn't recognize it, but he lived in the Corporate Sector near the military barracks.

They walked in and the lady, a younger woman, said hello to Khai right away.

"Hi, Joon," Khai said innocently.

"Who's your friend?" she asked, rather suspiciously.

"He's a hero," he said cheerfully. "He saved my life from that one creepy guy I told you about. You know; the one with the high-pitched laugh."

"I know the one," she said, less cheerfully. "My name's Joon. I haven't seen you 'round these parts."

"I don't come down this way much, but my name is Moon'Sinder Moore. And, uh, can I have two slices of pie please?"

"Sure thing. I swear that's all that kid eats," Joon said, turning to the cooling unit where the pies were stored.

"Where are his parents?" Moon asked.

Joon paused before putting the two plates down on the counter. "Don't know, to be honest. About a year ago, he just started coming in here alone and I would give him a piece of pie and take it out of my tips. The poor boy eats so fast it's like he doesn't eat otherwise."

"I found him cowering from a sexual predator between a couple trash recepts," Moon said. "Is he an-"

"Orphan?" Joon asked, almost accusingly.

"Yeah?"

"What if he was?" she asked defensively, sliding two pieces of pie onto the plates.

"You know why." Moon said, his voice almost pleading. "All orphans become wards of the state. Please, don't lie to me. Is he an orphan?"

"Yes," she said sadly. "His father was killed a while ago."

"Why didn't you take him in?"

"I already have four children and their father ran out on me. I couldn't afford to put another plate on the dinner table. I already work two jobs just to make sure they have what they need."

"You're a good mother," Moon said.

She turned to face him with two pieces of pie. It was obvious to him that it pained her not to be able to take the poor boy in.

"Thank you," she said, wiping a tear away. "Anyway, the pie's on me."

"No," Moon said. "Here, this should help feed your children." He dropped a wad of credit bills wrapped in an elastic band.

"You don't have to do that," she said, staring at more money than she made in two weeks.

"I know," he said softly. "But it's my duty to protect to the civilians of this planet, in any way I can. Besides, I have no need for money. The SCGF provides me with everything I need."

"Are you going to take him?"

"I have to," he said. "He will be cared for, fed, clothed, educated-"

"Trained to kill," she said, disdain filling her voice.

"Trained to protect this planet," he corrected her. "Would you prefer if we took *your* children from you?"

"No," she said, dropping her gaze to the counter, at the two pieces of pie.

"We take those with nothing, and give something; something to help them live a productive life, something to live for, to believe in. We give them hope. All the while, keeping the planet safe from the Vyysarri and keeping your children out of the war."

He was right, she knew it. But it didn't hurt any less. She had grown quite fond of little Khai.

"Enjoy your pie," she said and left.

Two days later, Khai and Moon arrived on Gor'Tsu Gorn, a planet named after the Naval Admiral who had discovered it two centuries earlier. The planet was three times bigger in diameter than Seryys, which meant that the pull of gravity was equally stronger than that on Seryys. The transition from Seryys gravity to Gorn gravity was enough to make Khai cry for days. But it was necessary to endure such pain. As their enemy, the Vyysarri, were superior in every physical way.

Compared to the average Seryysan, an average Vyysarri was two-to-three times stronger, faster and tougher. It took several slugs to bring a Vyysarri down and going toe-to-toe with one was inviting certain and painful death as they fed on the blood of their adversaries.

Though, there was nothing that could be done about the hardiness of Seryysans—short of giving them the best armor money could buy, there was something they *could* do about the other attributes, which was where Gorn became an essential part of military training. Putting them on a planet with such gravity forced their bodies to adapt, to weave tighter, more efficient muscle mass. A trained soldier in the SCGF was a lethal weapon from head to toe.

The sun in the Gorn System, and the planet's distance from that sun, was much like that of Seryys, which made Gorn a prime place to emplace Fort Gor'Dyyn Gorn, the namesake of the general who moved the indigenous species off the planet in a quick and decisive attack, and the son of Admiral Gorn. Though that was a darker chapter in Seryys history, most historians looked at it as a necessary evil in the cause of repelling, and one day, defeating the Vyysarri. The whole planet had its own economy and was self-sufficient. The soldiers had part-time night jobs to earn military credit, which was useless anywhere else. Credit was used to buy privileges, such as shore leave, entertainment and "special" visits. However, the essentials: food, clothes, housing, medical attention and household supplies were provided by the military.

Most of their time was spent in training, though. They endured long, grueling days of physical, mental and psychological trials and, in some cases, were deprived of sleep to push them to their limits. They had to be tough as nails to fight the Vyysarri.

Orphans were the primary source of enrollment, though there were those who chose to enlist at the age of consent, which was fifteen years. The orphans that were found earlier than that lived on base with a drill sergeant, who was responsible for up to ten children. They spent most of their days in school. There, they got the best education money could buy. Far superior to the public schools on Seryys available to civilians, these future soldiers received more-than-basic training in math, science, music, art, history, politics and social studies. But they also received advanced combat training for melee, hand-to-hand and firearms, military tactics and they also had access to optional ship-to-ship combat training (both in capital ships and dogfighters), theoretical science, quantum physics and general maintenance of military equipment from guns, to tanks, to capital ships.

Once they reached the age of consent, they were sent out into the field to implement their newly acquired knowledge and skills.

Khai lived on base with Sergeant Moore, who cared for him, both physically and emotionally. Moon was a tough soldier and even tougher drill sergeant. But he cared deeply for the kids under his command and would do virtually anything for them; even die for them, if it meant their survival. However, out on the training field, he was as impartial as they came. He pushed his kids just as hard as the others and produced some of the best trainees the SCGF had to offer, Khai included. Khai loved Moon as a father.

He was seventeen when the Vyysarri attacked Gorn Base. He and the other recruits were escorted to a bunker. The air raid sirens blared in his ears.

Suddenly, he realized it wasn't the air raid sirens, it was his alarm clock. It was time to get up and go back to work. *Damn, forgot the pills again.* This time, on his way out, he grabbed the bottle and popped two pills down the hatch with a full glass of water.

Chapter Three

"It's not an option," Prime Minister Puar said, putting his foot down. "The amount of money it would cost to relocate the entire population of Seryys City would cost more than the money we would make off of the Ti'tan'lium. Director San already said that and I agree with that assessment."

"It's not about the cost, Prime Minister. It's about the material beneath the city and what it can do for us in the war effort. Isn't that worth it, an end to the war?"

"This wouldn't *end* the war, Tran. You know that as well as I do."

"Can you really risk it?" Trall asked.

"More civilians will die in the relocation than in the last ten years of the war."

"That slab of ore can provide armor for almost twelve capital ships."

"I understand that, Tran, but I'm still not signing *anything* condoning a relocation, plain and simple."

"I think you're mistaken, Prime Minister."

"Duly noted. Now if you'll excuse me, I have an appointment in the Rec Room."

Tran'Ri Trall stormed out, fists balled in anger. How could the Prime Minister be so blind? *That arrogant fool,* he fumed. It took the whole lift car ride down for him to calm down. After all, he was the Prime Minister and he does have the peoples' best interests at heart. *This isn't a resignation,* Trall thought to himself. *He'll come around, once he sees the necessity of my idea.*

He exited the lift car and headed for his waiting hover car, stretched and luxurious with tinted windows and a glossy, jet-black finish. Once inside, he stretched his legs and barked an order to the serving computer, which chirped its compliance and poured his favorite alcoholic beverage on ice into a waiting glass beneath the nozzle.

After the large gulp of burning liquid cascaded down the back of his throat, he leaned back in his chair. *Now, how do I force his hand?*

Khai set his glass down after taking his pills. He was watching the Net'Vyyd and the news was showing a riot in the slums of the Residential Sector, the camera panned all the way around, taking in the destruction that had taken place only moments earlier. The reporter was standing with his back to the riot several blocks away and moving further away in that direction. The riots had been going on for several weeks since he discovered the deposit of Ti'tan'lium under the new casino. Construction had been halted until the government could decide what to do about it. So while the construction was stopped, he was on paid leave until they either resumed construction on the casino, or the company got another job. His discovery was big news for a while, but now these gang-led riots were tearing up the slums and threatening to move out farther than that.

The police were losing miserably. And they were losing ground faster than they could kill the gang members. These gangs, almost overnight, seemed to arm themselves with high-end sophisticated weaponry—military grade even—which should have been unquestionably and impossibly out of their price range. Yet somehow these thugs were wielding these weapons and effectively making minced meat out of the outgunned police. And even more bizarre, was that the military wasn't getting involved.

The new energy shield was definitely doing its job; the Vyysarri weren't getting through to the city. With the shield operational, the defense navy could focus on the drop ships and then watch the Vyysarri retreat to regroup.

Another reporter was showing hundreds of people fleeing the slums for the forests and prairies outside the city where they were setting up little tent communities and sharing whatever they had with each other. Khai saw children wearing dirty clothes and running through a small stream where people were washing what clothes they had. For the big tough guy Khai was, his heart broke for those families.

This had to stop. At that moment, he knew what he had to do. He picked up his com unit and called his boss, Captain Pig-face.

"Khail," he growled. "What the hell do *you* want?"

"To make your life a little easier," he said back.

"Oh yeah?" he asked, obviously amused. "How the hell are you going to do that?"

"I quit."

"What?"

"I quit, you worthless, annoying, fat-assed sack of shit-eating beetles."

"Why you-"

Khai wasn't going to listen to him anymore. He disconnected the call and felt a million times better.

The next day, he marched down to the police department and handed the man at the front desk an application.

"I'm sorry, we're not hiring," he said curtly, not even looking up at him.

"Have you been watching the news?" Khai asked him.

"Yes," he said, still looking down at what he was doing.

"Hey!" Khai snapped, slapping his open hand down on the counter. "Look at me when I'm talking to you! You guys are getting steamrolled out there. Looks to me like you could use all the help you can get."

"Fine," he said, standing up and directing his bored, lazy eyes in his direction. "I'll give it to the cap', see what he says. Can I get your name?"

"Khai'Xander Khail."

The man stopped in mid stride. "*The* Khai'Xander Khail?"

"Unless you know another one," he said with a shrug.

"Why are you here?"

"Are you stupid or deaf? I'm here to help. Those thugs are tearing apart this city and driving good people from their homes; people that I put my life on the line for every single day that I was in the SCGF. You need me."

"Let me go talk to the cap'."

Several minutes later, an older man, maybe in his nineties, waddled out of the back office. He was tall, almost six feet and was completely gray, both in his beard and what was left on his head. He wore an expression of almost awe on his face.

"The legendary Khai'Xander Khail."

"In the flesh."

"Indeed," the captain said with a smile. "You're really here to help?"

"Are you refusing?"

"No," the captain said, "Your reputation as the hero of Seryys Four is known throughout the system. "

"I just killed the Vyysarri general of the invading army on Seryys Four. The real victory came from everyone working together."

"Don't be modest, Khai," the captain said. "The quickest way to kill a Northern Bloodslug is to cut off its head."

"True," Khai said. "So when can I start?"

"You can start by addressing me as 'Sir,' recruit."

"Yes, sir!" Khai shouted, snapping a crisp salute and clicking his heels.

Captain Byyn'Doox Byyner forced a stern look. "At ease, soldier. This isn't the military, just local law enforcement."

"You got it, sir."

The next day, Khai woke up and sauntered over to the bathroom. He popped two pills with a glass of water and accessed the secret hatch behind the mirror. He took the pistol, A Seryys Combat 92-30:11-1 Assault Pistol (92 being the year it was made, 30 being the number of its series, 11 being its overall length in inches and 1 was the diameter of the shells it used, in inches). It was considered an antique by today's standards, being the year 13241—since Seryys became a space-faring race again. The high caliber and elongated barrel gave this weapon remarkable accuracy, distance and destructive power. The weight of the weapon felt all too familiar, and he liked it, missed it.

"Well, old friend, looks like it's time to go back to work."

He sat it down on the sink while he prepped himself for his first day of active duty in ten years. Being a man of about fifty years of age put him still in his prime. It wasn't his physical shape that put him out of the active duty with the SCGF, but his psychological status. He was suffering from severe Post-Traumatic Stress Disorder. He was medicated and it was controlled; but if he forgot to take his pills daily, he would lapse back into his days of being shot at and killing. It was something he would keep from Captain Byyner as long as he could. He hated being labeled as mentally unfit for duty; it was like having a gun without a firing pin.

He stood in front of the mirror, giving himself a once-over. He was wearing the blue uniform of a Seryys City Peace Officer, complete with a flak jacket, wrist restraints and utility belt. He holstered his beloved weapon and walked out the door.

It only took him a few minutes to get to the station. He walked in through the sliding door into a group of people who were standing in awe of the living legend who had just entered the building. After a few moments of hero worship, Captain Byyner came out and broke it up.

"All right, all right. We all know who this is, he clearly needs no introduction. However, he doesn't know any of you."

"Khai, this is the Seryys City Anti-Terrorism Team, or SCATT. Your commanding officer is Captain Dack'Tandy Dah. Your demolitions expert is Pual'Branen Puar-"

"Hey are you?" Khai interrupted to ask.

"Yes, he's my older brother."

"He's a good man. We fought side-by-side in many battles—including Seryys Four—I am honored to work with anyone from his family."

Dack'Tandy Dah was about the same height as Khai, same build too. His hazel eyes were cold and hard, his hair was black as night in the country, slicked back and he had a five o'clock shadow.

Puar was a spitting image of his older brother Prime Minister Pual'Kin Puar. Had they been born on the same day, one would have thought that they were twins. The only difference between the two was that Pual'Kin was brought up on Gor'Tsu Gorn Planet and was built like someone who was raised on a planet with a higher gravitational pull. Pual'Branen was still built and strong by Seryys standards but nothing like his brother.

The captain went on. "The other three are just good at shooting things. They're Koon, Naad and Brix."

Koon was a skinny toothpick with dark hair and eyes. He wore a cocky grin on his face at all times. Naad was of average height and build, his skin was a dark mocha and so were his eyes. Brix was a hulking man that rivaled Khai and Dah in size and almost in strength. He had blonde hair and green eyes that looked like nobody was home.

"Now everyone, this is *Colonel* Khai'Xander Khail."

"It's not Colonel anymore—technically, anyway, I'm a civilian now. Just call me Khai."

"You got it," Koon said.

"Now, quit your lollygagging! We work for a living here. Get suited up and ready to go. The slums are still burning and the gangs are in control. We have officers trying to contain the gangs twenty-four hours a day but we're losing ground. We're going to airlift you guys behind them and I want you to sneak up on them and kill every... last... one of them."

"Deadly force?"

"Extreme prejudice. Minster Trall gave me the order directly. Now that's not a charge card to go hog wild. We need to keep collateral damage to a minimum."

"Hey, Cap', it's us you're talking to," Puar said.

"That's why I felt compelled to say something," Byyner said, deadpan. "Now the chopper is waiting, get going!"

They filed into the backroom where the lockers were located. They suited up into their riot gear and brandished their own favorite weapons.

The captain favored a Seryys Combat Full-Auto, 23-10:25-.75, it was a standard military-grade machine gun that all soldiers were trained on. Khai's first weapon proficiency and expert status was on a 23-10.

"Were you in the SCGF?" Khai asked him.

"Did my five years and called it quits. I felt I could make a bigger difference planet-side, rather than on distant worlds."

"It's definitely not for everybody," Khai admitted.

"Why'd you retire?" Captain Dah asked.

Khai's stomach knotted up. "Got tired of killing Vyysarri and watching my friends, who I grew up with, die." It was the truth, just not the whole truth.

"That's it? I thought you hardened war vets didn't mind the violent lifestyle."

Khai took a breath to spout out a lie when Puar interrupted. "Hey! Is that a 92-30 series?"

"Sure is," Khai said, pulling it from its thigh holster and handing it over to Puar. "Your brother was big fan of this weapon, too."

"Man, they don't make 'em like this anymore," Puar marveled, feeling the weight. "How many in the clip?"

"It's an extended mag; ten in clip, one in the chamber," Khai explained, taking the gun back and putting in its holster.

"That's a sweet gun," Naad said. "But don't you need a main weapon? I mean, that's great for a sidearm and all..." he trailed the sentence off when he got an intimidating glare from Khai.

"It's all I need," Khai said seriously. "Now, what are you packing?"

"These babies." From two thigh holsters, he brandished a pair of Seryys Combat Super-Auto submachine guns. "These are 21-120 series. In fact, they're 121 and 122:10-.50s. Got 'em as a package deal."

"Are you accurate with them?" Khai asked.

"No need to accurate when you're firing ten rounds a second, baby!" Naad laughed, his brown eyes sparkling and crow's feet forming in the dark skin at the corners of his eyes.

"Those are nice popguns!" Koon said. "You want a good weapon that takes skill *and accuracy*? Check this out!" He tossed his weapon to Khai.

Khai caught it but knew exactly what it was before it was even thrown. He was an expert on this weapon as well. "It's a Seryys Combat Semi-Auto 31-54:35-1 Pro with a ten-ex zoom, electronic scope. I got one just like it in my storage unit; only its number is 31-1."

"The prototype?"

"You got it," Khai grinned. "How about you Puar? I know you all want to show off your toys, and you started this whole conversation, so let's see it."

Puar's eyes widened and he grinned. "This is my baby, a Seryys Combat 35-130:12-2.5, Grenade Launcher. I make things go boom."

"How about you, Brix?" Khai asked.

"You'll just have to wait and see once we're out there."

"Ooh," Khai said, rubbing his hands together. "The suspense is killing me."

They all laughed as they marched up the stairwell to the roof access point where their chopper was waiting. It was dual-propeller chopper, one on either side like wings, with an afterburner good for speedy evacs and surprise attacks.

They filed in and buckled up. Just as Khai fastened his restraints, the pilot howled a war cry and kicked in the afterburners once the chopper was less than a foot off the landing pad. The pilot swooped low between skyscrapers and under pedestrian bridges. At one point, he went almost belly up and skimmed the side of a building so close Khai could have reach down and touched the glass of the windows.

"Okay!" the pilot shouted. "Hang onto your hats!"

The pilot yanked back on the yoke and sent the chopper into an almost vertical climb and then dove down. Khai, sitting forward, could see the ground looming up and a crowd of angry rioters and gangbangers firing at an overwhelmed group of officers. Suddenly, the co-pilot opened fire with a high-caliber chain gun on the rioters, mowing them down.

The pilot pulled up at the last minute, so late into the dive that the wind force from the chopper blades knocked many of the gangbangers down.

The ones that didn't get mowed down by the first, and apparently only diving attack, were left for Khai and his fellow soldiers to clean up. This mob of people was only a fraction of what was going on all over Lower Seryys; this particular riot was threatening to move south into the Corporate Sector, which could have catastrophic consequences.

The chopper swooped about and hovered 20 feet off the road between two vandalized apartment complexes. Khai and Captain Dah simply leapt from the chopper, while the others repelled by rope to the road. Finally, Brix unzipped the bag in which his gun was stored. He flipped the strap over his head and popped the two clips in.

"Now that's a gun!" Puar said.

"It's a-" Brix was about to say.

"Seryys Combat Full-Auto 23-2:30-.75 Special with Dual Magazines and a bandoleer attachment," Khai interrupted. "I've trained on that weapon, too."

The gun had two magazines secured to the lower forearm, protruding downward at a forty-five degree angle. From the front, it looked like an upside-down "V". The gun was actually illegal, but the police force pulled some strings to allow him to have it.

"All right, ladies," the captain said. "We've got forty blocks to huff and then a tough fight. Let's get this over with and get our paychecks."

"So what's the plan?" Khai asked.

"Minister Trall suggested a surprise attack from behind. Catch them off guard."

"Are you serious?"

"Yeah. Why?" the captain asked with an angry tone.

"That's not going to work in the slightest. We won't take them by surprise, you know that."

"But that's what Trall-"

"To hell with what Trall said! I don't know him, but he's clearly an idiot," Khai spat out.

"Okay," Dah said, "What's *your* idea?"

"We take the alleys, get ahead of them. Then we take up firing positions in the abandoned buildings on both sides and rain bullets as they pass."

"That's text book," Captain Dah said.

"The only way to be," Khai replied.

They ran twenty blocks and then split up, ducking into the darkness of the alleys and covered the rest of the distance. From ten blocks out, they could hear the gunfire and shouting. Koon and Puar went with Khai on the north side of the street, while Captain Dah, Naad and Brix took the south side. They worked their way five blocks past the crowd and, by radio, signaled for a stop. They entered the buildings and made their way to their positions.

Khai ordered Puar to the roof and Koon, with his sniper rifle, to the top floor of the six-story building. Being an expert sniper, he knew that the key was to shoot and relocate and the top floor was perfect because most of the walls had been knocked out. Khai took up a shooting position from a fourth floor window that gave him plenty of vision of the whole street.

"Khai to Dah," Khai whispered into his throat mike.

"Dah here. Go ahead, Khai."

"You guys ready?"

"Affirmative," the captain said. *"We've taken up firing positions on the fifth floor."*

"Good."

"Make the call, Colonel."

"Wait for my signal then open fire."

"What's the signal?"

"You'll know it when you see it. Khai out." Khai switched channels. "Puar, you read me?"

"I'm here. Go ahead."

"How far can you launch a grenade?"

"'bout a hundred and fifty yards. Why?"

"As soon as they're in range, I want you to fire a grenade directly behind the crowd. Take out as many as you can. But I don't want the riot police to be harmed. And Koon, wait for my signal to start firing. Okay?"

"Got it, sir," Koon's voice came over the com.

In short order, the riot police came backpedaling into view. The sheer volume of rioters packed into the streets almost took Khai's breath away. Even from this distance, he could pick out the ringleaders- they were the ones carrying the military-grade guns.

"Koon," Khai whispered into his mike again. "Take out the guys in front, the ones with the big guns on my mark."

"I'm all over it!"

The riot police weren't even firing back by the time they reached the buildings in which Khai and the others were waiting. They were dragging injured away from the fight and radioing for help or evac.

The first line of rioters came into view when the first explosion echoed off the building walls sending the back ranks of rioters sprawling in all directions, and the front ranks surging forward directly into the line of fire. Almost immediately, Dah's team opened fire from the building across the street. The tough guys spun to that building and opened fire as Dah's team ducked for cover.

"Koon, now!"

Khai took aim, closing one eye and lining up a shot down the barrel of his pistol, when he saw the top half of a rioter's head disintegrate in a red dust cloud. Khai took the next one down, putting a bullet hole two inches in diameter in his forehead.

Thump... Kaboom! Puar fired again at the rear of the crowd and took down another few ranks. By that point, Dah's team returned fire. Brix boldly stood in his window and emptied both clips into the crowd taking down several dozen rioters. It was a massacre, Khai felt sick to his stomach, and in the middle of the fight, chewed down two pills to keep himself focused.

Khai took down three more rioters with head shots and ducked for cover as bullets chewed the wood around the broken window from where Khai was firing. After that volley, Khai popped out and took down six more —four with headshots and two with chest shots. He ducked down to reload. His reload was interrupted by ten rioters who had found a way to dodge the rain of bullets and get into the building. The sole of a boot was striking at his face.

Khai reacted with the reflexes of an expertly-trained killer. The boot, which was destined for Khai's head, glanced of his shoulder as he stood up. The attacker's foot was still on Khai's shoulder when he brought his elbow down on top of the attacker's knee, bending it the wrong way with a sickening dull crunch and prompting a tortured cry from the assailant. He dropped to the floor, crying and clutching his dislocated knee.

"Who's next?" Khai asked tauntingly.

Two guys attacked at once. The first attacker threw a right hook. Khai ducked under the wild swing, grabbed the knife from his boot and came up behind the first attacker, stabbing the knife upward into the soft tissue behind the chin of the second attacker. Blood bubbled and gushed from the wound as the attacker gurgled and choked.

Khai then kicked the first attacker as he removed his knife from the other's throat. The blunt force of his kick caused the guy to stumble and fall out the window to his death.

Seven rioters were left. They hesitated. Khai took their apprehensiveness to his advantage. He flipped the knife over in his hand and threw it. The knife buried itself all the way to the hilt in the next person's chest—all eight inches of it. He fell back, dead.

There was clearly a leader in the room with him. A dark-skinned fellow hung back, watching Khai's work. He shoved a fellow rioter directly at Khai, who screamed and flailed his arms in fear, knowing the end was coming. In a feeble attempt to defend himself, the screamer raked at Khai's face. Khai easily ducked under the attack, weaving his right hand under the attacking arm of the screamer and behind his head, putting him in a half nelson. With a powerful push forward on the screamer's neck, his shoulder popped and his hand fell uselessly to his side. He fell to the floor, writhing in pain and screaming even more.

With five left, and the odds were definitely in Khai's favor, three of the five ran, taking their chances with the hellfire outside. That left two; one rioter and the ringleader.

They attacked at once; the leader with a high roundhouse kick to the face and the other with a lunge to the midsection. Khai snapped his knee up in time to catch the would-be tackler in the chin, sending him crumbling to the floor and spitting teeth. However, the kick met its mark with a flash of light and the power behind the kick sent Khai reeling.

The leader followed up with a stabbing kick to the back of the knee, sending Khai to the floor for the first time in a long time.

The now-cocky leader paused to gloat. Khai got to his feet, grimacing, which produced crow's feet in the corners of his eyes.

"Getting slow, old man," the dark-skinned leader taunted.

"You're telling me," Khai said, standing up and wiping the blood from the gash on his cheek.

Khai stumbled into a support beam and the leader took the initiative. He moved in for the kill with a powerful front kick, it was too late for him to realize Khai's stumbling was bait. Khai sidestepped the kick and buried his heel into the thigh of the supporting leg. With a *crack*, his femur snapped and he went down.

"Never wound what you can't kill," Khai growled.

The leader still had some fight left in him. He struggled up to his good leg and swung uselessly at Khai. Khai wasn't playing around, he grabbed the wrist of the striking hand and jerked him down to his knee and then to his belly. Khai put his knee on the back of the leader's arm, just above the elbow and jerked back. The elbow gave instantly under Khai's overwhelming strength and he didn't stop until the leader's hand touched his shoulder. He cried out in pain to stop.

Khai wasn't done. He grabbed the leader by the back of his shirt and picked him up, broken arm and leg flopping painfully about. Khai tossed the guy out the side window of the building and found that all was silent. Whatever rioters weren't dead were fleeing, some leaving a blood trail as they stumbled away. Dah's team was out in the street and he could hear Puar and Koon stomping down the metallic stairs on the emergency staircase outside the building.

Khai leapt from one of the front windows facing the street and caught a rail halfway down. He then dropped to the street and reunited with his team. The riot police were regrouping as well.

"What the hell are you guys doing?" one of them demanded.

"Saving your asses!" Koon replied.

"You killed almost all of them!" another pointed out.

"We were ordered to use deadly force," Khai defended his team.

"By who?"

"Our captain got the order directly from Minister Trall."

"We got *our* orders from him, too. And he told us *not* to use lethal force."

"Must've been a miscommunication," Puar offered.

"I guess," the first one said. "It just makes all of us look bad, like we don't know what we're doing."

"'Bout sums it up," Captain Dah said, wryly.

"Well, I think we need to get to the bottom of this sooner rather than later," Khai said.

"Couldn't agree more," Captain Dah said.

Chapter Four

"You didn't say *nothin'* about Khai'Xander Khail leading the counterattack," a dark-skinned man growled through a clenched jaw that was wired shut from when he crashed face-first into the fire escape of the adjacent building. Due to the damage Khai inflicted on his arm, his underground doctor had to amputate it at the elbow. Six metal pins, four metal plates and eight hours of reconstructive surgery repaired the damage to his leg, and it would still be another week before he was able to walk on it without a crutch. "We're gonna need better guns and more people to deal with him. He's a fucking legend."

A tall, lanky man sat in a chair not facing the gangbanger leader. "What am *I* supposed to do about that?" he asked.

"You can arrest him or something. Right? I mean, *fuck*! You're the Minister of Planetary Affairs."

"You want a favor, Lyyn'Del Leer?"

"Yeah," he said.

"You were supposed to destroy the Ti'tan'lium processing plant, and you failed. Just for that, I should have you killed. But I'm willing to grant that favor and let you live. I've already supplied you with military-grade weapons and even paid some of the men in your gang to stick around despite your apparent lack of competence. Now get out of my sight."

"Whatever, man. Just keep the weapons coming. We'll get to the plant. You just hold to your end of the bargain and keep the police guessing. And when this is all over, I expect my payment. "

"You have to pull your head from your ass, first."

"I assure you, Prime Minister. Things are not as bad as they seem."

"Really?" Prime Minister Puar asked. "Because my little brother, who's been fighting these riots for over three weeks, seems to be telling me otherwise. The slums are all but deserted and people are leaving the city by hundreds—maybe even *thousands*. The only reason my brother's team is doing as well as they are has everything to do with Former Colonel Khail joining the police force to help with the riots."

"Colonel Khail is a loose cannon!" Trall hissed. "You know he suffers from Post-Traumatic Stress? I'm half tempted to have him arrested for reckless endangerment!"

"Khail," Puar chuckled. "First he finds the Ti'tan'lium and now he's fending off riot after riot. You must be mad; he's saved this city—this planet—and several other planets under the Seryys flag, more times than I care to admit. Hell, I've *fought* with the man. You interfere with that and I'll have *you* arrested."

"Of course, Prime Minister," Trall said, with a less-than-cordial bow.

Khai was in his element. Not only had he remembered to take his pills every day, he hadn't had a flashback in over three weeks. The wind blowing on his face as the chopper swooped low to drop him and his team off at another riot comforted him. He and his team were once again dropping into the Corporate Sector to rout another gang of unruly misfits with fully automatic weapons. There were ten riots raging at that exact moment, but the city risked losing the most if the Corporate Sector fell into chaos. So, despite Minister Trall's orders sending Khai's team to the north tip of Lower Seryys to protect it, Captain Dah and Khai both disobeyed direct orders and both agreed that the Corporate Sector was their target.

They were able to rout the riot in a matter of hours; it was at least six times bigger than the first riot they fought in the Corporate Sector almost four weeks earlier. This time Captain Byyner had the chopper provide air support and mow down rioters with every pass. It was all going according to plan until the chopper was taken down by a handheld surface-to-air missile that clipped the right the wing and rotor. The chopper went spinning out of control and crashed in a fire ball into the side of an abandoned building. The pilot barely had time to eject before the thing went down.

The man who fired the rocket was the same guy that Khai had messed up weeks earlier. He was now sporting power armor, designed to both protect and enhance the wearer.

"Shit!" Koon said.

"No sweat," Khai said. "Cap'!"

"Yeah?" Captain Dah yelled back, still firing his weapon at the surging masses that seemed to flood into the street as if a dam had broken. *They were waiting to spring the trap! Fuck! How could I have been so stupid! It was too easy!"*

"Can I borrow Puar for a few moments?"

"What's up?" Puar asked. Khai pointed at the gangbanger in the blue-gray power armor that covered all but his face, which was protected by a bullet-proof, clear metal sheet. His cocky grin was visible from under the visor. The Seryys Combat Bionic Exo-Armor, or BEA, was a revolutionary military development and the initial answer to the Vyysarris' overwhelming strength and speed, but it was later banned because of its unpredictable properties. The way the suit worked, was that it used sensor probes in the form of microscopic needles that penetrated the nerve endings at key points in the body and transmitted electrical currents from the brain to all the moving parts of the suit. Essentially, it read the wearer's mind and acted accordingly; if the wearer wanted to move his arm, he would simply try to move it and the sensors would detect the current, moving the arm of the suit. The problem was the effects of the probes on the body were detrimental. Eventually, the nerve ends would stop receiving currents from the brain and permanent paralysis would set in. "Well, now *that's* not something you can just pick up at the store."

"Can you hit it from here?"

"Who ya talkin' too?"

"Well, *do it!*"

Puar took careful aim and launched a grenade. *Thump!*

The grenade hit the suit dead center on the chest and the explosion sent the suited man sailing through the wall of the adjacent building.

"Nice, shot!" Khai hooted. "Your brother must have taught you a thing or two."

"Nah," Puar said, waving his hand. "I taught myself everything I know."

"Your humbleness floors me," Khai said wryly.

"Hey," Puar said with a haughty grin. "Modest is the hottest!"

"Are you two done?" Captain Dah asked. "'Cause if you are, I could really use some help here!"

They were surrounded, standing in a circle laying down fire into the massing crowds. None of them had weapons more sophisticated than a lead pipe or knife. But they were advancing without fear or hesitation, like the very whips of their masters were on them. They fell by the hundreds, but more would step up to take their place.

"Shit!" Naad yelled.

"What's wrong, Naad?" Dah dared to ask.

"I'm running dry!"

"Shit!" Dah replied.

"Exactly!" Naad replied to his captain's reply.

"Okay," Dah said, pulling a machete from its sheath, mounted to the back of his armor. "Take my gun and the rest of my ammo. Make 'em count!"

"Where the hell are *you* going?" Khai asked.

"It's time to get messy!" the captain yelled as he charged the crowd swinging left and right, hacking arms and legs. It was only then that he realized what was happening. "Ah, fuck!"

"What now?" Khai asked.

"I'm such an idiot. I should've guessed this from the moment we got here!"

"What?" Naad asked, still firing.

"It's a damned Psych-Pro!"

"Great!" Khai scoffed. "We need to find the user!"

"You think it was metal man?" Puar asked.

"It would take an enormous amount of concentration to control both the BEA and the Psych-Pro."

"Or some really trippy drugs!" Puar added.

"Good point. I need to find that guy and shut him down!" Khai yelled over the gun fire.

"By yourself?" Dah asked.

"Yeah," Khai said almost casually. "Wouldn't be the first time, probably won't be the last. You guys have everything under control here?"

"Go!" Captain Dah nearly screamed.

Khai ran off in the direction of the building where the grey-armored, drugged-up gangbanger leader flew. The enormous hole in the wall of the abandoned building was big enough that he thought for sure that the building should have crumbled in on itself. In the center, Khai could hear the servos of the armor working as Khai's target emerged.

"Well, well, well. You come for round two?"

"And three and four and maybe even five," Khai said, popping his neck. "I was going easy on you last time."

"Well, don't get soft on me now! Bring it!"

Khai took a step forward, removing the giant knife from his boot. "Tell me. How are you able to control the Psych-Pro *and* the BEA at the same time?"

"It's called Whither Crystal, the only way to fly! Now, you can't possibly tell me that you're gonna go toe-to-toe with me and with only that knife."

"Well, you're bullet proof. Bringing a gun to a fistfight didn't make much sense, so I brought a knife."

"Let's dance!"

Lyyn'Del Leer lunged forward, the suit augmenting his abilities. Khai acted without thinking, he took two big steps forward and slid feet first under the attacking man. The armored man tucked and rolled to his feet. By the time he got to his feet, Khai was on him. He knew from his training that the weak points on the powered suit were the joints. From behind, Khai jabbed his knife into the flexible material of the shoulder of the armor.

A slight yelp issued from the wearer, but when Khai pulled the knife out, there was no blood.

Damn! Khai thought ruefully as the metallic elbow whipped around and caught him on the nose knocking him back. The suited maniac pressed the attack hard and fast, using the augmentation of the suit's abilities to their fullest extent. A gauntleted hand wrapped around Khai's throat.

"Getting too old for this shit!" he growled, trying to remove the fingers from his throat.

"You got that right!" the dark-skinned man said from behind the visor. "Let me put this old dog down!" He squeezed harder. Khai thought that his eyes might literally pop out of his head when the guy bore down on him.

"*Khai, where the hell are you? We're getting overwhelmed over here!*" Dah's voice came over the com.

"Little... busy..." he barely choked out. "Almost... done..."

"What the?" Lyyn'Del almost laughed. "I don't think you really know what's about to happen here."

"I... beg to... differ," Khai whispered. Khai, still having his knife in his hand, buried it to the hilt into the joint where the leg met the body bellow the hip. This time a cry of equal parts surprise, pain and anger issued from the suit of armor and Khai was dropped immediately. As he fell back, he had the presence of mind to twist the knife as it pulled out to do the maximum amount of damage.

Blood gushed from the knife wound and the armor-suited man dropped to one knee.

The suit had the ability to mend wounds such as that one to keep the wearer from bleeding to death. It wasn't able to repair the internal damage, but it was the idea that if the suit at least got the bleeding stopped, the wearer wouldn't bleed to death while trying to get out of the suit.

Before the armored man was able to get up, Khai pressed his own attack and ran at his enemy. He leapt forward and connected with a solid flying sidekick that made the armor topple end over end and come to a rest on its back. Khai jumped on him and jabbed the knife into the separation between the two chest pieces that came together when the suit was put on. He twisted the knife and spread the sections of armor far enough to get his fingers in there. Planting a booted foot on the man's chest, he jerked back as hard as he could. Using his superior strength, he pried the suit open with his bare hands to reveal the wearer's body.

The man tried feverishly to get up, but with his leg unable to support any weight at all, that was impossible. Instead, Khai unleashed a flurry of bludgeoning punches to the man's midsection, breaking ribs and rupturing several organs. He didn't stop until the man spewed dark, red blood all over the inside of the visor. Khai got up and grabbed a piece of crete left over from the building crumbling and smashed it over the visor several times until it broke open like the shell of a Rush Mussel.

With the man's face exposed now, Khai gave him one bone-crushing blow to the face and it was all over. The man was dead and the suit went limp.

Khai straightened up with a grunt and grimace.

"*I don't know—and I don't care—how you did it, Khai, but you did it!*" Captain Dah's overjoyed voice came over the com.

"Just another day, Cap'. I'll be there in a minute."

He sluggishly walked out to the street and saw what appeared to be *thousands* of dead bodies and an equal amount of disoriented, bewildered people coming off the spell of the Psych-Pro.

The Seryys Combat Psychic Projector worked as a radio transmitter that projected thoughts into the minds of intended victims to gain their total submission by interfering with the frontal lobe of the brain, which was the reasoning center, making them more susceptible to suggestions and commands. It was yet another banned device designed by the Seryys Combat Research and Development Center, or the SCR&DC, which had long-term side effects brought on by extended periods of use. The worst case scenario was being lobotomized by the device.

After all the civilians were rounded up and sent to local hospitals for injuries and checkups to make sure the Psych-Pro didn't do any permanent damage, lighting streaked across the sky and struck a building, crumbling it to the ground with only one salvo.

"What the f-" Puar's reaction as was cut short as another salvo lanced through the sky and crumbled another building.

"Captain Byyner, what the hell is going on?" Khai shouted into his throat mike.

"*Don't know, Khai. Looks like the shield isn't working. The SC com came alive only minutes ago. Garbled reports of several ships jumping into the system and punching through the Defense Fleet and— wait, I'm getting something else.*" Khai's stomach knotted up waiting for whatever Byyner was going to say. "*One ship has punched through and is heading for the city. It's not slowing down. Oh the Founders! It's on a collision course!*"

That was when Khai and the others could feel the rumble of a ship breaking through the atmosphere. Khai immediately ran for the nearest building, and like a jungle spider, climbed up the emergency ladder on the side. On the roof he could get a clear view of the ship coming in. Several dog fighters swooped in to try shooting it down. They scored several hits on the large ship, but nothing was slowing that thing down. Finally, a volley of concussion missiles connected with the hull of the ship and it listed as a series of explosions cascaded down the starboard side.

The ground of the whole city shook when the ship crashed.

"*Now I'm getting a general distress coming from the RLD. It's ablaze.*"

The fighters swung around and started attacking other ships that were now in airspace above Seryys City. Khai got out his electrobinoculars and realized they had broken during his fight with the armored maniac.

"Koon," Khai said into his throat mike. "Look up, to your two o'clock at thirty degrees and tell me what you see."

A few seconds later, Koon reported back. "*They're drop ships, Khai. Four of 'em.*"

"Where are they headed?"

"*Right for us.*"

"Right for us or right for the *Corporate Sector?*"

"*Your guess is as good as mine.*"

"Damn! We gotta move—now! They're headed for the shield generator!"

"*How do you know that?*"

"Call it a gut instinct."

Khai clambered down the ladder and regrouped with the others. Without saying a word, they ran as fast as their legs could carry them. Khai and Captain Dah were having the least amount of trouble, having been raised on Gorn Planet. The others, however, were huffing and puffing as they ran.

"Come on, ladies. Move your asses!" Dah shouted. "We still have several more miles to run and no help is coming for us."

"Hey!" Puar snapped. "You carry forty pounds of Detonite on *your* back and see how well you do!"

"Shit!" Khai laughed. "A standard rations and munitions pack was easily sixty pounds. Stop running your mouth and run your legs some more!"

The drop ships soared overhead and rumbled by. Puar, in a desperate attempt, shot one grenade at the tail drop ship and connected. The ship rolled over on its topside and dived down into the pavement of the street several miles ahead.

"Dammit, Puar!" Dah shouted. "You had better hope those Vyysarri are dead, or we're gonna have to kill them first and that's only gonna slow us down even more."

"Yeah," Puar said. "But at least then, I can catch my breath."

"Amateurs," Khai growled.

"What the hell is happening?" Prime Minster Puar demanded from Trall.

"I don't know, sir." Trall checked his micro-comp. "The shield had a lapse in power for only a brief moment, long enough for those ships to get through."

"Get me the Minister of Planetary Defense on the com—now!" Puar growled.

An elderly-looking man, maybe a hundred and five years old, wearing a blue jumpsuit and hardhat, answered the com. "*Yes, Prime Minister?*"

"You're not the Minister! Where is he?"

"*He's fighting off the intruders, sir.*"

"Maybe you can tell us, then, what the hell happened."

"I can't, sir."

"Why not?" Puar slammed his hand down on the desk, promoting the water in his glass to jump out and pool up around the bottom.

"We don't know what happened. The power went down for three minutes and thirty seconds."

"On the shield?"

"No, sir. The *whole* facility grid. It's like somebody-" the transmission was lost.

"Dammit, Trall. What the hell is happening?" Puar asked, swiveling in his chair to face him.

"Vyysarri troops have broken the defense line at the shield generator. The com has been cut."

"Get some men down there on the double! Where's Khai's team?"

Trall grimaced at the name. "He's quelling with a riot on the east side of the Corporate Sector near the Slums."

"Raise him on the com. Order him to go protect the shield generator at all costs."

"But, sir." Trall said in a whiny voice. "He's *miles* from the west side. He'll never make it time. Even with airlift— which isn't available anyway."

"Damn!" Puar growled. "Who do we have over there right now?"

"Nobody, sir," Trall hissed. "The Corporate Sector wasn't the projected target. The Honorifical Office was. Which brings me to my next order of business, sir, you're not safe here. I suggest we move you to the Emergency Bunker in Kal'Hoom Karr Canyon. Just in case our initial projections still prove accurate yet."

It was only a thirty-minute ride to the bunker, which was the single most impenetrable fortress on the planet. It was located in Kal'Hoom Karr Canyon, named by the explorer who discovered it several millennia earlier. It only had two ways in and out. There was the main entrance, which housed a large retractable landing platform big enough to hold a capital ship in the event that the Prime Minister needed to be whisked off-planet. This entrance was fortified by an impenetrable force field and heavy-duty, high-caliber sentry guns. The other entrance was less known, though. It started several hundred feet at the bottom of the canyon, underwater. There was an airlock at the bottom of the river, which flowed through the entire surface area of the canyon floor. It was only accessible by submarine that docked with the airlock. There was a long shaft that went all the way up the engineering level of the bunker, which was the bottom level. When a sub docked with the airlock—and the entrance code was provided and confirmed—the water in the shaft was purged into the river and the lift car became accessible. The lift would take them up to the engineering level where the arrivals were greeted by Security Patrol Enforcement and Assault

Robots, or SPEARs—automated security forces, essential artificially intelligent sentry guns on treads.

The whole bunker was automated, and self-sufficient. From hydroponics, to air-scrubbers, to automated maintenance robots, there wasn't a single task that needed to be tended to by a Seryysan making it the perfect retreat for the Prime Minister if he wanted to escape marauding Vyysarri or insistent politicians. The automated security forces were impossible to bribe and the only way to control then was from the control/panic room deep within the rock walls attached to the main hanger.

"Do you really think that's necessary?" Puar asked incredulously.
"Yes, sir. I do."

"Knowing you, old friend, you're not going to take 'no' for an answer." Puar sighed. "But, I'm still the Prime Minister, and I'm staying here. I'm not going to add to a hysteria that will cost more innocent lives."

Trall sighed, then said, "Then will you at least go home for the day? I have your personal shuttle idling on the landing platform for you right now."

"I thought you might," the Prime Minister said with a warm smile. "Let's get going."

The Honorifical Office had a lift car that provided direct access to the landing platform on the roof in the event of a full assault on the Capital Building. This wasn't necessarily the by-the-book way to get the Prime Minister out, but with the invasion fleet broken through, there was a good chance that the enemy could've also sent a team to find and kill the Prime Minister.

Khai and his team ran. "We're... not gonna... make it," Koon said between gasps for air.

"We don't have a choice!" Khai snapped. "If that shield goes down again, we're all dead!"

"Quit your crying and get moving!" Captain Dah ordered.

They started running again. Suddenly, though, Khai stopped.

"What is it?" Dah asked. The others stopped, too—and nearly collapsed.

"I see our ticket to a faster mode of transportation."

The sun had just set, casting brilliant shades of pinks and oranges and blues across the horizon. It was getting dark enough now that the Vyysarri would not need protection from the sun's harmful rays. Khai peered down a deep, dark alley, between two tall apartment complexes and spotted a large tarp covering something that resembled the curvy lines of a classic hovercar, the hovercar that originally caught his attention. Khai ran over and pulled the tarp clear to reveal an older, classic car on wheels. That was both good and bad: good because it would be easier to steal, bad because they would have to dodge obstacles on the road which would slow them down. *But still—*

"It beats running!" Puar said with another deep breath, finishing Khai's thought.

Khai kicked in the window and pulled apart the dash. Using wires from the ignition switch, which was ridiculously easy to find on an oldie like this, he fired her up and unlocked the doors. The others clambered in and Khai hit the accelerator. The car fishtailed around the corner coming out from the alley and sped off in the direction of the shield generator, which was still several miles away.

It took nearly another thirty minutes to get there and it was now night in the big city. They passed the flaming wreckage that used to be the lander Puar shot down on their way. Puar had a very satisfied *I told you so* look on his face. When they arrived, Khai stopped five blocks short. "Get out." Khai ordered calmly.

"What? Why?" Naad asked.

"Because, I don't want to get anyone hurt."

"What are you going to do?" Dah asked, unbuckling his crash restraints.

"You'll see," Khai said with a roguish grin, waiting patiently. "Let's just say that I'm not about to let these Vyysarri bastards leave. Now hurry up and get out."

They filed out of the car. Khai spotted the drop ship and revved the engine. He stepped on it and the car sped off. He was less than a hundred yards from the lander when he hit a hundred and fifteen miles per hour. Just before the car collided with the ship, Khai jumped out and painfully rolled to a stop as the car rammed into the ship eliciting a huge explosion and grabbing the attention of the Vyysarri watching guard at the front entrance.

"Holy shit!" Dah nearly whispered. "He's crazy."

"You can say that again!" Puar agreed.

"Let's move!" Dah yelled.

The others ran for the building that housed the shield generator. The Vyysarri charged at them. From a lying-down position, Khai dropped two of the six with headshots from his pistol. But the others ignored him. They simply charged at the others.

"Drop 'em!" Dah yelled. They stopped their charge and opened fire on them.

The Vyysarri were hardy people. It took several shots to bring them down. The leader of the group took a full spray from Naad's guns before he even slowed down. Koon had the most luck, one-shot-kills to the head with his sniper rifle. Dah killed the one fighting him with his machete and felt younger than he had in a long time because of it.

"Still got it," he said, smiling and sheathing machete.

"What about Khai?" Puar asked, concern filling his voice.

"Go check him out, Naad," Captain Dah ordered. "*You're* the medic."

When Naad reached Khai, he was sitting up and grimacing as he stretched his sore muscles.

"Khai!" Naad shouted. "Khai. You all right?"

"I'm fine," Khai said flatly. "Is everyone else okay?"

"Yeah," he said as the others approached. "We made short order of them."

"Good," Khai said. "You leave any of them alive?"

"Why would we do *that*?" Puar asked.

"To find out why that building is still standing?" They all exchanged bewildered looks. Puar actually rubbed the back of his neck and looked away. "Brilliant. Well, it must be explosives. We just need to find them and disable them, preferably *before* they go off."

"So, what? We're going in?" Puar asked.

"Not all of us," Khai said, looking back at the building. "Just me."

"Are you crazy?" Puar yelped. "Do you even know what you're looking for?"

"Detonite—or a variant," Khai replied to Puar's question.

"So, what if it goes off while you're still in there?" Brix asked.

"Then you should have nothing to worry about," Khai answered, not an ounce of fear in his voice. "It'll be nice to be able to die with dignity."

"Ah, hell!" Puar said. "I can't let you go in there alone."

"You don't have to go either. You can just wait here. I'm going to be honest with you; I probably won't make it out alive. I can't let you throw your life away. Besides, you're the best the city has to offer and losing *any* of you will leave this city vulnerable if I fail."

"Well, here, then," Puar said, handing Khai a device with a small display. "This'll detect and track the electronic triggers for the detonite. It'll detect any triggers within a hundred yards."

"Thanks," Khai said, strapping the radar to his belt. "If I'm not out in twenty minutes, get clear of the building and find cover. Got it?" They all nodded. "Good."

Khai breached the front doors and was greeted by a bloodbath. Wires hung, sparking small discharges, and water dripped from ruptured waterlines for the fire suppression system. This was clearly the maintenance level, as there were hundreds of pipelines and conduits lining the ceiling, several workbenches with tools lying about and circuit breakers every few feet. Plus, the constant rumble of the power generator made listening for enemies increasingly difficult. Security guards and maintenance men lay about, dead. Puncture wounds—two, to be exact—

existed on each of the necks of the guards in the front area. *Bloody leaches were feeding on these guys!* The left-over blood made the floor slick and the stomach-turning odor filled Khai's nose. He took a breath through his clenched teeth and grimaced. Khai activated the radar and ventured deep into the bowels of the building searching for explosives that *had* to be there. The radar detected five within a hundred yards of his position.

Three of the five were on higher levels, so he went for the two on his current level. As he ventured deeper into the building, one more blip appeared on the radar on his level. So that made six bombs, total.

In short order, he had located and disarmed the first three bombs, which were placed at strategic places on the first floor—two of those being support beams that kept the place up, only one was placed on the power regulator. It was going smoothly, and the bombs' triggers appeared to be not set to a timer, but to a remote trigger that would set them all off at once. Why they hadn't been set off yet was still a mystery, but Khai knew not to let his guard down for even a second. Not only could a searing, fiery death call at any moment, Khai also didn't put it past the Vyysarri to leave some behind to die protecting their handiwork.

He worked his way up to the second of ten levels. There was nothing on this level; only offices of people who monitored the shield generator—some of those people present, but dead. Khai grimaced again. The Vyysarri did an exceedingly proficient job leaving nobody alive.

Khai pushed on.

The third floor was all computer equipment; server panels and diagnostic readouts. Thousands of blinking lights winked at seemingly random intervals. This particular room/floor was at least fifteen degrees cooler than the first two he had explored to keep the computers from overheating. His radar indicated that there was one charge on this floor. It was placed on the floor at the center of the room—hopefully to take out all the regulatory systems in one shot.

Moving to the fourth floor, he was taken aback. Though from the outside the building appeared to be ten floors, the next six levels were comprised of what looked like an engineering level. There were catwalks that hung like streamers at a party from one side to the next on multiple levels. The constant grind of machinery echoed off the walls. One large cylinder—probably fifty feet tall and twenty feet in diameter—was marked:

Generator Coolant. HOT! DO NOT TOUCH!

There was, according to the radar, one bomb placed on the cylinder. There was a ladder that led up to a catwalk that went right by the midsection of the cylinder.

"Great," Khai growled. "Why is it *always* heights?"

He clambered up the ladder and ran his white-knuckled hands over the rail as he walked up to the bomb. He was almost there when he heard the low roar of a Vyysarri warrior as he leapt down from the top of the cylinder. He landed right on top of Khai and drove him to the grating floor of the catwalk with a pained grunt.

"I will feast on your blood, Seryysan," the Vyysarri warrior hissed.

"Maybe later," Khai grunted, pushing himself up—to the astonishment of the Vyysarri.

Khai threw his head back whacking his assailant on the chin, eliciting a grunt of his own and the weight being lifted off his back. Khai immediately sprung to his feet, readying himself for another fight. The Vyysarri also stood to his full height of over six and a half feet. He took a threatening step toward Khai. But he was in no mood for games. He was far too tired and hungry to deal with this nonsense. So, with the lighting speed of a Kal'Hoom Karr Canyon Sabercat, Khai quick-drew his pistol and popped one shot dead on into his opponent's forehead. The force of the blast staggered him a bit, but certainly didn't stop him. To Khai's dismay, he lunged forward with more speed than Khai could have anticipated and knocked the gun from his hand.

The gun clanked on the floor three stories below.

Damn!

Khai grabbed the Vyysarri by the throat and his face betrayed his surprise at Khai's strength. Khai pushed him back several feet, before he caught his footing and was able to push back. There, a stalemate ensued; their equal strengths pushed at each other as their arms shook with exertion.

"You must be military," a deep, gruff voice said.

"Yeah," Khai said, maneuvering his enemy into what would be his finishing move.

"I have killed many of your kind," he said plainly.

Khai didn't say anything in response; he only grabbed the Vyysarri's arm and using his enemy's momentum, rolled to his back, flipping the Vyysarri over his head and onto his back behind him. For only one second, they lay head-to-head on their backs; Khai kept rolling into a backward somersault and ended up on his knees straddling his stunned opponent. One solid and bone-jarring punch sent the Vyysarri spiraling into a dark oblivion. As the Vyysarri stopped struggling, Khai pulled his knife and drove it straight down into the Vyysarri's heart, not stopping until the tip of the knife found the grating floor and twisted the blade to make sure the job was done. The Vyysarri rattled out a final breath and collapsed.

Khai finished the disarming of the bomb and slid back down the ladder, retrieving his gun on the way to the lift car. As he rode the car up, he consulted his radar again. There were two left. One was the tenth level and the other was on the roof, most likely attached to the shield emitter.

The lift car stopped and before the door could even open, it was instantly riddled with bullet holes. The doors separated and smoke billowed out. As the smoke cleared, the irritated group of Vyysarri realized they only things they had hit were air and metal.

"Grand," the leader grunted. "Go check it out." Grand gave him a terrified look. Without hesitation, the leader shot Grand in the face, killing him instantly. "Bash, now you go."

"At once!" he snapped, brining his weapon to bear on the lift car. He looked around inside the lift car. "He's not here."

"Where is he, then?"

Chapter Five

Khai had to chuckle to himself. Those Vyysarri idiots must be scratching their heads right now. On the ride up, he climbed up into the shaft and when the lift made it to the tenth floor, Khai climbed hand-over-hand up the safety cable to the roof. He knew that if he didn't disable the bomb on the emitter, his whole trip would be for nothing. The bomb on the tenth level, though damaging, would not disable the shield generator.

He ascended the stairs to the emitter platform and found the bomb waiting. He disarmed it and turned, packing the detonator into one of the pockets on his flak jacket when a foot, moving at the speed of lightning, caught him square on the jaw, sending him stumbling over the railing of the platform and falling six feet to the roof.

"You're a quiet one," Khai said, slowly getting to his feet.

"The first of many things you will learn about me, Colonel Khail," the Vyysarri said. "We met once before, on a distant battlefield, many years ago. You were a good fighter in your youth; you broke several of my bones and left me for dead. Do you not remember me?"

"I've killed a lot of you guys," Khai said casually, wiping the blood from his chin

"I am General Sledge, a Vyysarri Warrior!" he boomed.

"All you blood suckers look alike," Khai hissed. "Now are you gonna kill me, or talk me to death?"

The Vyysarri lunged with rage at Khai's apparent lack of respect for a fellow warrior. That Vyysarri didn't know the half of it. Once again, relying on his quick-draw abilities, Khai drew his pistol and put a bullet right between the monster's eyes. He landed face first, sprawled out on the roof of the building, a pool of dark red—almost black—blood collecting where his twitching body lay.

"Eat shit," Khai growled.

He took his knife and made yet another notch on his faithful gun. Holstering both the knife and the gun, he made his way back to the lift shaft to climb down into the building and clear the tenth floor and disarm that bomb.

Khai had been gone almost an hour when Captain Dah's radio crackled to life.

"Captain Dah, do you read?" Captain Byyner's voice was on the other end.

"I read you loud and clear," Dah responded. "Go ahead."

"How are things going down there?"

"Could be better," Dah admitted. "I believe we have neutralized the threat to the shield generator. How are things elsewhere?"

"There was also a more covert attack on the primary com tower near the SCMBHF."

The SCMBHF was the Seryys Combat Military Barracks and Housing Facility, where most of the planet's service men and women—and their families—trained and lived. It was a large-area facility ten miles north of Seryys City. It was its own self-sustaining city with a power plant, agriculture, shops and entertainment—much like Gor'Dyyn Gorn Base. Most of the planet's military operations were based out of the SCMBHF.

"Was it stopped?"

"Yes, it was. But not without bloodshed, as usual with the Vyysarri," Byyner sounded very disappointed. *"They were trying to upload something; but when they were caught, they destroyed the evidence, and those who didn't die fighting took their own lives."*

"Glad to hear they were stopped."

"Well, they did invade a military base. Perhaps they felt that they would have better luck in the confusion with the shield generator going down."

"I suppose. But it's not gonna go down anytime soon."

"Is Khai with you?"

"No, sir. He's neutralizing the threat inside the shield generator. The Vyysarri planted charges within the structure and Khai is in the process of disarming them. He refused to let anyone else go with him in the event that bombs went off. I'm assuming from the fact that the bombs haven't gone off yet, that he is having some success." There was a long, *long* pause. At first Dah thought that the com channels were down again. "Sir? Are you there?"

"Yeah," Byyner sighed and was very reluctant to talk. At last, he spoke, his voice taut with strain as if he was grimacing as he said, *"When he comes out, you need to place him under arrest immediately and bring him here to the station."*

"What? You *can't* be serious," Dah said.

"What Cap'?" Puar asked. "What's wrong?"

"Captain Byyner wants me to place Khai under arrest."

"Why?" Brix asked.

Byyner sighed, hearing Brix's question. *"Because of a* damned *technicality!"*

"You didn't answer his question," Dah said coldly.

"Apparently, Khai failed to mention that he suffers from shell shock. Falsifying applications to the police force—or any force, for that matter—is an offence punishable by jail time, and..." Byyner's voice broke for yet another long sigh, *"...in times of war, punishable by death."*

"That's ridiculous!" Dah snapped. "He's never shown a single symptom!"

"I have his mental health file in my hands right now. I'm looking at them. They were released from the SCPDTF and sent to me directly from the Minister Trall. It's his orders that I'm following."

The SCPDTC, or Seryys Combat Patient Diagnostic and Treatment Center, was allowed to release patient files on government orders when pertaining to the mental stability of soldiers in the field. So the information was obtained legally by the laws in place.

"He's the only reason we have a shield generator to protect us right now, and you're gonna tell me that he's going to be *executed?*" Dah practically spat with anger.

"Sorry, kid. It's not my call. The order came directly from the Minister of Planetary Affairs. Don't disobey this direct order, or you and you team will also be put to death."

"And if he resists?"

"Your orders are to use deadly force. You understand?" Byyner wasn't even trying to hide the disgust in his voice.

"Roger that, *sir.*" Dah cut the channel. "FUCK!"

"What're we gonna do, Cap'?"

"Follow our orders," Dah said bluntly.

"I'm not arresting him," Brix growled.

"Then you're gonna die, just like *him!*" Dah snapped.

Just about then, a large explosion blew out all the windows on the top floor in a fire ball.

They all stood, their collective chins hanging below their knees, their eyes wide open.

"Guess we're not gonna have to arrest him after all," Puar said both sadly and relieved all at once.

They stood just a little longer, staring at the smoke billowing from the shattered windows.

They were all so focused on the tenth floor, that no one noticed the dark figure emerging from the front doors of the building. When the dark figure slumped against the wreckage of the drop ship, they all snapped to fire positions. The dazed figure was unarmed but huge in stature and cast a huge shadow from the pale moonlight.

"Lay down on the ground-*now!*" Dah shouted the order. *Dammit! What the hell is wrong this guy? What do I do?* The thoughts in Dah's head swirled like a tidal pool in the Great Rush. What if it was Khai? *No!* Dah thought. *Khai would've identified himself immediately.* The figure didn't comply, only stumbled forward some more. "Get down on the ground, or I'll *put* you there!"

The stumbling man took several more wobbly steps forward and as Dah was about to fire, another single shot rang out. A single round plunged into the chest of the man shrouded in umbra. The shot man issued a grunt and dropped to his knees, but kept coming forward, now reaching out for them.

Koon had the crosshairs trained on the figure's face, just waiting for the word. It only took a second to realize, though, that the stumbling figure was *not* Vyysarri.

"Company! Open f-"

"Wait!" Koon shouted, dropping his gun and running up to the man.

They all followed suit, knowing that they had made a huge mistake.

Khai rolled to his back, wheezing and coughing.

"Shit," Dah breathed. "Khai, say something." He knew it was stupid to worry about it, especially once they got him into custody. He was a dead man one way or the other. But he would be damned if this world-renowned warrior died by his hand. "Come on, you stubborn bastard. Say something."

"I..." Khai coughed. "I missed one..." Khai said, then wheezed out a weak chuckle.

The others laughed with him.

"Yeah," Puar said. "We noticed. That's coming out of your pay."

"Good thing you were wearing your flak jacket," Naad remarked.

"Doesn't hurt any less," Khai said dryly.

"Oh shut it, you pansy," Dah said. "We've all been shot before."

"Why'd you shoot me?" Khai growled.

"I didn't," Dah said, throwing up his hands in defense.

"Then who shot him?" Koon asked.

They all looked at each other and only one wouldn't make eye contact with the others.

"Brix?" Naad asked.

"Sorry!" Brix almost whined.

"Damn, Brix!" Puar shouted. "It's amazing that the Seryysan Society has come this far with people like *you* in the gene pool!"

They all laughed except for Dah, who was surprisingly glum given the jovial mood of the situation, and Khai picked up on it immediately, despite his injuries.

"What's..." Khai coughed again, "...wrong, Cap'?"

"Do you have shell shock?"

The smile quickly vanished from Khai's face. "How'd... you find out?"

"Trall sent your medical records to Byyner. He ordered me to arrest you." Khai instinctively reached for his pistol. Dah saw the motion and stiffened. "Relax. I'm not bringing you in."

"You're not?" Puar, Brix, Naad, Koon and Khai all asked at the same time.

"No," Dah said. "In fact, you're already dead as far as I'm concerned."

"What do you mean?" Khai asked, grimacing in pain.

"You missed one," said Dah, with a devious grin.

"Think they'll buy it?" Puar asked with hope in his tone.

"For a while," Dah shrugged. "At least until they identify all the bodies in there."

"Where should I go?" Khai asked.

"Here," Dah said, tossing something at Khai. Khai winced in pain as he jerked to catch it. It was a codepad, and from the looks of it, the device went to a ship of some kind. "It's space worthy. I'd suggest making a break for Seryys Four or Five. Lie low for a while. At least until you can charter a ship with an Eve'Zon drive to get out of the system." Dah paused. "In fact, break in and make it look like a robbery. I'll file the paperwork in two days. The ship is located in a storage garage on thirty-one Saber Avenue, just south of the RLD."

"Dah," it was the voice of Captain Byyner. *"Do you have Khai in custody yet?"*

"No, sir," Dah answered, looking straight at Khai. "And I don't think we ever will."

"What do you mean?"

"Khai failed at disarming all of the bombs. One of the charges went off on the conference level of the shield generator building while Khai was inside. He didn't make it."

There was a very long pause. Then Byyner let out a sharp sigh. *"It was probably better that way anyway. He died an honorable death—the death of a soldier."*

"I agree."

Khai slowly got to his feet and removed his flak jacket. There was a dark, circular bruise the size of a man's fist on his chest right over his heart. "Damn, that hurts!"

They all looked at Brix. He shrugged with a boyish grin. "It was a good shot, though. Right?" They all shook their heads, rolling their eyes. "Besides, I knew Khai was wearing a vest. That's why I only shot once. If he was Vyysarri, he would have raged and charged us."

"Whatever helps you sleep at night," Puar said, eyeing the good-sized bruise and clapping a hand down on Brix's shoulder.

"Now get out of here!" Dah said to Khai.

"Here," Khai said, tossing *him* something. "This is how you can contact me anywhere, any time. It's a dedicated com unit to me. I need you to find out where Trall is, so I can pay him a visit."

"Khai!" Dah snapped. "You're a wanted man. You've got a death warrant on your head. And you want to march into the sabercat's den?"

"You are one crazy son of a bitch, Khai. You know that?" Puar asked.

It was barely dawn when Khai used industrial, hydraulic metal cutters to make a man-sized door in the garage door. He hadn't slept since the Vyysarri attack; he imagined his former team hadn't either. He went home briefly to fetch a few personal effects and, most importantly, his pills. With one last look at his small apartment, he turned his back never expecting to see it again. He felt a pang of regret as he used the codepad to disarm the ship's alarm system and fire up the hoverpads that lined the flat bottom of the ship and its engines. As the lights came on in the garage, detecting movement, Khai could make out the exact design of the ship. It was cylindrical with a slightly curved, flatter bottom, stout wings that jutted out from the sides at the rear of the vessel that housed engine pods and an aerodynamic bow where the cockpit was located. It looked like a heap with several patched up spots in the hull plating denoted by a slight differentiation in color between new and old plates. But, as long as it could make orbit, he didn't particularly care. The inside was nice enough, though. Not a presidential ship by any stretch of the imagination, but it had all the comforts of home. The ship, overall, was fifty feet long and fifteen feet wide. Behind the cockpit was a small, but roomy, kitchen/dining area where the hatch to the outside was also located. Moving aft, he had to go through the bathroom to get to the bedroom. The last fifteen feet of the ship was dedicated to the engines in the form of a small engineering section with hatches that gave access to the crawlspaces belowdecks.

As he settled into pilot's chair, the onboard computer spoke to him in a sultry female voice, "Welcome aboard the *Star Splitter*." *Catchy name,* he thought. "Please state your request."

"Give engine status," he ordered.

"Primed and ready, sir" she said.

"Open garage door," he ordered again.

"Complying," she responded as the garage door lifted.

"Transfer controls to manual," placing his hands on the control yoke.

"Controls transferred," she said.

"Let's see what this baby can do!"

"Colonel Khail?" the computer asked.

Khai paused, eyebrows raised, looking up at the roof of the cockpit. "Um, yeah?"

"I have a message left remotely from Captain Dah. Would you like me to play it?"

"Yeah, let's hear it," he said, looking at the main screen imbedded in the cockpit paneling.

The smiling face of his new friend Dack'Tandy Dah blinked into view. *"Hey Khai. I just wanted to say 'good luck' because you're gonna need it, buddy. And furthermore, take good care of the Star Splitter. She's only on loan to you."* The cordial smile whipped off his face in an instant. *"You so much as scratch her and I'm taking it out of your hide. Got it?"* The cordial smile returned. *"Now, I'll let you know where Trall is the moment I find out. Good hunting, and may the Founders smile upon you."*

Heeding his friend's word, he gingerly maneuvered the ship out of the garage and into the alley, making sure he was well clear of the building and lifted off. The air traffic was thick with hovercars, skybuses, shuttles and other ships. He pulled into traffic and headed for the departure area where ships waited their turn to leave orbit. Once he was in line to depart, he spoke: "Computer."

"Yes Colonel? And please—call me Joon."

Joon. Khai liked that name; he would never forget the nice lady who used to feed him free pie when he was nothing more than a street urchin. He had to smile... and he did. He could almost taste the pie again. For several decades, he had wanted to return to that little café in the slums, but it was destroyed by gang activity almost twenty years earlier.

"Okay, Joon. In return, just call me Khai. I'm not in the military anymore."

"As you wish. What is your question?"

"How long 'til we're cleared to leave orbit?"

"One hour."

"I need some rest. Please wake me up at that time. I'll be in my quarters."

"As you wish, Khai."

Khai kicked off his boots and lay down on the bed. It was quite comfortable. He grabbed the selector and turned on the Net'Vyyd. He saw something on the news that shook him to his inner-most core. Suddenly, he wasn't tired anymore...

Pual'Branen Puar, still in his riot gear, stormed the Hall of Justice with the burning fury of a hundred suns. He had walked all night to get there. He nearly sprinted up the stairs to the main entrance that was flanked with a long row of granite columns, six on each side of the grand, wooden double doors.

In each of the columns, a face was carved. Each carving represented one of the twelve Founders of Seryys. It was said that tens of thousands of years ago, the Seryysans—known by a different name then, had the ability to travel the stars and had come to the planet... legend said they actually crashed on Seryys and their ship was destroyed.

It was said that before they crashed, they were highly advanced—even more so than the Seryysans of the current age. It was said that there might be others out there, like the founders, but they were most likely in another galaxy, or at the very least, on the far side of this galaxy.

With no technology, they were forced to start over. They had to rebuild an entire civilization from the ground up. Over millennia, the knowledge of interstellar travel and the memory of gallivanting across the stars faded into a dim memory where only ships of wood sailed the rivers, lakes, seas and oceans of Seryys. But, like all intelligent species, the art was always present, just waiting to be discovered—or *re*discovered, in the case of the Seryysans. This civilization blossomed into what was known now as Seryys.

"Hey!" a gruff voice shouted.

"*What*?" Puar snapped.

"You can't have that weapon in here! Only authorized personnel are allowed to carry firearms in the Hall of Justice."

Not stopping, he pulled his badge and threw it on the floor. It slid up to the security guard's feet. "Read it!"

He sprinted through the lavishly decorated, marble floored, pillar-lined main lobby, literally punched the lift car button and then tapped his foot impatiently, still fuming. The door slid open and before the lift car could even *ding*, he was in and hitting the button to the Honorifical Office repeatedly.

His anger had not dissipated in the slightest by the time he reached the two-hundredth floor a moment later. He stalked out into the Honorifical Office. The chair was facing away from him, behind the lavish desk, flanked by the Seryys flags on either side of it.

"Brother!" Pual'Branen cried.

The chair turned. *How could you do this to Khai? What the hell were you thinking? You asshole!* were just a few of the thousands of angry phrases that came to mind as he prepared to confront his brother over Khai's warrant. But the person in the chair sucked every ounce of anger out of him like atmosphere from a breached hull in the dead vacuum of space.

Pual'Branen stopped dead in his tracks.

"Mother?" he whispered. "What are you...? Where's...?" Her emerald eyes betrayed the deep anguish she felt. And he knew that something terrible had happened. The sadness on her face made her aged features look even older.

"Something awful has happened. Your brother..." she cried. "Your brother..."

She couldn't go on. All she could do was turn on the Net'Vyyd to the breaking news. It was an aerial shot of Upper Seryys just outside of Aurora. Smoke billowed up from a luxury high-rise, a gaping hole spewing flames from its side like a glass and metallic serpent with fire for blood filled the screen.

"*It was several hours ago,*" the female newscaster said, her voice quiet and reserved—almost mournful, "*that our beloved Prime Minister lived his final moments in terror as he and his driver, and long-time friend, Ralm'Es Ra, careened to their deaths into the side of this high-rise. Eyewitnesses reported that something went wrong with his private shuttle.*"

"*There are unconfirmed reports of hundreds dead inside the building and a full-scale investigation is already underway. Our hearts go out-*"

Puar shut it off, dropping to his knees. *He's dead!* Puar's voice rang in his head as if he had said it aloud. Before he could even register what his inner voice was telling him, his mother was there with him, kneeling beside him. Together they wept on the ornate carpet of the Honorifical Office, the office that, as far as they were concerned, would never be filled with as much love and devotion for the common people of Seryys as it had been the day before.

Khai pulled out of the line for orbit and was headed for the luxury high-rise where Prime Minister Puar's shuttle had crashed. He had to see it with his own eyes to believe it.

"Is this wise, Khai?" Joon asked.

"Do I care?" Khai shot back at the mouthy computer.

"I suppose not."

"That's right. Now shut up and let me drive."

"As you wish."

He piloted the ship into a sky traffic that floated nearly a hundred feet from the building. From that distance, he couldn't see much at all.

"Computer, are there any binoculars onboard?"

"Affirmative, in the survival kit attached to the wall directly behind you."

Khai fished out the binoculars. "Take over. Swing around so I can get a closer look."

Khai worked his way to the hatch and opened it. It popped the seal and a rush of warm air filled the cabin. The hatch slid back into the ship and then slid to the right toward aft. Looking out the starboard side of the ship with his binoculars, he got a good look at the impact point. The shuttle was buried a good fifty feet into the building. Being heavily armored, the shuttle was still somewhat intact. But, as Khai certainly knew, it was clear that no one could have survived an impact like that. Smashing into a building at one to two *g*'s was fatal, regardless of how armored the car was.

"That's it." Khai said ruefully. "He's gone. He's gone and there's nothing I can do about it."

"Were you expecting to be able to?" Joon asked.

"I don't know. I was hoping... I was hoping that it was just a mistake. Or that maybe... maybe he would still be alive. Do you have a police scanner?"

"Affirmative. My owner is, after all, a police officer."

"I want to you to monitor the scanner for anything pertaining to the accident and transfer controls back to me."

Khai pulled out of traffic and headed back for the departure point to leave for orbit and relative safety. Once in line, he transferred controls back to Joon and went back to the bedroom where he took a shower and got some long overdue sleep.

Minister Tran'Ri Trall sat in his office looking over files pertaining to some highly classified information when someone buzzed him over the intercom. He grunted annoyingly as he pushed the blinking button on his desk.

"Yes?" he hissed, not bothering to hide the irritation in his voice.

"The press is looking for answers to Puar's death. They want to know if you have any comment on the situation."

He scoffed in annoyance. "Tell them that a full-scale investigation takes time. We shouldn't have any solid leads on a cause for at least another four days. Are you really bothering me for *that?*"

It had been only a few hours since his death. But he was already making plans to take over. As second in command, it was his civil duty to assume the mantle of Prime Minister in instances of impairment, untimely death or impeachment of the Prime Minister. He had his assistant compose the acceptance letter. All he was waiting for was confirmation of Puar's death to sweep the nation. Then he would swoop in and pick up all the pieces.

"No, sir. I have news on the invasion."

"Well, out with it, then."

"There were two invasions, not one."

"Indeed." That piqued his attention. He leaned forward in his chair, resting his folded hands on the desk. "Go on."

"As one might expect, one was on the new shield generator and the other was on the primary com tower near the SCMBHF."

"Was either successful?" He was fishing for an answer.

"No, sir." Trall's hands began to shake violently. *Can't those blasted Vyysarri* do anything *right? "Colonel Khail-"*

"Former Colonel Khail," Trall corrected.

"Excuse me, sir. Former Colonel Khail was able to thwart the shield generator attack, while the other was-"

61

"Is he in custody now?"

"No, sir."

"WHAT?" he shouted through a clenched jaw.

"He's dead."

"Oh." He smiled a predator's smile. "How... unfortunate."

"I agree, sir. Apparently, according to the report that Captain Dack'Tandy Dah of SCATT filed through his official channels, Khail died in an explosion on the conference level of the shield generator building."

"Has he any next of kin?"

"None, sir."

Good! At least some *good news came out of this!*

"And what of the second attack?"

"The Vyysarri were killed, but one of them seemed to be accessing the computer."

Trall already knew where this was going. "What information did he get? Are we going to have to revamp our communication protocols?"

"No, sir. It's nothing like that at all. He was trying to upload *something from a memory stick. Base law enforcement was able to stop him before he could do anything."*

Interesting, he thought. "Do you have the memory stick?"

"No. You should be getting it any minute. I took the liberty of having it delivered straight to you before anyone else could even breathe on it. You should be the first to see what's on it."

"Excellent work."

"Sir?"

"What now?" he asked impatiently with a roll of his eyes.

"Do you really think he's dead? I mean, the man's a legend. It just seems so wrong for him to die that way."

"We can only pray to the Founders that he somehow survived," he said, feigning sorrow. "But the cold, hard reality is that he's probably dead." He had to suppress another evil smile.

"You... really think so, sir?"

With any luck! Trall internalized. "Only time will tell. Thank you for your help."

"It was my-"

Trall cut the channel. Khai had, yet again, thwarted his plans. At least he was dead, now. But he effectively pushed Trall into enacting Plan "B"- which involved the classified files he was reading. About fifty years prior, the Vyysarri had committed a whole task force of Vyysarri ships to an attack. The ships weren't the attacking force as much as what the ships were escorting. The Vyysarri they captured in the ship being escorted was interrogated until he revealed that the ship was called the *Hammer Cannon*. It contained a weapon so powerful, that it could level whole cities with a single shot. It fired a high-density, focused energy beam that penetrated a planet's crust causing a catastrophic seismic shockwave that rumbled cities to the ground. According to the tortured prisoner, the Vyysarri had used it once on another world far outside of Seryys Space with devastating results.

However, the Defense Navy was able to destroy the small armada and capture the *Hammer Cannon*. It was currently sitting in the hanger of Orbital Station 12...

Someone wearing a delivery uniform quickly entered and dropped a package on his desk. Trall signed for it and opened the package. Though his plans for the *Hammer Cannon* were pressing, he couldn't help but see what was on the memory stick. He plugged it into his computer and uploaded the information. There was a single video file of some kind. He pulled the video and the visage of an attractive young woman—if not a little too nerdy for Trall's taste—wearing a lab coat, standing in a dimly-lit office with the expression of someone who had the weight equivalent to the gravitational pull of a black hole on her shoulders filled the screen; she was beaten, battered and bruised.

"This is Doctor Tash'Door Tashar," she said, her voice strained, *"and I am the leading physicist of Operation: Bright Star. If you are viewing this, then the Vyysarri were successful in their mission. This is a warning to the Seryysan People..."*

"How interesting..." Trall mused, rubbing the top of his index finger along the bottom of his chin.

After watching the video he was speechless. But he didn't have time to reflect. There was a visitor waiting for him in the lobby.

"Send him in," Trall said.

A man, dressed in business proper, strolled in with a folder of paperwork. It was the Chief Medical Examiner, Ran'Dell Rashad.

"How do you do, sir?" deep lines in his dark face betrayed the confusion he was obviously feeling. "I have the preliminary reports on the bodies from the shuttle crash."

"Good," Trall hissed. "Come, have a seat. Can I offer you a drink?"

"Oh, yes, please. That would be nice."

"Pick your poison," Trall said, gesturing to the wet bar in his office.

"Just some ice water, please."

"As you wish," Trall said. "Me, I'm more of a Sarian Brandy kind of guy."

"Normally, I am too. But I'm on the clock."

He poured himself a drink and dropped three cubes of ice in it. Then he poured the glass of water, and with a slight of hand, slipped out a small bag with different ice in it. He dropped four cubes of that ice into the water glass and as he stepped away, knocked all the ice cubes to the floor.

"Ack! Blast these old clumsy hands." He smiled, walking over to Rashad. "Here's your water, sir. Now please, give me a moment to clean up my mess. I want to be able to give you my full attention."

He walked over to the sink and picked up every ice cube that hit the floor and put them all in the sink. He pumped the hand sanitizer past his hand into the sink while he ran hot water to melt all the ice, feigning that he was washing his hands. The "hand sanitizer" was a law enforcement-grade forensic cleanser used to clean up biohazards. He ran a cloth under the water stream and pumped some of the cleanser on it and cleaned the floor vigorously. None of this seemed uncommon as Minister Tran'Ri Trall was well known as a bona-fide germaphobe and was also known for having ridiculously potent cleaning agents in his possession.

"So, how's the wife and kids?"

Rashad took a big gulp of water. "Oh, they're the usual. My wife is just doing her usual mom thing; my oldest will be going off to college in two months and my youngest will be entering her final year of secondary school."

"Where does the time go?" he asked more of himself than Rashad.

It had been almost ten years since he lost his family to the Vyysarri. They were vacationing on the beaches of the island planet of Seryys III. The planet was less than two percent landmass and the rest was fresh water. In fact, the water was so pure there that the Seryys government shuttled if from there to the outlying planets with thousands of huge ships that literally landed in the water and pumped it into their gigantic tanks. It was quite the spectacle to watch.

The Vyysarri knew that it was a hotspot for vacationers and knew that it was also lightly guarded, as most of the defense fleet was surrounding Seryys. They punched through and simply started bombarding the planet from orbit, targeting high population spots where casualties would be highest. It was a sick and cowardly attack whose only purpose was to cause death and destruction.

The hotel where Trall and his family were staying was among the first to be hit. As Trall went to the local market to buy some fresh flowers for his beautiful wife, the first laser cannon blast flashed through the clouds and turned the sand near the flower hut to molten glass. The next two or three shots, Trall missed as he was still trying to get to his feet.

The moment he stood, he looked up at the hotel just in time to see a cannon blast rip through it. He cried out for his loved ones. He couldn't hear a thing—not even his own anguished cries, as the initial blast had deafened him. Two more volleys and the hotel was nothing more than a smoldering, twisted pile of metal girders and crete. No one still in the hotel at the time of the attack survived. What was worse was the fact that the bodies of his loved ones were never recovered, most likely having been incinerated by the cannon blasts. In hindsight, he decided that that was a better way to go than being slowly crushed to death.

"That's a good question..." his sentence trailed as he realized he was having trouble breathing. He started making struggled gargling, choking sounds and feverishly clawing at his throat. He looked imploringly over at Trall who watched with an almost disinterested, detached expression, his mind still on his lost family. Eventually, he moved into action and called his assistant to bring in the EMRT, or Emergency Medical Response Team.

They were there within minutes. They got a brief summary of the events leading up to his collapse and then took over. They worked diligently on the poor man, but it was too late. He died of heart failure half an hour after the EMRT arrived. Trall suppressed a smile.

Chapter Six

"Heard your ship got stolen yesterday," Captain Byyner said to Captain Dah.

"Yeah," Dah said, stirring his soup and sighing.

"I thought you'd be a little bit more upset about it."

"What's a ship versus someone's life?" Dah asked ruefully.

"Dah!" Byyner almost whined. "You gotta move past that! He was a soldier! He died an honorable death. What more would you want for him?"

"I don't know, a clear name, perhaps."

"Well, that's not gonna happen. He lied on his application; he would have been put to death. I rather like the idea that he died a hero protecting the city rather than by lethal injection as a traitor."

"I guess you're right," Dah said, feigning sorrow. "So, have you heard anything about Puar's crash?"

"No," Byyner seemed genuinely puzzled by this. "Trall's being very hush-hush about it. No official press conference or anything."

"That's unusual," Dah said, after spooning some soup into his mouth.

"Yeah. What's worse is the Chief Medical Examiner died in Trall's office from heart failure. He was perfectly healthy before."

"I also heard that Sam'Ule San, Director of D-PAG was arrested for embezzlement."

"Really?" Byyner asked, shocked. He had met the man once. Young and ambitious—and honest almost to a fault, Byyner couldn't picture San as the type of scum who would steal from a company that was already paying him probably six times what Bynner made in a year.

It was all so weird how things were coming together and swarming around Minister Trall. Even Trall was the one who ordered Khai's arrest. Trall was the last person to see Puar alive; the last person to see Rashad alive and... the last person alive who can claim the...

"Ti'tan'lium." Dah said.

"What?" Byyner asked.

"The Ti'tan'lium. I think that's the lynchpin. Trall is now the only one alive to lay claim to the Ti'tan'lium deposit under the city."

"Yeah, but there's a *city* over it. And the last report I saw said that it would destroy the city."

"So why not speed the process up? Come on, Cap'! Think about it. The riots with gangbangers using military-grade weapons—*outlawed* weapons, the shield dropping momentarily to let in a force that would have maybe permanently disabled the shield generator if it weren't for Khai's efforts, it all makes sense. I'd bet my meager paycheck on it!"

"So what do we do? I can tell you that I'm not the hero Khai was."

"No, but we can still make a difference!" He thought for a moment. "You know, Cap'. I think you shouldn't get involved. I might have to do things that would be considered... oh, I don't know, illegal."

"So what are you going to do?"

"I'm officially going on a leave of absence, sir. I'll be honest—I don't expect my job to be waiting for me when I get back. But I don't want you to get implicated in any way."

Byyner extended his hand and Dah took it. "Good luck."

"Thanks. I'm gonna need it."

"Bet your ass you will."

The next day, Dack'Tandy Dah, former police officer, set out on a task to help Khai get to bottom of... well, whatever it was that he needed to get to the bottom of. He knew the first person that he needed to talk to was Sam'Ule San. He had a hunch that the guy was innocent. And there had to be someone who saw Ran'Dell Rashad alive before he left for Trall's office. He wasn't interested in how he died, because Trall killed him to cover something up.

He got into his hovercar and left his garage—the garage attached to the house, that is— and pulled into traffic. He was headed for the Seryys Governmental Lockup within the city limits. It was a minimum-security facility to hold less dangerous individuals.

He pulled out that dedicated com unit and thumbed it on. "Uh, Khai? Are you there?"

"Yeah, Cap'. What's up?"

"I'm not a captain anymore. I took a leave of absence to help you investigate. And I have my first lead."

"Sam'Ule San?"

"Yeah," Dah didn't hide surprise in his voice. "How'd you know?"

"A hunch. I saw his arrest on the Net'Vyyd. He just struck me as the innocent type. Do what you can. I'm just laying low until I have a target."

"Where are you now?"

"Just floating around."

"You taking care of my ship?"

"Of course, what kind of a guy d'you think I am?"

"The type who's hard on bad guys, ships... um, cars. I don't know."

"Point taken. I have to go, though. This link can still be traced, if used too long."

"Got it. I'll contact you when I have more information for you."

"Good. Thanks, buddy. Talk to you soon."

The line went dead. He was almost there. *Time to make a difference.*

"Good. Thanks, buddy. Talk to you soon."

Khai killed the link. He wasn't entirely truthful with Dack. First of all, the com unit couldn't be traced; he used it on several worlds across the galaxy, but he needed to focus on flying the ship. Second, he wasn't in orbit; he was dropping from orbit into the atmosphere of Seryys IV, the planet where he became a household name. It was an arid world where water was as valuable as Ti'tan'lium. He was there to meet an old friend. But what Dack didn't know, couldn't hurt him.

The ship dropped into the atmosphere, her bow white-hot from re-entry. The *Star Splitter* soared for a small, out-of-the-way spaceport on the north pole of the desert planet that only the locals knew about. There, he would meet with his old friend and there, he would get some more help—not in the form of manpower, but in weapons.

"This is *Star Splitter* requesting permission to land."

"Reduce altitude to one thousand feet and then stay on your course until permission is given," a curt voice said.

"Roger that." Khai dropped the ship to one thousand feet, where powerful scanners buried in the ground scanned the ship for weapons—of which she had none—and finally allowed him in.

"Star Splitter, state your business in Dune Spaceport."

"I'm just here to meet with an old friend. Perhaps you know her, Joon'Kind Joom.

Suddenly a voice came on that made Khai immediately smile. *"Khai'Xander Khail! Is that you?"*

"Yes, ma'am."

"You're clear to land in... docking bay ninety-four. And I'll have some pie ready for you when you land."

"Sounds great, Joon. See you in a few."

Khai piloted the ship expertly into the tight opening of the docking bay and landed it on the designated pad. He secured his pistol into his thigh holster. After all, it was still a tough neighborhood. He stepped out from the ship and used the codepad to lock her up tight and activate the anti-theft system. Immediately, he was swarmed by urchins begging for coin. It didn't take long to realize that these urchins weren't just begging for coin, they were *insisting*. Khai felt the cold steel of a gun muzzle press hard against his back.

"You don't want to do that," Khai growled.

"Oh, I think I do. Now give me the cash."

There were four of them, one on either side, one in front and one behind. The one behind seemed to be the only one armed.

The thief on his right spoke up. "Holy shit, Max! This guy's packin' some serious heat!"

"Max?" Khai called out. "You don't want to do this."

"Shut up! You don't know me!"

"Apparently, you don't know me either."

With that, he threw his head back and hit Max right on the nose. He instantly crumbled to the sand. The others reacted wildly, pulling knives and clubs and attacking immediately. The three remaining thugs all lunged recklessly at Khai at once. Khai honed his finely tuned skills and leapt forward in a high somersault over the would-be attackers. They all collided with each other and hit the ground in a tangled mess of arms and legs.

The only female in the group, being more flexible, was able to detangle herself from the others and brandished her knife again.

"Look, little girl. You are seriously testing my never-hit-a-woman clause. If you want to get messed up, keep pushing."

She charged him, thrusting the knife forward. Khai caught the girl's wrist and used her own momentum to flip her on her back, knocking the wind from her lungs. She gasped as her diaphragm went into a stunned spasm. With the girl effectively out of the fray, he could focus on dumb and dumber.

Dumb swung a club horizontally at Khai's head. Khai ducked under and came up with a devastating uppercut that sent him flying back, spread-eagled, spitting teeth and blood. Dumber attacked with a knife much like the gasping girl's. The blade barely glanced Khai's arm and Dumber whooped a victory. That victory was short lived. With blurring speed, Khai swept the guy off his feet. He lost the knife mid-fall and Khai caught it, bringing it down through Dumber's thigh and into the dirt. He cried out in pain.

"Oh, quit your crying!" Khai spat. "It's only flesh wound. I made sure not to hit any arteries." The guy said nothing, just writhed in pain grasping at the knife. "Don't pull it out, stupid. You'll bleed to death."

"Khai," Joon's voice came from behind him. "You causing trouble already?"

"No, ma'am. I was just teaching the kids how to win a fight when the odds are stacked against you. Though this one here may need a medic."

"I'll send for one. You guys picked the wrong guy to rob. This is the legendary Khai'Xander Khail. He could have taken on like six more of you at once. You didn't stand a chance."

They left the bloodied bunch behind at the docking bay and convened in a local cantina.

"How long has it been, Khai?"

"Fifteen years," said Khai, then downed a shot of something that burned all the way to his stomach. He set the shot glass down on the bar. "I'll have another... of whatever that was."

"So what brings you here after fifteen years?" Joon asked.

"Weapons, not to put too fine a point on it."

"Ah," Joon said in mock disappointment. "And here I was thinking that you were coming for a social call."

"Well, I did come for some pie, too."

"I guess that's about as social as you get," Joon mused, then turned serious. "What kind of weapons are you looking for?"

"Anything in particular?"

"Big ones?" Khai joked.

"Well, that narrows it down a bit."

"And pie," Khai added.

"All right, all right," Joon said, putting up her hands in surrender. "Let's go back to my place. The pie I made should be ready."

A short ride later, they arrived at Joon's little hovel. It was only her living in the house. Her husband, a former black market weapons dealer, was killed five years earlier when a rival dealer put a contract out on him. Joon left Seryys several years after Khai was taken into the custody by the government and after her oldest kid flew the coop. She fell in love with a dashing and mysterious man and was swept off her feet.

They went on adventure after adventure, smuggling weapons to the frontier colonies outside the Seryys System, running from the law and hitmen and making money hand over fist. Since her husband's death, she was doing odd jobs here and there, but kept her husband's cache of weapons... just in case. Khai had bought weapons from him before when he was marooned on Seryys IV the day his carrier crashed. He was on his way home from a long campaign against the Vyysarri and a saboteur caused the crash. The saboteur was a high-ranking member of the crew and claimed that he had learned the "truth" about the war and the Vyysarri. Khai didn't care about the particulars, only that he was a traitor and needed to die. It puzzled him how something could send this well-respected officer and half the crew into a frenzy of conspiracy.

He and just about half the crew had allied against Khai and the rest of the crew. More importantly, they held the downed ship and all the weapons. That was when Joon's husband came into the picture. The fight lasted two days. When Khai won the battle, the ringleader went on and on about knowing the "truth" and all he wanted was to show them. Khai put a bullet into the back of his head before he could say any more and turn some of the currently-loyal crew members against him.

Khai and Joon sat at her table, a bowl of something that smelled incredibly spicy sat in front of them.

"Dig in," Joon said. Khai took an exploratory bite and nodded in approval. It was delicious. He had a cup of ale with his dinner. His watch chimed; he quickly pushed a button on it and the alarm shut off. "What was that?"

"My alarm," Khai said curtly, pulling a pill bottle out of his pocket, unscrewing the lid and dropping a pill into his hand. He popped the pill in his mouth and downed it with a whole cup of ale.

Joon eyed the bottle and snatched it before Khai could put it back. As she read, Khai poured himself another cup of ale. He sat down and started chugging the ale.

"Do not take with alcohol," she read, before Khai could finish his fourth cup of ale. He offered her a sheepish shrug. "You suffer from Post-Traumatic Stress Syndrome? And you're asking me for weapons? You must be crazy."

"Yup," Khai agreed. "I also have a warrant for my arrest."

"Ah. Who'd you piss off?"

"Apparently the Minister of Planetary Affairs."

"Tran'Ri Trall?" asked Joon in a surprised, but almost impressed tone. "*That* takes talent."

"A talent I have, apparently. But I think he's up to something, and I swear to the Founders that it's sinister."

"Why do you say that?" Joon asked, just before taking a long, enjoyable gulp of cold ale.

"Have you been watching the news?"

"Yeah, Puar dying, these crazy riots, the shield generator having a very convenient temporary shutdown and the most recent news of the medical examiner working on Puar's case dying in Trall's office."

"I hadn't heard about that last one, but it further proves my theory. He's up to no good. I can feel it."

"You're not..."

"Yes, I am. That's why I need the best weapons your husband had. I'm about to take on the whole planet."

"Well, in that case. Follow me."

"Ah!" Khai stopped her. "*After* pie."

They both chuckled.

The trip to the prison had been completely unhelpful. San swore up and down he had no idea where the money came from and that he hadn't taken a single credit from D-PAG. He clocked out one day and the next morning, the police were busting down the door of his Upper Seryys condo. Dah used the prison's computer to try tracking the large deposit, but without the backing of the police department, the banks were somewhat unwilling to give him the information he needed. The only promising information San provided was that Trall had come to visit him the day before inquiring about the Ti'tan'lium deposit beneath the city. He was looking for the amount in tonnage.

Suspicion sunk into Dah's stomach like a brick of crete. Trall was dirty, he knew it. But he needed proof, a smoking gun. He had one other stop to make before going home for the day. He was going to talk to Rashad's assistant. His backup plan, of course, was to do a full forensic analysis on Trall's office. On his way to the Seryys City Morgue, he called Byyner and got even more bad news. When presented with an official search warrant, Trall trumped that with a bullshit immunity clause that kept forensic investigators out of his office. With his backup plan officially screwing the pooch, he had to put all his eggs in the current investigation basket. He didn't like that at all, but what choice did he have?

A moment later, he landed on a landing pad designated for police on the main SCBI Building. The Seryys City Bureau of Investigation had one main office and several satellite branches all over the city, planet and system. More than a million workers strong, from administrative, to lab techs, to special agents, they were in charge of every investigation in the whole system. They did, however, leave smaller, less important investigations to local law enforcement agencies.

He exited his car and made his way to the entrance. A burly security guard stepped out in front of him. "You can't park there! It's reserved for-" Dah flashed his badge, "police."

He stepped aside and let Dah past. Dah caught a reflection of himself in the mirror-like surface on the windows in front of him. He was wearing dark shades, a long black duster, combat boots and a shoulder holster where his service piece was snuggly secured. *I look like a hitman*, he thought to himself with a slight chuckle.

The double doors slid open at his approach and he entered the building. There was a desk with a pleasant-looking woman sitting, filing her nails.

"May I *help* you?" she asked, eyeing him—and not hiding it in the slightest. The way she asked gave him the distinct impression that she was looking for more than just helping him find his way around the *building.*

"Uh, yeah." He put on a charming smile and showed his badge again. "I'm Captain Dah of the SCPD. I'm looking for Doctor Rashad's office."

The flirtatious smile was swept from her face as if he had slapped it off. "It's off limits, by order of the Honorifical Office."

"Who placed the order?"

"Minster Trall. No one is allowed in or out of his office, his lab or his residence."

"Did he have any assistants?"

"He had one," she said, looking almost nervous. "Bria'Nah Briar. But she disappeared before his death."

"Hmm." He scratched his whiskered face. "Okay. Thank you for your time. Can you direct me to the restroom?"

"Down the hall and to the right."

"Thank you."

Dah moved on. Once he rounded the corner, he slunk off to find Rashad's office. There had to be a sign somewhere that said where his office was. As if his prayers were answered, a sign hung from the ceiling saying that Rashad's office was one floor up in room 703.

Upon picking the electronic lock with a small device that overloaded the door's servos, he started snooping around. There was paperwork scattered about. It looked as though the place had already been ransacked. *Damn! I'm too late!* Dah thought ruefully. He fruitlessly sifted through piles of crumpled papers, overturned furniture and wrecked equipment. He was about to leave when an electronic chime nearly scared him out of his skin. He shook his head and rolled his eyes, silently berating himself for being so jumpy. He dug through the garbage all over the floor and found the jingling device, a com unit. It registered a missed text message. He thumbed through the com unit's data base and found the message. It had been sent right around the same time of Rashad's death and it was sent from Bria'Nah Briar.

It read: Come to the house, Lover.

Lover? That's odd. Dah knew that Rashad was married—and happily so... at least he thought.

He pocketed the com unit and snuck out.

He walked by the front desk and the flirty secretary called out to him.

"What?" he asked, his skin flushing a bit.

"Did you find the restroom?" she repeated.

"Uh, oh, yeah! Thanks. Have a nice day."

"You too," she said with a pleasant smile.

Dah lowered his hovercar onto the private landing pad attached to the Rashads' house in Upper Seryys. He entered the house, ducking under the orange caution tape denoting a crime scene. The house was in far better shape than his office. The house wasn't huge by any means, but definitely was bigger than Dah had expected. He stealthily moved through the house. The kitchen, living room and bedrooms were empty. He only had one room left.

He moved down the hallway to what he thought was Rashad's den. He slowly forced the door open after overriding the servos. It was open about six inches when gunshots rang out, hitting the door inches from his hands. He ducked back and pulled his sidearm from his shoulder holster. He risked a look into the den. There was someone hiding behind the huge wooden desk. He was surprised that his attacker hadn't taken that opportunity to put a bullet in his head.

He acted on a hunch. "Bria'Nah Briar?" he shouted the question.

"Who are you?" a frightened, female voice shakily called out.

"Please. Put your weapon down. My name is Dack'Tandy Dah. I'm with the SCPD."

"Prove it!" she shouted.

Dah took it on faith that she wanted to believe him. The first thing he threw was his gun, then his badge. He heard footsteps skitter up to both. He held his breath, thumbing his backup pistol within his boot.

"You see?" Dah said. "I'm not here to hurt you. I'm investigating Doctor Rashad's death."

"You don't look like a cop. You look like a hitman."

"I'm doing this off the record because Minister Trall has deemed it an open and shut case. But I don't believe that it's as black and white as he's making it out to be."

The woman's voice was right at the crack in the door when she spoke, soliciting a slight jump from Dah. "I have proof."

"What kind of proof?"

"Throw in your other gun, and I'll tell you."

Dah's eyebrows shot up. "How did you know?"

"You're a cop," she said plainly. "No respectable cop would throw in his *only* gun to someone who was just shooting at him." He heaved a long sigh and rolled his eyes, pulling his backup from its boot holster and tossed it in as well. "Go ahead and open the door."

Dah got to his feet and pried the door open. A very beautiful woman, with tight curves, wavy brown hair with red highlights, smooth, pale skin, vibrant green eyes and in her mid-thirties stood in the office, a small gun in her trembling hand.

"You mind, maybe, putting that down, first." She nodded and put the gun down on the desk. "Thanks," he chuckled. "That's better. So what proof do you have?"

"This," she said, holding up a memory stick.

"What am I going to find on that memstick?"

"Look for yourself." She plugged the memory stick into Rashad's computer. Dah walked around to look at the screen. "I thought that maybe they were his financial records. But when I heard of his death..." her voice began to break and tears rolled down her cheek. She took a deep breath and wiped the tears away. "When I heard of his death, I checked it and..."

Dah picked up where she left off. "Found out why he was killed." It was all right there in front of him in black and white. The bodies found in the hovercar were that of Ralm'Es' Ra and an unknown male, definitely *not* Prime Minister Pual'Kin Puar.

"This is it!" Dah gasped. "This is the evidence I was looking for."

"What's Minister Trall up to?"

"I don't know yet, but I think it has something to do with large Ti'tan'lium deposit beneath the city." She nodded thoughtfully. "So, how did you avoid Rashad's fate?"

"He sent me a letter. The memstick was with it. The letter only told me to go into hiding. I just figured that his wife found out about... us."

"He must have foreseen the possibility of Trall making this kind of move. Ballsy for sure, but he could've gone straight the Magistrate and bypassed Trall all together."

"Maybe he didn't want to arouse suspicion," Bria offered.

"I guess it's possible. It could also be that he wanted to make damn sure he had a backup. Maybe he didn't expect to die, but he might've expected Trall to falsify the documents."

"Either one of them makes sense," Bria said with a shrug. "So now what?"

"I gotta get you out of here, like *now*," Dah said, escorting her down the hallway back to his car. "You're not safe here. You'll be safer at my place."

"Okay," she said, stuffing her pistol back into her purse as they walked.

"Why *did* you shoot at me right away?"

"I don't know." Bria shrugged. "You're dressed like a hitman."

Dah laughed. "I said the same thing to myself as I entered SCBI Building earlier today. I'm actually off-"

"You were at SCBI Building today?"

"Yeah," Dah shrugged. "Why? I was on official police business."

"Did anyone see you?"

"Well, yeah. The security guards, that super-hot receptionist who directed me to the restrooms, a handful of workers. Why?"

"Shit!" she scoffed, looking around, scared stiff.

"What? What's wrong?" Dah stopped and gently grabbed her arm, forcing her stop and look at him.

"Any one of those people could have been a spy! Did you tell anyone where you were going next?"

"No," he promised. "Not even my superiors know where I am."

"What's that supposed to mean?" She fixed him with a very incredulous gaze.

"Like I said, I'm not really on official police business." Dah looked at the floor, unable to look Bria in her beautiful green eyes. "I knew Trall was dirty from the moment he authorized the use of deadly force on the rioters weeks ago. So I was willing to go the extra distance to get the evidence I needed. I knew, as a cop, that I couldn't touch Trall. But as a civilian, I could get away with certain things. My superiors know I'm up to something, just not what."

"So, who's getting this information I gave you?"

"A friend," Dah said and started walking again.

"A friend?" Bria asked, falling into step.

"A friend in high places... *literally.*"

"So are you-" Bria's question was cut short when a high-velocity bullet ripped clear through her abdomen, lodging in the wall behind her.

"Bria!" he shouted.

She dropped to the floor, a steady flow of blood issuing from the wound the size of a man's thumbnail. He instantly dropped to the ground, too, pulling his side arm. It was definitely a sniper. Someone must have followed him to Rashad's residence.

He grabbed Bria by the shoulder of her shirt, and dragged her along the carpet below the view of the windows. Some random shots ripped through the walls near them. Clearly the sniper got the impression that he was crawling on the floor. Another bullet ripped through the wall inches from his head and he stopped for moment.

A loud crash came from one of the spare rooms that led to the hallway.

Ah crap! Dah thought.

He could hear footsteps, booted and running. They rounded the corner and looked at the two of them lying on the floor. Suddenly another bullet ripped through the hallway and dropped one of the approaching bad guys. Then another bullet came and another man dropped. Dah opened fire on the remaining and, between him and this unknown, friendly sniper, they were able to clear out the house.

Suddenly, Dah's com unit chimed. Dah checked it and it indicated that Koon was calling him.

"Thought you could use some help!" his voice came through.

"And not a minute too soon. What are you doing here?"

"Caught wind of a break-in on the scanner. Your name came up and I knew that you weren't going to be able to take 'em all by yourself."

"Did you get the other sniper?"

"Come on, Cap'!" Koon sounded almost hurt... *almost.* *"I took care of him first."*

"I owe you a drink," Dah said, picking up the barely-breathing Bria'Nah Briar.

"And I'm gonna order the most expen-" Koon's reply abruptly turned into an agonized cry followed by a gurgled moan.

"Koon?" Dah called. "Koon, you there?"

"Captain Dack'Tandy Dah?" a sultry female voice asked over Koon's mic frequency.

"Who is this?"

"Who I am isn't important. Your friend Koon, here... well, let's just say he's a good shot, but he hit the wrong target... and paid for it with his life."

"You bitch!" Dah growled. "He was just a kid." It was true; he was barely twenty-five years old.

"Easy, Captain. I can see you quite clearly. Let's cut a deal. You give me the memstick and the girl, and I let you go and forget that you violated a federal law to obtain the information you're carrying."

"And if I tell you to go fuck yourself?"

"Then I put a bullet between your eyes and you both die."

Dah was feeling a little bolder than usual today. He started flapping his arms and bobbing his head like a bird. "What am I doing right now?"

"Acting like an idiot," the velvet voice answered pointedly.

"Ah! But you didn't say *what* I was acting like," Dah pointed out. A bullet blasted through the window and grazed Dah's face so close that he could feel the heat emanating from it. "Okay, so you *can* see me."

"That's right, Captain Dah. Now what's your choice?"

"So I hand over the girl and evidence, and I walk away clean as a baby's butt?" Dah was only really interested in buying some time to activate his car's homing equipment to zone-in on his location and fly to him.

"That's the idea."

"Hmm, that's a gracious offer; the type that only a *fool* would decline. But, then again, I was never accused of being the sharpest tool in the shed. Go *fuck* yourself!" he shouted as the car crashed into the hallway and the hatch popped open. While bullets rained down on him from a distance, he loaded Bria into the car and took off for heavy traffic in hopes of losing any other tails that he might have picked up his trail. He felt a pang of regret for not picking up Koon's body, but he wasn't in the mood for a straight up fight and Bria needed medical treatment.

He knew just the place.

Chapter Seven

"It's bad," the doctor said. He went solely by the name Medic. Dah never knew his real name, but understood that it was essential for his protection. With as many enemies he had, it was a miracle he could go to the corner store without getting dragged into an alley and beaten to death. He used to be a mob medic, but got out of the business when he ratted out a major crime boss on a plea bargain.

Now he did basement treatments for low-income people. He would take payments in food or goods or, of course, cold, hard cash. But he lived in a constant state of fear that mafia muscle would knock down his door at any time. That's when he changed his name and had his face surgically altered in an attempt to disappear. So far, it had worked.

"How bad is 'bad'?"

"I might not be able save her. She's lost a lot of blood."

"I got her here as quickly as I could."

"That's probably why she's still alive." He closed the wound using a small laser device that cauterized it. It was a field medic's bandage used for closing bullet wounds quickly. "I have her hooked up to an IV with synthetic but if her body doesn't assimilate it, I don't have enough real blood to save her. Right now, it's going to be a waiting game."

"How long until we know?"

"Maybe tomorrow morning," he said with a shrug.

"Okay. Give me a call on my com unit when you know for sure. I have to make a call."

"Khai!" Dah said when Khai answered.

"You got something for me, Dack?"

"As a matter of fact, I do. I've got the dirt on Trall that we needed. I have it here on a memstick. I'm transmitting it to you now. It's encrypted, but Joon's onboard computer will decrypt it for you."

"Okay, I just got it... the computer is decrypting it..." Khai paused for a long time. "Are you shittin' me?"

"No," Dah said plainly. It was certainly wasn't a time to joke.

"The body in Puar's shuttle wasn't him?"

"You know what this means?"

"Yeah," Khai growled. *"Puar's alive and I'm in for a world of hurt."*

"There's just one problem. We don't know where Trall is."

"We'll know soon enough," Khai said.

"How can you be so sure?" Dah asked.

"Now that the populace thinks Puar's dead, he'll make his move. And with any luck, he'll give away his position."

"I hope you're right."

"Trust me," Khai said and cut the transmission.

"'Trust me'," he mocked. "How can I trust you when you won't let me in on the plan?"

Life blurred into view as the drugs that Trall had injected into Puar's system began to wear off. The injection was a concoction that slowed the body's processes down to a crawl; for all intents and purposes, he had been almost legally dead for three days, slumped over, comatose in a plush chair in the control/panic room deep within the rock walls of the canyon bunker. Trall sat across from him, leaned back in an equally plush chair, legs crossed, a pistol trained on him. All the muscles in Puar's body ached with oxygen deprivation.

"Good morning, Prime Minister. 'Bout time you came around."

"Trall! What the hell is-"

"Shut up!" Trall screamed. Puar complied. "I didn't want it to come to this, but you've left me with little choice! It was I who bribed a lowly, underpaid engineer to drop the power in that grid long enough to let a couple Vyysarri ships through, not to mention the military-grade weapons supplied to the Slum Gangs. I so hoped they would rid me of the insufferable Colonel Khail and my prayers have been answered. Though his selfless death did save the shield generator—and prolonged the life of this city, I was not without a backup plan. Now, I'll just have to use the *Hammer Cannon* instead. Despite Khail's efforts—it's inevitable, the city *will* fall and I'll be rich! Rich beyond my wildest dreams!"

"This is about the *Ti'tan'lium*?" Puar did nothing to hide his disgust.

"Oh!" Trall laughed maniacally. "Bravo, our fearless, *brainless* leader! Seryys law dictates that any minerals not claimed by the government, can be claimed by its discoverer. And since *Former* Colonel Khail isn't around to claim it for himself, and with Director San being arrested for embezzling millions of credits from D-PAG, I'll be the only one to claim it. I'll sell it to Seryys Combat and they'll be more than happy to buy from me to avenge the travesty of Seryys City."

"I'll never give you the fire code."

"I beg to differ, Pual." An evil scowl graced his gaunt face. "I don't want to bring your family into this. It would be most unfortunate if your brother's armor failed to stop a bullet, or if your mother's house was to burn down, or even... your nephew's school was terrorized by Slum Gangs... How is your wife these days?"

"Why you little..."

"Oh please," Trall hissed. "What are you going to do, huh? I've programmed the security to kill you if you leave this room. And I already have 'people' watching every move your family makes. If you value their lives, you'll give me the code."

"Fine," Puar relented, fearing for his family's safety. "It's Puar-seven-seven-five-alpha-tango-two. But the Board of Directors will never let something like that happen without my consent, even *with* the fire code."

Seryys Combat was a corporation, contracted by the government, to produce, build and maintain the military that protected the Seryys System. Though the Prime Minister had supreme power of the military, there was also a board of directors, which was made up of equal parts, retired military, civilians and retired government officials, who could accept or deny a declaration of war or a commission to build a weapon of mass destruction as a kind of checks and balances. Seryys Combat was the largest employer in the system being on all five of the habitable planets in the system and on countless other colony worlds within their boundaries. The government gave SC a yearly stipend and whatever overhead the company had, was out of pocket for them, not the government. That meant less deficit spending and more production.

"Oh," the Minister of Planetary Affairs sang. "Prime Minister, I'm afraid that you don't have any authority anymore... you see, you're *dead*. It was just unfortunate that your body guard and driver had to die, too. Who would have thought that your personal shuttle's hover pad array would malfunction?"

Puar instantly felt for his family. Ralm'Es Ra was another veteran with PTSD. He was fired from a construction company working in the Corporate Sector on the shield generator project. After Ralm was fired and arrested—and being a former soldier himself—Prime Minister Puar took pity on him and gave him the job. That, and he and his family had been good friends with the Ra family for decades and when an opportunity came up to help that family, Puar hired him in a heartbeat. He was a good soldier and dear friend to him... and Colonel Khai'Xander Khail.

"You son of a bitch!" Puar rumbled as he jumped up and tried to wrest the gun from Trall's hand. He didn't make it far. A security robot stunned him with a taser jolt that sent him falling, stiff as a board, to the floor.

"That's better."

Trall turned his back on his Prime Minister and left. He had a date with a multi-trillion-credit destiny and he didn't want to be late. He was headed for Orbital Station 12, in low orbit around Seryys to watch the city fall from a good safe distance.

"Trall, you piece of shit! This isn't over!"

Trall stopped and spun on his heel. The lighting in the bunker accentuated every deep line and wrinkle on his sickly face. "You are so right, Prime Minister. Things are going to get a whole lot worse before they get better. And don't worry, my friend. You'll die soon enough. The *only* reason you're still alive is because I feel that you might still prove useful yet. "

"You bastard," Puar seethed. "You'd sell your soul to the Vyysarri if it meant turning a profit in your favor."

"Now, Prime Minister. How ignorant that violent, little brain of yours is." A large smile crept across his gaunt features. "My actions will not only make me rich beyond my wildest dreams, they'll save this system and help to eliminate the Vyysarri threat through new ships and weapons. In all actuality, I'm a *true* patriot."

"Listen, Trall. I know that the death of your family was hard to cope with, but this is not the way to avenge their deaths. I can't tell you how many friends I lost in the SCGF, but that doesn't give me the *right* to kill my own kind as a means to justify an end."

"Your words are true, but the real world doesn't work that way. There's *always* collateral damage... *always.*" Trall took a menacing step closer. "You're too soft. I will be a strong leader, one who can make those tough decisions. You should thank me, Pual. You will be the Prime Minister who everyone loved and mourned the death of, as a hero and someone who truly loved his people, while I'll be the Prime Minister who everyone hated because I was the one who sent innocent people to their deaths, but ultimately saved the planet. And when the people realize that the *Hammer Cannon* was a Vyysarri attack, they'll cry out for blood and revenge. The cause will have renewed strength and conviction, and we will push harder than ever to end the Vyysarri threat forever."

"You're *so* selfless," Puar growled.

"I know," Trall said, his smile becoming more sinister. "What can I say, Pual? I'm a giver. Now, if you'll excuse me?"

A space-worthy shuttle was waiting for him on the platform when he got there. He climbed in and ordered the pilot to break for orbit as soon as he had clearance.

Once he arrived at Orbital Station 12, he marched straight to the commander's quarters and sat in the chair. He had relieved the current commander of his duties for the time being. He activated the com systems and overrode the systems communication broadcasting channels.

Every Net'Vyyd, com unit and any other communication device on every planet in the Seryys System broadcasted Trall's image and voice. When he spoke, his even tone was impeccable and he put on his best derjik face. Trall's ability to bluff during any game of derjik was legendary. It had served him well over the years no matter what kind of hand he was dealt, both in games and in politics.

"My fellow Seryysans," he started, feigning deep sorrow. "Three days ago, SCBI's Chief Medical Examiner, Ran'Dell Rashad, died in my arms, an unfortunate allergic reaction was to blame. Even sadder was the information with which he presented me."

"Ladies and gentlemen, it is my most upsetting and sorrowful duty to inform you that the bodies found in the Prime Minister's personal shuttle were those of Ralm'Es Ra and..." he faked choking back tears, "Prime Minister Pual'Kin Puar. Our hearts and prayers go out to their families in this time of great emotional turmoil. Though I can never replace Prime Minister Puar, it is my most profound honor to succeed him. As of oh-eight-hundred hours, today, I have officially taken my place as Commander in Chief of the Seryys System and all outlying colonies."

"This is a dark time for Seryys. The Vyysarri knocking at our front door weekly, slum gangs terrorizing out streets, our greatest hero, Colonel Khai'Xander Khail, dying in the line of duty, are only a small taste of what we face. But I know that the resolve of our great society is strong; stronger than the Vyysarri savages, stronger than the slum gangs and stronger than our heroes. I know, as Seryysans, we can come together and overcome any obstacle. I am a patriot. I live to serve the people of this great nation. And I will personally take the Vyysarri threat head-on. I am giving you my solemn oath that the Vyysarri monsters will be eliminated. That is why I am mobilizing a major offensive against the Vyysarri as soon as our forces are consolidated."

"This will be a time of great victory for the Seryysan People and time when we will make every last Vyysarri regret the day they were born!"

"May the Founders smile upon you. Good day my friends."

The moment the transmission ended, Khai knew exactly where he was going and where he would find Prime Minister Trall.

For the first time, Khai called Dah.

Dah was sitting next to Bria's bedside, watching her intently. She had stabilized the night before, now she was just resting. Dah knew she was going to be all right, but wanted to see her when she woke up. He was drawn to her like a bug to a flood light. When she slept like that, she looked like an angel. He had just watched Trall's state of the union and fought incredibly hard to keep the bile from creeping up to the back of his throat.

The rhythmic beeping of Bria's heart monitor began lulling him into a light sleep. But the sudden sharp blare of his com unit jerked him out of the almost nap-like state.

"Dah," he said.

"I know where he is, Dack."

"What? How could you possibly know where he is?"

"I don't have time to explain, but I'm on my way to go get him right now."

"Wait! Come get me. You're gonna need my help."

After a long pause, he said, *"All right. I'm coming to get you right now."*

"You need the address?"

"No. Your com unit also has a tracking device in it. I'll be there in five minutes."

"Oh. Okay. I'll be on the roof waiting for you."

"Roger that."

Dah was sitting on the roof, fidgeting with his sidearm when a ship came to a hovering stop just above the roof. It was the *Star Splitter*, or at least he thought. If it *was* his ship, Khai had made a couple changes. For one, the exterior was bulkier, it was still aerodynamic, but it was boxier with ablative armor. It was also bristling with weapons. Exterior missile launcher, forward and aft Mark II laser cannons, and a cannon turret mounted to the top. The hatch popped open and Dah jumped inside.

There were wires hanging from ceiling of the ship, wires he *knew* weren't there before. When he got the cockpit, his jaw dropped. Hundreds of wires were bunched together with zip ties and haphazardly fastened to the ceiling. There were two new consoles attached to the bulkhead with adhesive tape.

"What the hell did you do to my ship? This was a pleasure yacht!"

"Well, now no space pirate will dare mess with you."

"What's with all the wires?"

"Hey, this was the best I could do in four days, okay?"

"But my ship..." he Dah said, waving a hand over the controls.

"I tried to talk him out of it, but he shut off my vocal processor," Joon whined.

"You didn't..." Dah gasped.

"Well, she wouldn't shut up," Khai said defensively. "I just increased your market value by, like, three times. Are you really gonna bitch about it?"

"I guess not," Joon replied, but her tone left that open to debate.

"Is there anything else I should know about?"

"Uh, no." Khai paused for a bit. "Except for the engine upgrade... Oh, and we installed an Eve'Zon Drive, too."

"She has an Event Horizon Drive, now?"

"Yeah, that's why she had to have ablative armor made of Ti'tan'lium—we can't save the planet if we get cooked in our seats, can we?"

"Where did you get Ti'tan'lium?" Dah frowned. "No. Strike that. I don't want to know. Is there anything else?"

"Uh, yeah."

"Are you going to elaborate?"

"A Mark I Shield Generator. I know it's not the best, but we had very limited space to work with."

"And where did you get the extra space for an Eve'Zon Drive and shield generator?" Dah scowled at Khai.

"Well, let's just say that you'll be sleeping on the couch for now."

"You took out the bedroom?"

"It's still there. There's just a lot of equipment installed back there. It's better if you don't look."

"I'll take your word for it," Dah said, relenting. "So where are we headed?"

"Orbital Station Twelve."

"What's Orbital Station Twelve?"

"It's a top secret space station built into a hollowed-out asteroid. It has its own Eve'Zon and thrusters, an array of defenses and is about three miles in diameter."

"How do you know Trall's there?"

"He was in the commander's quarters when he gave his little speech. I had been in there six times during my time with the SCGF. Admiral Dran'Gyyl Drannig was in command then, may still be, too."

"Clever. So I'm sincerely hoping you have an equally clever plan to get us in before they blast us to space dust."

"Yep. I'll tell you that plan once we've broken atmosphere."

"Okay," Dah said, leaning back in the copilot's chair. "So, really, how did you obtain all this weaponry?"

"Not legally, if that's what you're fishing for."

"I was afraid you were going to say that."

"Yeah." Khai gave Dah a roguish grin. "An old friend owed me a favor."

"So, you've got us in," Dah said skeptically. "Do you have a plan for finding Trall and then getting us the hell out of there?"

"Nope. I'll figure something out when we get there. I have no idea how much resistance we'll encounter there. As far as leaving goes... run like hell and pray the ship makes it out in one piece."

"That's not very reassuring, Khai," Dah growled.

"I'm sorry. You asked to come along. From the start, I had a strong impression that this was going to be a one-way trip." Khai admitted, pulling into line to leave orbit."

"A one-way trip? *A one-way trip?* You could've told me that *before* I volunteered to come along, you know."

"Well, if you play your cards right, it might not be for you."

"You have a death wish, you know that? A *death wish*," Dah spat out, pointing an angry finger at Khai.

"You're the second person to tell me that this week," Khai said, his voice full of sarcasm.

"Yeah? Who was this genius?"

"The person who sold me the weapons and helped install them. She also gave me some other... *supplies* we may need."

"What kind of supplies?" Dah eyed Khai suspiciously.

"Go in the back and check it out." Khai jabbed a thumb toward the aft of the ship.

Dah unstrapped himself and sauntered into the back. There was an armory back there! The thing that immediately caught his eye was a Seryys Combat Mark III Gatling Gun, one thousand rounds per second. There were RPGs, stun grenades, knives, armor and who knows what else in the converted bedroom.

Dah worked his way back up to the cockpit and sat down. He stared at the console for a moment, then looked at Khai. "We're a flying fortress."

"More or less," Khai said, taking the controls. "Strap in. We're about to break atmo."

Dah buckled up his crash restraints and Khai pushed the *Star Splitter* into orbit. There was that brief moment of discomfort when real gravity loosened its grip and the ship's artificial gravity kicked in. They were in orbit, headed for Orbital Station 12.

"So... are you going to let me in on the plan now?"

"Yeah," said Khai. "Hit that button over there."

Dah pointed at a small red button on the navigational console. "This one?"

"Yeah. Hit it."

Dah pressed the button and the ship listed dramatically. Dah panicked.

"We've just lost the starboard thruster! We're losing attitude!"

"It's okay," Khai said.

"What?"

"How is this letting me in on the plan?"

"Kinda busy here..." Khai growled, trying to the keep the ship from spinning out of control. "We're almost there."

The asteroid loomed. The giant bulbous rock looked completely out of place in the empty skies above the planet.

"So, what's so special about this rock?"

"Several years ago, the Vyysarri sent a ship to destroy Seryys City. They thought that if the system's capital was destroyed, the military would go into disarray. This ship was called the *Hammer Cannon*. It possessed a weapon that cracked the planet's crust and sent a seismic wave that would level entire cities in one volley. This event spearheaded SCR&D development of the shield generator that now protects the city.

"Fortunately, the Defense Navy was able to disable the ship and commandeer it before the Vyysarri could use the weapon on Seryys City."

"You don't think..."

"I don't. I *know* he's gonna use it. And we have to stop him."

Suddenly the com crackled to life. *"Unidentified ship, you are entering SCNDF space. Turn your ship around or you will be destroyed."*

"Negative," Khai said. "We came out of Eve'Zon and clipped a stray asteroid. We won't make it to ground. Requesting permission to land so we can make quick repairs."

There was a long pause. Then the com spoke again. *"Stay on your present course and power down your engines. We will bring you in with a hauling beam."*

"Thank you, control." Khai feigned gratitude and relief. "I'm not sure how much longer I could've held her together." The com went dead. "Get suited up. As soon as we land, we're busting out guns blazing. You got it?"

Dah nodded.

They suited up in flak jackets and armed themselves to the teeth with knives, grenades, guns, everything that Khai had bought.

"How did you afford all this stuff?"

"I gave the owner his planet back. He owed me."

"I'd say that some damn good credit," Dah joked.

"You got that right."

The ship bucked as it dropped down on the hanger floor. Khai made his way to the cockpit and looked out the front canopy. There were hundreds of troops, in full armor, armed with standard machine guns.

Dah came up behind him. When he saw the number of troops waiting for them, butterflies whirled up in his stomach and lodged in his throat as if he had bitten off more than he could swallow.

"We can't get past that," Dah said, dread filling his voice.

"Yes we can," Khai countered. "Remember what I said?"

"Guns blazing."

"I never mentioned which guns..." With that, Khai brought the new targeting system online for the dorsal cannon. Putting the crosshairs right in the center of the bubble of troops, he fired. The blossom of energy blasted a hole in the hanger floor as hundreds of bodies, and body parts, went flying in every direction. Klaxons blared loud enough for them to hear them from inside the ship as the fire-suppression systems came online to douse the flames.

"You ready?"

"As ready as I'll ever be," Dah shrugged.

They hit the hatch button and they came down the ramp, gun blazing. They quickly mopped up the remaining soldiers and Khai used a codepad built into his left gauntlet to lock the ship up. Dah was sporting his usual machine gun but also had two pistols, two hunting knives, four throwing knives, a grenade launcher and a bandoleer full of grenades. Khai was wielding the Gatling gun, but had the same type of machine gun as Dah strapped over his shoulder and just as many pistols, including his personal one, and knives.

"Where to, now?"

"The service lift is straight down the corridor. That takes us to the main deck. There's a lift at the far end that leads to the command center. Off that room is where we'll find Trall in the commander's quarters."

"Oh, and I thought this was going to be hard," Dah didn't bother hiding the sarcasm in his voice.

"Let's move," Khai said, heading for the main cargo doors that led to the main corridor.

The doors slid open slowly into a very quiet hallway... *too* quiet. Khai, being the leap-before-you-look type of guy, tossed a grenade about fifty feet down the hallway. Suddenly, like a mound of army ants, men scurried to avoid the blast. As soon as they left their cover, Khai opened up on them with the behemoth gun and they started dropping like flies. Dah followed suit.

At that moment Khai had a glimmer of hope. *This might actually work!* They advanced into the corridor, blast marks scored the walls and a giant crater in the floor signified where the grenade had gone off. They had just made it past the hole the floor when the service lift doors yawned wide. Behind the doors were three, count them, *three* power armor soldiers, bristling with weaponry. They were the new Mark Vs, bigger and stronger than the one that Khai fought earlier that week... but *slower.*

"Ah, shit!" Khai growled. "I had to say something..."

"What?" Dah asked, not taking his eyes off of the three harbingers of death in their way.

"Nothing. Just find cover."

Their first move, before they even took a step, was to send a volley of grenades into the hall directly at the intruders.

Khai and Dah looked at each other and bolted back to the hanger for cover. The explosion sent them sliding across the floor and tumbling to a stop. Before they could even get up, another volley peppered them with shrapnel. Dah cried out as a piece ripped through his side. Khai finally got to his feet and pulled a piece of bulkhead from his chest plate, the tip dipped in a crimson liquid. He could hear the thunderous footsteps echoing into the cavernous hanger. Khai dragged Dah to his feet.

"You okay?"

"It's just a scratch," he said with a grimace.

"Good. I need you to get into the ship and use the cannon turret."

"I'll hold 'em off here."

Khai hit the button on his gauntlet and the hatch opened. Dah staggered into the ship and made his way to the cockpit, leaving a trail of blood behind him.

The power suits stomped into the hanger and Khai opened up with the chain gun. A thousand rounds a second battered the armor of the lead soldier, its grey-blue armor sparking as bullets bounced off and ricocheted in all directions. It seemed to be having little effect on it, the others stayed behind in single file using the front man as cover.

The lead Mark V suddenly dropped to one knee; servos whirred louder than usual as it struggled to get to its feet again. Khai was about to shout a victory whoop when the cannon came online. The thundering laser bolts caught the first soldier square, sending him flying back twisting and tumbling end over end. Khai thought that he could actually hear the soldier inside crying in pain.

The other two scattered. Textbook formation, one in each direction to confuse the attacker, returning fire and running as fast as the suits would allow. Dah tracked the one moving off to the left flank, while Khai took the one going right. As Khai thought things couldn't get any worse, another fifty soldiers entered the arena, thirsty for blood.

Khai swung the big gun around at the newcomers and dropped several of them before they could even register they had been shot. The others took up firing positions using cargo containers and other ships as cover. Khai threw another grenade into a cluster of men ducking behind a large crate; some actually jumped out of cover to avoid the blast while the others stayed and died a fiery death. But, he took his eyes off of the suited warrior who was now not on the run, but on the offensive.

Opening with a barrage of attacks from multiple ranged weapons, the armor-clad soldier pressed the attack. Several bullets splashed across his chest, being absorbed by the chest plate, but stealing the air from his lungs. He gasped a raspy breath and ran for the relative safety of the *Star Splitter*.

Dah wasn't having much luck. Now that the suits were aware of the ship's capabilities, they were able to dodge the cannon blasts as they came. The regular soldiers were keeping Khai pinned down with heavy fire, which allowed the Mark Vs to approach.

"Dack!" Khai shouted over the fire. "Dack, do you read?"

"Loud and clear, good buddy. You sweatin' out there?"

"Can it, soldier. Do you see a small, blue button on the weapons console?"

Dah's eyes darted across the black panel looking for the little blue button. There it was! Like a little blue planet in a blackened sky of meaningless stars. "Found it!"

A grenade went off against the side of the ship, raining sparks down on Khai's head. "Well, *hit it!*"

Dah pushed the button and the ship powered down. The dorsal cannon fell silent. All the lights winked out in the cockpit. "What the hell was that, the instant-death-for-us button? Everything's offline! We're sitting ducks!"

"Wait for it," Khai whispered, thumbing off his gun. "Shut down your mic."

"Okay. Nice knowing you."

It started as a prickling, tingling pressure- though Dah didn't feel that because he was protected by the armor plating of the ship. Then the pressure was released in a conflagration of a blue-and-white blossoming ball of energy. To living flesh it was harmless, but to the Mark Vs, it was game over. The electromagnetic pulse hit them, all their electrical parts shut down immediately, trapping the helpless soldiers within. The regular soldiers went on a rage and fear-fueled frenzy, firing wildly at the ship.

"An EMP? You installed an EMP on my ship?"

"Works wonders in space and apparently in hangers as well."

"You crazy son of a bitch! Joon, why didn't you tell me?"

"Khai threatened to sell me for scrap if I did."

"You're welcome. Now, if you're not too busy. I could use some help out here." Dah swung the cannon around and sent a barrage of fire that reduced the entire area, and every living thing in it, to molten slag. "Thank you. Now get off your lazy ass and get down here."

"I'm on my way." He stood and slumped against the damage-control panel.

"Captain, Dah?" Joon's sultry voice sounded concerned. "I detect internal bleeding. I estimate you have five hours to repair the damage to your abdomen until you expire."

"I'm fine, Joon. Thanks for your concern. Like you said, five hours."

"As you wish."

Khai was literally tapping his foot when Dah descended the steps. "Are you with me? Do we need to abort?"

"No!" Dah snapped. "It's just a flesh wound. Let's move and just get this over with."

They ran.

They entered the service lift.

The doors opened to reveal the main deck. Yet another cavernous expanse housing most of the engineering sections; service shops where parts were repaired and manufactured; barracks to house the thousands of soldiers, engineers, laborers, scientists of all kinds and some of the lower officers—the higher-ranking officers had personal quarters one deck up just below the command center. But the most spectacular sight, that stopped Dah dead in his tracks, was the enormous ship that hovered in the center of the main deck.

The *Hammer Cannon* hung like an oppressive titan over his head. A complex network of catwalks crisscrossed the area above him. Most of them were attached to the ship itself. He could only look up and gawk at it. The ship, simplistic by design, was flat and rectangular except for a large sphere that sat in the center, where a large circle was cut out to house it. The "bottom" of the sphere had what appeared to be an iris of some kind.

It looked much like a laser emitter. The rear of the ship fanned out to house powerful engines that were humming as if warming up.

"The *Hammer Cannon,* I presume."

"That's it, all right." Khai pointed at the center. "The sphere houses the seismic cannon."

"So *that's* the ship that's gonna level Seryys City."

"Yeah."

"So, are you going to destroy the ship, too?"

"Nope."

"No?"

"Once I kill Trall, I'm taking down the whole the facility."

"You're gonna kill all these people. Some of them *are* innocent, you know," Dah said, using his cop voice.

"Don't worry. This facility has *hundreds* of escape shuttles. I will send an evacuation call before it blows."

"Okay." Dah seemed pleased with that answer.

They moved swiftly through the bustling deck, thousands of people were running scared for bunkers within the base for protection. The bunkers were designed specifically for the event that intruders busted their way in. The insanity going on around them was the perfect cover. They went unnoticed, just moving with the ebb and flow of the living tide of people scurrying about.

The lift was only yards away, after climbing several sets of stairs and ladders to get to the catwalk that led to it.

Suddenly the sound of creaking metal filled his ears. Khai looked in the direction from which the noise came and instantly, his heart froze. A catwalk, overloaded with people, began to bow under the extreme weight as the bolts holding it to the wall started popping out.

The catwalk was ten feet above Khai and Dah.

"Follow me!" Khai jumped into action. He climbed a ladder that led to that level and a catwalk that ran parallel to the one that was failing. Khai used his antaean strength to leap the distance. Dah followed. When Khai landed on the catwalk, it swayed dizzyingly. The people on that catwalk cried out and surged one way or the other. The catwalk jolted and dropped a few inches.

People screamed.

Khai looked around desperately for anything that would help. The catwalk was anchored to a crete hallway that led to a control room for a crane. Khai ran for a more-stable section of catwalk in the opposite direction, pushing past panicking people. Dah again followed. The whole catwalk was going to come down if all those people stayed.

Just to his left at eyelevel, a chain with a hook hung from a pulley. Khai took the hooked end and wrapped it once around the railing on the left side of the catwalk and repeated the same motion on the right side.

Then he took the hook and tossed it onto another, stable catwalk. The hook caught and Khai pulled it tight. The catwalk shuddered as it was about to give. He wrapped the other side of the chain around his forearm several times and grabbed the railing next to him.

The catwalk gave and sagged. People screamed but quickly realized that they weren't falling to their deaths. But the panic didn't subside any. And now, Khai was calling on every ounce of that strength he had developed on Gor'Tsu Gorn Planet to keep the catwalk from plummeting by anchoring himself to the more-stable catwalk and holding on tight to the chain.

"Run!" Khai shouted through a clenched jaw.

Dah wasn't sure what to do. The people were all standing, screaming, crying. Dah, then knew how he could help. He pulled his gun and fired rounds into the air. The sudden terror of gunfire made the people move with purpose. It worked! But the now running masses on the catwalk were shaking it so violently, Khai was having trouble hanging onto the railing. His grip slipped and the pulley jerked him up toward it. Dah reached out and grabbed Khai's hand and anchored himself to the same railing. Now his strength was being put to the test as well, honed on the same soil as Khai's.

Finally, all the people made it to the crane control room.

Khai's strength finally failed and he dropped. But Dah was still somewhat fresh and kept his grip tight, hauling him up over the railing to safety. About that time, the failed catwalk crashed hundreds of feet below.

"Let's not do that again," Dah said, his voice heavy with fatigue. That five-hour window was narrowing with the exertion. Though somewhat clotted on both ends, he was still bleeding badly and working that hard made his blood pump even harder.

"You need to get back to the ship and get planet-side."

"I'm not leaving you to die here."

"Look, there are a hundred ships in here. I'll get out of here before it blows. Now get out of here. That's an *order!*"

"You forget—I'm still *your* commanding officer."

"Really," Khai folded his arms defiantly. "'Cause the last time I checked, neither one of us is employed by the SCPD."

"You have a point." Khai gave him a stern I'm-not-backing-down look. "Fine." Dah growled, making his disapproval very apparent. "I'll get you to Trall. *Then* I'll leave."

"Deal," Khai said and turned, entering the lift.

A short lift ride later, the door slid open into pandemonium. The command deck was bustling with officers not rated for hand-to-hand, or firearms combat, arming up to stop the intruders. Most of them didn't even know how to hold the weapons they were handed.

A single man—a lieutenant, by the looks of his uniform—was the only man barking orders that were even intelligible. Khai boldly stepped out into the command center, shouted an attention.

The men all stopped, even the young lieutenant. And when he spoke, they listened.

"My name is Colonel Khai'Xander Khail, the hero of Seryys Four. I'm here for Prime Minister Trall; to stop him from leveling Seryys City. You have one chance, and one chance only, to surrender and aid in the evacuation of this station. If you do not heed my word, you *will* die today."

"Don't listen to this traitorous, has-been, lousy excuse for a veteran!" the lieutenant cried. "He's-"

Khai drew his beloved pistol and dropped the young man with a single shot to the forehead. He fell to the floor, twitching and bleeding. He pulled his knife to make another notch on his pistol, then paused and put his knife away, taking a step closer.

"Anyone else want to follow the young lieutenant?" There was silence deep enough to hear his own heart beating. "Good. Drop your weapons and leave the command center."

Most of them complied immediately, some stayed behind to be defiant.

"You're making a mistake," Dah said to those who stayed.

"He's a traitor," an older man said quietly.

"What if I told you that the man found in Puar's shuttle wasn't Puar?" Khai fired back.

"But Prime Minister Trall said-"

"That Puar's dead?" Khai interrupted, holding up the memstick that contained the truth. "I have proof right here that CME Rashad found conclusive evidence that Puar was *not* in his shuttle when it crashed."

"How can we believe you?"

"If you don't, I'll kill you where you stand."

That seemed to squash the stragglers' defiance. They left.

"Dah, follow them. I'll see you planet-side."

Dah hesitated, Khai gave him a look. "Fine. I'm on my way."

"Hurry," Khai said. "I'm blowing this thing as soon as I kill that bastard... which won't be long."

Dah nodded and stumbled back to the lift. A small pool of blood had gathered where he was standing. He paused and looked back at Khai.

"I was gonna shoot you," he said.

"What?" Khai asked, completely confused. "What are you talking about?"

"At the shield generator," he clarified. "I was going to shoot you, but Brix beat me to the punch."

"That's good to know..." Khai said, leaving an upward inflection as if it were a question.

"Just had to get that off my chest... You know, just in case you..." Dah visibly squirmed and shrugged. "... die..."

"I'll see you planet-side. Get out of here."

As soon as Dah entered the lift, Khai pressed his arm-mounted codepad.

"Yes, Khai?"

"Dack isn't going to make it planet-side conscious. I want you to pilot him directly to his friend Med's place. Got it?"

"As you wish, Khai. Good luck."

Chapter Eight

Khai closed the channel and strode for the door that led to the commander's quarters. He expected Trall to have a trap set for him, but he wasn't concerned in the slightest. The door slid open into a dark room. He could hear Trall's labored, sickly breath. He moved toward it. From deep within the shadows, a figure emerged holding a short, sharp sword. It glinted off the dull lighting in the room. The sound of another sword leaving its sheath drew Khai's attention the opposite side of the room.

"Former Colonel Khail, it's nice to finally meet you in person... well, as in person as watching my personal guard dice you to pieces."

"You think these guys are good enough to stop me?" Khai was honestly amused. "Bring it on."

They weren't guards; Khai knew immediately that they were Kyyl'Jah Assassins. Trained in ancient martial arts, they were extremely dangerous and deadly. The Kyyl'Jah Assassins were a highly secretive, highly organized society of ex-Seryysans who left to form their own culture and government on a planet outside Seryys Space. Each assassin was trained individually to master their arts, and then assigned a life-partner, with whom they would finish their training and become a nearly undefeatable pair. The Joining, as they called it, matched a male assassin with a female assassin based on a highly scientific genealogy and their individual fighting profiles. They not only became combat partners, they became lovers. They would train, live, love and die together. And those that made it long enough, would bare genetically strong children to carry on the assassin way of life. They were deadly, a force to be reckoned with, but Khai had one major advantage—he grew up, and trained, on a planet with several times Seryys' gravitational pull. His strength was far superior, even to these deadly assassins.

They attacked in tandem, one high, one low, knowing exactly what the other was going to do, like lovers making love. Khai jumped and leaned back so that the low attack passed under him barely grazing his hamstrings and the high attack barely grazed his chest plate. The maneuver left him vulnerable for only a split second. To keep himself a moving target, he continued back rolling backward to his feet and kept moving.

The assassins were relentless. They pressed the attack harder. Simultaneously, he caught swords on his gauntlets, high and low, front and back. Finally, Khai found a split second where the assassins were vulnerable. They made their customary high-low attack, Khai twisted his body yet again, only this time he jumped, twisted more and caught both swords with his boots. The woman on Khai's right held tight to her sword as it was kicked up over her head. The other was broken in half and dropped when Khai's boot forced the tip into the floor.

Khai jumped to his feet and pressed the attack on the armed assassin. She swung the blade wildly, struggling to work on her own. Eventually, she was able to calm herself and fight like the assassin she was. She swung a horizontal attack that Khai blocked with his gauntlet and followed up with a solid chop with his other gauntlet down on the blade, breaking it. Khai's strength was tremendous.

Khai yelped as the man silently came up behind him and kicked him on the back of his knee causing it to buckle. He dropped to one knee with a grunt but kept fighting. The man put him in a choke hold and bore down on him. The woman came up to Khai and drove a serrated knife into the gap of his flak jacket between the chest plate and rib protection. He growled in pain as the tip of the knife struck one of his ribs.

Khai struggled to get free, but he was running low on oxygen. He was fighting, holding his breath. His head began to swim and another knife strike found its mark. Khai felt a painful *pop* as the tip of her knife punctured his left lung. Khai was running out of time. Out of desperation, he kicked his feet and amazed himself by wrapping his legs around the woman's neck. With a powerful twist of his of his strong hips, he flipped the woman over on her head.

"Turn him around," Trall said. Khai was losing consciousness. His vision narrowed and his strength began to fail, because, without oxygen, even the strongest muscles will fail. The male assassin turned Khai to face Trall. "A pity," he chided, holding a pistol leveled at Khai. "All that work, all that fighting to die here when you were so close."

Trall fired. The bullet struck his chest plate, lodging deep into the metal and breaking a few ribs. Since he had no wind to be knocked out, he only felt the pain of the impact... a weird feeling.

The female assassin was coming around. She slowly got to her feet and walked unsteadily over to her life-partner. Khai was finished. He tapped his gauntlet and it sent a pre-written message to the *Star Splitter* notifying Dack that he wasn't coming back. While Khai sent the message, Trall was too busy to notice, bashing Khai's face in with the butt of his gun. Once Trall was done, he pressed the muzzle of the gun hard against Khai's forehead, breathing heavily from his exertion.

Trall squeezed the trigger. Khai was still lucent enough to time the shot. From the time the hammer hit the bullet to the time the bullet left the barrel, Khai tilted his head just enough and the bullet ripped through the assassin man's throat. The man instantly dropped Khai and clutched at his throat, applying pressure to stop the bleeding. He had seconds to live. Khai watched in smug satisfaction while Trall watched in realizing horror as the male assassin took his last gurgled breath. The female cried out in anguish. In a rage, she rushed Trall and disarmed him so fast, that Khai's returning sight barely registered it.

Tears of pain—deep emotional pain—streamed down her face as she put the gun to her head and pulled the trigger, painting the far wall with blood, skull fragments and brain matter. She dropped dead.

Trall now had the look of an innocent man walking the green mile on his face. Fear gripped his gaunt features and his dull green eyes. He dropped to his knees. Beyond him, Khai looked out the huge bay windows and saw escape pods jettisoning into space. Only a few had launched so far, but it was only a matter of time before they all launched and the innocent people of the station would be safe from the blast that would inevitably consume the asteroid.

Khai took a menacing step toward Trall, who was shaking like a leaf on a tree in a hurricane.

"You piece of shit. Where's Prime Minister Puar?"

"He's dead, you moron," he hissed.

"Bullshit!" Khai threw the desk that Trall was hiding under and picked Trall up with one hand by the collar of his lavish, silk shirt. "I saw the findings of CME Rashad. I know he's alive. Where is he?"

"I... don't... know," he rasped between coughs.

Khai threw him over the conference table and he crashed in a heap over a comfy chair.

"Where... is... he?" Khai bellowed.

"Okay, *okay*!" Trall literally cried. "He's at the bunker in Kal'Hoom Karr Canyon."

"Thanks," Khai growled. "Now it's time to die!"

He grabbed Trall by the wrist and picked him up. He twisted Trall's arm until it popped and hung dead by his side. Trall cried out in pain and terror. "Wait!" he cried. "There's other things I can tell you! Things you might find interesting." Trall held up a memstick. "Things on this memstick I already knew. Others were new to me. I'll give it to you, if you spare my life."

"What do I care about political bullshit?"

"There are things about how the war started that you might want to know."

"I don't care," Khai said, snatching the memstick from Trall. "I was a soldier. I followed my orders and never asked questions. Why the war started is none of my concern. And now that I'm retired, ending it isn't my concern either."

"I'll give you a cut of whatever I make on the Ti'tan'lium!"

Khai actually laughed. "You can't cash in on something you never possessed."

"The *Hammer Cannon* is programmed automatically to launch in two hours. Seryys City's demise in inevitable."

"I beg to differ," said Khai with a devious grin. "Computer? Voice recognize."

"Colonel Khail, Khai'Xander. Active reservist in the SCGF."

"And who, at this exact moment, is the ranking military officer aboard Orbital Station Twelve?"

"Colonel Khail, Khai'Xander." Trall's eyes narrowed to slits. If he could kill with a look, Khai would have died a thousand times in that instant. "Computer, activate auto-destruct sequence. Ten minute trigger."

"Produce authentication code."

"Tango-tango-alpha-three-nine-nine-four-beta."

"Code accepted. Auto-destruct sequence activated, ten minutes and counting."

"Now, Trall, time to meet the Founders, you worthless sack of..."

A distortion in space caught Khai's attention for a brief second. Five black holes yawned wide, spewing forth five Vyysarri capital ships. They instantly started firing on the escape pods. *No!* Khai seethed. Trall took Khai's distraction to his advantage and kicked Khai square in the groin. As Khai doubled over for a brief moment, wishing he were dead for that minute, Trall jumped to his feet and sprinted to the wall. He kicked over a bust of some famous bureaucrat and a secret hatch popped open. Trall disappeared inside and the hatch sealed behind him. Trall had escaped.

"You can run, Trall! But you can't hide forever!" he shouted angrily.

An instant later, the station bucked and rumbled as the Vyysarri ships undoubtedly traced the pods back to the station and opened fire. Khai felt the strong tug of guilt and regret on his heart as he watched as one escape pod after another made the faintest popping flash. All those people—*civilians*—blinking out of existence in only a second or two, it made Khai's stomach turn. Then, his stomach *really* turned. The floor rumbled.

"Computer! Status!"

"Station's main gravity generator has been hit, loss of gravity in five seconds; critical damage to main engines; station is now in a decaying orbit around Seryys, reentry to planetary atmosphere in ten minutes; structural integrity failing, complete hull failure in seven minutes, thirty seconds."

"Great!" Khai growled as his feet left the deck and weightlessness took over.

He reached out to the giant conference table and positioned his feet, poised to push off toward the door. He waited for the table to rotate toward the door and pushed off. The mass of the table far outweighed Khai's solid frame and he quickly drifted for the door. It opened as he approached and he caught the door frame to keep himself from drifting into the center of the command deck where he would have very little to grab a hold of to navigate himself through the dying station.

He glided his way to the lift. The door slid open at his arrival and he flew in. He pressed the button for the main deck and braced himself for the lift's ceiling to hit him. As the lift moved, Khai repositioned himself within the lift so that when he the door opened, he could push off and glide quite a distance to the service lift that led to the main hanger.

The lift stopped and the lights went out. Khai slammed into the floor of the lift and saw stars for a moment. He activated the entry light on the machine gun that was strapped to his back and shone it around, looking for a way out. It wasn't hard to find, the emergency hatch was clearly marked. He kicked the hatch out and climbed out of the lift car. He worked his way around the side of the car and started moving toward the main deck, using the emergency ladder along the side.

The station rumbled again. The pressure within the lift shaft changed drastically and a whoosh of air sucked him back down the lift shaft toward the lift car. Suddenly, as if matters weren't already bad enough, the computer's voice chimed in.

"Backup systems activated."

The lift car started moving again. The air escaping the lift shaft and the car moving at him with a high rate of speed, he was about to become a bug on a windshield. He had to think fast. At the last second, he was able to the grab the ladder and pull himself into a nook where the lift would miss him. As the lift passed by, he reached out and grabbed anything on it he could grasp and got jerked off the ladder away from the hull breach in the shaft. The lift came to a stop at the main deck. At that point, all the air had left the shaft and he was blacking out. He barely had the time to crawl back into the lift car and force open the door with what strength he had left.

Another great gush of wind slammed him into the back of the car and threatened to suck him out through the hatch. But now he had air filling his lungs and his muscles were no longer running on only lactic acid. He climbed from the car and hit the manual close button on the outside of the lift. Suddenly, he was free floating again, with oxygenated blood coursing through his veins and arteries.

"The hull has been compromised. Hull integrity will fail in two minutes."

Shit! Khai scowled. He knew that there were SCGF soldiers stationed on the asteroid station. The SCSCSFSs, or Seryys Combat Self-Contained Space Flight Suits, were standard issue on about any space-faring vessel. He would just have to find them. They were mostly used for orbital skydiving. They were made mostly of a fiber woven with strands of Ti'tan'lium to absorb the heat from reentry. Each suit was equipped with an air supply good for five hours, maneuvering thrusters for limited movement in space and a steel-fiber parachute that would automatically deploy at a 2500 feet above ground level.

He pushed off toward the barracks, thinking his best chance would be to find one stowed in a footlocker. He had his eyes on the prize. The barracks were looming up quickly; straight ahead and directly below him. All he would have to do is catch the catwalk directly above and push off in that direction.

"One minute, thirty seconds." The computer's voice was breaking up. The station rumbled again and Khai panicked. The impact from the dying Vyysarri warship crashing into the asteroid had caused the station to rotate on its x and y axes. Khai was near the center of the asteroid when the impact happened, and what was directly in front of and below him was now thirty degrees to his left and above him. Khai closed his eyes for moment as the spinning station forced his stomach to turn yet again. He fought off the strong urge to vomit. "Correction: forty-eight seconds until full structural failure."

Khai hit the wall on the far side and held on while he matched the spin of the station. He then pushed off and headed, once again, for the barracks. He hit the barracks and tumbled along the roof until he found something to grab. Once he stopped himself, he crawled to the main door and it slid open for him. The door slid shut behind him and he went to work checking the rooms for the flight suits. It didn't take him long to find one.

"Eighteen seconds until structural failure."

He struggled to the get the flight suit on. It was usually a two-person job, but, obviously, he was flying solo on this one.

"Ten seconds until structural failure," the computer said. "Nine, eight, seven, six, five, four, three-"

The computer cut out as the asteroid shook and shuddered. The reverberation resonated in his chest. The door leading out from the barracks flexed outward and then there was only complete silence. Khai knew that the hull had failed and the only thing keeping him from the cold, hard vacuum of space was a flimsy steel door sealed airtight. He scrambled to get the suit on. Once the clasps in the front of the suit touched, they automatically sealed, forming an airtight bond from the helmet to the boots.

Khai floated over to the door and stuck a grenade on a timer to the door and kicked off. The grenade blew and the door blasted out with the last of the air in the barracks. Khai was sucked out into the expanse of the main deck. Khai was right, the hull was compromised. A Vyysarri capital ship crashed nose first into the asteroid. A good two-hundred feet of the wedge-shaped ship was buried into the main deck. It also crashed through the *Hammer Cannon*, completely destroying that ship and cleaving it in two.

The positive side of the ship careening into the station was that it left a gaping gash in the hull and a direct route out into open space. Using the wreckage as leverage, he pulled himself to relative freedom. As soon as he left the ship, he was smack dab in the middle of a space battle. *Raptor*-Class dogfighters were chasing down Vyysarri dogfighters and the other way around.

Khai's attention was immediately drawn to an explosion and he immediately hit the suit's thrusters. He emerged from the fissure in the hull between a Vyysarri battle cruiser and a Seryysan battle cruiser. They exchanged cannon fire and silent blossoms of molten slag filled the dead, airless space between them. Khai was stuck in the middle for the longest forty seconds of his life. Finally, his thrusters pushed him up above the ships' dorsal sides to relative safety. At least that was his hope. Two squadrons of *Raptors* zipped by so close Khai could see the pilots doing double takes. The engine wash of the ships sent him into an uncontrolled spin away from Seryys.

Once he was able to get himself under control, he watched as what was left of Orbital Station 12 entered Seryys' upper atmosphere and started burning up. Only the sounds of his breathing and his heart beating were what he heard as the asteroid broke up into several pieces and vaporized in several balls of fire. After the fireworks were over, and the battle above Seryys raged on, he traversed the labyrinth of dead ship hulls and battle formations. After a few minutes, and almost all of his thruster fuel, he started to feel the tug of Seryys' gravitational pull. He hadn't made an atmo jump in years. He would only admit to himself that he was a little nervous.

Silence enveloped him.

His heart rate jumped; his breathing accelerated.

Then... a burst of sound so loud, his ears rang. That was reentry. Suddenly, his innards did backward handsprings as he hit the mesopause of the atmosphere. The noise only increased as he hit the mesosphere and his suit began to heat up. Though the suit was insulated and protected by the Ti'tan'lium, he was not immune to the effects of dropping at several hundreds of miles per hour.

Almost entering the troposphere, he hit supersonic speeds. The sonic boom was the worst part. In his youth, he would be whooping an exhilarated cry to buffer his ears from the pop. Now all he could do was think, *I'm getting too old for this shit!*

At five thousand feet from the ground, the remaining thruster fuel kicked in to bone-jarringly slow his descent enough for his chute to do the rest. At that point, he was only falling at terminal velocity and could relatively control his descent. He knew that the shield was still up and he would most likely be vaporized on contact. He spotted a good, safe drop zone between the city and Kal'Hoom Canyon. At 2500 feet, the chute deployed jerking him around a bit.

Everything was going smoothly until a lingering fragment of Orbital Station 12 came burning down and clipped his chute.

Subsequently, he went spiraling out of control toward the canyon, his strings hopelessly tangled. He pulled up on the chute and he was able to regain some semblance of control, at least long enough to ditch the chute and pull his back up.

He swiftly fell into the canyon.

He hit the rock wall, rapping his helmeted head on the red rocks and his world went dark, slipping into the unknown oblivion.

It had only been twenty minutes since Joon had relayed Khai's "not coming back" message. He was sitting in Med's clinic getting his innards sealed up with a tiny surgical laser that mended individual capillaries and organs. Bria was awake and mostly on the mend from her wound at the hand of the mysterious woman that shot her. The assassin's voice was eerily familiar, though. He knew he'd heard it before. He just couldn't put his finger on it.

"I'm sorry to hear about your friend," she said softly. "Really."

"Thanks," he said. "It's weird, we only knew each other for a couple months, but..."

"But it's..."

"Yeah," Dah said, sadly. "Ouch!"

"Well," Med admonished. "If you would stop moving..."

"Okay. I'm sorry."

"It's fine," Med said as he leaned back wiping off his blood-covered, gloved hands with a rag. "You're done. I want you to stay here tonight, but you should be right as rain tomorrow."

"Thanks, Doc." He rolled over on the bed to face Bria. "So, uh, when do *you* get out?"

"Tomorrow," she said, blushing.

"Yeah?"

"Mm-hmm. Why?"

"I thought, maybe, you and I could, you know, go have a... drink or something."

"I suppose that would be the *least* I could do for my rescuer."

"Yeah? That's great! Ooh!" He winced in pain. "Guess I should take it easy for the night."

"See you in the morning?"

"Yeah. Night."

"Night."

"Dack?"

"Yeah, Bria?"

"I'm glad you went to the SCBI Building to find Ran."

"Me, too." That was it! The SCBI Building. That voice! It was the receptionist at the front desk. That was the voice of the woman who tried to kill them both! "I gotta go! I know who she was!"

"You're not going anywhere," Med remarked, filling Dah's IV with a strong sedative. "You *need to rest.* Whatever it is you were going to do, it can wait!"

"No, I need to go back... to..." He was out.

"What'd you give him?"

"Oh, just a sedative... that's used on desert bulls."

Chapter Nine

An explosion rocked the ground under his feet. He dropped to the ground, covering his head as bullets whizzed over. It was only the two of them left. Two lone soldiers out of two hundred that landed on Planet 128 facing an entire legion of Vyysarri troops, it seemed like impossible odds.

"Corporal!" Ralm'Es Ra shouted. "Where do we go from here?"

"I don't know," Khai admitted, another volley of bullets chewing up the dirt above his head.

"We've got to get to the command center," Ralm shouted.

The command center was once in the possession of the Seryys Armed Forces, but in a recent skirmish, the Vyysarri proved to be a violent and unwavering force. Planet 128 was a Seryys colony, a stronghold and a military complex/staging ground for the Seryys Combat Expeditionary Naval Fleet, or SCENF.

"I realize that," Khai yelled back. "Maybe you didn't notice the hundred-or-so Vyysarri troops surrounding it!"

"Oh, I did. Just didn't think that was the problem," Ralm retorted, firing back at the Vyysarri.

"You didn't think that... that was a problem?" Khai said, pulling the pin on a grenade and tossing into the mass of Vyysarri troops. "You're a cocky smart ass, aren't you?"

"Guilty as charged, sir," Ralm gave him a mock salute. "Captain Smart Ass reporting for duty, sir!"

As Khai saw it, he had two options: sit there in the ditch and die, or charge the castle, retake the command center and die. A Vyysarri dogfighter came blazing into view and crashed, leaving a large dust cloud and digging a deep crater just outside the front entrance to the complex. Khai wondered how the battle was going topside. He gathered his courage and loaded another magazine into his machine gun. They nodded at each other, knowing exactly what the next step was, the crater.

"Okay, Smart Ass, you first!"

"That's *Captain* Smart Ass to you... sir."

"Fine, *Captain.* Go!"

"With pleasure, sir!"

After a mortar shell exploded on the ground, Ralm made his move. Khai provided cover fire while Ralm ran for the destroyed hulk of a load hauler. Then, while Khai ran for cover on the opposite side behind a leveled building, Ralm laid down a consistent rain of fire. Khai looked over at Ralm and he nodded his head toward the grenade in his hand. Ralm nodded and grinned, pulling out his grenade.

Khai mouthed a countdown, then together they threw their grenades. The combined explosion took out several Vyysarri and in the confusion they ran like crazy to meet up on the far edge of the crater, closest to the front doors. The Vyysarri recovered quickly and started pouring fire into the crater trying to hit them.

"So what's out next move, Corporal?"

"Get in, or die trying?"

"Sounds... inevitable."

The word inevitable was about as close to correct as possible, especially when a grenade landed right at Khai's feet.

"Ah, crap! Run!"

They scurried out of the hole and ran headlong straight at the Vyysarri, firing their guns and praying to the Founders. What transpired next was nothing short of miraculous. Another Vyysarri dogfighter, its angular features gave it the look of a jagged tooth, crashed into the ground killing the rest of the Vyysarri that stood in their way. The mangled doors lay open before them, smashed off their slides and still smoldering.

They pressed on.

Covering one another as they had many times before, they were able to communicate without using words. They moved quickly and quietly through the dark and battle-damaged corridors of the complex, sweeping their weapons from left to right, scanning the immediate area for enemies. It didn't take long to for them to find some. A squad of troops came out of the shadows, not wearing protective helmets and masks, their pale faces, long fangs and red, light-sensitive eyes gave them a truly grotesque visage.

The Vyysarri running point caught Khai almost flat-footed. The monster actually sunk his teeth into Khai's neck, it was the first time that had ever happened to him. He had heard stories about it from other, less fortunate soldiers, that it was not a pleasurable event by any stretch of the imagination. That was the understatement of the century! The venom contained within their saliva felt like acid running through the veins in his neck, spreading both up toward his head and down toward his shoulders and arms. His body was gripped in spasms from the paralytic nature of the venom.

Khai yelped. Ralm moved into action. He crushed the butt of his rifle into the base of the attacking Vyysarri's skull. He crumbled to the ground like a card house. The others attacked with the ferocity of Canyon Sabercats. One pushed the dazed Khai to the floor while Ralm started firing his weapon at point blank range at the remaining Vyysarri. Each Vyysarri took several rounds at that range before they finally went down. But the victory did not come without a cost. Ralm took a jagged knife to the gut. Rather than pulling it out and bleeding to death, he broke the knife off inside him and then used a surgical laser to cauterize the wound around the knife. It hurt like hell, but it was better than the alternative.

"Thanks," Khai said, as Ralm helped him up.

"Hey, even the great Corporal Khai needs some help sometimes."

"Don't let that get out," Khai grinned. "Got a reputation to uphold."

"Understood, sir."

Ralm followed Khai through the maze of corridors and intersections. The bodies of Seryysan Soldiers littered the halls. The Vyysarri resistance was curiously limited. They only encountered two more squads of troops before they made it to the door of the command center.

The layout of the building consisted of the command level and officers' quarters on the main level, with lower crew quarters a level down and the engineering level one below that. The upper level was a massive hanger, big enough to house two *Dagger*-Class dreadnaughts, several wings of *Raptor*-Class fighters and *Shark*-Class interceptors. On top of the hanger were several high-powered, orbital laser cannons that could reach, bombard, disable and/or destroy capital ships in orbit over the complex.

The command center, mission control and com relays were located at the center of the gigantic, rectangle-shaped facility. When the facility was fully manned, the command center was the safest place to be on the whole planet.

The door was jammed open and there were several Vyysarri inside. In the split second that Khai peaked in around the corner, he counted fifteen total—seven to the left of the door and eight to the right settling into firing ranks. They were ready for Khai and Ralm.

"These guys are making one huge mistake," Khai said, dabbing a rag at the wound in his neck.

"Yeah?" What's that?"

"They obviously don't know who the *fuck* they are dealing with!" Khai said, grinning. "You ready?"

"Born ready, sir!"

"Then let's get to it!" Khai was surprised that they had made it this far; but, with the uncharacteristically light resistance, they made it all the way to the command center relatively unscathed.

Khai, being the shoot-first-shoot-some-more-throw-a-grenade-or-two-and-try-to-ask-questions-from-body-parts type of guy he was, tossed a flash-bang, followed by a frag grenade, and then charged in guns blazing. It was, after all, his style... and it had worked for him so far.

The initial blast disoriented several Vyysarri; the disorientation was a perfect distraction for the actual grenade that splattered Vyysarri parts of at least seven soldiers all over the walls, consoles, bulkheads and floor of the command center.

Then, as the Vyysarri were finally getting their heads back in the game, Khai threw more chaos at them by charging in. In the first second of Khai's charge, he counted eight Vyysarri left, including a general. Khai put eight rounds into the Vyysarri general's chest and watched him fall to the floor. Ralm was right behind him. Khai leapt ten feet into the air in a front somersault with a half twist over a grouping of three Vyysarri, raining bullets on them as he performed his acrobatic feat. All three of them fell dead where they stood.

Ralm, being a bit older than Khai, opted for just running up and kicking a Vyysarri in the back sending him flying six feet into a support beam; his body wrapped painfully around the beam with a muffled *crunch*. The Vyysarri fell to the floor in heap and tried clawing his way back into the fight, but without the use of his legs, he was worthless. So, rather than dying many years later as a useless cripple, he opted to eat a bullet instead.

Khai never skipped a beat. After landing his flashy, showboat move, he somersaulted over a consol bank for cover as the remaining Vyysarri tracked him and fired. Khai fired back blindly from his cover point to get the Vyysarri to back off a bit. It worked, they all dived for cover. Khai continued to fire until he heard the telltale *click-click-click-click* of his gun running out of ammo. He was out of extra magazines so he opted for his baby, the 92-30 pistol. He waited for the Vyysarri to stop firing and reload; he popped up, like a rodent from a hole, firing. With three quick shots, he put one in the head of an enemy—who was dead before he hit the floor—and two into the right leg of another. Khai was going to question that guy later... *if* he lived long enough, that was.

There was one left. He was a particularly large Vyysarri with a missing eye and more scars on his face than Khai could count. At the moment, he was wrestling Ralm to the ground and rearing up to bite Ralm on neck. Khai took a step to intervene when a strong, taloned hand wrapped around his ankle. At that point, he knew this Vyysarri was indeed *not* going to live long enough to be questioned. He put a bullet hole the size of a man's thumbnail in his forehead and an exit wound the size of a man's fist out the back of his head. Black-red blood spattered all over Khai's face, boots, armor and the floor.

"Khai!" Ralm screamed.

The Vyysarri had overpowered Ralm and was straddling him trying to get his fangs into the Ralm's neck. Ralm had both hands wrapped around the Vyysarri's neck trying to keep him away, and even though Ralm was superiorly strong measured against a normal Seryysan, this Vyysarri was simply stronger. But he wasn't as strong as Khai. Khai pushed himself harder than most Seryysan soldiers when it came to lifting weights; he wanted to be the strongest and fastest of his platoon, and he was, by quite a large margin.

Khai rushed over to help.

The Vyysarri was too into his blood frenzy to even care that Khai was there. All he could see was the neck, pulsating with each rapid heartbeat, of Lieutenant Ralm'Es Ra. Using the Vyysarri's single-mindedness, Khai put the muzzle of his gun to the Vyyysarri's head and squeezed the trigger. The Vyysarri was more aware than Khai thought;

before the bullet could leave the barrel, the Vyysarri ducked and bobbed out of the way, rolling to his feet and pulling a jagged knife—the same kind of knife that was buried in Ralm's belly—called a Judac.

Khai reciprocated by pulling both the knife from his belt and the knife from his boot. Ralm stepped in with his knife as well. The two attacked at once, the Vyysarri was well trained in hand-to-hand combat. He was clearly trained in the Kyyl'Jah Assassin Art. They fought for several minutes in a flurry of flashing steal so fast, the eye would have to strain to follow the movements. Despite their fighting prowess, they couldn't get through the Vyysarri's defenses. Eventually, the Vyysarri began to tire, fighting two foes of equal strength and comparable training. That was the plan all along: let the Vyysarri punch himself out and then go in for the kill. And that was exactly what Khai did. He nodded at Ralm who immediately feigned an attack. A fresh Vyysarri would have seen it for what it was, but with battle fatigue setting in hard, he missed it entirely and moved to block the attack with his steal gauntlet.

While the Vyysarri blocked the fake attack, Khai struck with deadly speed. He first jabbed a knife into his side between the ribs into his left lung and the second knife into the stomach. He then followed up with a two-fisted uppercut that snapped the Vyysarri's head back. He flailed, reeling from the blow and spitting teeth. Khai didn't stop there. He let his hate of the Vyysarri people take over. He charged forward, tackling the Vyysarri with a roaring war cry.

As the Vyysarri landed, he wheezed, coughing up blood that splattered all over his face. Khai pulled the knife from the Vyysarri's stomach, prompting more hemorrhaging, and pressed the blade firmly against his throat. Khai held it there long enough for the Vyysarri to register that his life was about to end and then ran the sharp blade across his throat, leaving a deep and gory gash that sprayed blood all over Khai's face.

Once it was all over Khai stood up, his chest heaving from the fight and fire in his eyes. Ralm had never seen Khai quite so fired up, though he had only been fighting beside him for a year—which really wasn't a long time considering that the war had been going on for centuries and Seryysans lived to be roughly a hundred and twenty-five years old.

Khai stared vacantly at the dead Vyysarri lying in a pool of his own blood. Ralm approached him and put his hand on Khai's shoulder.

"Khai?" he asked.

Khai spun around so fast that Ralm didn't even have time to register the movement and put the knife to *his* throat. Ralm threw up his hands. "Whoa! Khai, it's me Ralm." Khai still held the knife to his throat. "*Sir!* Snap out of it." Nothing. Ralm, with almost as much speed as Khai, swung around and slapped Khai across the face so hard it left a handprint on his cheek. Khai blinked several times and shook his head.

"You still with me, sir?"

"Y-yeah. I..." He frowned, drawing his eyebrows together and shaking his head. "I don't know what came over me. I'm sorry."

"It's okay," Ralm said, taking a step back from the blood-soaked knife. "Let's just finish what we have to do here and get the hell out!"

"Agreed. You know how to use a targeting computer?"

"Yeah-I mean... yes, sir."

"Good," Khai said. "Target the Vyysarri warships in orbit while I bring the cannons online."

"Yes, sir!"

There were four *Dagger*-Class ships losing a battle to the seven Vyysarri *Fang*-Class battleships in the space above Planet 128. Two of the four ships were venting atmosphere, but still fighting, one was still fully functional and the other was in the process of breaking in half from several internal explosions that rocked the ship from bow to stern. Only two Vyysarri ships were showing any signs of damage. One was missing the starboard wing and the engines and lights were flickering. The other was in far worse shape having gaping holes all over the hull that were venting atmosphere. The lights were out and main power was gone. It was dead in the water.

The two remaining Seryys ships staggered their formation to overlay their shields and give them a little time for reinforcements to show up. Things were looking grim, Khai realized as he checked the tactical display. The cannons were warming up, eventually the screen showed full power.

"Ralm!"

"Sir?"

"Pick your targets and fire at will. I'll join you and take half of the cannons after I send another distress signal."

"Yes, sir!"

Khai worked the com panel sending a general distress signal to SC Command. He transferred the view of the battle to the main screen at the front of the command center, then ran over to the targeting computer and helped Ralm bombard the Vyysarri ships from the ground.

From the main viewer, Khai watched as their efforts changed the course of the battle. Ralm and Khai focused their attacks on one ship at a time, each. Khai's first ship started to break apart sending flames and debris out into the space around the battle. Ralm's ship wasn't far behind.

"Sir, you see that?"

"Yup. I got it!"

One of the *Fang*-Class ships broke formation and headed toward low orbit. The cannons Khai controlled focused on that ship, but since it was in the best shape out of all the ships, Khai couldn't deal enough damage to stop it before it got within firing range of the complex. When it did fire, it rained hell on them. The ground shook violently as salvo after salvo struck the massive building.

Pieces of crete fell on the two soldiers as they poured fire into the shields of the enemy ships. They were going to stay there until the building fell on them or the ships were destroyed.

"Khai! Take that ship down!"

"I'm trying! Its shields are only at sixteen percent!"

Finally, Khai broke through its shields and started hammering the unprotected hull. Khai thought it was over. But in its death throes, the ship launched a warhead that connected with and blasted through the facility's shields, striking the power generator. The lights went out—except for the emergency lights—and the guns fell silent. Though the Vyysarri ship was dying and moving into decaying orbit around P-128, it still continued to fire, connecting with the base.

Khai and Ralm could do nothing more from there, so they ran for the door. Just as they left the command center, a cannon blast ripped through the ceiling and engulfed the room with superheated plasma. The force of the attack threw the two soldiers several yards down the corridor slamming into the wall. As they struggled to get to their feet, another salvo rocked the foundation and knocked them to their backsides again. They both started crawling for a door jam in the hopes of avoiding getting crushed to death. Debris was falling all around them and the ship in orbit, though dying, wasn't letting up.

They waited for a lull, and when it came, they ran as fast as they could back the direction from which they came. Each blast that followed jolted them both and they bounced into the walls of the corridors and each other. Another volley collapsed the roof directly behind them. A *Shark-*Class interceptor slid down the sagging, slanted ceiling straight toward Khai and Ralm. They scrambled to their feet and ran as fast as their legs could carry them. The ship crashed and tumbled and fell through the floor behind them.

They ran.

The front door was within sight; the light at the end of the tunnel, as it were. There was a squad of Seryysan medics waiting for them, large piles of freshly-dead Vyysarri soldiers all around them. The Vyysarri must have had an ambush waiting for them and were intercepted by the squad of medics. When the medics caught sight of them, they ran to help them. The two soldiers were battered, bleeding and tired.

As they approached, Ralm slid to a stop and yelled something to the medics. They didn't hear him and in a split second, Ralm spun and pushed Khai as hard as he could. Khai flew back, confused and frustrated. Then, in a split second, a proximity mine went off vaporizing the medic behind Ralm and the force of the explosion ripped Ralm's left arm clean off. Then, the roof collapsed from the explosion crushing Ralm's other arm.

Khai hit the floor sliding and watched helplessly as Ralm got buried alive under rubble.

"No!" Khai screamed as he ran to start uncovering his friend. Another mine went off further towards the door and Khai dropped to his knees, staring at nothing, his eyes glazing over. The world around slowed down and all he could hear was a loud ringing in his ears.

Another loud crash and he felt himself falling. The last thing he remembered was hitting the ground.

And then, darkness took him.

Chapter Ten

He woke up under a pile of rubble. Instantly he started screaming and kicked as hard as he could as fear and panic took hold. He kicked at his dark prison with all of his strength. Suddenly, the sound of rocks rolling filled his ears. Then, a small beam of sunlight shone in. He clenched his fist and took a deep breath. He placed his hands on the rocks in front of him and pressed. His body started to lift and suddenly, he realized that he was facing down. Basically doing a push up, he was able to remove some of the rock laying on him. After another great effort, he was able to roll to his back and press up with his legs.

The giant slab of rock hefted and fell off to the side. Then, it was just a matter of digging his way out. He climbed out of the hole and stretched his back, looking around at his surroundings. The first thing he saw was the last thing he remembered: the wall into which he crashed and caused the rockslide that buried him.

The first thing he did with his freedom was run to the river, stick his face in it and take a long drink. Once his thirst was quenched, he was able to gather his wits about him. He shed the excess weight of his armor and extra guns, keeping only rations, his water canteen, his 92-30, a broken com unit and a small hand-held computer called a Seryys Combat Personal Micro Computer, or micro-comp.

He took the transceiver out of the dead com unit and fused it to the circuit board of the computer. Then, he used to the micro-comp to uplink a satellite in orbit to give him his exact location. He also checked the news and learned a couple things: one, he was a wanted fugitive—so contacting the outside world would mean insta-death, and he had been unconscious for three days under that rock pile. He had to get back to the city and find Dah. Unfortunately, the broken com unit was the dedicated, secured one to contact him, so he would have huff it by foot back home and find him.

The only problem was that Khai had managed to crash-land himself a hundred miles from Seryys City and eighty miles from the nearest city, which was Tanbarder, a small mining town of three thousand people twenty miles southwest of Seryys City along Kal'Hoom Canyon. He could use the micro-comp to send a text message to someone asking them to come scoop him up, but Seryys Combat Interplanetary Intelligence Administration, or SCIIA, would most certainly intercept that message and track it to the canyon. Most likely, now that he had essentially two death sentences on him, he would be shot on sight. So that was out of the question. He would need to get to Tanbarder and contract a shuttle to get him back, no questions asked.

It was nearly night and he had a choice to make. He could travel under the cover of night or travel during the day, sticking close to the canyon walls for cover. Each option had its merits and flaws. Traveling by night was dangerous; most of the canyon's top feeders did their business at night, not to mention all he would have was the light of Seryys' two moons to aid him. Going by day would mean ample light and less predators, but he would be more visible from the sky. Either way, he would have to skirt the canyon wall, because the satellites in orbit all had thermal imagers that could trace his body heat. And since he didn't move like a Canyon Sabercat, it would be pretty obvious that he was running through an uninhabitable canyon... and he knew that Trall wouldn't count him as dead until his head was on the man's desk.

After five minutes of mulling it over, he decided to move at night. He wasn't sure if that was the right choice, but he felt that, if nothing else, a patrol wouldn't simply spot him running through the canyon. He sat for the next two hours until the sun went down. All he could do was sit there and think. He thought about that day. The day they dug him out of the rubble that was once the military facility on P-128. Six days later, a military psychologist diagnosed him with Post-Traumatic Stress Disorder; the day they promoted him to the rank of colonel; the day they discharged him from active combat duty and the day they put him behind a desk.

He was a fair tactician, but nothing like the generals of the ground forces or the admirals of the fleets. He felt like a fifth wheel. He lasted at that job for about two years before he couldn't stand it anymore. He couldn't take sending thousands of soldiers to their deaths in his stead. He wanted to be out there fighting with the others, bleeding with the others as he had fought and bled hundreds of times before on hundreds of planets across this section of the galaxy.

The sun had finally gone down, one moon was already out in full and the other was rising in the west. That was his cue. He packed up and headed out. It was a quiet night; the sound of local insect life chirping filled his ears and the cool night air enveloped him. He took a deep breath through his nose filling his lungs with the fresh air, and let it out through his mouth. *I should retire out here*, Khai thought. *I could get used to being out here. No traffic, no jobs, living off the land. I could get used to this.*

He had been sluggishly walking for nearly ten hours. He decided to call it quits for the day. There was no sense in pushing himself after falling several hundred feet and being buried alive under a pile of rocks. Besides, after the first two hours of walking, he realized that he had indeed suffered some injuries in the fall on top of the injuries he acquired on Orbital Station 12. He was pretty sure that his shoulder had been dislocated in the fall, but it had set itself. The wound in his chest from the shrapnel had dug in pretty deep, deeper than he originally thought—which was just shy of two inches. His neck hurt where it met his shoulders, he had broken ribs, a puncture wound from the assassin's knife that hit his ribs and the one that found its mark had punctured his lung. He was still dribbling blood, and his breathing was wheezy. At this rate, he wasn't going to make it to Tanbarder.

Maybe, after some rest, he would have more strength to go on. He had suffered worse injuries than this on the battlefield and pushed on. But that was when he was in his twenties and he was able to shrug off pain more easily. He found a spot to set up camp under a large jutting outcropping of rock that would protect him from the rain and satellites.

He slept like the dead. No dreams or nightmares entered his slumber.

He slept through the next day, the next night, and into the following day. When he woke, he slowly ate some rations and took another long draught from the river. He then realized that he needed more rest. So he slept.

He slept like the dead. No dreams or nightmares entered his slumber. And when he woke, it was nightfall once more.

He was barely able to get to his feet. He couldn't decide if waiting and getting some more sleep was a great idea or the complete opposite. All he knew was that now he was in so much pain, he could barely walk, whereas yesterday he could push on for almost a whole day. He rummaged through the medikit for anything that could help. He found about six feet of bandaging and, thank the Founders, a full bottle of Kryylopax, powerful painkillers that were so potent, they were illegal to citizens in the Seryys Sector. They were mostly used on the battlefield to ease a soldier's passing if he was mortally wounded.

He popped two of the pills and waited for them to kick in. When they did, he wished they hadn't. His head spun. Or... was it the planet that was spinning? *The planet is* always *spinning, stupid,* he told himself. So... maybe it was just the canyon...

Khai shook his head and fell to his backside. As the world began to slow down—or was it his head or the canyon? —he wasn't able to form single, cohesive thoughts or perform simple functions. He used the gauze to patch up his wounds the best he could. Now, feeling absolutely no pain whatsoever, he pressed on. It was a weird feeling, he had the distinct impression that when he walked, the world moved with him. Like a giant treadmill, he could control the spin by how fast he walked, or how slow. If he sprinted, he got the hilarious image of people being sucked, face first, into a wall and sticking there like the GravDefier ride at a carnival as he ran.

His jovial, laughter-filled romp through the canyon was stopped by the sound of a single shot that echoed in his ears. He froze, looking around at the canyon walls for the shooter. He instantly ducked into an alcove in the rock wall and pulled his 92-30.

Another shot rang out. Khai scrambled to a large boulder for cover.

When he peaked around his cover, he saw the ugliest sight he'd seen in years.

Vyysarri! *Hundreds* of them. They were marching in ranks down the canyon corridor. They all seemed to be looking straight at him. He turned to run when he realized that he was standing on the edge of another cliff. He turned to face the Vyysarri. His cover was gone and only one man stood between him and the now *thousands* of Vyysarri warriors. That man was Sergeant Moon'Sinder Moore.

Moon looked back at Khai and gave him a wink and a grin. He charged in, cutting down Vyysarri by the tens and twenties. He mowed down several hundred with his machine gun. Khai watched in sick satisfaction as his former commanding officer/father figure/mentor tore the Vyysarri scum to shreds. But, all good things must come to an end. The tide turned and Moon was struck by a bullet that passed straight through him. He froze, eyes wide with surprise that these lowly scumbags could even touch him.

Khai screamed, noticing his voice was cracking like that of an adolescent boy.

"Moon!" he cried out.

"Run, Khai!" Moon shouted. "Get the others to the bunker—now!"

"Not without you!" Khai screamed.

"That's an *order*!" Moon snapped, kicking a Vyysarri soldier to the ground and killing him execution-style.

"Yes, sir!" he said, snapping a crisp salute and moving into action.

He rounded up the other recruits and herded them into the bunker. He spared one last look at his mentor. He was as good as dead. A Vyysarri had his fangs deep in Moon's neck. Crimson blood ran freely down the front of his camouflaged shirt. He reached out for Khai. Khai closed the impenetrable door of the reinforced, Ti'tan'lium-covered bunker.

Moon died that day along with Khai's innocence.

Khai'Xander Khail found himself sitting with his knees drawn up to his chest, rocking forward and back, his clothes stuck to him with cold sweat, cornered in a small cave-like alcove. Tears streamed down his face freely. He hadn't had his pills in days now and the Kryylopax was compounding the problem. He forced himself to stop crying and stand up.

He walked to the river, drank and splashed water over his face, head and back. *Get a hold of yourself, Khai!* He had lost precious time in his incapacitated state, and now, he had to make up for it. He popped another two pills and started running. After consulting his computer, he still had over sixty miles to cover.

He ran.

It had been three days since Khai's final transmission. If he had survived, he would've contacted Dah by now. All this he thought about as he walked through a bustling market with Bria. This was their second date and he was growing quite fond of her. They were both on the mend from their ordeals and were trying to get out and find some peace and quiet. Beyond the market was a city park with a medium-sized reservoir where people came to swim, sunbathe and play with their pets.

"What's on your mind, Dack?"

"Huh?" Dah asked, his voice distant. "I'm sorry. What'd you ask?"

"What're you thinking right now?"

"Oh, sorry," Dah shook his head. "Just... thinking about Khai."

"I'm sorry," she said sincerely.

"Not your fault," Dah said, wrapping an arm around her shoulder and squeezing her gently.

"He died to save the city, you know."

"No one knows that more than I do. But..." Dah took a very contemplative expression. "Did he really save the city or just delay the inevitable? I mean, Trall lived. He's still the Prime Minister."

"Yeah, but two of his attempts to destroy the city were thwarted. He's going to be hard pressed to come up with another idea."

"So," Dah said, with a very concerned look on his face. "Khai really only bought us some time."

"It kinda looks that way."

"So, it looks like I need to up the ante. I still have Rashad's findings on a memstick. But how do I get them authenticated? You *know* Trall's first reaction will be to discredit the information... *and* me. And he has the power to do both with the flip of his limp wrist."

"So, we need more evidence," Bria said simply.

"Like what?"

"I don't know! *You're* the cop, not me."

"Oh," Dah laughed. "*That's* helpful!"

"Hey," Bria said, changing the mood. "Is this our first lover's quarrel?"

"Are you saying we're lovers?" Dah asked, hope filling his voice.

"I..." She turned away from Dah, pulling herself out of his grasp. "I don't know. I'm sorry I brought it up."

"Don't be," Dah said. "If you're not ready, you're not ready. I understand."

"That's just it," she said. "I *am* ready. But I *shouldn't* be. It's only been like a week since Ran was murdered. I should still be upset about his death."

"Well," Dah asked pointblank. "Did you love him?"

"I don't know," she admitted. "I mean, he was a great man and he was an amazing lover. But he still didn't leave his wife. He kept telling me the timing wasn't right. But, was it love that drew me to him, or was it stability?"

"Well, if you have to question it…" Dah let his sentence trail off meaningfully.

"I know," she said, her voice filled with guilt.

"Let's not talk about these things anymore," Dah said cheerfully, trying to change the subject. "Let's go for a dip and forget about our troubles for a day."

"I think that's a great idea." Bria shoved past Dah. "Race ya!" She ran for the water.

"Oh!" Dah laughed. "You little…" He ran after her.

They make a cute couple, she thought ruefully. *Too bad I have to kill them both.* But not now. All she was ordered to do at this point was survey and report. It was obvious that Captain Dack'Tandy Dah and Bria'Nah Briar knew too much and she was sure that Trall would have her kill them in time. It was a pity, she thought. Captain Dah was a fine specimen. Under different circumstances, she might have taken him as a mate. But that skinny, weak bitch he was with had captured his heart with her batting eyes and charming smile. She was attracted to Captain Dah the moment he came in to the SCBI Building to investigate Rashad's death… and she let him know at that point.

She almost had him that night at Rashad's residence, but he proved to be more resourceful than she originally thought. That move with the hovercar was clever. And the one named Koon, well, he was just practice. It was regrettable that her counterpart had to die, but he served his purpose to give away Koon's sniping position. Running her blade across his throat was a very satisfying, almost orgasmic, feeling; her arousal only heightened by licking Koon's blood from her knife.

The other regret she held was that Colonel Khai'Xander Khail, the legend and savior of Seryys IV, had died on Orbital Station 12 and would not die by her hand. It would have been a great battle, worthy of songs and films. Maybe, if she was lucky, he would have fallen for her in the heat of battle and bedded her at that moment, covered in each other's blood.

Kay'Lah Kayward, code name: Agent 13 of the SCIIA, was a highly-trained, physically-altered, cold-blooded killer who stopped at nothing to accomplish a mission. She reported directly to Prime Minister Trall, and had served Prime Minister Puar during his time in office. Though Kay didn't know the particulars of Trall's ascension to power, she didn't particularly care. She was trained to follow orders at all costs, whether it was morally right or not. She knew she was a monster. And she forsook the Founders so the Seryys System would remain a safer place to live. She saw herself as a messiah of sorts, she sinned so others wouldn't have to, and that suited her just fine.

Once she was done with her surveillance, she secured her binoculars in her utility belt, pushed her jet-black hair away from her green eyes, stood then turned and ran, swan-diving off the far side of the building. In her freefall, she flung a grappling hook that latched onto the roof of an adjacent building. She swung on the line from building to building until she reached her dwelling, her home. Outside this place she was a fearless, deadly warrior. But inside... inside she was a frail, vulnerable girl. The couch and bed were covered in colorful stuffed animals; the walls were covered with posters of the latest teen heartthrobs. Inside this room, Kay'Lah Kayward was a sixteen-year-old girl, taken from her home at a young age and trained to be an unstoppable assassin.

When she was ten, she took a test; a government-issued, standardized test designed to evaluate a child's aptitude. Kay's results were off the chart. She was "recruited" by a highly secretive society for "gifted" children several decades before Puar's terms started, but Puar was not happy to hear that the government was turning children into highly-trained killers. He tried to do away with the whole program, but the cabinet vetoed him only a few hours after his proposal. They felt that a child made the perfect assassin because one would never expect a child to be such a brutal killer. And, someone would have more qualms with killing a kid than an adult. And Kay was no exception.

She sat on her bed, legs crossed, hugging one of her biggest stuffed animals. It was time for her conditioning. She hated this part. She could kill and it didn't bother her, but watching it was another story all together. The Net'Vyyd automatically turned on and she was forced to watch horrible videos of death and dismemberment. People getting cut open and their heads being cut off and Vyysarri feeding frenzies were among the desensitizing material she was required to watch. Every night, she sat there and cried, watching these videos, wishing she were dead in those moments. Then, the next morning, she was better and could go about her life as a killer.

There were days she wished she could eat a bullet. But under the ever-watchful eye of her superiors, she didn't dare do so. The terms of her service—no, *slavery*—were that upon any attempt to do away with herself, to end her own life, her family would be the ones made to suffer. She had a mom, dad and two little brothers. From time to time she would spy on them. She liked to see what her family was up to. Her little brothers would grow ever bigger every time she saw them. She loved them more than anything and would never do anything to jeopardize their safety. As far as they were concerned, Kay was killed in an airbus accident. There was even a body. A girl, very close in appearance to her who died in a similar fire, was her body double and coroner documentation was falsified to prove it.

Someday, maybe she would be able to come back from the dead. But until then, she had work to do, people to kill.

Khai had been running all day and most of the night. He stopped to eat. The cool night was no comfort at this point. He was still losing blood and the consistent taste of blood in his mouth was starting to get old. *To hell with safety,* he thought. He would keep moving whether the thermal scanners could track him or not. He stopped for a long drink from the river and kept running. Come hell or high water, he was going to get to Tanbarder, or die trying.

His trek along the canyon floor was taking its toll, especially with the laundry list of injuries Khai had suffered on the station and from the fall into the canyon. His body ached and protested with every step. He had to dig down deep and muster that youthful resilience he once possessed.

"Keep moving, cadet!" Moon's voice echoed in his head and ears.

Khai stopped. He looked around and there he was. Sergeant Moon stood with his fists on his hips and a scowl on his face.

"Sarge?"

"Did I say 'stop'?"

"No, sir," Khai said, straightening.

"Then Move... Your... *Ass!*"

"Yes, sir!" he shouted.

He started running, Moon keeping up with him.

"Come on, Khai! You're running like a fat, old general! Move like a soldier!"

"Yes, sir!"

Khai ran as hard as he could. He wasn't about to give up with Sergeant Moon on his heels. The last time he did that, he got whooped with a baton until he caught up with the others.

After several hours of running, he stopped for a breather just as it started to rain. It began as a small trickle and quickly escalated into a deluge—which was typical of Seryysan weather this time of the year. Khai ducked back under a long ledge along the wall of the cliff. The rain pattered down. He popped another pill and leaned back against the rocks.

"Now that was a good run, son!" Moon said. "I expect nothing less from you."

"Thanks," he said, breathing hard.

"You're gonna make it," Moon remarked. "You don't know how to fail."

"Yeah?" Khai asked, pulling out the micro-comp. "According to this, I have about forty miles left."

"Hell!" Moon said. "You've run that several times in boot. You'll make it and still have energy to give me fifty pushups!"

"I'm not as young as I used to be," Khai admitted.

"Bah!" Moon's scoffed with a dismissive wave of his hand. "You still have another thirty good years in you!"

"I hope you're right."

"I know I'm right." Moon's stern features softened a little, showing the side of him few people had ever seen. "Now, get some rest, son. You need to be ready for another hard day tomorrow."

"Yes, sir," Khai said, his eyes already growing heavy.

His eyes slowly became slits, then eventually shut. He slumped over and dozed. He dreamed of the old days, but certainly not the good old days.

Khai woke up to a foreign sound; it was the sound of a window being broken in. Khai was immediately on his feet and walking down the short hallway of their very small two-bedroom apartment to his dad's room.

"Dad?" he called quietly.

Suddenly, a loud clatter made him jump. Looking straight ahead into the bathroom, he saw bottles fly across the view of the door. There was frantic scuffling coming from that room.

"Dad?" There was still no answer.

As Khai approached the bathroom, the man made himself known. He stepped out into the doorway downing a bottle of pills and chewing frantically. His hair was disheveled and greasy, his eyes wide with some kind of wild rage, his hands shaking violently, uncontrollably.

"Dad!" This time it wasn't a tentative murmur as much as it was a terrified cry.

The man, suddenly snapped from his drug-induced daze, gazed at Khai. His pupils were so big, they almost filled their irises. He charged wildly at the boy, with a guttural half-scream, half-bellow. Khai's dad, Khai'Sola Khail, stepped out from his bedroom just in time to bring the crazed druggie down.

"Run!" he yelled to Khai. "Xander, run!"

Khai didn't listen. He just stood there crying as his dad struggled with the crazed man, hopped up who knows what. Sola was a big, imposing man, who worked as an engineer on the ship yards outside of Seryys City, and shared a lot of the same features as his son, the same eyes, build and chin. Khai's nose was his mother's. Sola was a single father. Khai's mom ran out on them when Khai was only two years old. Khai was too young to even remember what she looked like.

The fight raged on across the top floor of the apartment and finally ended up back in the bathroom where it all started. The intruder shoved Sola into the sink, crashing his head into the mirror. Shards of glass flew everywhere cutting the two men. Sola scored a bone-jarring left hook that sent the druggie to the floor, whacking his head against the tub. The intruder was so high he didn't even register that his jaw was hanging slack, broken. He simply grabbed a piece of glass from the mirror and charged Sola.

The glass sank deep into Sola's chest. He cried out and Khai jumped on the intruder's back, sinking his teeth into his neck. The drugged man started jumping up and down, screaming something about a Vyysarri. Sola tried to wrest the glass shard from his hand to keep the man from injuring his son. Khai was thrown off into the tub.

The man pushed Sola off and went after Khai in the tub. Sola came up behind him and wrapped him in a bear hug. The intruder screamed and kicked like a captured sabercat. And like a trapped sabercat, he became even more aggressive. He slashed wildly at Sola's arms, cutting them up— some all the way to the bone. But he held strong, knowing eventually the man would pass out from asphyxiation. That didn't stop the man from making every attempt to escape.

Eventually, Sola's persistence paid off. The main stopped struggling and was dropped to floor in a heap of sweaty, filthy grime.

"Xander, are you all right?" Khai only nodded, crying and staring at the amount of blood everywhere, his dad's blood. "Good. Call the police and tell them we have an intruder."

Khai did as he was told. He went downstairs and used a com unit to call the authorities. He told them exactly what Sola told him and gave them the address. They told Khai that they would be there in about six minutes, no longer.

Khai came back to the bathroom where his dad was cleaning his wounds. The cops showed up much faster than they said, meaning that a unit was somewhere in the neighborhood. They used a device to override the lock on the door and charged in, guns drawn.

They started to collect the junkie when he, very suddenly, regained consciousness and flailed about, knocking down the officer that was carrying him. He charged back into the bathroom, running over one of the two cops there, and picked up that same piece of glass. The third remaining cop put a bullet in his back, but it didn't stop him. He lunged on Sola stabbing viciously down on him. Blood spattered everywhere. He stabbed Sola twenty times, got shot ten times and knocked Khai back into the bathtub, breaking off the faucet and filling the tub with cold water that shocked the wind out of Khai's little lungs.

Khai was getting wet, his eyes fluttered open and suddenly, Moon's voice was booming in his ears.

"Khai!" Moon shouted, shaking him. "Wake up!"

"What's going on..." Khai asked, groggily.

"Uh, you're *drowning*!"

The cold water rushed up over his head and jolted Khai out of his stupor. Immediately, he started flailing his arms and legs trying to keep afloat.

"What the hell happened?" Khai asked, spitting out water.

"Flash flood!" Moon yelled, swimming next to him. "We need to get to higher ground!"

"No shit!" Khai spat back. He was being rushed down stream, which was good, because that was the direction he needed to go. If he wasn't worried about drowning, he would have ridden the tide all the way to Tanbarder. He finally was able to grab a jutting rock. Using that strength of his, he was able to haul himself out of the waters and start crawling up the cliff face. Once he found a ledge, he stopped to catch his breath. The pain was overwhelming. When he rolled to his back, there was Moon, just standing there, grinning at him.

"Just like basic, right, kid?"

"Yes... sir..." he said, between gasps. "And look at you. You're not even *tired.*"

Moon beat his chest with his fist, full of pride and a cocky grin. "Strong as a desert bull."

"I guess so."

Khai looked out over the rushing river that filled the entire bottom of the canyon. There were places in the canyon where that was normal, but not here, and those heavy deluges could make even a little stroll in the canyon a life-and-death situation in an instant. He was only about ten feet from the raging rapids and the rain continued to fall. It would only be a couple more hours before the place where he was lying wouldn't be safe either.

Looking up, he saw another ledge about fifty feet higher. He was confident that he could make the climb now and then be able rest a little longer. His injuries weren't making this trip any easier and he would die soon if he didn't get medical attention. But, for the time being, he was stuck.

The typical rainstorm in Seryys lasted about six hours or so, and he could wait that out.

"Ah, shit." Moon said.

"What? What's wrong?"

"We have company..." Moon pointed.

Khai followed Moon's finger to the spot and rolled his eyes. "Man! Can I catch a *break*?"

A full-grown, female Kal'Hoom Karr Canyon Sabercat approached, her hind side high and her head low, her red fur—designed to blend into the walls of the canyon—on end. She hissed a warning; there must have been a cave somewhere nearby—otherwise she would have attacked already. A mother sabercat never picked a fight that might jeopardize her cubs.

Khai slowly got to his feet; he risked a glance over his shoulder and Moon was nowhere to be found. *Figures!* Khai thought. He popped another pill in his mouth, knowing he was about to be in a world of hurt and took a step back, hands up in the most non-aggressive posture he could muster.

"Okay... *Nice* kitty. I'm not gonna hurt you." The cat roared another warning. Apparently, Khai was not leaving fast enough. "No need to get fussy. I'm leaving, see?" The cat glided closer, hissing and baring her large fangs. "Damn! What do you want me to do, jump back in the water?"

The giant feline's ears flattened and Khai knew an attack was coming. It was then that he realized that the cat was simply pushing him further from her den so that the fight wouldn't endanger her cubs. She hissed one more time.

"All right, if *that's* how you want to play it, then *that's* the way *I'm* gonna play it! AHHHHHH!"

Khai recklessly charged the cat, taking it slightly off guard. She bounded forward and Khai caught her front paws in mid-lunge. Khai growled at the beast while it hissed at him, snapping at him occasionally. Khai shoved the cat backward; she twisted acrobatically and landed on her feet, her eyes still on the prize.

Khai.

Dinner.

She lunged again. The cat was damn fast, faster than Khai by a long shot. Honing his skills as a well-trained soldier, he flattened out to his stomach and the cat flew over, gracefully landing behind him and spinning for another attack. Khai only had time to roll to his back before the full two hundred pounds of cat landed on him.

With one hand, Khai fought off the cat's bite by grabbing her throat. With the other hand, he was striking the beast in the ribs as hard as he could. He could tell he was breaking ribs, but the cat was tough; she wasn't showing any signs of injury. Khai, on the other hand, was tiring. He couldn't keep this up for much longer. He needed a miracle...

...And a miracle he got.

A bolt of lightning struck the cat's broadside sending tens of thousands of volts through both the cat and him—mostly the cat. It was both the most relieving experience and painful experience he'd endured in a long time. The cat leaped off and limped away, only stopping to weakly hiss at Khai saying, *you're lucky, buddy.* Khai had to agree. That sabercat was going to make dinner, for her and her cubs, out of him. Now, he had to make a choice. He could climb to the next ledge, stay there and be eaten later or jump back into the river and pray to the Founders that he didn't drown and hope that he made it to Tanbarder.

"Jump in!" Moon said, now suddenly standing next to him again.

"Where the hell were you? I could have used your help, you know."

"I'm your drill seargent, I don't help you. I throw you to wolves— or in this case, sabercats—and watch you get out of it yourself, soldier!"

"Convenient," Khai said sarcastically.

"Hey!" Moon said admonishingly. "You could have taken that job on Gorn Planet, doing what I was doing, but *no*! You wanted to see *more* combat."

"It just seemed like the right choice. Things are so much clearer for me when I'm getting shot at. What can I say?"

"You've got a death wish."

"Why is it that everyone seems to think I want to die?"

"Because you do," Moon said, not skipping a beat. "You're alone. You have no friends because they're all dead or vegetables; you have no love life because you won't let anyone get that close and now, you can't fight anymore because you're a head case! Does that about sum it up?"

"You'd make a lousy head doctor, you know that?" Moon was right, though. It wasn't as clear until that moment. He did want to die. But all he could do was use a sense of humor to deflect the truest statement that Khai had heard in months.

"A fact I'm quite proud of," Moon said, a broad grin spreading across his face. "Now, are you going to jump in, or not?"

Khai got up and swayed. "Whoa. I'm not in any condition to be swimming-"

Suddenly, he was in the water and Moon was waving at him, smiling. "Good luck, buddy!"

Khai rushed down the river, swallowing water, coughing, flapping his arms in a feeble attempt to stay above the current. The current was strong. On several occasions, he was pulled under by invisible fluid hands that would wrap around his waist and jerk him down. He would break their grip and kick to the surface for a deep breath and the hands would bring him down again.

He got to the surface. Another deep, rasping gasp filled his lungs with air and he spotted it: a log in the water and it was big enough to hold him up. He swam for it. He wrapped his big arms around it and rode it for a while, catching his breath and thanking the Founders to be alive.

After an hour of riding the log, the rain stopped. But that didn't stop the river from pushing him downstream. He would ride as long as he could, or until he reached Tanbarder. Hour by hour, the rapids subsided. He was slowly floating down the river now, and he could finally breathe easy. He kicked himself away from obstacles and drifted along. He dared not kick to shore and rest there, for the river would soon run itself down into a stream again, barely waist deep; he needed to keep going.

Eventually, his feet began to drag along the bottom and he knew that his ride was just about over. He let the river take him as far as another few miles and finally, it became more work to kick himself along than it would be to walk it. So, he kicked himself to shore and sat on the beach. It was still a little overcast outside and the air was cool. He pulled out his computer, some rations and his gun. The rations were soggy, the computer was fried from the lightning bolt and his gun was soaked. So, he threw the computer into the river, ate his rations anyway and took apart his gun to clean and dry all its parts. He shook out the chamber of the gun as he wondered how far he was from Tanbarder. Without his little micro-comp, he had no idea what his location was.

"Well that's just perfect," he grumbled.

"Ah, keep your head up, soldier!" Moon's voice came from behind him.

Khai blew the water out of the barrel and said, "What were you thinking back there? You *pushed* me in!"

"Well," Moon shrugged. "I knew you wouldn't make the decision on your own, so I made for you. You should thank me, really. You probably traveled twenty to twenty-five miles in only a few hours."

"I don't care how true that is," Khai growled. "From here on out, *I* make the decisions. Understood?"

"Hey," Moon laughed, holding up his hand in surrender. "You're the boss!"

"Good. Now, as the *boss*, I say it's time for a nap."

"Good idea, I could use a few hours of sleep."

Khai swallowed another painkiller with some river water. Once he was finished, he lay down right there on the riverside and slept.

Chapter Eleven

Dah awoke the next morning and a gorgeous, naked woman lay to his left—Bria. It was an amazing night! He had never felt this way about anyone. He got up and made breakfast while she slept. The wonderful aroma of breakfast cooking woke her up. She lazily slid out of bed, put on a robe and sauntered out into the kitchen. He was wearing nothing but his underpants as he cooked and whistling a tune she didn't recognize. She had never felt this way about anyone. Bria came up behind him and ran her hands under his arms and held him around the chest, resting her head on his back.

"Good morning," he said, twisting to give her a kiss.

"Good morning to you," she said back after the kiss. "What's on our fun-filled agenda for today?"

"Nothing with you, unfortunately."

"Aw," she jutted out her lower lip. "But I want to be with you today."

"I know," Dah said, sympathetically, slipping some breakfast onto her plate. "But I really need to check something out today."

"Like what?"

"Listen," Dah said, taking a more serious tone. "I don't want you getting wrapped up in all this mess. Okay?"

"Oh no. What are you going to do?"

"I'm going after that woman who tried to kill us," Dah said.

"But-"

"No buts," Dah said strongly. "She may know where Puar is. And if she does, I'm getting it out of her."

"She could kill you!" she almost cried.

"So could this breakfast, but you're not stopping me from eating it."

"That's different. That will kill you over time by making you fat and out of shape. By then, *I'll* be fat and out of shape, too. So then, we can die together. But that lady will kill you a hundred different ways with her pointer finger."

"She could also kill me with a gun, or knife, or grenade..."

"That's not making me feel any better."

"Look, I'm a cop. I protect people. And the city'll be a safer place with her six feet under. And I might be able to find the *real* Prime Minister in the process. This is who I am, take it or leave it."

"I'll take you with whatever character flaws you may have."

"Character flaws?"

"Well, yeah. I mean, you think you're a superhero!"

"Well, in a way, I suppose your right. But, seriously, stay here where you're safe."

"But-"

"*Please*. Stay here. At least until I deal with this assassin girl. Okay?"

She slumped in her seat. "Fine," she whined.

"Thanks," he said as he headed for the bedroom to get dressed. He stopped and looked over his shoulder. "And please, feel free to stay naked while I'm gone. It'll give me something to look forward to when I get back."

"You're so bad," she said, laughing and throwing some cereal at him.

He dressed and came back out into the kitchen.

"Sit tight," Dah said, putting on his trench coat. "I'll be back in a while."

"How are you going to find her, anyhow?"

A broad grin widened on Dah's face. He knew something, she could feel it. "I won't have to…"

With that, the door slid open and he was gone. *That crazy fool!* Bria thought to herself.

There he was. *Like clockwork,* Kay thought.

Kay'Lah Kayward was standing atop a building adjacent to the high-rise where Dack'Tandy Dah lived and she knew—because she watched them—that he had bedded Bria'Nah Briar last night. She couldn't help but feel a little jealous. *She* wanted Captain Dah. *She* was worthy of his love. *She* was a strong woman who matched Dah's combat prowess. She could kill Bria with almost a look, but that wouldn't accomplish her mission. Her new orders were to capture Dah and interrogate him. Trall, who survived his narrow escape of Orbital Station 12, wanted to know if Khai'Xander Khail survived as well. It filled her heart with hope that he did. She wanted the honor and privilege of crossing blades with him and killing him herself. And Dah was the key. He infiltrated OS 12 with Khai. He was injured and Khai sent him back planet-side. Where he went from there, she didn't care. That wasn't her concern.

Dah strolled almost casually along the pedestrian walkway. Whereever he was going, he wasn't in any hurry. He was easy to track as she bounded from building top to building top. He stopped at a food stand and bought some meat on a stick, munching on it as he walked.

Come on, Dah! Kay scoffed to herself. *What are you up to?"*

Dah swung right into an alleyway, throwing the stick away in a trash recep on the way.

Now was her chance! She ran to the edge of the building, did a handspring off the ledge, threw her grappling hook, caught it on the next building's roof and slid down the rope to the ground below. Immediately, she pulled a short, serrated sword. She scanned the immediate area and found no sign of him. She was puzzled. She saw him enter this alley only seconds ago.

That was when she heard the tell tale *click* of pistol being cocked.

"Turn around, nice and slow," Dah growled.

"Impressive, Captain Dah," she said with a genuine smile as she turned. "Not many can get the drop on me... or even detect me following them."

"I've been at it awhile," he said, emotionless. "Now, let's start with a few questions."

"Whatever you wish, Captain Dah," her velvet voice betrayed no fear because she felt none.

"Why were you at the SCBI Building that day?"

"I would have thought that was obvious. To keep people like *you* out of Doctor Rashad's office."

"Who's your superior?"

"Now, now, Captain," she sung, swinging her athletic hips as she took a few steps toward Dah. "You know I can't tell you that."

"Fine. What do you want from me?"

"More than you can give, my dear. But, if you want to survive this encounter, I suggest you answer a question for me."

"I'm not answering shit for you," Dah spat. "You're just a mindless assassin who takes orders like a domesticated lupine."

"Now, Captain," she smiled, stepping another few feet closer and coming into the light. Dah got a good look at her. And he faltered for only a second. She was just a *kid*! She must have put on a lot of makeup or something at the SCBI Building, because she looked older there. Without so much as a simple effort, Kay swiped her sword across Dah's gun and cut it in half. The barrel fell to the ground with clank. "You shouldn't hurt a girl's feelings. It's rude and quite un-chivalrous."

Dah took a step a back raising his hands. "What do you want to know?"

"Colonel Khai'Xander Khail's location."

Dah actually laughed. "I'll give you Colonel Khai's location! He's in the forests of the Truhar Oasis about two hundred miles northeast of Seryys City, just outside the city of Klomehaven."

Kay pulled out her computer and keyed in that location and she frowned. "You think you're funny." She was not amused. According to her computer, several thousands of acres of forest were set ablaze when OS 12's remains crashed there. Firefighters were doing what they could to keep the fire from spreading to Klomehaven, using the water from a two-thousand-square-mile lake on the shore of which Klomehaven stood.

"I do," Dah said simply. "And now I know who you're working for. You tell Trall that, even if Khai *was* alive, I would rather *die* than tell him, or you, where he was. And you can also tell him that I know Puar is alive and I *will* find him."

"Not likely, but I'll relay the message."

Without so much as another word or a second glance, Kay spun on her heels and ran off. She grabbed the rope to her grappling hook that still hung from the roof and climbed up like a spider. Before long, she was out of view. Dah turned and ran home as fast as he could.

Kay had to smile. As good as Dah was, she was better. She was already on her way to her ship. She knew he knew where Colonel Khail was. And now he was going to lead her right to him.

Dah was running home as fast as he could. Not only was he in danger if he had drawn the attention of an Agent, but Bria was in danger, too. He ran, looking back over his shoulder to make sure he wasn't being followed. With his attention behind him, he nearly ran over a teenage boy.

"Hey, gramps! Watch it!" he snapped, after regaining his balance.

"Sorry!" he said as he kept running.

He made it back to his apartment and sure enough, Bria was still there and had followed his orders to the letter. If circumstances weren't so dire, he would have taken her right there on the floor of the living room, but they needed to get out of there as soon as possible.

"Hey, big boy," she said seductively. "What's the hurry?" Dah said nothing, just ran for the bedroom. "Oh! I see." She followed with a smile on her face.

That smile disappeared quickly when she saw her lover packing a bag with enough weapons take down a police station.

"Get dressed! We need to leave like ten minutes ago!"

"Why? What's wrong?"

"We've attracted the wrong kind of attention and we're in danger!"

"Who's after you?"

"Please, no questions right now. I just need you to trust me and get moving."

"Okay," she replied.

They were packed and dressed in five minutes. Dah was carrying all the bags and still running faster than she could. It was the military training on Gorn Planet; it made him stronger than the average man and she found that out last night.

Using his codepad, he started the *Star Splitter* before they even got there. The engines were humming and hot when they arrived and the hatch was open for them. He threw all the bags in and helped Bria up into the ship. Once he was in, he slapped the button that closed the hatch and ran for the cockpit.

"Joon," Dah yelled. "Engine status!"

"Engines are primed and ready, sir. Though I don't particularly like the urgency in your voice."

"We're in trouble. Run pre-flight checklist while I get Bria strapped in."

"As you wish, captain." Bria was strapped in with her crash harness and so was Dah and it only took about thirty seconds when Joon's voice broke the silence. "Checklist complete, sir. All systems nominal."

"Good. Let's get the hell out of here!"

He kicked the throttle hard, left the garage attached to his apartment, and soared for one of the higher, less-traveled sky lanes heading southwest.

"Where are we going?" Bria asked, stress and fear filling her voice.

"Tanbarder. It's a small mining town along Kal'Hoom Canyon. I have family there. We should be safe there for a while, at least until I can figure out what to do. Joon?"

"Yes, captain?"

"Patch me through to my brother's com unit. I want to let him know we're coming."

"As you wish, sir." A few seconds later, Joon's voice came back. "I have him, sir. Patching him through to the cockpit com station now."

A mirror image of Dack'Tandy Dah stood in view of the camera. Dack'Tander was Dack'Tandy's identical twin brother. They even had the same build, though Tandy was stronger only because he was in the military. Tander was a miner, and hard labor was his trade. "Tandy!" he laughed with a big smile. "It's good to see you!"

"You, too, bro."

"So, to what do I owe the honor?"

"I need a favor," Dah answered honestly.

"Anything. What do you need?"

"I need to hide out for a few days. I've pissed off the wrong people and I have an Agent after me."

The smile swept from Tander's face. "I'll have a spot ready for you." He was dead serious now. "You watch your back, okay?"

"Will do." Tandy nodded with a slight smile. "And Tander?" He was about to cut the channel and looked up at his brother's image. "Thanks."

"Anytime. You know that. See you soon." Tander smiled warmly and cut the channel.

Khai woke from a dreamless sleep and packed up. Moon was standing there beside him, ready to go.

"Let's get a move on," Moon said. "We could be there by nightfall tomorrow if we hurry."

"I'm not disagreeing," Khai remarked.

They walked in silence. The sun was high overhead and there wasn't a cloud in the sky. A large predatory bird made lazy circles in the sky above them.

"That's never a good sign," Khai said.

"What?" Moon asked.

Khai pointed at the bird above them, stalking them, waiting for them to die so it could pick at their remains.

"I wouldn't worry that," Moon said plainly.

"Yeah? Why not?"

"Give me your gun."

Khai followed orders and Moon shot the bird out of the sky. It landed about a hundred yards ahead of them. When they got there, they realized the bird was pretty big; at least eight pounds. Khai used his knife to clean it and cut it into more manageable portions. The temperature was climbing. Khai figured it was about a hundred and twelve degrees.

"Man! It's a hot one today, isn't it?"

"Sure is, sir."

"Remember that time we went out into the wilderness on Gorn Planet?"

"How could I forget?" Khai laughed. "Our thermometer said it was a hundred and twenty degrees outside, *and* we were lost without water reserves."

"We weren't *lost*," Moon said defensively. "I just momentarily lost my bearings."

"Momentarily?"

"Yeah."

"We were out there for three days, one of which we had no water or food."

"I was able to find food; we just had to cook it on a rock. You were so picky back then."

"Well, I've had far worse now."

"I would imagine," Moon agreed. "Oh look! I see a perfect rock to cook on!" Moon wiped the rock off with his hand and quickly jerked it away. "Yikes! That's hot!"

"Well, I guess that means it's primed for cooking," Khai said ruefully as he slapped the lean bird meat on the rock and listened to it sizzle.

"So tell me," Moon said, taking a seat on the rocks. "Why are so you bent on getting yourself killed?"

"I would rather die in battle, for a good cause, than in a bed—old and decrepit."

"You don't have *anything* to live for?"

"Not that I can think of," Khai was being honest. "I just want to make a difference."

"Well," Moon responded with a sincere smile. "I'd say you made a difference on that space station."

"Felt good," Khai admitted. "If I just could have gotten that son-of-a-bitch, Trall... I know Puar has to be alive somewhere."

"So you don't think that you have anything to live for? You don't think you're making a difference right now?"

"No," Khai grumbled. "I'm eating bird, walking through a canyon with more injuries than I can count and talking to someone who's been dead for decades."

"So what's your next step, then, Captain I-have-nothing-to-live-for?"

"Go after Trall. It's obvious he survived, or there wouldn't be a huge price on my head."

"Okay, and then what?"

"Go find Puar-"

"*If* he's alive."

"He's alive," Khai said, popping a piece of bird in his mouth.

"You're so sure," Moon said, standing up and looking down the long the canyon. "Why?"

"I don't know," Khai grumbled. "Call it a hunch."

"A hunch?" Moon actually laughed. "A hunch? That's ridiculous!"

"It's not. Trall's got intel with Puar. As long as Puar is useful, Trall will keep him alive."

Prime Minister Pual'Kin Puar sat in the heavily-fortified bunker within Kal'Hoom Karr Canyon, a SPEAR sitting at the exit to the room where he had sat for weeks. He had no idea what was going on in the world around him. All he knew was that if he made any sudden movements, that SPEAR would reduce him to bloody goo.

Suddenly the SPEAR moved, prompting to Puar jump into action, triggering his training and fight-or-flight reaction. When the SPEAR didn't attack, Puar looked out from his cover position. He found Trall's scrawny form standing in the doorway, a satisfied grin on his face.

"What's the matter, Pual?" Trall chuckled. "A little jumpy?"

"You try getting shot at for nearly your whole career and let's see how well you do. I suggest we start right now."

"Thank you, Pual," Trall said as another, more sinister grin stretched across his sunken features. "But I think I'll pass."

"You don't look well, Trall," Puar growled. "Being the Prime Minister taking its toll?"

Trall ignored the dig. "What do you know about Colonel Khail? I can tell you that I've learned a great deal about him in the last week or so. Like that he still has an active status in the military, or that he has access to sophisticated weaponry from *somewhere*."

"Giving you a little trouble is he?" Puar mused, not bothering to hide his pleased tone.

"More than you could ever imagine," Trall grumbled.

Puar laughed. "He must've destroyed the *Hammer Cannon*!"

Trall slammed his hand on a desk. Puar thought he heard a bone break in his frail hand. "This is not funny! I need to know everything you know about Khai'Xander Khail and I need it *now*!"

"He's the most resourceful, well-trained, determined soldier the SCGF has ever had. He's killed more Vyysarri by himself than some entire platoons. You can't stop him. Nobody can."

"Does he have any family? Any loved ones?"

"No," Puar didn't have to lie about that. "His father was killed when he was a boy, and his drill sergeant was killed by the Vyysarri. He has no one."

"What about this Dack'Tandy Dah?"

"Who?" Puar feigned. He knew Dah because he worked with his little brother.

"Oh, Pual. I know your brother worked with him. I have an Agent following him now. If you don't help me, I'll have to recruit *his* help."

"You leave my brother alone, you-" As Puar leapt to his feat to strike Trall, the SPEAR tazed him again.

When the tazing was done, Trall knelt down beside Puar. "Now, are you willing to help?"

"All I know is that he was trained as a soldier, but he dropped out to help the Seryys people planet-side rather than on a distant battlefield. And he works with my brother for SCATT."

"Yes, yes. All that I can get from the main computer. What I want, are the names of family, friends, allies. What is his relationship with Khail?"

"I don't know." He was being honest again. "Khail only worked for SCATT for a couple months."

"No matter. Agent Thirteen will get the information I require," Trall said casually. "Now, what do you know about Operation: Bright Star?"

"Tandy! It's good to see you!" Tander looked over at Bria. "Oh! Who is this?"

"*This* is Bria'Nah Briar. She's my..." he looked at her and she nodded with a warm smile, "girlfriend."

"Well," Tander said, putting his most charming smile on and kissing the top of his hand. "It's always a pleasure to meet Tandy's friends."

"Well, it's a pleasure to meet his twin brother. How will I tell you apart?"

"Oh, that's for me to know, and you to find out!" Tander said, playfully.

"Great," Tandy said. "I'm watching you closely." Tandy gave his brother a serious look, then they both laughed heartily and embraced.

"It's been too long, little brother!"

"Wait, little brother?" Bria asked Tandy.

"Tander came out first. He's 'older brother' by about three minutes. He's been rubbing it in for decades. Anyway, how's business?"

"Not so great. Now that the Seryys City is protected by the energy shield, everyone else has been the target. The last attack knocked out one of my biggest mines in the canyon. And others have reported the same. The Seryys Miner's Guild said that civilian losses have doubled in the last week. Meaning that the Vyysarri are attacking anything else they can find. Three other cities have activated their own shields, but the smaller cities are struggling to get theirs online.

"Even our town with all its resources is still lagging to get ours up. We received the schematics package, but labor is hard to find at the moment and it's slow-moving. I have personally sunk *millions* of credits into this project and have brought people from the outside to finish it. It's stimulating the economy, but crushing my bank account and the accounts of those who are helping. We may be the richest city on Seryys, but there are even limits to what we can do."

"I'm sorry to hear that," Tandy said. "I wish there was something I could do to help."

"Well, if there is, you'll be the first to know. Now, how about we go back to my place and we catch up on the last year over a warm dinner."

"Sounds great."

They followed Tander to a stretch shuttle that wisped them off over the city to the private estate where Tander lived. It was a huge mansion, on several acres of land surrounded by a large stone wall that traversed the entire perimeter of the estate. They flew overhead to a personal landing pad attached to the side of the house on the third floor.

"Hmmm..." Bria murmured, looking out the window.

"What?"

"I think I made a huge mistake," she admitted.

"What are you talking about?" Tandy asked, leaning closer to her.

"I think I may have fallen for the wrong Dah..." she said, turning to her man and smiling playfully.

"Oh!" Tandy laughed. "Very, *very* funny!"

"Hmph!" Tander laughed. "If you like this, just wait 'til you see the *inside.*"

"How did you afford all of this?" Bria asked.

"Well-"

"Sir," the pilot interrupted. "We're about to land."

"All right, we'll have to save that story 'til we get inside."

They were escorted inside and the doors were locked behind them.

"What's with all the security?" Tandy asked.

"Being a big contributor to the military makes me and my business a target. They're providing me with protection in the event that the Vyysarri, or perhaps a competitor, gets any funny ideas."

"Wait," Tandy said. "You mean these guys are *military?* What part of '*I have an Agent after me*' don't you understand?"

"Take it easy, brother. I would *never* rat out my own brother. You know that."

"Do I?" Tandy was obviously hurt.

"You *should*," Tander shot back, obviously just as hurt. "I would die for you."

"You should've told me they were here."

"Think about it, Tandy. If you're on the run from the government, this is the *perfect* place to hide."

"In plain sight," Tandy realized.

"In plain sight," Tander repeated.

"Okay," Tandy agreed reluctantly. "But it's only for a few days until I can figure out what to do."

"So," Bria tried to break the tension. "You were saying about your operation?"

"Of course," Tander said, grateful for the distraction. "Most of it came from my mining operations all over the western hemisphere. Both Tandy and I were left a large sum of money from our parents when they passed. Tandy bought a house, a ship and a car, while I invested my money in this mining operation. It was in shambles when I bought it, but now it's one of the top ore providers for the military. Our family was not happy with Tandy's choice of spending, but he was an adult. They didn't like the fact that he wanted to become a soldier and, later, a cop instead of a business owner like the rest of us."

"I like helping people, making a difference in the lives of the common people," Tandy defended himself.

"But you are so much smarter than that!" Tander pleaded. "You know, Bria. I offered to make him a partner in my business, but he refused."

"I don't like being a blue-blood. I like working for my money."

"You call what I do 'not working'?"

"No!" Tandy was losing his patience with his brother's stubbornness. "I just don't like being in charge of hundreds of others' lives."

"You are, just in a different capacity."

"I *protect* them," Tandy corrected his brother. "It's different. I put myself in harm's way, so others don't have to."

"You were just destined for more, little brother. That's all I'm saying."

"So you bought a mining facility and Tandy bought a ship?" Bria, once again, tried to break the tension.

"Yep," "Tandy beamed with pride. "And I still have that ship."

"You mean *that* was the *Star Splitter*? What the hell happened to it?"

"A friend of mine upgraded her."

"That's some friend."

"Well, he *was*."

"What's that supposed to mean?"

"He's died on... Base Twelve"

"You mean, Khail, the traitor?" Once the base burned up in the atmosphere, the base's existence was released to the public.

"He's not a traitor!" Tandy snapped. "Trall was going to use a highly classified weapon called the-"

"*Hammer Cannon*?"

"How do you know about that?"

"Oh come on!" Tander laughed. "Don't you ever watch the Net'Vyyd? *True Conspiracy* is one of my favorite shows. They've covered that ship several times. But, of course, they never had any solid proof."

"You've got it now."

"Huh! That's very interesting. But what does it have to do with Khail?"

"Trall was going to use it on Seryys City. Khai stopped him and died doing it. He sent me a prerecorded message in the event that he didn't make it."

"I can't believe it..." Tander said, his breath taken away.

"That's not all," Tandy added.

"What do you mean?"

"Puar is still alive somewhere. I have proof that his accident was staged."

"This can't be..." Tander couldn't believe what he was hearing. "So what was this all about? Power? Money?"

"Maybe both," Tandy said with a sigh. "Only Khai knew the answer. My suspicion is that Trall was after the large Ti'tan'lium deposit under the city. With Director San from D-PAG out, and Khai dead, he's the only one who can lay claim to it."

"You can't possibly expect me to believe that the government wanted to destroy this world's greatest city for money!"

"I do, because it's the truth."

"You said you have proof..." Tander said.

"Right here," Tandy held up a memstick. "It has Doctor Rashad's autopsy reports. The two bodies recovered were that of a Puar's driver and an unidentified male not matching any description even close to Puar."

"Let me see that," Tander demanded.

"No," Tandy refused. "I'll put it into the computer for you to look at. Too many people have died for this for me to just give it up to anyone."

"Fair enough," Tander relented.

An hour later, Tander was speechless. The findings were conclusive. Puar was definitely alive somewhere.

"I don't know what to say," Tander admitted.

"You can start with 'I'm sorry'," Tandy said.

Chapter Twelve

"Painkillers aren't working as well as they were a while ago," Khai said to Moon.

"Well," Moon replied sarcastically. "You've been popping them for days now. You need to back off of the pills."

"I've got to be getting closer to Tanbarder," Khai said. "We've been traveling for days."

"Well, maybe you're right," Moon remarked, pointing off into the distance.

Khai looked, squinting against the sun's rays. That's when he saw it, a glint on the top of the canyon wall several miles away. "That's gotta be it!"

Khai started running. Moon stayed with him.

It wasn't long before the glint turned into a large building with tubes hanging out over the canyon and running down the canyon wall. A large service lift was bolted into the rock wall as well. That was his key up.

Just about an hour later, he had arrived. The building was in far worse shape from this distance. The lift was operational, and had power, but the rest of the facility was in shambles. He took the lift up. It was a rickety ride of about twenty feet up the hundred-foot wall when the lift chunked to a stop. The metal railings bolted to the wall were old and rusted; they creaked with fatigue and the bolts holding them to the wall started popping out.

"Figures," Khai said with a sigh!

He looked around, knowing he only had seconds to find a way out. Ten feet to the right of the lift was a service pipe about three feet in diameter. Every five feet there was a support strut that fastened the pipe to the canyon wall. Khai took three steps and leapt for the piping. He caught a strut and the lift stopped its fall. Apparently it was his weight that stopped the lift. He climbed up the pipe the rest of the way and crawled over the ledge.

When he stood, Moon was there, smiling and not in the least bit tired.

"A little help would've been nice back there, you know."

"Not my style," was all Moon said.

"No," Khai grumbled, his voice full of sarcasm. "Of course not."

The mining facility was abandoned. Not much remained except broken tools and antiquated mining equipment. There were several ore haulers all around the compound, but Khai was convinced that he wasn't going to find an operational one. And a quick visual survey confirmed that assessment.

A quick reconnoiter of the compound revealed that the facility still had partial power and was once a facility owned by Dah Ore Extraction.

Dack's family? Khai thought. He knew his only hope at this point was to venture in and see if there was a working communication console somewhere within the bowels of that building. There were several ways in, and all of them were viable options. He also found what appeared to be a small administrative office outside of the main building.

The office had been ransacked at one time, though nothing seemed to be stolen per se. It looked like this place hadn't been in service in about fifteen years; there was a newspaper sitting on a desk next to a console dated fifteen years ago. The office itself was ruined, stripped of anything of value. The only things that remained were papers, office supplies and one remaining console—which was active.

He accessed the computer and got nothing more than a schematic of the mining building. He called up the building's internal sensors and got a reading on the facility. It was large facility, several hundreds of thousands of square feet, three levels tall above ground and seven levels below ground. As most designs were, the communication tower was on the top floor of the building and the consoles to operate it were there, too. The computer gave him the most direct route to the communication tower and he moved out. He managed to find a small codepad that would open any door inside and provide him with a map to his destination. The codepad also had a wireless earpiece that gave him a hands-free interface with it and the facility's main computer.

The most direct route wasn't direct at all. There were two main lifts in the building. One was down and according to the computer wasn't going to be operable anytime soon. The other lift was in working order, but wasn't accessible from the main level or five levels below it. The main reactor on level five had ruptured and flooded levels three, four, five, six and seven with high levels of deadly radiation.

The facility possessed two stairwells, one on either side. The one on the far side, same side as the operational lift, looked to have collapsed and the one on his side was visibly destroyed due to the large hole in the side of the building where he could see at least two levels of stairs were gone. It looked to be a rather large explosion from something that looked less like a mining charge and more like an RPG. The stairwells were lead-lined and the only safe place to be in the event that the reactor melted down. Most safety protocols instructed the miners to remain in the stairwells until radiation relief teams came to their aid.

So his only course was to traverse the lower levels of the mining facility—which was definitely not the most ideal path—and brave the brief exposure to radiation on the lift ride up—again, not the best situation. He pried open the huge iron door; it creaked open sending an echo reverberating the down the stairwell and into the long, abandoned corridors of the facility.

He peered in, his flashlight in one hand and his trusted pistol in the other. He was not prepared for what he saw. What he saw was carnage. Dried blood was all over the walls and floor of the corridor. Though long decomposed, dismembered skeletons lay everywhere. They wore tattered mining uniforms belonging to Dah Ore Extraction.

"What the hell happened here?" he asked himself, realizing that Moon was nowhere to be seen.

It was dead silent, only the sound of dripping water echoed in the lonely corridors. The musty smell of stale air with a slight accent of decay assaulted his nose. He grimaced as he slowly stepped in. This was definitely *not* just a core reactor going critical and the workers abandoning it; *something* came in here and tore these men apart, limb from limb. Small and large arms fire had riddled the area with bullet holes and there was definitely evidence of both mining-style charges and military explosives going off in the area. *Maybe it was a Vyysarri attack,* he thought. Though, this didn't exactly fit the bill for a Vyysarri attack. Vyysarri didn't tear their enemies apart—they simply drained them of blood.

He pressed on, not venturing deeper into the facility to avoid the radiation. He slowly moved down the stairwell. He stopped only for a second to investigate the corridor of the next level and saw much of the same scene played out there; evidence of a struggle and more death. Whatever did this was *not* Seryysan or Vyysarri. Curiosity was eating at him, but the radiation levels were still too high. He knew that he would get his chance to find out once he reached the top level.

The next level had some lighting; a few fluorescent light banks flickered and blinked hanging by their wires. Still, though, nothing new had surfaced; only the same dismembered skeletons everywhere.

"This place is a tomb," he said to the darkness and moved on.

He reached level two and the codepad indicated that the radiation levels were safe enough to traverse the corridors.

"Computer," Khai called out. "What is the radiation level on this floor?"

The garbled, male voice of the computer spoke back to him. "Radiation levels are measured at seven REPs." REPs were Radiant Energy Particles in parts per million.

"What REP level is fatal to humans?"

"Five to ten REPs."

"How long will I survive on level two?"

"Roughly one hour."

Not nearly long enough to find out what happened in here. "What about level one?" He was almost afraid to ask; the longer he was there the more uneasy he felt.

"Two REPs, roughly three hours until effects of radiation felt."

"Damn," he whispered. *Plenty of time.*

He marched down the stairs to the bottom level. The stink was strongest here. The lighting was minimal but more than enough for him to see what had happened. He ventured deeper into the labyrinth of corridors. Immediately, he came across more evidence that he didn't like. Skeletons in SCGF fatigues and armor, armed with the standard array of weapons. The farther he dived into the facility, the worse he felt. He found gashes, deep, long and about two inches wide along the walls. *Definitely* not *Vyysarri*.

He was about an hour into the investigation, when the flat walls gave way to rougher, cave-like walls. "Computer. Where am I?"

"You have entered the mining corridor. This is where the building meets the mine. It also houses the entrance to the mine itself."

As he walked deeper into the rocky corridor, he happened upon a large metal door about ten feet tall and fifteen feet wide. It was sealed shut. "Computer, what am I looking at?"

"This is the entrance to the mine."

"What's behind it?"

"I'm sorry. My files on what exists behind the door have been corrupted."

"Convenient," Khai grumbled.

"Can the door be opened?"

"Negative. Power supplies are only at reserve levels. Without the core, powering the motors for the door will be impossible."

"What happened here?"

"The crew tunneled into a new cavern not charted on any geological map of this area and..."

"And what? What did they find?"

"... I'm sorry. My files on what exists behind the door have been corrupted."

"By who?" Khai shouted.

Before the computer could respond, Khai heard some skittering from behind the large, metal door. Khai pressed his ear against it to see if he could hear anything from beyond. He rested his head against the door when a solid *thump* came from the door. Khai jumped back, tripping over a skeleton and falling backward, rapping his head against the wall.

"Fuck!" he gasped.

"Computer, what is *behind that door?*" he shouted.

"I'm sorry. My files on what exists-"

"I get it! I get it!" Khai shouted over the suddenly-consistent pounding on the door. "What is the structural integrity of the door?"

"The door is constructed of Ti'tan'lium. It is ten feet by fifteen feet by two feet. The door is undamaged, and, given the nature of the material from which the door is made and the nature of the organisms behind the door, it is highly unlikely that the structural integrity will ever fail."

"Organisms? What kind of organisms?"

"I'm sorry. My files on what-"

"Shut up!"

The thumping became deafening! The constant pounding against the door turned to scratching at the door. Nails screeching against the metal door assaulted his ears. He instantly thought of the scratch marks he found on the walls of the corridor before he found the entrance to the mines. He put his hand on the door and felt it flex with every blow. Suddenly, he didn't want to know what was behind the door, he only wanted to get the hell out of there.

He started moving through the corridors, following the map on his codepad. He found the lift and punched the button for the top the level. The lift started moving and in short order, he made it to the communication room and all the equipment was in working order. It seemed that whatever was behind that door wasn't able to get into the upper levels of the facility.

He keyed in the frequency of the dedicated com unit he had given Dah. It patched through.

"Tell me I'm dreaming," Dah's voice came over the com.

"Okay, you're dreaming. Now that we've got that out of the way, come get me."

"Where are you?"

"I'm in the com tower of the mining facility time forgot. Oh, and I think it was owned by your family."

"Why do you say that?"

"Because it's called Dah Ore Extraction."

There was dead silence, then, "Activate the beacon for that facility. It should be next to the communications console. Do you see it?"

"Yeah," Khai said, stepping over to it. "Give me just a second to turn it on."

"Is he really there?" Tander's voice was full of dread. The map of every mine owned by Dah Ore Extraction materialized in the empty space in the room. The mine in question was blinking. Dah Ore Extraction Mining Facility 11 blinked red as the beacon was activated. "Damn!"

"What? What's so important about that mine?"

"I'm not allowed to discuss it with anyone for any reason. It's been deemed classified," Tander said cryptically.

"Is Khai in danger?" Tandy asked.

"No... Well, not immediately."

"What's that supposed to mean?"

"I can't tell you. But we have to go—*now*. If the military gets that signal, they'll be all over it like Vyysarri on blood."

"Khai are you there?" Tander yelled into the com unit.

"Yeah. I read you."

"Turn the beacon off right now. We're coming to get you!"

"Right. Turning it off. Dack?"

"Yeah?" Tander asked for his brother.

"You have a cold or something?"

"No. I'll explain later."

"Prime Minister!" Trall's aid shouted, panicky.

"Go ahead."

"I have an urgent message from Commander Hoom!"

"Patch him through." There was an audible *click.* "What can I do for you Commander?"

"Sir, the beacon on DOEMF Eleven was activated for only a moment then turned off! What are your orders?"

"Send a team to investigate. We can't have anyone ruining our plans. Got it?"

"Yes, sir! I am dispatching the soldiers now."

"Good," Trall hissed. "Do not fail me. Trall out."

No sooner did he close the channel when his aid called again. "What now?"

"Now I have Agent Thirteen on the line for you."

"Very well, patch her through."

"Sir, I'm tracking Captain Dah to-"

"DOEMF Eleven?"

There was a long pause. *"Y-yes, sir. How did you know?"*

"That's not important. Just track him and don't engage him until I tell you. If Khail survived his fall to Seryys, he'll be there, too."

"I'm on it, sir. I'll keep the channel open so you can give me the word."

"Very good, Agent."

Kay was elated. Khai'Xander Khail survived his ordeal on OS 12 and now she was going to meet him in battle. Her mouth watered with anticipation. She would taste his blood and take him for her mate. Captain Dah would be there, too. Him, she would just kill outright, along with that skinny bitch Bria'Nah. She throttled up her ship and soared for the Dah Ore Extraction Mining Facility 11.

Tander, Tandy and Bria were in Tander's luxury shuttle, headed for the facility.

"What the hell is going on, Tander?"

"I don't know," Tander said, taking a sip from an ice-filled glass with amber-colored liquor. "But, in light of what you've told me and showed me, I think I know why the military has taken a sudden interest in my operation here."

"What's so special about this mine?" Bria asked.

"It's better if I show you," Tander said, throttling up the shuttle. "And if I'm right, it won't be long 'til the military gets there, too."

"Should you be drinking and driving?" Bria asked.

"Look," Tander said deadpan." If you knew what I was about to show you, you'd be drinking, too."

Within twenty minutes, they made it to DOEMF 11. The place looked deserted, almost ransacked. There was a landing pad on the upper level near the tower. Khai was sitting on it, waiting for them to arrive. The shuttle set down on the landing pad and the side door swung up to open. Out stepped Dack, another Dack in an expensive suit and a girl.

"What the hell took you so long?" Khai grumbled.

"It's still a drive from Tanbarder, you know," Tandy said. "Anyway, let me introduce you to my twin brother, Dack'Tander Dah and Bria'Nah Briar. Everyone, this is the legendary Colonel Khai'Xander Khail."

"A pleasure," Tander said extending his hand with a charismatic smile.

"Good. Now that we've gotten the pleasantries out of the way, let's get the hell out of here!" Khai said forcefully.

"No," Tander replied to Khai firmly. "We need to check on the status of the door."

"Relax," Khai growled. "Your computer told me that the door is holding whatever the hell is in there."

"I'm not worried about the strength of the door," Tander snapped. "The military has a code key to open that door. What they don't know, is that I have an override code to lock it permanently."

"Why would the govern..." Khai almost instantly understood. "What the hell is behind that door?"

"Let me show you." Tander moved past Khai into the control room. He sat down the main computer. "Computer," he called out. "Unlock terminal."

"Please provide unlock code," the male voice spoke back.

"Tander-one-seven-seven-Tandy-alpha-nine-six-tango-four, enable."

"Authorization accepted. Welcome Dack'Tander Dah. Please state request."

"Display Reaper."

From the hologram projector in the center of the room, a monstrous being appeared.

"What the *fuck* is that?" Tandy asked.

"A Reaper," Tander responded, his eyes gazing at the monstrosity with a haunted expression. "Killed my whole crew here. There were hundreds, maybe even thousands of them. You're looking at the original inhabitants of Seryys. Samples taken from the rock in that cavern were dated hundreds of thousands of years ago. We know nothing about them except that they're incredibly strong, and fast, too. We believe they feed on the little rodent-like creatures that feed on the lichen on the walls; a very simple food chain, by our standards, but an effective one. We also know they're cannibalistic, as we watched them eat their dead and wounded on their retreat back into the cave. We think, being strict carnivores meant that they had to feed several times a day, but the rate at which the rodents reproduced, they had a nearly unlimited supply of food. As you can see, it hunts by sound and smell, but it knew the layout of the facility well enough to navigate it. So that made us think that they must have had some other kind of sense, like sonar or the ability to sense bioelectric currents. No studies were ever conducted out of fear of one of these things getting out. But the military required that we have a plan to let them out, in case someone, sometime down the road, wanted to study them."

"Is this to scale?" Khai asked.

"Afraid so," Tander replied.

The beast was humanoid, about seven feet tall, completely white with no hair on even an inch of its body. The head was elongated slightly from the chin to the back of the head, with a smooth, shiny surface all over. It had no eyes, two small slits for a nose and a mouth full of needle-like teeth. The ears were like small flaps that ran the length of the head.

Its torso was more humanoid than the rest of its body. Lean and muscular, it had very similar features to that of a Seryysan. They could see the vertebrae of a spine, ribs, collarbones, shoulder blades and muscles. The arms were longer than that of a normal man's and ended in oversized hands with six-inch talons on the ends of the four long, bony fingers that seemed to have an extra knuckle. The imposable thumb had only a small claw.

The bottom of the creature was more alien. It had a small protruding tale less than six inches long. The legs reminded Khai of sabercat's legs. It had thighs, knees and calves. But it had a third joint below the calves that bent forward like a sabercat's leg and ended in large feet with imposing big toes.

"Fifteen years ago, we tunneled into a large cavern, several hundred miles long and wide. It ran along the canyon but was several hundred feet from the canyon wall. I was here in the control room watching from the helmet cams of every miner I had in there. The whole area had its own ecosystem. It was like nothing I had ever seen! Water filtered down into large underground lakes from small, inch-wide fissures in the rock. The rock was incredibly hard. We had to develop a new drill bit just to cut through it. Small lichen grew along the rock where the water ran down. This lichen was eaten by these small rodent-like creatures. They were everywhere! They seemed to reproduce at an exponential rate, faster than anything my scientists had ever seen.

"We brought one back with us and closed it up for the day. This little, harmless creature seemed to have only two purposes: eating lichen and reproduction. And it did so asexually."

"You mean, like without-" Khai was about to ask.

"Without mating," Tander answered.

"Where's the fun in that?" Tandy asked jokingly.

"Anyway, what my scientists couldn't figure out was why they were there and, more importantly, how their population was controlled. Because at the rate at which they bred, there should have been *millions* of them down there, but we only found a couple hundred.

"The next day, we went back in. Things were going fine. Our geological survey team was making considerable progress when one of the monitors I was watching went straight to static. I called out on the com channel to raise the others. Suddenly, helmet cams started going out all over the monitor station. Gurgled cries came from all channels.

"One of the helmet cams caught a short glimpse of our attackers; *that* was the first time I saw one. I almost threw up, but I kept my composure and called for military help.

"The creatures slaughtered my men and started working their way up to the main entrance from the bottom level. I had the door closed and locked, regrettably before all my men got out. These creatures were immensely strong and started pounding down the door. Military aid was on its way, so all I could do was pray to the Founders that the door would hold until they got here.

"It did, thankfully, but the military was unprepared for what they met. *Hundreds* of those monsters came rushing out of the door when they opened it. I could hear the gunfire from here. The explosives from both my men and the SCGF soldiers shook the floor beneath my feet. I remember specifically a soldier yelling over the com that one got by and was heading up the east stairwell. A soldier fired a grenade into the wall and blasted the stairwell from the outside using thermal tracking goggles.

"Eventually, the soldiers were able to kill enough of them that they retreated back into the mine. They grabbed their wounded and dead and began eating them on their way. The military held them at bay until a new door could be manufactured and put into place. We lost six engineers during the installation of the door."

"You said that you knew why the military was suddenly taking in interest in your operation," Bria pointed out. "Why?"

"After the evidence you showed me, I had a bad feeling about this whole thing. If Trall was willing to the use the *Hammer Cannon* to destroy

Seryys City, maybe this was another backup plan. If you released even fifty of the things into the city, they would tear it down brick by brick. And I'll be damned if those engineers lost their lives for nothing."

"So what's the plan?" Khai asked.

"We go back down there and permanently disable to the lock."

"So then what's going to stop Trall from just blasting a hole through the canyon wall?"

"Without a controlled spot to get them out, they would simply rush out and kill everyone. They need the door so that they can manage the flow of Reapers at any given time."

"Good point," Tandy said. "So how do we disable it?"

"From the source," Tander responded.

"Why did I know you were going to say that?" Khai almost shuddered.

"It shouldn't take more than-" Tander was cut off by an alarm.

"What's that?" Khai asked.

"Proximity alarm. Looks like we have company. I have a ship—no, *two* ships—coming in hot. One is definitely military; the other looks almost civilian!"

"Trall knows we're here. That supports your theory, Tander," Khai said checking his 92:30. "You guys go down there and get the door sealed! I'll hold them off as long as I can."

They nodded and headed for the lift that worked.

Khai walked out to the landing pad and could hear the high-pitched sound of engines rushing his way. He cocked his gun and waited.

Kay caught the military vessel, bristling with weaponry, on her scope the minute they both came within range of the mining facility. She sent them a friendly code and then promptly a cease-and-desist code. These kills were *hers* and she wasn't about to let some Neanderthal take them from her!

"Commander," a young private called from the com station. "We're getting a high-authority cease-and-desist code from that civilian contact on our radar."

"What?" Commander Hoom squawked.

"There's a friendly code followed immediately by the cease-and-desist. I think it's an Agent, sir."

"Hail that ship, private."

"Sir," the private punched in the code and the screen flickered to a young woman—no, a *girl*!

"Agent, this is Commander Hoom of-"

"I know who you are, Commander. I'm telling you to back off and provide support only if I need it."

"With all due respect," Hoom protested. "This is a military operation."

"My clearance far outreaches yours, sir. Pull back and wait for my signal. That is an *order*!"

Hoom grimaced, furrowing his graying brow. "Yes, ma'am. Pulling back now."

"Thank you for following your orders, Commander. I will send my regards to your commanding officer about your superior ability to follow orders."

The screen went blank. "Damn! Fucking *kids* with more superiority than me! I don't get it!"

"What do we do, sir?" the pilot asked.

"We hang back, but just outside the facility. If she shows even the slightest sign of trouble, we swoop in and help her."

"Yes, sir."

Khai watched the military ship break off and land just out of view, but the civilian ship kept coming. Khai popped another painkiller as the ship slowed to a hover about thirty feet above the landing pad. Suddenly a figure emerged from the ship, falling toward him. He wasn't sure until she landed into a crouching position that she was even Seryysan. But when she did land, Khai had to pinch himself. It was a girl, a little girl. She stood straight up and Khai got a good look at her. She was lean and muscular, wearing a body-tight, black-and-red flight suit.

She unsheathed a sharp sword called a Kit'ra, a blade originally designed by the Kyyl'Jah Assassins as a remarkably fast and deadly weapon, and advanced in its design. The blade was fashioned from carbon steel by a laser for the sharpest edge possible and then coated in a Teflon-based film to ensure the edge stayed as sharp as the day it was made by easing the blade's path through whatever it was cutting. Khai wasn't in the mood for games; he pointed the gun and squeezed the trigger. The girl whipped the sword around and literally blocked the bullet. *Ah shit! An Agent!* He should have known. Only an Agent would be that young and that deadly all at the same time.

As an Agent, she was put through rigorous training, pushing her into the peak of perfect physical condition. She was schooled in hundreds of different styles of fighting; she was put through cognitive training to push her reflexes beyond that of a normal person and a cognitive microchip was installed in her brain to give her reflexes that bordered on precognition—the reflex package interface detected bioelectrical signals within the brain and acted accordingly, much the same way bionic prosthetics worked (in fact, they both used identical interfaces); she was beaten relentlessly—sometimes to within an inch of her life—to make her tougher; it was an awful life, but she was faster, stronger, tougher and smarter than the average person. She was faster than Khai, but she wasn't nearly as strong or as war-hardened as he. Khai holstered his pistol and pulled his knife. He advanced, she matched. They circled. She swung and Khai blocked, their blades crossing. Khai kicked her square in the gut, sending her tumbling back. She quickly got to her feet and grinned. She was *enjoying* this. Khai took no pleasure in roughing up a child, but it was either him or her. She lunged forward, plunging her sword forward. Khai barely had time to twist out of the way and bat the blade away with his knife. As he spun, he was caught at the base of the spine with a powerful side kick that issued a pained grunt from the old soldier. He somersaulted forward to put some distance between them and rolled to his feet. He was a good fifteen feet away from her and bringing his knife up into a guard position.

Suddenly, faster than he could blink, she covered that distance and attacked with a lateral swipe with the sword. Khai barely had time to register the attack when the blade sliced into his abs.

The blade was so sharp Khai barely felt it. It was only when he spotted his own blood pooling up at his feet, that he realized just how injured he was. That was also when he realized she was playing him, feeling him out. She knew from step one that she was faster than him. She was just playing it safe until she knew she could score the final blow. He had only minutes to use his field medic cauterizer before he bled to death. He had an idea. He pulled one of the remaining grenades from his bandoleer threw it at the Agent. Like he expected, she was able to bat the grenade away, but she left herself wide open and Khai made his move. He drew his pistol and put a bullet just below her ribcage. It would have been her head had his head not been spinning.

She squawked and stumbled over the ledge, falling forty feet to the ground. Khai knew she wasn't dead, but he now had an opportunity to buy his friends downstairs a little more time. He jumped into the shuttle and called Tandy.

"Hey Dack-uh, Tandy?"

"Yeah?"

"There's an Agent lying unconscious on the ground below the landing pad, I'm taking the shuttle to draw her and the military ship off of you guys to buy you some more time."

"Be careful."

"I will."

Khai fished through his bag and found the cauterizing tool. He bit down on a piece of leather and ran the searing hot tool over the slice in his stomach. He could feel that it was only into the muscle, that it didn't hit any major organ, but he was still losing a lot of blood. The cauterizing worked and the hemorrhaging stopped.

Once he was able to regain his composure, he started the shuttle, brought it up on its hover pads and spun it around a hundred and eighty degrees. He punched the throttle and sped off toward Tanbarder. The military ship gave chase and started firing immediately. Khai upped the ante by piloting the shuttle into the canyon. The larger, less maneuverable military ship followed, but wasn't as agile as the shuttle. The ship opened fire on Khai the instant they were both in the canyon. Khai juked and jinked and the cannon bolts passed by, hitting the canyon walls.

Finally, a shot found its mark. The bolt of laser fire ricocheted of the hull of the shuttle and struck the canyon wall. *Ti'tan'lium hull plating* and *shields? This guy knows how to ride in style.* The pilot of the military ship learned quickly and moved to solid rounds and started peppering the shuttle with bullets. The shuttle bucked and shuddered as bullets lodged into the hull and actually got through.

"Damn!" He punched the console. More bullets found their mark and he had to pull out some old tricks, tricks he hadn't used in years. He pushed the throttle to full and took a smaller canyon that shot off to the right. He had to spin the shuttle up on its side to squeeze through the small opening. He looked back and saw that the larger ship simply left the canyon and followed from above. Khai knew it was only a matter of time before the pilot figured something out. Inevitably, the ship rained fire on the shuttle with missiles. Khai pulled up on the yoke and the shuttle left the canyon.

The shuttle was spouting smoke now. Khai was losing hope that he was going to make it to Tanbarder in one piece. Finally, as if the Founders answered his prayers, Tanbarder loomed up on the horizon. He coaxed a little more power from the engines and the ship soared as fast as it could toward the city. Khai performed evasive maneuvers, flying low to the ground. The larger ship wasn't able to fly that low without crashing, so Khai kept it up. Missiles exploded all around him as he swayed from the left to right dodging attacks.

"Computer, are you still operational?"

"Yes, sir," the male voice responded.

"Where's the *Star Splitter* located?"

"Docking bay sixteen."

"Show me on a map."

A map popped up on the screen. It showed a blinking light near the center of town. Khai had his destination. He was approaching the city limits when the military ship was about to overtake him in the shuttle. He dived down into the city. *The military wouldn't dare fire on civilian buildings to bring down a criminal*, Khai thought. He was wrong, *dead* wrong.

Chapter Thirteen

The lift doors opened; the smell was the first thing to assault them.

"Ugh! What *is* that?" Bria asked, covering her mouth.

"Decay," Tandy answered. "Breathe through your teeth."

They worked their way through the lowest level, finding the same skeletal remains that Khai had found hours earlier. As they drew closer, the loud banging became clearer.

"What's making that noise?" Bria asked, fear in her voice.

"The Reapers," Tander replied. "Single-minded, they are."

"Are they in the complex?" Tandy asked.

"No. They're still behind the door. We need to make sure it stays that way... *permanently.*"

"And how do we do that, exactly?" Tandy asked his brother.

"There's a hidden security panel *inside* the rock next to the door. That panel is a failsafe. I had it installed in secret. I was always afraid that someone might try to release these monsters. We have to chip away some rock to get to it, but it was the only way to keep it invisible to scanners."

"And you know where it is?" Tandy asked.

"Yes, I marked the spot."

"Good," Tandy said curtly. "The quicker we get out of here, the better. This place gives me the creeps."

"Get in line," Bria grumbled.

The pounding got louder and louder the closer they got, until they had to yell to be heard.

"Ok, now!" Tandy shouted. "How do we get to it?"

Life smeared into view. The ground was the first thing she found. She rolled over onto her back, pain shot to every nerve in her body. The fall was bad, the bullet in her stomach was worse. She used a wristband computer to call her ship down to her. The ship landed next to her. She crawled on her belly up the ramp and into ship. The onboard computer scanned her injuries immediately and a medical robot descended from the ceiling and lifted her into the medical bay.

Surgical arms went to work on her right away. One extracted the bullet, while another set her broken leg and another administered a liquid form of Kryylopax. She cried and squirmed as the robotic arms worked away on her. Strips of metal were placed on the broken bone to reinforce it and the bone was fused back together after the leg was cut open to administer aid. The bullet hole was cauterized to stop the bleeding. As the anesthetic took hold, she became more serene. The surgical arms finished their work and she was well enough to go back out and fight. She could only hope that Khail was still out there.

An initial scan of the area showed that the shuttle and Commander Hoom's ship were both gone. *Damn! He's gone!* She looked at her display and found something else, a consolation prize. Captain Dah was still in the facility, somewhere below her. She focused the scan on the building and she found him on the bottom level of the facility near the center. She pumped some more anesthetic into her system, landed the ship on the landing platform and headed off into the bowels of the building.

It took a several minutes, but they finally found a pick that would be strong enough to chip away the six or seven inches they needed to find the secret panel. Tandy started picking away, swinging with all his might on the completely obscure marking on the wall indicating that that was where it sat, waiting. His superior strength gave him an edge and he was blasting holes in the wall with every strike.

The door slid open into the remnants of chaos. Skeletons lay everywhere, signs of a struggle filled the room and the pungent stink of years-old decay filled her nostrils. Using the entry light on her gun, she worked her way through the labyrinth of corridors following the blip on her tracking device. It was only a matter of time before she found them and killed them. She pressed on, ignoring the pain and looking forward to the time when she licked Captain Dah's blood from her sword.

As she drew nearer, she could hear two very distinct pounding sounds. One sounded muffled, while the other sounded more defined and like metal on rock. Both grew louder the closer she got to Dah's location. Finally, she found them. Captain Dah, Bria and… Captain Dah? No. He was wearing a fine suit and had his hair combed differently. A twin brother?"

"Well," she said seductively. "Hello."

"Ah crap!" Tandy growled.

"Who's that?" Tander asked.

"That's the Agent that's after me," Tandy responded.

She holstered her gun and drew her Kit'ra.

"Whoa!" Tander took a step back and raised his hands. "Do you have any idea what's behind this door, little girl?"

"It's not my concern. My concern to eliminate all of my targets, Captain Dah and his *girlfriend* are two of those targets. You are not, but if you interfere I will kill you as well."

Tandy swung the pick once more and he hit metal.

"That's it!" Tander shouted.

"Good," Tandy said. "Get that door sealed and I'll hold her off as long as I can."

"Come on, Captain Dah. I've been waiting for this for a while now."

"Well, come and get it," Tandy said, waving her in and pulling his knife.

She moved so fast, Tandy didn't even have time to register he was injured. The sword was placed perfectly under his left collarbone, missing the shoulder and any organs, and pinning him to the wall. He cried out in pain and Tander went to aid his brother.

"No!" he cried. "Seal the damn door!"

Tander stopped, looked at him and nodded, getting back to work. Kay twisted the sword causing the blade to bend within him, Tandy cried out again as blood began spurting out from the wound.

"This is not fatal," Kay stated. "You will live if you do exactly what I say."

"What's that?" Tandy asked, grimacing in pain.

She leaned in closer to him; she was nose to nose with him. He could smell her perfume and thought how weird it was that a trained killer would wear perfume. Tandy was no idiot. He noticed immediately that she was injured. Despite her trying hard to cover it up, Tandy saw her limping slightly and saw the smear of blood surrounding what appeared to be a bullet hole in her flight suit just below her ribcage. As she leaned in to apparently *kiss* him, he wound up, put his military-honed strength behind it and struck that bloody spot.

The gasp that came from the Agent was both pain and surprise. She stumbled back into the wall, rapping her head on a rather large pipe. Tandy had only seconds to react. He tried pulling the sword out, but it was stuck into the wall of the corridor too deep; he didn't have the strength necessary to do it. So he did the only thing he could think of... he grabbed the handle of the Kit'ra and bored down on it. The blade bowed and he cried out. Eventually, the blade gave and broke. Tandy roared as he leaned forward and the broken blade passed through him, staying in the wall.

He slumped forward and fell to his knees. By that time, Kay had recovered and bashed him in the face with her knee. Tandy flipped to his back, spitting blood as he flew. From his back, he saw the Agent approaching, his knife in her hand. All he could do was kick at the left leg she was favoring as she walked. The girl cried out and fell to the ground. Tandy quickly got up and pressed his attack. He kicked her in the stomach while she was down and she slid down the hallway. Tandy kept it up. He picked her up by the neck with one hand and pounded her in the bullet wound several more times with his balled fist. He dropped her in heap.

She was barely able to get to her feet and was wobbling back and forth; blood covered her face from a large gash above her right eye; her eyes were only slits and she was swinging sluggishly at him to try to fend him off. She dropped to her knees and lowered her head, as if surrendering and asking for death.

Tandy did not comply.

Kay looked up at him. "Why do you not finish it?" Why do you not end my life?"

"I don't kill kids," Tandy said deadpan, then punched her in the forehead, knocking her out cold.

"Got it!" Tander shouted, elated. "The failsafe has been activated!"

"Good," Tandy said, carrying the girl over his shoulder.

"You didn't kill her?" Bria asked.

"No," Tandy said. "She's just a confused kid, brainwashed into thinking what she's been doing was right. Do you have an infirmary here?"

"Yeah, it's on the top level right of the control room."

"Good. We'll leave her there for the robots to mend her, and then take her ship. I'm sure she can find a ride home."

They got into the lift and it started taking them back up to the top level.

"So what was the failsafe?" Tandy asked.

"The panel within the wall governed heating coils within the door's mechanics. The heating coils kept the lubricants warm so the door would work properly when activated. I had to reprogram the panel to tell the coils to superheat. Eventually, they will melt the gears that lift the door together so they'll never move again."

"So, why did you have to hide the panel deep enough in the rock to hide it?" Tandy asked.

"Because that panel was designed to power and regulate heating coils that could melt iron and steel. If they found the panel, it was possible that they would have also discovered that the heating coils within the door were far too strong for their intended purpose and replace them with weaker ones that would not melt the gears."

"Clever," Tandy said.

"Thank you," Tander responded. "Those degrees finally paid off."

"*Degrees?*" Bria asked.

"Yeah," Tandy said with an unimpressed tone. "Captain smarty pants, here, has ten degrees."

"That's incredible!" Bria marveled. "In what?"

"Well," Tander sighed, "five of them are in some sort of engineering, mostly pertaining to mining. I thought that if I was going to own a mining company, I should also learn to how run every aspect of it, including the machines. I also have to a degree in economical structure, political structure, geology, philosophy and galactic languages and cultures. I do have some dealings with other cultures outside of Seryys space and though Seryys is mostly isolationistic, I do find it necessary to export some goods."

"Basically," Tandy growled, "he's a genius."

"And a billionaire," Tander added.

"Rub it in," Tandy grumbled.

They reached the top level. Tandy gently placed the child on a medical bed, wrapped himself with field bandages, gave himself an injection of a Kryylopax-based painkiller and activated the infirmary's automated medical response robots on his way out.

He returned to the control room to the middle of a conversation between his brother and Bria.

"... it's not that I disapprove of Tandy's career choice," Tander said defensively. "In fact, in a lot of ways, we do the same type of work. We both serve Seryys in our own ways: I serve her through innovation and provision, while my brother provides her with protection. It *is* a noble occupation, just a dangerous one. I live in fear that one day I'll get a call from Captain Byyner telling me my twin brother was killed."

"I understand, but he's a good man and fine officer. He's resourceful, a quick thinker and a survivor. You have nothing to worry about."

Tandy decided to break up the conversation and pretend that he didn't hear it. He was inwardly relieved to hear Bria defend him against his brother. He was worried that Tander might try to steal her by flashing his money and brains. But Bria knew who she wanted.

"All right, guys. Time to head to out."

"What about your shoulder?" Tander asked, his voice full of concern.

"I'll have Med take a look at it when we get back to Seryys City. Right now, we need to get out of here before she wakes up. I pumped her with enough sedatives to put her out for days, but I can't be too sure she hasn't developed an immunity to it."

"Agreed," Tander said.

They entered the ship and Tandy settled into the cockpit. The controls were very similar to that of the *Star Splitter*'s. Tandy swung the ship around and headed for Tanbarder.

"Shuttle is approaching docking bay sixteen," the computer's voice announced.

Khai was piloting the shuttle just above the building line—roughly thirty feet up. Once he got the signal, he put the shuttle on autopilot. The military ship pounded the shuttle and it was threatening to just fall out of the sky. Khai popped the hatch open. He saw the *Star Splitter* coming up and just before he was completely over the docking bay, he jumped.

The ship scored a shot on the shuttle and it veered off course into a vacant lot and exploded in a cloud of dust on contact with the ground. Khai hit the ground about thirty feet from the *Star Splitter* and tumbled several times before coming to stop near the ship face down in the dirt. He didn't move for some time, but eventually, he convinced his body to get up and limp up the ship's ramp. He was certain several bones were broken from the fall. But he knew someone who could fix him up, if he could just get back to Seryys City.

He started up the ship. The computer ran the preflight checklist and confirmed that everything was ready to go. He lifted the ship up on its hover pads and spun around to head toward Seryys City. He punched the throttle and the ship took off. He was only a few minutes' flight from Seryys City, especially with his military codes to bypass sky lanes and take a direct route to Medic's hidden clinic.

He was just about to enter Seryys City space when the ship bucked hard and listed to the right. Khai grimaced. Even the bucking of the ship caused him incredible pain. From all the injuries he suffered, to the days of travelling with them, his body was finally giving up. Blood dribbled from his mouth. But that was the least of his worries. That same damned ship caught up to him. His little decoy worked for a while. He made a snap judgment and yanked back on the yoke heading for space.

The ship followed him right up.

His ship bucked again and pain shot to every inch of his body. He went evasive trying to dodge any of the attacks coming from the military ship. He pushed the throttle to a speed that was barely tolerable to the structural integrity of his ship. His pursuers were falling behind, not willing to push their ship that far. But no matter how fast Khai could fly, no matter how many ships he could outrun, he couldn't outrun their radios and a whole squadron of *Shark*-Class Interceptors was waiting for him.

As soon as he broke orbit, they opened fire. Damage lights lit up across the damage control board in the cockpit. Khai had only one more option: make a blind jump and pray. He primed the Eve'Zon drive and activated it.

"I strongly advise against this, Khai," Joon's voice chimed in.

"You wanna blow up?"

"Not particularly," Joon responded.

"Then shut up!"

"As you wish," Joon said, slightly defeated.

"Is the Eve'Zon primed?"

"Yes, Event Horizon Drive is ready."

"Activate it!" Khai yelled as sparks flew across the cockpit.

A gigantic maw yawned, revealing a black nothingness beyond. The ship rocked again. "Shields down, hull integrity at fifty-five percent."

Khai pushed throttle and the ship went nowhere. "Computer! What's the problem?"

"We are caught in a hauling beam. A *Grind*-Class frigate has joined the fight. They are attempting to keep us from entering the black hole."

"Reroute all power, even from life support, to engines. I want to break away from them—*now!*"

The ship shuddered and bucked as she started pulling away toward the black hole. The singularity began to close. Khai rotated the cannon to face aft. "I really didn't want to do this..." he pulled the trigger and the cannon blast hit the beam emitter on the frigate. The *Star Splitter* lurched forward, sucking Khai into his seat. The ship entered just as the maw closed and he was catapulted into the unknown. When his ship emerged on the other side, it spun powerlessly. Adrift in space, he may never be found, but he wouldn't know even if he was. Due in part to the explosive entrance into the event horizon and to his injuries, he blacked out. His heart rate was slowly dropping and he was running out of oxygen as the ship's systems all went down.

Kay'Lah Kayward came to in an infirmary that was not familiar to her. She immediately sat up and looked around. There was chirping equipment all around her and medical robot arms hung from the ceiling. She felt fine. As she explored the sickbay, she found her x-ray results. The metal plates in her leg were removed and the bone was mended properly. The bullet wound was still on the mend, cleaned properly and bandaged well. Captain Dah went through great pains to make sure she was treated for her wounds, and comfortable. Why? Why would someone whom she was trying to kill take such good care of her, show her mercy?"

She had to find out. She checked her wrist band and was not surprised to see that her ship had been taken. It only made sense that Captain Dah would take the only mode of transportation available. She wandered out to the control room and found the communication console and called for help.

The screen blinked to Trall's gaunt—and now, angry—face.

"I told you *not* to engage the targets until I said so. Not to mention the fact that you called off a military craft in pursuit *and* you let Khail escape *and* since you're calling me that means you allowed Captain Dah to escape too!"

"I'm sorry, Prime Minister. Khai proved to more resourceful than I anticipated."

"And what is your excuse for Dah?"

"I-I was injured from my fight with Khail. Dah exploited that."

"What were Khail and Dah doing there?"

"I don't know," Kay admitted. "But when I found Dah, his twin brother was doing something to a large door inside the facility on the lowest level."

"What did he do?" Trall's voice betrayed both fear and anger.

"I don't know."

"Well, get down there and find out!"

"Yes, sir."

She did her scans of the door and waited for her ride. A group of engineers and soldiers were there within the hour. They also made scans of the door and transported Kay back to her home where she curled up on her brightly-colored bed and slept off her injuries.

The next day, she reported to Prime Minister Trall's office.

"I have the reports from both you and my team. You know what it found?"

"No, sir. I don't."

"Of course you don't! Because you're an *idiot!*" Trall spat, slamming his fist on the desk.

Kay recoiled. Despite her ability to snap Trall in half, she still feared the man, like a child fearing an abusive father. "I'm sorry I failed you."

"Captain Dah managed to the permanently seal that door holding back something very important to me! That was my last plan and you let them ruin it!"

"I'm sorry, I was injured. I don't even remember them leaving."

"If you were injured, why are you perfectly healthy now?"

"I don't know," she admitted. "I woke up in the facility's infirmary. The automated system healed me."

"And how did you get there?"

"Captain Dah spared me. He knocked me know out and he must have left me in the infirmary."

"So let me get this straight," Trall hissed. "You disobeyed a direct order, let both targets get away, allowed one of them thwart my plans *and* one of them saved you?"

"Y-yes, sir."

"Great. Just wanted to clarify your roll in this complete failure."

"I don't know what else to say, sir."

"You have failed me. Failure of this magnitude must not go unpunished."

"What are you talking about?"

"Your family. Your family will pay for your failure."

"You... you can't!" she sobbed, standing, balling up her fists with rage. "They have nothing to do with this!"

"You should have considered that before you failed me!" he roared.

"Kill me!" she cried. "Kill me instead, *please!*"

"No," Trall grinned. "*You* are still useful to me."

"Please..." she whispered.

"Get back to your hole," Trall seethed, standing and turning his back to her. "You'll be contacted when I find a use for you. Now get out of my sight!"

Kay sat on her brightly-colored bed, hugging her stuffed animals, rocking back and forth, crying and trying to figure out what she was going to do. She didn't dare defy Prime Minster Trall, but if she didn't, her family was going to die. She couldn't possibly fight off an entire attack team. She could try to employ the help of another Agent, but she knew that it would be nearly impossible to get them to disobey orders or even go out of their way to help one another while on assignment. It took an act of congress to have another Agent "bump" into Dah and place a bug on him...

"That's it!"

She knew where Dah was and she could ask him for help. He could bring the entire police department to bear on the military to save her family! She pulled up the tracking device on her computer. There he was; in the Residential Sector.

She left her home and set out to find him, to get him to help. He showed her compassion once, why wouldn't he show it again?

Dack'Tandy Dah sat up in Medic's private recovery suite attached to the main building. He got up and walked naked to the shower. Bria was still in the bed, and she stirred ever so slightly as he got up. The shower felt good and he needed it badly. After almost an hour, he turned the water off and stepped out into the bathroom. He toweled off and wrapped that towel around his waist. He stepped into the suite.

"Last night was..."

He couldn't believe it! There she was, *again*! She had Bria in a chokehold with a gun to her head.

"What do you want?" he asked the Agent.

"I didn't come for a fight, not this time."

"Then my question still stands."

"You showed me mercy before. Why?"

"You're just a kid," Dah replied. "I don't kill kids, and your disposition isn't your fault. You were programmed that way. You still haven't answered my question."

"Sorry," Kay said. "My name is Kay'Lah Kayward and I need your help."

"I'm sorry," Dah half chuckled. "Can you repeat that?"

"I desperately need your help," she pleaded. "Trall is going to kill my family for not succeeding in my mission to kill you. He said that I allowed you to thwart his plans by sealing that door in the facility."

"Why didn't he just kill you?"

"He said that I was still useful, and that killing my family would be a far better punishment."

"Okay," Dah sounded like he was considering it, which filled Kay with hope. "Let Bria go first. Then we can talk."

Immediately, she let Bria go and she ran over to Dah. Kay dropped the gun without with being asked and sat down. Dah nodded and was pleased with her behavior so far.

"Will you please help me?" she asked, tears welling up in her eyes.

"You Agents have been known to be very convincing actors. How do I know you're not just luring me into a trap?"

"I can't prove it," she admitted. "All I can do is give you my family's address and hope you show up."

"Do you know when they're supposed to be attacked?"

"I don't. I'm just going to sit there and wait."

"You're not giving me much to work with here," Dah said, heaving a sigh and crossing his arms. "But you didn't come here looking for a fight. That I can tell."

"So you can help me? You can bring your police friends and help me?"

Dah stared at her for a good long while. If she was looking to ambush him, she wouldn't have asked to bring his "police friends" with him. *Maybe she's telling the truth.* "I can't bring any other officers into this. I'm on leave. Furthermore, without proof, they can't do anything anyway."

"Oh." Dah could feel the hope drain out of her.

"What's wrong?"

"I'm afraid they may send another Agent, or a team of Agents, to do the job."

Dah changed gears on her. "How did you find me?"

"On your way home from our first encounter, you bumped into a young man. That young man was an Agent and he planted a device on you."

"Is that how you found me at my brother's mining facility?"

"No. Trall's people detected the facility's beacon when Colonel Khail activated it," Kay answered plainly, hoping that her being this forthcoming would help her case.

"Tander said that might happen." Dah nodded, thumbing his chin.

"Look," Kay said. "I know you don't trust me, I wouldn't either. After all, I tried to kill you— though it would seem that you have mostly recovered from our encounter."

"I would say the same about you," Dah said, eyeing her.

"That leads me to the other reason for coming here. Thank you."

"For what?" Dah was sincerely confused.

"For sparing me. For so long, I've been brutally beaten and tortured to harden me for the life I was selected to live. My family has been used as leverage over me for the last four years of that life. If I ever deserted, they were as good as dead. Now that Trall has ordered their deaths, I have no reason to stay. No one has *ever* shown me an ounce of kindness since I was taken from my home until you. I owe you my life and in return I give it to you."

"Wait, what? You're pledging your life to me?"

"If you help me save my family," Kay amended.

Dah sat for a long while, his jaw twitching as he thought about her words and what they meant. She seemed sincere enough. Maybe she was telling the truth. There was really only one way to find out.

"Okay," Dah said definitively. "I will help." Kay looked like she just opened the present she always dreamed of and was about to jump up to give him a hug. "But!" She stopped. "If I even *smell* a backstab coming, I'll kill you myself. Understood?"

"Perfectly," she beamed. "Thank you!"

"You're welcome."

She approached Dah, who immediately recoiled, then loosened up. She reached out and grabbed his sleeve. He tried to jerk back, but her grip was stronger than he anticipated. She jerked back and ripped the sleeve clean off. Before Dah could snap some colorful line of curses, the girl removed a small patch of transparent, fiber mesh that was stuck with adhesive from the sleeve. The fiber mesh was filled with microscopic circuitry that was used as a tracking device. When Dah looked at her, she smiled sweetly. "So they don't find you and Medic."

"Thanks. Now, get out of here!"

"Right away!" She dropped a piece of paper on the table and ran out the door so fast Dah could have blinked and missed her exit.

"Are you crazy?" Bria snapped as soon as she was convinced the girl was gone.

"A little," Dah replied with a shrug. "Why?"

"She's going to kill you," Bria stated frankly. "You realize that, right?"

"I'm not so sure," Dah disagreed. "I can usually tell when someone is lying."

"How so?"

"I don't know, it's like a... sixth sense I get when they're lying. Call it a gut instinct."

"So, you're psychic?"

"Oh, you're funny. No, I've just been doing this job for long enough to know."

"You're going, aren't you?"

"I have to," Dah said. "It's my job. If her family is really in danger, then I have no choice but to protect them... even it *is* from our own government. I just wish I could find Khai; I could really use his help right now. He was able to defeat her."

"But you were, too."

"I targeted the wounds that Khai inflicted. She should have been able to slice me into a hundred pieces in under ten seconds."

"Well *that*'s reassuring. Now she's a hundred percent, and she may have friends."

"She could have done it right now..." Dah gave it a moment to set in. "And her friends would've definitely busted in by now. Remember? They probably want the both of us, since it was your late lover who discovered the truth and died for it."

"That doesn't mean she can't knock me off later after you're dead."

"We're just gonna play it by ear," Dah said with a sigh.

Chapter Fourteen

It was quiet. Dah couldn't tell if Kay had seen him yet or not. If she had, she wasn't making any move to attack him. But that didn't at all mean that he wasn't in danger. Even if she was telling the truth, that meant that other Agents could possibly be on their way. If she was lying, that meant other Agents could possibly on their way. Either way, his danger sense was prickling with... well, *danger*. He found a good perch on an adjacent building to that of Kay's family's. They were on the tenth floor of fifteen. The stealthiest way in would be achieved by repelling down the side of the building and going in through the window. Kay obviously felt the same way. She was perched atop the stairwell access point to the roof. Chances were very likely that the people coming may not even use the stairs; they would probably drop in from gunships or BASE jump from a higher building. But her position gave her the ability to defend from both high and low attacks.

Dah had several thumbnail-sized motion trackers placed on several of the surrounding buildings to track any attack coming from those directions. Essentially, he was covering both his and Kay's rears simultaneously. His only hesitation was whether or not to warn Kay if they came, or wait to see if they attacked her. If they attack her, then out comes the sniper rifle he brought with him to take them down from a distance. If they don't attack, then he kills Kay outright and makes a hasty retreat. Either way, it was favorable for him.

About an hour into the stakeout, Dah's motion sensors picked up movement and displayed the information into the HUD through his sniper scope. Four individuals were approaching from the south, moving fast—faster than normal. *She was right. Agents. Damn!* He was north of Kay's position, so he wasn't in immediate danger just yet. As if reading his mind, Kay responded immediately. She moved into the shadow of night for cover. So far, her story was checking out. If she was acting this whole thing out, she was being most convincing. The four other kids leapt from a dangerous height and all landed, tucking into a roll that ended up with all of them on their feet. Kay was invisible.

They started unraveling lengths of rope. Dah was right; they were repelling. Suddenly, Kay emerged, slowly and quietly sneaking up behind them. She unsheathed a new Kit'ra and threw it. The blade connected and plunged deep into a young blond boy's back. Kay didn't skip a beat to celebrate. She ran up, jumping into a front flip, planting her feet on the boy's back, grabbing her sword and pushing off, pulling the sword out. The boy fell forward off the building as Kay landed on her feet after performing a back flip off the boy's shoulders. Dah was wholly impressed with her abilities.

However, the others responded immediately. The remaining three Agents (a boy, a redhead girl and a brunette girl) swarmed her. At that point, there wasn't a doubt in Dah's mind that she was telling the truth. And only then, did he provide assistance. He squeezed the trigger and the brunette girl's blood splattered all over Kay and the other two Agents as the bullet passed through the right side of her chest, collapsing a lung and shattering several ribs. He still refused to kill any kids, even if they were trying to kill others.

For about two seconds, which seemed longer than that, they all looked around with bewildered expressions. Then Kay realized what was going on and she smiled, pressing the attack. She thrust her sword forward and the boy twisted out of the way while the girl flew in with a flying sidekick that was blocked wide to the right by Kay's foot swooping through an arcing kick.

The girl tumbled to the ground and rolled to her feet as the boy swung horizontally with his Kit'ra. Kay bowed forward to duck under that attack and while kicking her feet back, connected with the girl to stop her approach. Kay landed on her belly and rolled out of the way as the tip, and about six inches, of the boy's Kit'ra drove into the floor. Kay thought quickly and kicked the blade, breaking it into three pieces. Dah tried to get a clear shot, but with them moving so bloody quickly, it was hard to home in on one and he certainly didn't want to end up shooting Kay, or killing the others.

Suddenly, a proximity alarm displayed in his HUD. Another two Agents had flanked him and were less than twenty feet behind him. He expected that. The Agents weren't stupid; they wouldn't send in their entire force and give away their numbers. He had incapacitating charges placed around him to act as a buffer for just such an event. As they moved into range of the charges, Dah set them off and virtually shattered the Agents' ear drums instantly—without causing damage to the roof or killing them. They may be deaf for the rest of their lives, but they wouldn't die... and with any luck, they'd be cut loose because they wouldn't be of any use again. But, what Dah didn't anticipate was the sheer number of Agents Trall sent. His proximity alarm went off again, two more from the west and one from the east.

Dah risked being spotted by popping up from his prone position to survey the situation. He spotted the one coming from the east and took him down with a well placed shot to the knee that pulverized it. The other two made it to him quickly and pounced. Dah was outmatched basically ten to one. He used their overconfidence to his advantage. The first kid, a boy, simply grabbed him by the neck and tried choking him to death. Dah was superior in strength by three times. He simply grabbed the boy's arm with both hands and snapped it. The boy yelped and fell to the ground, his radius and ulna protruding from the skin, blood gushing.

The other saw what Dah had done and took a step back to reassess the situation. Clearly, Dah could tell that this boy now knew he had military training. He had already proven to be more cunning than he appeared. What other surprises could he be hiding? Dah had to grin, because now the boy *was* overestimating his abilities. After all, he was just an ex-soldier turned cop. Dah used that to his advantage.

"Listen here, boy," Dah said in the most intimidating voice he could muster. "You're in way over your head here. Don't make me hurt you."

"I must follow my orders!" he cried, his voice still squeaking from puberty.

Dah felt an overwhelming sense of pity for this boy. *His head is so fucked up...*

"What's your name, son?" Dah asked.

"That doesn't matter! I have to kill you!" he cried again.

"No you don't!" Dah insisted. "You're not a soldier, you're a *kid*."

"I have to complete my mission at all costs!" he shouted, adolescent hormonal rage filling his voice. "You don't understand!"

"What's your name?" The boy, no more than fifteen years old, started to shiver like it was a ten below zero outside. Dah took a step closer and he matched it backward. "Come on, kid. What's your name? Mine's Dack."

"I know," he responded. "I memorized your profile. Prime Minister Trall made you required reading after you, your twin brother and your friend Colonel Khai ruined his plans."

It wasn't his name, but it was a good start. "Then you have me at a disadvantage. I don't know *your* name."

"Six," he said.

"Okay, Six. That's a start. What about your birth name?"

"Gav'Vin Garmin. Gav for short."

"Gav," Dah nodded with a slight smile. Dah took a step closer and extended his hand. The boy recoiled so much that he stepped backward off the ledge of the roof. "No!" Dah cried, lunging forward and grabbing Gav's hand. Dah was more than strong enough to pull the boy back up to safety, but as Gav dangled there, his eyes kind of glazed over and his face took on a haunted expression. His lips moved as if he was talking to himself and reached behind his back.

"At any cost..." the boy murmured. He pulled himself closer to Dah and brandished a polished knife. Gav swung the knife at the exposed man, who was his lifeline at the moment. The knife sunk three inches into the soft tissue just behind his collarbone.

Out of pure reflexes alone, Dah jerked back with a grunt. He instantly lost his grip on the boy's hand and he fell, screaming, all the way to his death. "No!" Dah cried. *No! No! NO!* It was too late, he was dead.

That poor haunted kid was dead. *At least now Trall can't hurt him anymore.*

The Kit'ra was broken and Kay was on the move, rolling out of the way of the girl's next attack. Kay sprung to her feet from her back and spun kicked the girl's sword away and located hers at the same time. Once armed again, she pressed the attack. She attacked the boy with a high, horizontal attack with her sword and as anticipated, the boy ducked under it. Kay kept her momentum spinning and swiped her foot low to floor wiping the boy's feet out from under him. She went to drive the killing blow into his chest when she was bashed in the side of the head with a brick of crete.

Kay stumbled back and that gave the boy enough time to get to his feet. The girl took an attack of opportunity on Kay, dazed from the blow to her head. Kay barely ducked under the fast blow. The blade cut through her hair still suspended in air. Just before Kay could really recover, the girl attacked again, this time low. Kay jumped over the blade as it cut through a heating exhaust pipe behind her. During the jump, Kay spun and swung her foot around catching the girl Agent in the face and sending her spinning to the ground. Her victory was short lived, though. As she landed, the boy kicked her into a network of ducts for the building's ventilation system.

She emerged from the wreckage to find both of them ready for her. She sighed, rolled her eyes and waded through the broken ducts. Once she was out, she saw what appeared to be two large explosions on a rooftop adjacent to her. *Dah!* Kay though immediately. Then she realized that the others were also looking in that direction. Kay moved quickly. She lunged forward and connected with a bone-jarring kick to the side of the boy's face. He crumbled to the floor. The girl responded quicker than Kay had thought she was going to and swiped her sword down at Kay's exposed leg. Kay kicked her leg down fast enough to avoid it getting cut clean off, but it left a deep wound across her thigh. Kay refused to let it slow her down. She dug deep and found that inner strength to survive. She pressed the attack, a barrage of rage-fueled attacks, high and low, vertical, horizontal and diagonal. The boy recovered.

The two were backpedaling as fast as they could, batting away the attacks. Then, at once, they turned the tables with a coordinated flurry of attacks meant to overwhelm their attacker. It worked. Kay made a fatal error and thrust her sword forward to run the defenseless boy through, but left her right arm exposed to the girl with the sword. Kay knew it was a calculated risk, but if she could dispose of at least one of them, her chances of survival increased exponentially. Her gamble, unfortunately, did not pay off. They were baiting her to attack, and when she did, the girl chopped down on Kay wrist. The only thing that kept the blade from slicing her hand completely off was her quick reflexes. She jerked her hand away, but had to drop her sword.

She took several steps back, trying to put some distance between her and her attackers. The boy picked up her sword and together they attacked. Using every ounce of strength, constitution and heart she had, she defended herself knowing full well that if she failed, her family's fate was sealed... and it would be a brutal and painful death. The thought of her brothers and mother and father being tortured to death gave her even more strength.

"Give it up, Agent Thirteen!" the boy yelled as he swiped the sword at her.

"Never!" she cried as she kicked the blade the away.

"We promise your family a quick death if you surrender," the girl said, her sword swooping down diagonally at Kay.

"I can't!" Kay snapped, dancing out of the way of the attack. "I love them!"

Blood was gushing from the open wound in her leg. She needed to end this now before she lost the ability to defend herself. She heard a faint scream and risked a glance over to where she saw the explosions. It appeared to be an Agent falling to his death. Maybe Dah—if that's who it really was—had come out on the winning side. She decided to find out.

"Dah!" a girl's voice called out from a building over. "If that *is* you out there, I could really use some help!"

Dah looked up and saw her fending off those same two Agents. She was in bad shape.

Dah found his sniper rifle and zoomed in on her. She had lost her sword and was batting the others' swords away with her hands and feet, bobbing and weaving away from attacks. She was bleeding from a large gash across the front of her thigh, her right wrist and her nose. Dah zoomed out a bit and focused on the two Agents. He took a couple deep breaths to slow his heart rate down and then held it as he lined up his shot. The bullet fired from his gun hit the sword hand of the boy and pulverized it. Only a bloody, twitching stump remained. The boy cried, clutching and staring at the spurting stump of bone and mangled flesh. In shock, he started futilely to pick up the piece of his hand to try to reattach it somehow.

Kay used the distraction as an opportunity to attack. She pivoted on her left foot and struck the girl in the face with her roundhouse kick and followed up with a spinning back kick. The girl stumbled back and tried to bring her sword to bear on Kay, but Kay was too fast. Performing the same attack as before only starting with the other foot and the first kick was meant to knock the sword out of her hand. The attack did exactly as it was designed to do and the follow-up back kick connected with the girl's now-bloody face, snapping her head back.

Moving faster than Dah could track with his scope, Kay rushed forward and flipped over the girl Agent as she fell backward into a back handspring. The end result was Kay standing just behind the girl. When the girl straightened up, Kay grabbed her by the hair and jerked her backward off her feet. On the Agent's way down, Kay chopped her in the throat crushing her windpipe. The Agent spent the last moments of her wasted life writhing on the floor, grasping at her throat and gasping for air. Kay watched with detached satisfaction as she took her last breath.

Dah slumped as the fight ended. As the adrenaline wore off, the pain of the knife still stuck in him overtook him. He stumbled backward and slid down a short wall to his backside. He tried to pull the weapon out, but every time he even touched it, he cried out. The awareness of his surroundings was starting to fade. The last thing he saw, or maybe hallucinated, was Kay kneeling down into his face and kissing him.

Chapter Fifteen

As Khai's ship drifted through dead space, he slept. His injuries were grievous, and the sheer shock of traveling through a closing black hole overloaded his nervous system. Though his body was broken, his mind still wandered in the form of a dream. His mind's eye saw many things, travesties, miracles and horrors no man should ever experience. One dream in particular caused him much distress as he slept. When he was young lieutenant in the SCGF, he and his division were deployed to Planet 276. The planet itself was a gas giant, completely uninhabitable, but it contained a precious gas that Seryysans used to power their vehicles. Litha'no'gen was a combustible gas only found on three planets within safe range of the Seryys System, P-276 was the biggest by ten times and seemed to provide an almost unlimited supply of the gas. It had special properties that, when passed through the catalyst chamber of a ship's exhaust ports, produced no harmful byproducts during atmospheric flying. Once in space that was less of an issue as there was no atmosphere to damage.

P-276 had several moons, ten to be exact. Seven of them were dead rocks of useless minerals. One was a smaller gas-based moon, speculated to be a fragment that broke off of P-276 and settled into orbit like a moon. The remaining two moons were habitable; one had an indigenous species that lived there. They were humanoid, short, slender, frail, covered in black or brown fur and highly primitive. When Seryys discovered this species—which they named Furrans for their fuzzy appearance—and made first contact, they developed a bond with the people of Seryys. By all intents and purposes, they were "cute" little creatures, sentient, but not developed.

They lived off the land, hunting and gathering; they lived in small huts made of earth and wood; and they worshiped the Seryysans as gods. Upon first contact, the representatives of Seryys refused to be treated as gods and only wanted to befriend them. They mostly communicated with a series of clicks and whistles. It took one of Seryys' leading anthropologists over a year to learn their language and develop a translation device that made communication with them possible. In time, they were able to convince the Furrans that they were just mere mortals who only possessed higher technology. They were a peaceful race, friendly and trusting. Even Khai had grown a liking to them with their pleasing nature. And the moon itself was breathtaking. Khai had visited the Furran Moon a few times for shore leave. The moon was probably much like what Seryys might have looked like thousands of years earlier, before the Founders colonized it.

Due to their frail and peaceful nature... *and* to protect their interests, the Seryysans couldn't leave them to be dominated by another species like the Vyysarri—and they certainly couldn't lose the valuable resources contained within that planet they orbited—so they set up an outpost on the Furrans' sister moon to monitor the system.

When the fleet to which Khai was assigned emerged from their black holes, they found what was left of the defense fleet. Broken, flickering hulks that were once Seryys capital ships tumbled aimlessly through the vacuum of space above the Furrans' home and its sister moon where the outpost was located. Accompanying the flaming pieces of Seryys ships were the broken hulls of Vyysarri ships.

"Sensors indicate a substantial lack of radioactive isotopes in the immediate area. I would say that this battle took place about twelve hours ago, maybe more," a young tactical officer said.

"Scan the surface of both moons," Fleet Admiral Takkir ordered, his forehead creasing with stress above his bushy, white eyebrows. "See if there are any survivors."

"Right away, sir!" the young man said, working the console like a prodigy instrumentalist.

"Lieutenant Khail," the elderly man, wise beyond even his years, turned to face him.

"Sir?" Khai straightened to attention.

"Prepare your men. You're going down to reconnoiter. Check on the Furrans first, then move on to the outpost on the other moon. There will be another unit there already, you will assist them upon your arrival."

"Sir. Yes, sir," Khail saluted, spun on his heel and marched off to the lift at the back of the bridge.

"Life signs are minimal, sir," Khai heard the young officer announce. "I'm reading, Seryysan, Furran and... *Vyysarri.*"

"Did you hear that lieutenant?" Takkir called after Khai.

"I did, sir," Khai stopped to say, grinning over his shoulder. "I wouldn't worry about that, sir."

"And, Lieutenant?"

"Sir?"

"Remember. *No* prisoners, per order of the Prime Minister. Understood?"

"Perfectly, sir. Just means less paperwork."

The lift doors opened into the hanger where troops were assembling and ships were being loaded up. Captain Dremyyl was prepping his *Shark*-Class Interceptor for a solo flight around the immediate area for remaining ships from either side.

"You going out?" Khai asked him.

"Yeah," Dremyyl said, wiping his hands off with a rag. "Admiral Takkir wants to know what's out there."

"Be careful, Cap'," Khai said, slapping him on the back. "Those *Raptors* are pretty fast."

"Not faster than *her*," he said, nodding his head back at his ship with a cocky grin. "I'll outrun 'em all."

"I believe it!" Khai laughed. "Just watch your tail rudder, okay?"

"Is that an order?"

"Oh, I can't order *you* around, *Captain*," Khai chided. "I'm just a lowly grunt still."

"Well, congratulations on your promotion, *Lieutenant*," Dremyyl said with a crisp salute. "And good luck. You're gonna need it."

"I make my own luck, Cap'!" Khai said, walking away. "But thanks for the gesture!"

His unit was made up of twenty-five soldiers. Many of them had been working with Khai for the last eight years of his career. Most of them had outranked him at one point or another, but his hard work, ferocious soldiery, bravery and unwavering loyalty to Seryys and his men catapulted him up the military ladder very quickly. They were all geared up in their armor and armed.

"Ten-*hut!*" Sergeant Baccar shouted over the chaos and chatter of the bustling hanger.

"Thank you, Sergeant," Khai said to his friend. "At ease." They relaxed. "We are the first wave. Our job is to assess the damage and engage any remaining resistance. I am under orders from the Admiral to show no quarter to any injured. Just put 'em outta their misery. Got it?"

"Yes, sir!" they shouted in sync.

"Good," Khai said, shouldering his machine gun. "Move out!"

They loaded onto a troop drop ship and it left the hanger, breaking through the invisible barrier between the hanger and space. The ship bucked and shuddered the whole way down into the atmosphere of the small moon. As they dropped into the lower skies above the forested moon, they could see smoke billowing up from small Furran villages that now burned. The drop ship touched down on its landing struts and the ramp dropped to the ground.

Khai led his men out into the forest. The sight that greeted them was something Khai would never forget. They had landed within the capital village and, as far as they could tell, everyone was dead. The little Furrans were literally torn to pieces. Arms and legs were everywhere, decapitated heads sat on spikes and many of them had been bled dry. And not just the men were killed; the women and children were treated equally.

Rage boiled up like bile to the back of Khai's throat; at that moment Khai was glad that Takkir had given the order to take no prisoners.

"What kind of monster does this?" Baccar asked, his voice haunted and almost distant.

The sound of rustling drew their attention to a large hut off to their right. They all pointed their guns at it. A pasty-white hand reached out from beyond the door. That hand dug into the ground and pulled a white body out from the innards of the hut. It was a wounded Vyysarri. Khai noticed right away that the debriefing he received was correct; Vyysarri could survive in the twilight of P-276's sun. The moon didn't spin and took the same amount of time to orbit P-276 as the gas giant took to orbit the sun. This meant that the Furran Moon was in a constant state of twilight, never experiencing complete day or total darkness.

The whole unit moved in to kill him.

"No!" Khai shouted the order. "This is one is *mine.*"

He stalked up to the Vyysarri and glowered down at him. He had several arrows in his chest and a short spear-like weapon stuck through its leg. Khai looked inside and there were several frightened Furrans, shaking and whimpering.

Khai looked down at the Vyysarri. "Why?"

The question prompted a gurgled laugh. "Anyone who aids the Seryysans deserves to die!"

"Where are the rest of your buddies?"

"They left already. We did what we came to do and left."

"Then why are you still here?" Khai growled, grabbing the Vyysarri by the collar of his tunic.

"Stupid boy!" he laughed. "Vyysarri always leave their wounded, they are weak."

"So that would be you," Khai pointed out, shoving the Vyysarrri back down to the ground.

"So it would seem." The Vyysarri sat up against the wall of the hut.

"These beings were defenseless! They had no technology!" Khai's rage boiled over.

"Made for an easy kill," the Vyysarri mumbled.

"You piece of shit!" Khai grabbed the Vyysarri by the throat and slowly pushed one of the arrows deeper into his stomach. He growled in pain, but refused to give Khai the satisfaction of crying out. Once that arrow was punched all the way through, he moved onto next one.

"Yessss!" the Vyysarri hissed, spitting up blood. "Give me an honorable death, young one."

To Khai's pleasure, the Vyysarri still lived. After all the arrows were pushed all the way through, Khai moved onto the spear through Vyysarri's leg. He picked the Vyysarri up by the spear and got what he was looking for... a cry of pain. That set Khai off. He dragged the Vyysarri out of the hut and swung him around by the spear, throwing him to the ground.

The Vyysarri tried to stand, but Khai wouldn't let him. He straddled the Vyysarri and pounded his face in with a rock. The body bucked and twitched as the Vyysarri's face caved in from the blows. Eventually, Khai stopped. His men all stared at him with horror in their eyes. He was covered in black-red blood when he stood, staring down at the Vyysarri in the death throes of his final minutes.

When the Vyysarri finally died, Khai looked up at his troops. "Fan out! Kill anything pale!"

Khai went back into the hut where the Furrans were being held hostage. There was one female Furran dead on the floor, a small pool of pink blood gathered under her. He took a step closer to the family of Furrans and they recoiled, crying a high-pitched squeal and clicking like mad. They threw household objects at him to fend him off. The translator wasn't doing its job, so Khai figured they weren't saying anything intelligible, just scared gibberish.

"It's okay," Khai said, dropping his gun, wiping the blood of his face and dropping to his knees. "We're here to help. We're here to stop those monsters."

They listened to the translator click and whistle and they calmed a bit. One got up, he was older than any Furran Khai had ever encountered. He started clicking away.

"My name Brubee, I chieftain of village," the male voice of the translator said. It determined the sex of the speaker by the tone of its voice.

"I am Lieutenant Khai'Xander Khail. You're safe now."

Brubee shook his head and clicked and whistled.

"No. Monsters hiding in woods. Watched go."

"They're still here?"

"Yes."

"Sergeant," Khai called into his mic.

"Sir?" Baccar's voice came in on his ear piece.

"Stay alert, my Furran friend here says that they're hiding in the forests. Proceed with caution."

"You got it, sir."

"Okay, Brubee. I want you to gather all of your wounded and bring them to the village square. I have two very skilled medics who can tend to them. Understood?"

"Yes, Lieutenant Khai'Xander Khail. We bring them as we find them. Thank you for helping."

"You're welcome, Brubee. I'll be back in a few hours."

Khai went into the forest and found Baccar.

"Report."

"Well, sir. The Furrans were right. They did flee into the woods, but we don't think they're hiding."

"Why not?" Khai asked his friend and folded his arms.

"We found very distinct markings in the ground in a clearing about two hundred yards off in that direction. I'm confident that they landed there and left from there."

"So they *have* left."

"Yes, sir."

"Lieutenant!" a faint voice yelled out.

Baccar and Khai looked at each other and ran.

They came upon another injured Vyysarri. This one had fewer injuries than the last, but a spear had been lodged into his back diagonally and severed his spinal cord at the tailbone. Even without the use of his legs, he was doing a fine job of warding off the Seryysan soldiers.

"Enough!" Khai shouted. "Leave him alone."

"What?" Ralm asked.

"It has come to my attention that a crippling wound is a fate worse than death. Let him crawl about the forest."

"You are a coward!" the Vyysarri hissed. "Give me a warrior's death!"

"No!" Khai snapped. "*You* are the coward. *You* attacked a defenseless race of peaceful inhabitants. For that..." Khai left his actions to finish the sentence. He reared and stomped on the Vyysarri's arm, snapping it in half. The Vyysarri grunted and the others cheered. Next, he broke the other arm. More cheering ensued. As a final insult, he spat on the Vyysarri and left him for dead.

"Come back!" the Vyysarri actually cried. "Finish what you have started!"

Khai turned his cheek and left. His troops followed, letting the screaming Vyysarri lie where he was.

They returned to the village to find *thousands* of injured Furrans lying about. Most of them with bite marks. Their primitive healers were doing whatever they could, but most of their healing efforts were herbal and only served to ease their passing. As the last of Khai's unit emerged from the trees, Brubee approached, clicking and whistling.

"You find them?"

"No," Khai said coldly. "They left on ships that were hiding in the woods. They are all gone."

"Good. Have you healers?"

"Yes, they're here. I've ordered them to tend to your wounded."

"You have thanks."

"No problem," Khai looked around at the hopeless numbers. "Where did they all come from?"

"We have hideaway. Very secret."

"Good. Don't tell *anyone*, not even me, where that is. You understand?"

"Yes."

"Good."

Khai patrolled the square, watching his men do what they could. His two medics were overwhelmed. Khai clicked on his com unit.

"Khail to Admiral Takkir."

"Takkir here, go ahead, Lieutenant."

"We have *thousands* of injured down here, sir. Requesting full medical teams to be dropped in."

There was a long pause. *"Granted, Lieutenant. Medical teams will be dispatched in a few moments. In the meantime, do what you can."*

"Will do, sir. Khail out."

Khai moved about again, almost pacing, waiting for the medical relief to arrive. In his pacing, he came across a young adolescent Furran. He was whimpering as he spoke, pink blood gushing from a gaping wound on his neck and matting his brown fur.

As he approached, Khai's translator began working to decipher what he said.

"I not want death. I frightened, father."

The father responded, cradling the youth.

"Be brave, little one. It over soon."

The translator stopped and the frantic clicks and squeaking picked up. Though Khai couldn't understand what the boy was saying, he could certainly see the fear in his eyes. His end was near. The look his father had was one of hoping the boy would die to be out of his misery, but also filled with anguish, hate and rage.

"Can I get a medic over here?" Khai cried out.

No help came. They were so overwhelmed, they couldn't get away. The drop ship carrying medical backup was still en route. He knelt beside the boy and his big brown eyes looked up at Khai. Khai grabbed his hand and held it tight. The boy jerked and gasped. Gasped. Gasped... gasped... His eyelids grew heavy. *It's almost over, little one,* Khai said inwardly. *Be strong.* He gasped again at length. Gasped... then nothing...

The father squealed, clicked and whistled an anguished lament that came out so quickly, the translator couldn't even begin to keep up. The boy's hand loosened its grip on both Khai's and his father's hands and he was gone. That sent Khai over edge. His young and foolish mind raced with rage and loathing of these monsters. He stood and let out a bellowing roar that seemed to echo off trees and mountains miles away. He picked up a small cart and threw it into the woods. He stormed off back into the forest to find that worthless cripple. And he found the Vyysarri right where he left him, he pulled his trusted pistol and put two bullets in each leg. Khai knew he wouldn't feel a thing, but he didn't care.

Khai picked the Vyysarri up under the arms and started dragging him deeper into the forest, leaving a trail of blood from the shot-up legs. Fueled by rage, he dragged the Vyysarri tirelessly until they reached the clearing where the Vyysarri ships had landed earlier. He dragged the monster to the center of the clearing and dropped him.

"What are you doing, Seryysan," he demanded.

"Lining you up to be a hot meal," Khai grumbled, striking the Vyysarri in the face. "The way I see it, that blood trail should attract some rather hungry predators..."

Without saying another word, Khai once again turned his back on the Vyysarri and walked back into the village. Upon his return, the drop ship with emergency medical personnel had shown up and they were tending to the wounded. Things had calmed considerably since his storming off. It was only a matter of time before the medical staff had every one they could save on the road to recovery.

Khai looked up at P-276's hypnotic, swirling gases and wondered when this war would be over...

Trall stalked up to the boy with no hand and backhanded him across the face.

"Your failure *disgusts me*!" he roared. "Your failure, *all* of your failures will not go unpunished. Since you failed at killing Agent Thirteen's family, I have no other choice than to kill yours."

The only Agents not present were the three killed by Dah and Kay. They all looked at each other with real fear in their eyes, for their families were the only thing that really mattered to them. This was true for all of them because several questions in that test rated their loyalty to their families. The higher the score, the more easily they could be manipulated.

"Furthermore, your visual desensitization will quadruple for the next six months. Now leave my sight before I kill you myself."

They all left and went straight to their homes. And they all at once called Kay for help.

Dah woke to the sound of a com unit beeping in his left ear. A voice answered it and Dah immediately knew to whom the voice belonged. He sprung from his bed and looked about frantically for a weapon.

"Whoa!" another familiar voice called out. "It's okay!"

Bria stepped in front of him.

"Bria? Kay?"

"Don't forget me. I mean, after all, I only saved your life. That knife went in pretty deep. An inch to the left we'd all be glimmering in sparkling silks of the Founders," Medic said.

"Why is she here?"

"She also saved your life," Bria pointed out. "She brought you here before you bled to death."

"Really?"

"Yeah," Medic said. "She even removed the knife and field-dressed the wound."

"Wow. I guess I owe her an apology." She pocketed her com unit and approached Dah with an even more grim expression than the first time she approached him. "I don't like that look, Kay."

"The surviving Agents collectively called me. They need our help." Dah sighed. "Let me guess?"

"Trall is coming after their families now."

"Damn it!" Dah snapped. "He doesn't know when to quit!"

"I agree. They need our help, though."

"We're just two people, Kay! How the hell are we supposed to protect that many targets?"

"We need *help*!" she cried. "Or innocent people are going to die."

Dah sat there for a long moment, mulling it over in his mind.

"Dack," Bria said, touching his shoulder gently and looking at him with those beautiful, marble-like green eyes. "She needs help."

"Fine," Dah said, pulling out his com unit. "I'll make some calls and see what I can brew up."

"Really? That's great! Thank you so much!"

"Don't mention it," Dah said wryly.

After a call to Captain Byyner and a few hours of negotiating, Dah was able to get the Agents to agree on a couple of things as a bargaining chip if Captain Byyner wasn't going for it. When Dah heard what the Agents had to offer, he had to fight a strong urge to storm off on his own and protect the families single-handedly. The information they possessed was enough to bury the present administration and complete Khai's mission.

"You know I can't do that, Dack!" Byyner said, folding his arms and turning to look out the window of his office.

"Come on, Captain. These people need our help. I can't do it alone."

"That's just not *possible*, Dack. You're asking me to interfere with a government operation."

"You're right, I am. And *I* am interfering, because it's the right decision," Dah argued, driving his index finger in Byyner's desk.

"I can't, Dack."

Dah held his wildcard for last. "What if I told you that the Agents whose families you save will offer their services starting with the location of Prime Minister Puar?" That stopped Byyner dead in his tracks. "That's right. They'll turn their backs on Trall and help us. They'll help us get him back."

"Where?" Byyner asked.

"They won't tell me until we agree to help them and carry it out."

"And what about Colonel Khail? Where is he in all of this?"

"I don't know," Dah said sadly. "I haven't seen or heard from him in several days, not since our encounter with Agent Thirteen."

"You think he's dead?"

"No," Dah said more hopefully than definitively. "He doesn't know how to die."

"I hope you're right," Byyner said. "Seryys needs heroes like him."

"I couldn't agree more, sir. So what do you say?"

Byyner turned to face Dah and said, "I don't think we have a choice. If they can track down Puar, then we have go along. I'll give you six men per family. I don't have any more men than that."

"That'll be enough, sir." Dah gave his commanding officers a crisp salute, spun on his heel and made his way for the door.

"Captain Dah!" Dah stopped and twisted to look at Byyner. "Good luck, you're gonna need it."

"Thank you, sir!"

Khai stirred, groaning, his brow furrowing.

"Rest, child," a gravelly voice rumbled. "Your injuries were grave, but you will mend in time."

"Where am I?" Khai murmured.

"You are safe for now. That is all that matters. Now, rest."

Khai did not like the dark places sleep took him recently. He was back in his house, his old house when he was a child. His father sat in a reclining chair that faced the front door to the apartment, a gun lay across his lap. Khai was supposed to be in bed, but he was sneaking up on his father.

"Dad?" Khai's little voice called out.

A man with long, braided white hair stood, his back to Khai. Khai's heart fluttered and butterflies flurried up as the man turned. He was Vyysarri, elderly and but still muscular. He had deep crow's feet at the corners of his eyes and his fangs gleamed white. He towered over the young boy. Khai stumbled back over some toys and landed on his back.

The Vyysarri man stood over Khai.

"Easy, child. I won't hurt you. Be still."

Petrified with fear, Khai couldn't even scream for help. The large Vyysarri man reached down and Khai blacked out. When he woke, he was in an infirmary on a Seryys ship. The bright lights hurt his eyes and he squinted against them. Due to his frequent visits to the infirmary, he knew exactly where he was. He was laying in bed on a *Dagger*-Class Dreadnaught.

"Doc?" Khai asked, his head pounding. "Can I get something for the pain, here?"

"Of course," an eerily familiar voice rumbled. The doctor turned around and it was that same Vyysarri. He had a small, white cup with some pills in it. "You realize that you don't actually *need* these pills right?"

Khai scrambled from the bed and stumbled over several trays on his way to his back. When he hit the floor, there were two other Vyysarri there to pick him up.

When he was on his feet, the dream was over. He was being held by two Vyysarri and that same old Vyysarri. He struggled against them, but he was still in a lot of pain.

"Here," the gravelly-voiced man said, handing him a metal cup with two pills in it. "You don't need it, though. You are addicted to them. You have been suffering from withdrawal the last two days."

"Let me go!" Khai growled.

"I can't," the man said. "Not until you are healed."

"Thanks, but I'll take my chances out there," Khai hissed. "Now, let me the hell out of here. You can't keep me here forever."

"I know. That's why, when your wounds are healed, you are free to leave."

"What did I just say?" Khai snapped then, that question was completely irrelevant the instant it left his mouth "Wait, what did *you* just say?"

"When you have mended, you can leave at your leisure. You are among friends here."

"But... you're *Vyysarri...*"

"Not all Vyysarri are warriors bent on your destruction," he said.

"Who the hell are you?" Khai growled, wincing in pain.

"My soldier name is Sibrex."

"Soldier name?" Khai asked.

"We do not give our real names to outsiders."

"Fair enough," Khai said, shrugging off the two holding him down.

"And what is your name, stranger. We do not see many Seryysans this far out."

"What do you mean by 'this far out'?" Khai asked. "Where am I?"

"You are in one of the last remaining, drifting *free* colonies of the Vyysarri," Sibrex answered, "in the outer sector of the galaxy. But you still have not answered my question."

"Oh, yeah," Khai said, slowly reaching for his weapon. It was gone.

"Now you are being rude. You must think we are stupid, if you thought that we would let you keep your weapons, stranger. Now, how about your name."

"Colonel Khai'Xander Khail."

"Ah, the 'savior' of Seryys Four. Your reputation precedes you."

"Apparently," Khai said, dryly. "So where am I, exactly?"

"I honestly do not know our exact location. Hence, *drifting* colony."

"How'd I get here?" Khai asked.

"We found your ship adrift in space. Your life-support was failing and your ship was without power. We used a hauling beam to bring your ship into one of our hangers. How did you come to be out here on the outer edge?"

"I was on the run," Khai explained. "My ship was damaged and I was about to be captured. My only option was to make a blind jump and pray I didn't die."

"Well, you have accomplished at least that, my friend. Now, come and sit so that I may tend to your wounds."

Khai sat back down on the bed and let the elderly man examine him further.

"So what exactly is a drifting colony? Why aren't you on Vyysar?"

"Do you not know, boy?"

"Know what?" Khai answered with another question.

"The entire Vyysarri race lives in colonies of one sort or another. Some are not drifters, but ours is. We have no propulsion; we go where the solar winds take us. Though, we do exercise a degree of anonymity."

"Why? What're you on the run from?"

"Our own people," he said frankly. "We are an undesirable caste of Vyysarri who are mostly imprisoned for our beliefs."

"Whoa, slow down," Khai said, adjusting on the bed and flinching as another Vyysarri doctor drew some blood. "You mean, you're on the run from your own government?"

"We are," Sibrex admitted.

"So am I," Khai said.

"What have you done that has you on the run from the Seryys Government?"

"I destroyed the *Hammer Cannon* to keep it from falling into the wrong hands," Khai said, rubbing his arm where the needle pricked him.

"The *Hammer Cannon*..." Sibrex looked almost nostalgic for a moment.

"You're familiar with it?"

"Oh yes," Sibrex said. "I was on the team that developed it. I am pleased to hear it was destroyed."

"Why?" Khai asked, confused as ever.

"That is why I am here. I defied my government when it came to the use of the *Hammer Cannon*—amongst other methods. I was not interested in genocide. Not even when it was our sworn enemy."

"You're an awful decent person... for a Vyysarri."

"As I said," Sibrex repeated, "not all Vyysarri are blood-thirsty killers. In fact, most of us are just civilians." Sibrex finished patching up some of the superficial wounds. "There, now follow me. I will give you a brief tour on our way to what will be your quarters as long as you are here."

"Uh, thanks, but I really need to get going."

"You're not fully mended yet, sir. And your ship won't be repaired for at least another week. The damage was quite extensive."

"You're fixing my ship?"

"Of course. It was damaged."

"Why? Why are you showing me so much kindness?" Khai stopped walking.

"Because I hope that you will return the favor in due time," Sibrex said honestly. "Now, come. Your quarters are over here."

They emerged from a corridor that was apparently the medical wing, as injured people were being carted in and bandaged people were leaving. The corridor opened into a vast expanse of several hundred levels. People, from children to the super-elderly, walked about. It was the first time Khai had ever seen a Vyysarri child; they looked and acted much like Seryys children. He was having trouble wrapping his brain around the idea of "normal" Vyysarri, as in regular people just going about their lives.

"This is the Hub, where all Vyysarri congregate to trade and purchase goods. It is also where we educate our young. Over there, see?" Sibrex pointed to a gathering of children, which Khai would have guessed were in the range of eight to twelve years of age, who were all sitting around a very elderly Vyysarri female—something else Khai had never seen —who was telling an apparently entertaining story. The children laughed wildly as she spoke.

"How many of you live here?"

"Roughly fifty thousand... give or take a few. Our population is ever expanding. You are free to roam this area as much as you please. But, please, for your own safety, stay out of the feeding area; you will not like what you see."

"You still drink blood?"

"Yes," Sibrex said, his tone of voice almost regretful. "We have to."

"So, what am I supposed to eat?"

"We have some food stocks. It may not be much, but it will suffice until your ship is repaired."

"How is it possible that you have food stocks when you don't eat it?"

"This colony used to be a military installation. Several hundred years ago, it was abandoned and left to decay in space. My people found it and refurbished it. Now we call it home."

"You didn't really answer my question," Khai pressed.

"Quite right. It used to be a research and development facility. It was here that the *Hammer Cannon* was designed and manufactured. When your people captured the ship, we abandoned the project and left the station to rot. I went into hiding for years, but one day, I found it again and that is when I founded this society for people who opposed the war."

"Why would you oppose a war *your people* started? That doesn't make any sense."

"Oh, my young one," Sibrex actually had pity in his eyes. It angered Khai. "That is a story for a different day. Follow me. We are almost to your quarters." Sibrex led Khai into a network of corridors and intersections. After a few turns, they came to what looked like a detention center. There was a bunk made up with blankets and other basics. "This is where you will stay. I apologize for keeping you here, but we have little room."

"This is why you have food reserves, huh? You used to have Seryys prisoners here."

"Yes," Sibrex answered sadly. "Most of them were tortured to death. The food is dry-frozen, that way it stays good forever."

"Is that why you really left? You didn't like the torturing of the Seryysans."

"That is part of it. But I learned the truth, and I could no longer continue to fight."

"What do you mean by that?"

"That... is a story for another day. Now, get some rest we will speak more tomorrow. We have much to discuss. You have brought us an opportunity. Good night, Colonel Khail."

"Just... call me Khai."

"As you wish, Khai. Sleep well."

Chapter Sixteen

It was unanimously decided that, due to his recent injuries, Dah would lead the defensive from a secured location behind the scenes. Each Agent was posted at their family's home with six others from the police department. Byyner came through on his word and supplied all the men he promised, including Puar, Brix, and Naad, they were the team leaders for each unit along with the Agents. Dah's intel indicated that the attack was going to be comprised mostly of Special Operations Soldiers accompanied by Kyyl'Jah Assassins. To Dah's relief, no Agents were going to be involved with the attack on these homes.

Dah was in Kay's ship hovering above the city, the back area of the ship behind the cockpit was like a miniature bunker lined with monitors, computers and communication consoles. There was even a secondary pilot's station in the event that the cockpit was compromised. The sensor package on her ship was top-notch; he could monitor the movement of nearly anyone from that seat. So far, it had been eight hours since they set up the motion trackers and nothing so far.

"Cap', you sure about this?" Puar's voice came over the radio. *"We've been out here eight hours and nothing."*

"Listen, the Agents who asked for our help wouldn't have if they weren't sure about Trall's attack on their families. I would've thought that you of all people would be more willing than most to help out, given your current situation."

"Hey! I want to find my brother just as much as—if not more than —the next guy. I just don't think Trall is that stupid... or that brass."

"If the Agents said they're coming, they're coming. Now cut the chatter before I..." A blip showed up the radar heading in from the south of Naad's position. "Naad, they're coming your way. Heads up, everyone. Looks like they're coming. Stay sharp!"

Four blips appeared in each of the areas. The families were spread out across the city. Most resided within the Residential Sector but were randomly dispersed. One was on the southernmost end of the Residential Sector, skirting Corporate Sector. There was one in Seryys Heights and even one in the RLD. Dah's men were positioned as close as possible to each family. However, some of the families weren't easily accessible. The family in Seryys Heights was in a gated community, so the soldiers had to find a more discrete way in and now they were waiting in the sewers beneath the house.

The radar beeped again and then there were eight each, then ten!

"Shit! Heads up, everyone! You will be meeting heavier opposition than we originally anticipated; apparently Trall learned from his last mistake. We need to move these people somewhere safer. I want you to hold out as long as you can while I get a bigger ship."

The sleek, black ship cut through the night sky as it soared for the Police Impound Lot. Dah remembered that a large smuggling ship had been confiscated two months ago and was due to go to an auction to fund the smuggler's defense. It would be perfect for getting those people out safely and comfortably. It even had a small hanger big enough to house Kay's small ship.

As he flew, Dah pulled out his com unit and keyed in an identification code. He then plugged the unit in the communications console and the unfamiliar face of an older woman filled the screen.

"Who is this?" the woman demanded curtly.

"My name is Captain Dack'Tandy Dah of the Seryys City Police Department and I-"

"Look," she interrupted rudely. *"I'm not in that business anymore. I stopped smuggling weapons when my husband died. Why can't you just leave me the hell alone? I don't have time for glory seekers! Now, goodbye!"* the woman started reaching out to close the channel.

"Wait-wait-wait! You misunderstand. I'm a friend of Colonel Khai'Xander Khail! The ship you modified, the *Star Splitter*, was mine. I'm the one who helped him destroy the *Hammer Cannon*."

She eyed him suspiciously. *"How did you get this ident?"*

"Khai gave it to me in the case of an emergency. And I have one."

"Where is Khai?"

"I don't know," Dah said sadly. "I haven't heard from him in several days. This is the second time he's died."

"Then what do you need from me?"

"Refuge. I have seven families that need a place to hide out until things calm down here."

"Why do they need refuge?"

"They're marked for death. Prime Minister Trall ordered their deaths for the failures of their children. I'm trying to protect them, but Trall sent far more men than I anticipated. I'm on my way, right now, to steal a ship from the impound lot to carry them all. It would be nice to have a place to bring them."

After a long few moments, and a very heavy sigh, she said, *"All right. A friend of Khai is a friend of mine. When will they be here?"*

"I don't know for sure," Dah admitted. "But I should have the ship within the next five minutes."

"Okay. I'll have some warm beds ready for you when you arrive."

"Thank you, Joon. You're a lifesaver! I owe you one!"

"We'll square up later. For now, just get those people here safely."

"Will do. Dah out."

Dah swung the ship in low around the impound lot and landed at the front gate. A security officer approached the ship, his hand resting on the butt of his sidearm.

"You can't park that here!" he shouted over the hum of engines. Dah emerged from the ship, his face troubled. "Sir! I'm sorry, I didn't know it was you."

"It's fine. But I need to ask you a favor."

"What is it, sir?"

"I need that smuggling freighter we impounded a while back."

The security officer frowned. "You know I can't do that, sir."

"I was afraid you'd say that," Dah said, sighing and taking a step closer to him. "Unfortunately, peoples' lives depend on it."

"Why is that unfortunate?"

"Because I have to do... *this*!" Dah struck the man in the throat just hard enough to incapacitate him, but not kill him. The man dropped like a bag of bricks.

Dah used his code to open the gate and then piloted Kay's ship in. He landed it right next the freighter. Dah had to admit, it was a good ship, sturdy and well-armed. It was fifteen feet tall, sixty feet wide from wingtip to wingtip and seventy feet long. The front of the ship was flat like a bus and the cockpit was located there. The bus-like body of the ship was twenty feet wide. On either side of the bus-like hull were what, from the top of ship, looked like half circles, each fifteen feet wide, with recessed gaps between the half circles and the bus-shaped portion. The wings were mounted atop the ship like a spoiler of a sporty hovercar near the rear of the ship that curved smoothly downward. The wings housed some serious weaponry. Hanging from the bottom of each wing were cannon turrets and missile launchers. At the aft of the ship were the engines. Rated at those of a capital ship, those engines could move that small ship so fast it would break apart.

Located on the side of the ship was the loading dock that fed directly into the small hanger. There was once a hovercar in there, but that car crashed and the pilot was captured during a high-speed chase. Dah piloted the ship in and used his code to power up the big ship.

"Welcome aboard the *Bolt Bucket*," the computer said as the ship started up.

"*Bolt Bucket*, huh? Well, at least the guy had a sense of humor."

"I don't particularly like the name, but he took care of me."

"Are we ready to fly?"

"Affirmative."

"Great." Dah pulled back on the yoke and the ship lifted up on its hoverpads. He spun the ship around and left the impound lot.

"Captain Byyner?"

"Yes, officer?"

"I have an unauthorized launch from the impound lot over in East Seryys Residential Sector."

"By whose authority?" Byyner demanded.

"Uh…"

"The *code*. Whose code was used?"

"Captain Dah's code is what activated the ship. Shall I call in a pursuit?"

"No," Byyner said with a grin.

"Sir?"

"You have a hearing problem, officer?"

"Uh, no, sir. I don't."

"Good. Let him go."

"Yes, sir."

Give 'em all hell! Byyner thought.

"Dah! Where the hell are you? We're getting creamed out here!" Brix's strained voice came over the radio.

"I'm on my way. I've got a ship and I'm picking you all up! Just hang in there a little longer. Get the families out for pickup!"

"We don't have a little longer!" Brix yelled over the sound of gunfire. *"We're pinned down by military forces and we can't retreat anymore! These assassin guys are practically dodging our bullets!"*

Checking the map, Brix and his team were not the closest, but it sounded like he was the most in need of a pickup.

"Okay, Brix. I'm coming to get you first! I'll be there in two minutes tops! I need you to not die in that amount of time. You think you can swing that?"

"Yes, sir, I can!"

"Good. Dah out."

Dah punched the ship's throttle and was forced into his seat. The whole ship shuddered as it sped towards Brix's position. He swooped down low, skimming the building tops.

Brix, the Agent and only a few of the police were left. They had the family out in the open and were trying their best to defend them, but they were getting overwhelmed and fast. Dah armed the cannons and opened fire on the ground between the soldiers and police, then landed in the debris field where he fired. The main ramp was already down as the ship touched down.

"Get in!" Dah yelled into his throat mic.

He heard the thumping of several sets of feet running up the ramp along with the sound of bullets ricocheting off the hull of the ship. After a few agonizingly long seconds, Brix gave the signal.

"We're all in! Get us the hell out of here!"

"With pleasure!"

Dah yanked back on the yoke and the ship hefted off its landing skids, bullets still clanking against the hull. Dah homed in on the closest team and headed for them. Brix came up to the cockpit and sat in the seat next Dah.

"Thanks for the speedy getaway," he said, slumping down in the seat.

"No sweat," Dah responded, not taking his eyes off the canopy. "Is the family secure?"

"Yes, but they're scared and trying to resist."

"Damn," Dah whispered. He was worried about that. "Can you fly a ship like this?"

"No," Brix said honestly. "And I won't try. But if you would like me to bring them up here, I can."

"Go get them."

"Yes, sir."

A moment later, Brix came back in with a man, a woman and one other child.

"What is the meaning of this?" the man demanded. "Who are you people?"

"Sir, my name is Captain Dack'Tandy Dah of the Seryys City Police Department. I am here because your missing son is not missing at all. He is one of the people back there right now."

"Bull shit!" the man yelled, nearly foaming at the mouth. "He was kidnapped!"

"Your child is back there right now, he's here to protect you. He was taken from you by the government and trained to be a killer."

"That's not possible."

"Go back there and find out, then!" Dah yelled. "Go back there and call out his name. I guarantee he'll respond. Brix, go ahead and take them back there. Help them find their son."

"You got it."

After about two hours, Dah had finally rounded up everyone. They lost ten police officers in the various skirmishes, but the Agents, and their families, were safe and sound. Some of them gladly boarded the ship, while others had to be subdued and dragged aboard. As Dah was making for orbit with almost a whole squad of atmospheric fliers on his tail, Kay came to the cockpit and sat beside Dah.

"I know you have already done a lot for me and my friends, but there is one more thing that I would ask of you."

"What's that?" Dah was almost afraid to ask.

"Can we pick up my family, too?"

"Are they not safe?" Dah asked, trying fruitlessly to dodge the rain of bullets peppering the hull.

"No," Kay said fearfully. "And I didn't get a chance to see them when we fended off the others."

"Why not?"

"Because you were gravely hurt and I couldn't justify letting you die to speak with my family."

"Wow," Dah gasped. "I... I had no idea. I really do owe you one, don't I?"

"Not really," Kay said, looking down at the communication console. "It's still your choice."

Dah didn't even have to think about it. "Fine. Let's go."

"Really?" she squeaked.

"Yeah, really. I owe you at least that. But you have to make it quick."

"I will move so fast, you won't even see me."

"I would expect nothing less. But remember, your friends need to give us Puar's location."

Dah juked hard to the right and pulled back on the yoke sending the ship into an inverted nosedive. The ship picked up speed and it dived down back into the city. The atmo fliers matched his maneuver and tried to keep up. Dah kept the dive going until he was certain that only a ship with hoverpads would be able to pull out of it in time. He was right. The jets pursuing him pulled out of the dive long before he did.

Dah flew the ship to Kay's home. He was a few miles away when Kay spoke up again.

"Just slow down, don't land. I'll call you when I get them. You can swing around and land briefly just to pick us up. Okay?"

"You sure you don't need help?"

"No," Kay said confidently. "I can handle this on my own."

"You got it, kid."

Dah slowed slightly and Kay disappeared into the ship. Then he heard and felt the wind whip through the cockpit as Kay opened the hatch and lowered the ramp.

The wind whipped about her as the ramp lowered. She could see her family's complex and when the ship passed over about thirty feet up, she jumped. During the freefall, she let her body go limp and when she landed, she tucked into a roll and rolled to her feet in a dead run. She kicked open the door leading to the stairwell that led down into the building. She knew the layout like the back of her hand from years of running up and down the halls when she was a child. She found the door leading to her apartment and knocked frantically.

A woman answered the door, her mother.

She stood there for a few seconds just staring at her mother. She had waited a long time for this moment and had rehearsed what she was going to say at this moment a thousand times over, but now she couldn't say anything. She could only stare into her mom's eyes.

"Kay'Lah?" she gasped. "Kay'Lah? Is that really you?"

"Yes, mom!" she cried. "It's me!"

"This... isn't possible! We..." Her eyes darted about trying to grasp the situation. "W-we were told you died. We had a funeral and everything!"

"It was a ploy. But I'm here! We have to leave. You are in danger. I don't have time to explain. Grab some essentials and follow me."

Kay forced her way into the home and started rounding up her family. Her brothers and father were just as bewildered as her mom was only a few minutes before.

"Where are we going?" her dad asked.

"To the roof. There's a ship waiting for us there to take us to safety."

"Are we in danger?" her youngest brother asked.

"I'm not going to lie: yes," she took the honest approach. "Any minute, there will be soldiers breaking down that door, armed and ready to kill all of us. I've already repelled them once, but I don't think I can protect you again. Dack, you there?"

"More or less," Dah answered. *"We're dodging jets left and right up here. How much longer?"*

Kay's mom came out with a suitcase crammed full.

"We're leaving now!" she shouted. Kay opened the door and looked down the hallway. It was clear at the moment, but that was subject to change very quickly. "You know where the stairwell that leads up the roof is?" she asked her brother.

"Yeah."

"Good. That's where we're going. I need you to lead mom, dad and your brother there. I'll be right behind you. Okay?"

"Yeah."

"Good. Now go!"

They left the apartment and turned left down the hallway toward the stairwell. To the right was the lift at the end of the hallway. The lift chimed and Kay just had a bad feeling about that. The lift doors opened and five soldiers in combat gear emerged. The first thing they did was throw a flash-bang right at her. She quickly pulled her Kit'ra and deflected it back down the hall at them. They all dived out of the way as it went off.

The soldiers recovered quickly and pulled their machine guns. Kay could deflect one or two bullets at a time, but not a full-on barrage from three machine guns. She pulled a knife and flung it into the face of one of the soldiers. He fell dead in mid-step as the others opened fire.

The hallway turned ninety degrees to the right and the door to the stairwell was directly on the left. Her family made it around the corner before the men opened fire.

But Kay didn't.

When Kay made it through the door, she barricaded it with a piece of the stair railing. It wouldn't hold forever, but it would hold long enough for them to escape. She met her family on the roof just as Dah dropped in with the *Bolt Bucket.* They ran up the ramp. Kay gave Dah the signal and the ship lifted off as Kay ran up the ramp and hit the button to close it. The jets were making a strafing run across the ship with their guns blazing.

Bullets ricocheted off the hull again as Dah made for orbit as fast as the ship could go without flying into a million pieces. The atmo fliers wouldn't be able to keep up and eventually would have to break off their pursuit simply because they weren't rated to fly in the vacuum of space.

"I've got a missile lock!" Brix said.

"Get the energy shield up!"

Naad punched a few buttons and a dotted line traced the outline of the ship on the tactical display.

"Shields are up!"

The ship bucked hard as the missile impacted on the shields. A chorus of cries and screams echoed from the main hold of the ship as they were all thrown again when the ship bucked once more. An alarm went off on the damage control console.

"What is that, Puar?"

"I don't know. I've never been in a ship like this before. I think it's saying-"

"Computer, damage report."

"Gravitational field crippled. Total gravity failure in ten seconds."

"Damn!" Dah growled, slamming his fist down on the navigation console.

"Buckle up, everybody! This is about to get really bumpy!" Dah called into the inter-ship com system.

The gravity failed and all those who weren't strapped in were now floating helplessly though the cabin.

"I'm punching the coordinates for Seryys Four. I have a contact there who's making room for everyone."

"Who is this person?" Naad asked.

"Her name is Joon. She was a friend of Khai's," Dah said, remembering Khai and that he hadn't heard from him in almost a week.

"Ah shit!" Brix growled.

"What?"

"*Sharks,* coming our way."

"Naad, that console controls the cannon turrets hidden inside the hull. Keep them off of us long enough to make the jump into the black hole."

"Got it!"

The Eve'Zon Drive thrummed with power as it ramped up to punch a hole in the fabric of space time. The shields were holding and Naad was doing a hell of job keeping those *Shark*-Class fighters off their backs. The particles collided several thousand yards ahead of the *Bolt Bucket* and after a small flash, a micro black hole yawned wide enough for a ship to pass through.

The thrusters fired and the ship started passing through. This was the most vulnerable moment for any ship. Any cannon fire coming from the entering ship was sucked into the black hole leaving it incapable of defending itself. Naad stopped firing and the ship bucked and rattled as the *Sharks* took small bites out of the ship's shields.

"Aft shields aren't doing so hot!" Naad announced.

"She just has to hold together long enough to get through. We're entering now!"

And just like that, they flew in and flew out just outside of the Seryys IV's gravity well.

"Computer," Dah called out. "Call Joon."

"Channel open."

Joon's strained face appeared on the view screen. "Captain Dah. You're just in time for dinner."

"Good! I'm hungry. Is everything all right?"

"Yes, just tired. You asked a lot of me here today. Finding places for several families to stay was no walk in the park."

"I appreciate all your help, Joon. I know Khai would appreciate it, too."

"Well, if your credentials hadn't checked out, you wouldn't have been appreciating anything. But I have contacts in almost every government branch on Seryys. They were able to verify your identity within the police secured database."

"You could've just looked me up in the general SCPD personnel file through the net."

"That can be altered or falsified. Going to the source was the most reliable way to go about it."

"Point taken," Dah said with a nod. "Now, we should be dropping in on you within the next five minutes."

"I've already cleared a spot for you in docking bay fifty-one. The doors are open and the beds are made."

"Sounds like a plan. See you soon."

"Captain Dah!" Kay's mom ran to the cockpit.

"What's wrong?"

"Kay's dying!" she cried. "I guess she got shot trying to save us. There's blood everywhere and..."

"Naad," Dah snapped. "Go back and try to stabilize her. I've gotta land this bucket. Computer, raise Joon again."

Joon's face appeared on the screen. "Now what?"

"One of my passengers is badly hurt. We'll need medical team to meet us there."

"Okay, I'll send for one."

"Thanks. See you in a few minutes."

Naad came back to the cockpit, his face betraying a grim prognosis.

"That bad?"

"She was shot six times," Naad answered his captain. "I can't get the bleeding to stop. I don't think she's gonna make it."

"Damn it!" Dah growled through his teeth.

Khai had been wandering the expanse for about an hour. He wasn't talking or interacting with anybody, he was simply observing his surroundings. Even in day two, he couldn't fathom Vyysarri as "normal" people. A man and woman walked along a catwalk roughly forty feet above him, looking into shop windows and holding hands. Kids ran by, giggling and shouting at each other. They were playing Tag. How could a race of people get so strong and so violent? Why did they hate the Seryysans more than they loved themselves. Yeah, Khai still heard the propaganda that was crammed down his throat, but this wasn't the picture those vyyds portrayed. The vyyds only showed the Vyysarri warriors, bloodthirsty— literally—and relentless. After seeing this whole station, he was even questioning how the war started. According to his education, the Vyysarri attacked without provocation; they mercilessly slaughtered millions on a far outlying colony; they were a warrior race that stopped at nothing to achieve total control of the entire galaxy. He had to wonder how they evolved the way they did. How does a race evolve to a point of only drinking blood, or being allergic to ultraviolet light? It was a question he would have to ask Sibrex.

He strolled past a class of younglings, maybe ten years old, and listened. They were being taught about their history. It intrigued Khai so he sat with them and smiled at the children. It astonished him how accepting they were of his presence. The children just smiled back at him and went about their business.

"Who knows why we are here?" the teacher asked. A little girl raised her hand. "Yes, Anya?"

"Because we do not believe in killing our Seryysan Brethren."

Brethren? Khai was confused. *What does that little girl mean?*

"That is correct, Anya. We are through with the killing, the war. We need to reunite with our Seryysan brothers and sisters."

Vyysarri sick of war? Is that possible? Every Vyysarri he encountered on the battlefield fought with the rage of a sabercat mother protecting her cubs. This wasn't making any sense; it was shattering all his beliefs about the Vyysarri. They weren't stabbing each other in the back for advancement; they weren't eating their young; they were just... *people* making their way.

The teacher continued. "Do we hold the Seryysans responsible for starting the war?"

"Yeeeees," the children almost chanted.

"But do we take our vengeance on them?"

"Nooooo," they all answered.

Is he teaching these kids that my people started the war? Anger boiled up from Khai's stomach. *They struck first!*

Khai opened his mouth to shout an anger-fueled retort when a soft hand fell on his shoulder. It was Sibrex. Khai stood, his hands balled up into fist, shaking with rage.

"Follow me. We have much to discuss."

"You got that right," Khai growled through a clenched jaw.

"Please, I beg you, not here. You may yell and shout all you wish once we get to a secured area."

"You might want to bring guards," Khai warned.

"If you let me speak, I guarantee you will not feel that way."

"You have shown me nothing but kindness and hospitality since I got here. So I'll go on a little faith right now. But if I don't like what I hear, you'll have to kill me or die trying."

Khai followed Sibrex to a small room off of the Hub. A desk with two chairs was in the room, one for Sibrex and, presumably, one for Khai. Sibrex moved in first and sat in the chair to the left of the door; Khai took the chair to the right, directly across from Sibrex.

"First of all," Sibrex stared. "Let me give you my real name: Broon'Kur Broor."

Khai frowned, taking a moment to assimilate that. "But that's..."

"A Seryysan name," Sibrex finished Khai's statement. "I know. There's more. What I am about to tell you is the reason I left the military. The teacher, to whom you listened, spoke of 'Seryysan Brethren'." Sibrex sighed and shifted uncomfortably in his chair. He tossed a picture to Khai. It slid gracefully across the polished table and stopped under Khai's hand.

"What is this?" Khai asked contemptuously.

"Just look," Sibrex requested.

Khai did just that. The picture was clearly old, printed on a type of paper that didn't even exist anymore. It was faded, tattered and the corners of the picture were worn down. To make this picture a fake would have taken a lot of time, money and special equipment... all of which were things these particular Vyysarri didn't have.

The picture had three hundred or so people standing in front of a giant ship. Khai had to squint to see the image clearly. The ship was of ancient design with a bulbous nose and cockpit canopy. Just below the canopy was some lettering in ornate script. This word shook him to his core. The name of the ship was the *Vyysar*. Khai looked up at Sibrex, dumbstruck.

"We are of the same ancestry." The six-word statement hit Khai like a speeding hover train. His jaw was slack; his eyes were wide and darting back and forth as he tried to grasp the gravity of what this Vyysarri just told him. Sibrex continued. "What would you say if I told you that the Seryysans actually started the war?"

"I would say you're full of shit!" Khai snapped, slamming his hand down on the metallic table.

"I am not lying to you. I have no reason to. That picture is proof that I tell the truth."

"I thought Vyysar was a planet," Khai breathed.

"It was, at one time," Sibrex said with a nod.

"What happened? Where do your people live?"

"In colonies," Sibrex said sadly. "Let me start at the beginning."

"No better place," Khai said, leaning back in his chair and folding his arms defiantly.

"It started nine thousand, seven hundred and twenty-one years ago..."

Chapter Seventeen

We have a detailed record of our evolution. The crew of the Vyysar was commissioned by the Seryys Government to explore the outer regions of the galaxy when the whole government-funded exploration race began. They set out with a faulty Eve'Zon Drive that failed as the ship passed through the event horizon. The cataclysmic failure of the Eve'Zon sent the ship hurtling farther than any ship had ever explored by several hundred lightyears.

The pilots of the ship fought to get her back under control but lost that battle when she was gripped by the gravitational pull of a planet several times bigger than Seryys. They crashed on that planet and were forced to live there for millennia. Planet Vyysar was a giant world, with a dying sun. No ultraviolet light bathed this barren planet. The first generation had the hardest life. Using only the technology of the *Vyysar*, they built a small colony. They couldn't live off of the land, because there was no plant life, at least not that they found right away. Fortunately, as part of the initiative to encourage exploration, each ship was assigned specialists to be a part of the crew. One of our specialists was a brilliant geneticist. He was the one who helped us "evolve" into what we are today, though some of our features came from actual adaptation. The next wave of colonists were given strength to handle the extreme gravity of the planet, the forefathers struggled daily with the extreme gravity and if they were going to make this new planet their home, they were going to have to make things easier for the next generations.

Food was scarce on the planet and the rations were running thin. Upon exploration of the area, the colonists found caverns deep underground where watersheds existed, and where there was water, there was plant life. The plants lived off of carbon dioxide, water and geothermal energy—rather than sunlight. Many colonists died slow, horrible, agonizing deaths from poisoning from the toxins contained within the plants. The toxin attacked the brain stem, causing bodily functions to cease over time. Despite their best efforts, they could not remove the toxins from the plant life. They had to find food and time was of the essence. They finally found some indigenous life within the caverns... rodents. These small rodents, through millions of years of evolution, adapted to the plant life and grew glands on their livers that scrubbed their blood of the toxins. At first, they tried grafting that gland to their own livers; that only ended in disaster and more colonists died. The next logical step was simply trying to eat the animal, but the meat on these animals was also toxic. It appeared that their muscle tissue absorbed the toxins but the glands purified the blood. It took several years to adjust to living on only water and blood, but in time, our people were able to stomach it and now, through thousands of generations, we cannot live any other way. Our bodies simply rejected the genetic manipulation.

Now, as I said before, our new sun was a dying sun, in its death throes, if you would. Over several generations, our skin adapted to the different light and our eyes were genetically altered to make it easier for us to see in our low-light environment. Over the generations, we began to outgrow our colony and spread out to other areas of the planet. Before long, we had made our new civilization and named ourselves the Vyysarri to honor the ship that brought us there and sustained our lives for so long.

With the specialists' knowledge being passed on from generation to generation, we built cities and eventually were able to obtain enough resources to begin a space program here. We started exploring the local systems and found nothing of value. Almost overnight, our civilization grew too big for our planet's meager food supply. We needed to expand. And expand we did. We used our superior strength to dominate populations of smaller planets. And we thrived. I am not proud of our history; we could have found a way to peacefully coexist with the peoples upon whom we relied. But our bloodlust got the better of us.

Once we were able to make our own Eve'Zon drives, we decided to reconnect with the Seryysans, to regain that past we lost for thousands of years.

A little less than a thousand years ago, we traveled to the nearest Seryysan colony. We made first contact with them and Prime Minister Castur flew out personally to greet us. Together we sat and had several days of talks. Castur wanted to subjugate us, turn us into servants to labor in the mines of Seryys and put us into the military. He said it was "the easiest way to reintegrate our civilization into theirs" and said that we had lost our way, that we needed to be "tamed, domesticated" like animals. He truly felt that he was doing us a favor.

Needless to say, our leaders were *not* pleased with this proposal. We left and returned to our home to rethink whether joining the Seryys society was really what we wanted. After weeks of internal strife, including protests, riots and more unnecessary violence, we decided to never make contact with the Seryys people again, that we did not need their companionship to fulfill ourselves. That planted the seed. Your people watered that seed by continuously encroaching on our space, sending small teams to assassinate our world leaders and plant your own operatives in their places to convince our people to be slaves to yours. We had almost five hundred years to build our ships and our armies in the event that you conducted an all-out invasion.

And then there was the final blow, the reason we live in space colonies adrift in the stars rather than with our feet on the ground, the soil we called home.

Chapter Eighteen

Sibrex produced a laser disk, rather old by design and handed it to Khai, his hand trembling with subdued rage.

"This vyyd disk is carried by every Vyysarri warrior. Nearly every attack on Seryys City was to plant this in one of the major communication relays that would broadcast a signal to every colony in Seryys Space. Watch this," he said, his voice shaking. "And you will know our pain. You will know what fate befell us. Now go. There is a video device in your room."

Khai silently stood, disk in hand, and left. Every eye was on him as he walked back to his quarters. He did not stop to observe anything; in fact he didn't even look beyond his boots. His curiosity was killing him. He so desperately wanted to get back so he could watch it, but didn't want to run, to look too eager.

After what seemed like forever, he finally rounded the corner into the deserted detention block and bounded the rest of the way to his cell. As Sibrex indicated, a vyyd unit was waiting there for him. He plugged the disk into the drive and waited anxiously for it to start.

"This is Doctor Tash'Door Tashar," she said, her voice strained. Her face was badly bruised and she looked to be malnourished, *"and I am the leading physicist of Operation: Bright Star. If you are viewing this, then the Vyysarri were successful in their mission. This is a warning to the Seryysan People.*

"Operation: Bright Star was sanctioned and funded by the Seryys government to wipe out the Vyysarri people in a preemptive strike to eliminate the Vyyarri threat before it became one. I was chosen to ensure that the plan was carried out to the letter and it was successful."

"Roughly four thousand years ago, the brightest scientific minds Seryys had to offer developed a method of saving the Seryys System—and several other systems at the same time—by stopping the aging process of a star. The unforeseen results were that the aging process was actually reversed. It was speculated that we could exploit the Vyysarris' susceptibility to UV light by doing the same to their sun and rendering their planet uninhabitable to them. We had hoped that the Vyysarri would spread out into the galaxy and die off. As I said before, the mission was a success and the Vyysarri have fled their planet."

"Unfortunately, by the time this attack was planned, the Vyysarri had spent the last five hundred years building their war machine and were ready to retaliate. I was captured along with the crew that delivered the weapon. The crew is dead and I will be by the end of the day. I am sending out a warning to the Seryys people. They have the Bright Star Schematics and are not afraid to use them! You must stop them at all costs! Mom, if you see this-" her plea was stopped short as the Vyysarri slit her throat and

drank her blood right there in front of the camera. Khai had to turn it off, as the gargled sounds of her screams and the blood orgy that ensued were still too much for him to watch.

"Founders help us..."

Dah stood outside the makeshift operating room, pacing back and forth like a nervous father waiting for a child to be born. It was almost ten hours after the surgery began when a doctor came out, blood smeared over his scrubs.

"How is she, doc?"

"She's a tough little girl. I was able to remove the bullets and stop the bleeding. But she still has multiple internal injuries. Bullets ripped through pretty much every non-vital organ in her body. How they missed her heart and lungs, is quite beyond me. I guess the Founders were smiling on her."

"Is she going to make it?"

"I think so," the doctor said, prompting a relieved sigh from Dah. "Can I see her?"

"Maybe tomorrow. For now, she needs sleep."

"Okay. Thank you, doctor."

The next day, Dah sat with every single person he rescued, including the officers of the SCPD, in Kay's room. He was getting impatient. It was touching to see all these people being reunited and all, but Puar was still out there somewhere and he needed Dah's help. *Man! I could really use Khai right now,* he thought.

"Okay, guys," Dah said, standing up. "I came through with my end of the bargain, probably at the cost of my career. So now it's your turn. Where is Trall keeping Puar?"

All the Agents huddled around Kay's bed for a little discussion. It only took a few minutes, though it seemed like a whole lot longer than that. When they emerged from their huddle, Kay spoke for all of them.

"Puar is being held at the Bunker. We have the exact location on this digital map right here." She handed him the device. "It's not easy to get in. In fact, that would be the biggest understatement of the millennium. It's heavily fortified with SPEARs and more security protocol than the Honorifical Office."

"Is Trall with him?"

"No," Kay said. "He is under close watch at the Honorifical Office. But I wouldn't worry about him right now."

"Why?" Dah asked.

"Your priority is to find Puar. We'll take care of Trall."

"How?"

"We have our ways."

"So who's with me to save Puar?" Dah asked, renewed hope filling his heart.

"I have to go. That's my brother out there," Puar said, prompting a satisfied nod from Dah.

"Who else?" Nothing. "Don't all jump up at once!"

"If we're going to meet as much resistance as we did protecting these people, it's suicide!" Naad pointed out.

"Not to mention those SPEARs protecting the place," Brix added.

"Are you kidding me?" Dah asked shocked.

"We're brave, Captain, not stupid," Brix continued, then frowned as everyone looked at him incredulously. He ignored them and continued. "We would need nearly an army to get in there. It is, after all, the place where the Prime Minister goes during an invasion."

"But we have the element of surprise, and intel," Dah said jabbing a finger at the Agents. "They know every way in and out of that bunker. Hell, we could probably get in, get the Prime Minister and get out before they even knew we were there."

"Not likely," Kay said. "There are motion trackers imbedded in the walls throughout the facility. The moment you step in, the building's defenses will activate."

"You're not helping me, here," Dah growled at Kay.

"It's insane!" Naad snapped. "We'll be dead before we breach the first door."

"Fine," Dah said stubbornly. "Then it'll just be me and Puar. To hell with the rest of you guys!"

"Dack, come on!" Naad grumbled, his dark eyes betraying the guilt he felt. "Don't be like that!"

"Then what should I be like, Naad, huh? Just tuck tail and run? Leave Puar to his fate? No! I won't do it!"

While Puar and his friend fought over who was helping, the Agents huddled again and spoke amongst themselves. Kay interrupted them.

"Captain Dah!" she said as forcefully as she could. "*We* will accompany you."

"No. Not you, Kay. You're too hurt and won't be ready. I can't let you put yourself in jeopardy. Trust me, you've done more than I could have asked. But the rest..."

"We will fight for you, Captain Dah," another Agent spoke up. "You saved our families and helped us break our bonds of servitude. Trall must be punished for his crimes, but this nation needs a leader first."

"Thank you, guys... really."

"Ah shit!" Naad growled.

"What?" Dah asked.

"I can't go letting kids risk their lives for this. If they're going, *I'm* going."

"Now you're talking," Dah said slapping him on the shoulder.

"Well," Brix grumbled. "I suppose I can't let you guys take all the credit. I mean, this is like real hero stuff."

"Then it's settled," the Agent said. "We will all go together. We will fight together. We will bleed together and we will die together."

"Well," Naad interjected. "I'm not dying."

"Okay," Dah said. "We need schematics of the bunker, weapons, armor... and a miracle."

Khai sat in his cell the rest of the day. He replayed the video over and over again on the Net'Vyyd and in his head. Now he understood the hatred that the Vyysarri felt for them. Their home was destroyed and they were forced to scatter to the solar winds and regroup. They practically had to rebuild their entire civilization. It occurred to him that that was yet another reason they appeared to be so aggressive. Without the ability to eat food, they were forced to raid other civilizations and harvest their blood to sustain themselves. Khai's heart almost broke for them; he would seek revenge, too, if his planet had been destroyed. The next day he emerged and found Sibrex waiting for him, his hands tucked into the sleeves of a long, dark cloak. His face betrayed nothing; it was motionless, emotionless, like chiseled stone. Khai approached, saying nothing. The look on his face said it all. Khai couldn't believe he fought so long, so hard for Seryys when *they* were the ones who precipitated the war to begin with.

At length, Sibrex broke the silence. "What do you think of our people now?"

"I don't know," Khai answered honestly. "Do you really have the Bright Star technology?"

"We do," Sibrex said bluntly.

"Then..."

"Why haven't we used it?"

"Yeah."

"Because we were not interested in genocide, just to be left alone."

"Live and let live," Khai said.

"Precisely. That recording was designed to scare you all into leaving us be."

"So then why have your people made so many unprovoked attacks on Seryys Colonies and on Serrys herself?"

Sibrex showed the first emotion since their conversation began. "For some commanders, somewhere along the line, the message was lost and it became more about wiping you out, exacting revenge. Though the majority of the attacks on Seryys were solely to upload this message."

"And that's when things like the Furran Massacre happened," Khai said folding his arms.

"Yes," Sibrex looked down at his feet. He clearly didn't like the history that played out.

"So what do we do now?"

Sibrex looked up him, a twinkle of hope in his red eyes. "You mean... you'll help us?"

"Yes, I will. The truth needs to be known. A long time ago, I asked myself when this war would end. Now I think I know the answer to that question. But I do have one question for you."

"Ask."

"You said you left when you learned the 'truth' about something. What were you talking about?"

Sibrex nodded, fully understanding his confusion. "It was just over a hundred years ago when a radical faction of renegades called the Crimson Truth revealed information that shook the Vyysarri people to the very foundations of their beliefs. Until that moment, we all thought that we evolved on our own, on that planet. When pictures of the Starship *Vyysar* and its crew, captained by Vyys'Ari Vyysar, began circulating, people began to protest the war outright. They began defying our government. Riots gripped the streets and our whole society began to tear itself apart.

"Two major factions emerged, the Warmongers and the Reluctants. The Warmongers pushed to retake Vyysar and set up a strong defense parameter around our space, while the Reluctants hesitated because they were not sure that further bloodshed with your kind was the answer. However, the hate for your people ran deeper than our blood and the Warmongers became the new government while the Reluctants disbanded."

"But for four hundred years of the war you had the weapon and didn't use it. Why?"

"The government knew who you were," Sibrex explained. "They didn't want to wipe you out, just scare you into leaving them alone."

"But you were never successful," Khai murmured, regret filling his voice. "Whatever happened to Vyysar?"

"The armies of Vyysar tried several times to retake what was rightfully ours, but were repelled on every attempt. We just-"

"Wait," Khai interrupted. "You tried *retaking* your homeworld? From who?"

"The Seryysans. Why?"

"What planet was once Vyysar?"

"I do not remember," Sibrex said, his eyes darting back and forth as if searching his mind for the answer. "No. I cannot remember the name, but I went there once... when I was a young, foolhardy boy itching for blood. I sustained an injury to my head which has wiped most of that memory clean... *thankfully*."

"The name! What the hell was the name?" Khai growled, clenching his fists in frustration.

"All I can remember was that a training facility sat on it." That didn't narrow it down much. There were ten planets in the outer regions that had military training facilities on them. But...

"There's only one planet in the Seryys System that has a high-grav training facility, Gor'Tsu Gorn Planet."

"Yes!" Sibrex whispered. "Yes, that is it."

"That's where I was trained..." The realization was almost more than he could handle and the cold, hard truth socked him in the gut hard enough to actually steal his breath.

"You can imagine the insult we suffered, knowing that our homeworld had been made into a facility to train soldiers bent on our destruction. We almost used the weapon on you when that happened. But, fortunately for you, cooler heads prevailed."

"You should have," Khai said, ruefully.

"I'm sorry?"

"You should have used the weapon on us, forced us to leave our home."

"You have," Sibrex said.

"What do you mean?"

"Our historical records indicate that we all came from another planet. The Founders discovered Seryys and colonized it."

"Well, every child knows that," Khai said.

"But is that not the same thing? At some point, tens—possibly hundreds—of thousands of years ago, our people left another planet to come here. Perhaps their planet was destroyed by an enemy."

"I see your point," Khai relented. "But that still leaves the issue of what we do about this."

"Play the recording. Show the Seryysans the truth about their Vyysarri brethren."

"You have my word I will. But in the meantime, I still have five more days until my ship is in shipshape. What's there to do around here?"

"I'm sure we could find *something* for you to do."

Sibrex led the way to the Hub. Khai followed. Sibrex's long, white hair was braided behind him and the tail flopped back and forth as he walked. They entered a small room that appeared to be a cantina of some kind. A dull roar filled the room as people conversed, sharing drinks. Sibrex led Khai to a booth and gestured for him to sit down.

"I will return."

In just under minute, Sibrex returned with two drinks. He sat them down on the table and slid onto the seat.

"What's this?"

"Can you hold your drink?"

"I've been known to drink people under the table from time to time."

"Then drink and we shall see."

Khai took the small glass and quickly downed the green liquid. The burning that followed took Khai completely by surprise. He nearly spat it out and started coughing profusely.

"Good, yes?"

"I've had worse, that's for sure."

"Would you like another?"

"Absolutely!"

Sibrex signaled for someone to come over and assist them. The person who came to serve them nearly took Khai's breath away. She was beautiful! Even the pale white of her skin was attractive! She was just about Khai's height, her white hair pulled back in a ponytail. She wore tight-fitting black pants that shimmered in the light and her shirt was cut off just above the belly button and sat low enough to show her busty cleavage.

"What can I get you, gentlemen?"

"Four more of these, please," Sibrex asked.

"Right away," she said in flirty tone, eyeing Khai.

"I think she is taken with you," Sibrex said playfully.

"I'd be lying if I said I didn't look," Khai said with a laugh.

"She is fine a woman," Sibrex agreed.

The ridiculously attractive woman retuned with four more of... whatever it was, and smiled at Khai.

"Thanks," Khai said, doing everything he could to keep his eyes on her eyes.

"Anytime," she said with a smile.

Sibrex held up his glass. "To the future of our peoples."

Khai reciprocated. "May they leave each other the hell alone!"

"Well put!" Sibrex said.

They both downed their drinks.

"Ah! Whew. What the hell *is* this stuff?"

"We call it Broshia. It is very popular."

"I can see why!" They both laughed.

Khai went to take his next drink and a piece of paper fell off the bottom of the glass. He unfolded the paper and read it aloud.

"Brindee'Lyyn Brook. Com unit identification: 3387? Did she just give me her Com-Ident?"

"I believe she has. Will you call her?"

"I... don't know," Khai admitted, shaking his head. "She's very beautiful, but..."

"But what?" Sibrex seemed puzzled.

"She won't... you know... uh... *bite* me. Will she? I mean, I've been bit and I did not like it at all!"

"No," Sibrex answered definitively. "For us, feeding is no longer a pleasurable experience. There are those, especially those who fight your kind, who take pleasure in feeding on you, but they are an anomaly."

"Interesting..." Khai said, thumbing his chin.

"We have rallied more people to our cause," Kay told Dah. "Within four days, more Agents will be answering the call."

"More Agents?" Dah sounded genuinely surprised.

"Yes," Kay said. "After hearing our story about Trall coming after our parents, actually carrying out what we were threatened with, they have also changed sides. Though this strengthens our numbers, it also raises the stakes. We must be successful. If Trall lives, *their* families die."

"That is *exactly* why he won't," Dah insisted as he reassembled his gun.

"Do you promise?" Kay asked from her hospital bed.

"I will complete the mission, or die trying. You have my word."

"I wish I was coming with you."

"You need to recover from your injuries. Your bravery came at a steep price."

"I had to save them. Again..."

Dah nodded. "Again. But now they're safe and you're with them at last."

Kay nodded. It was a bittersweet reunion for the families of the Agents.

There was a heated argument that included virtually everyone else in the next room. The parents were refusing to let their children go into the bunker to most likely die. Both sides had compelling arguments. Before the argument started, Dah made it abundantly clear that any Agents who did not want to go would not be seen as cowards, that it was their choice to make. But their parents, despite the fact that some of them hadn't seen their children in almost ten years, still seemed to think that they knew what was best for them. Most of the parents were in denial that their children were trained as cold-blooded killers and that their programming was still mostly intact. They were compelled to engage in combat like a compulsion.

The argument was getting heated. The voices escalated into full-on shouts from both sides. Mothers and fathers, brothers and sisters, sons and daughters, all fighting for what they believed to be the right course of action. Dah eventually heard individual voices shouting above the rest.

Dah stood, slapping the magazine into his gun. "Stay here. I'll be back."

"Where are you going?"

"To stop a fight."

Dah stalked into the room. The consistent roar made Dah's ears ring.

"Enough!" he shouted, but was drowned out by the constant bickering of over forty voices. Losing his patience, he fired a shot into the ceiling, which, after Dah was disarmed, punched in the face and lying on his back, was probably a bad idea in a room full of Agents trained to react violently to just such events.

"I'm sorry," the boy said, offering a hand up. "I didn't even think..."

"It's okay, son. I know." Dah stood and looked at everyone in the room, blood trickling from his nose. "Now that I have your attention, I wanted to share a couple things with you."

"Like what?" an angry father spat out. Clearly, his voice was one of the voices that Dah heard stand out from the other room.

"You're still not safe," Dah simply put. "Trall *will* find you here. You *will* be tracked wherever you go and I can't continue to find safe havens for you every couple of weeks. Your children have been taken from you, and wrongfully so. But they are killers... cold, calculating, relentless killers. They have been conditioned to carry out gruesome things. Though they may be standing right beside you, the people who you call your children died a long time ago. These kids are what's left. Now, you can forbid them to go, reduce our chances of success and be on the run for the rest of your lives, or you can let them go and let them make a difference. If we succeed, Puar will be reinstated as Prime Minister and you will be safe to go about your lives with your children."

"How can you say that?" the same father asked. "You're not the government. Who's to say Puar won't take them from us again and put them back to work?"

"My brother would never do that!" Puar shouted. "He's a good man!"

"Nonetheless," the father said. "He is only one man and the senate has to approve any major changes like that. Who's to say that he hasn't already tried and failed?"

"It's entirely possible. But don't you think that's worth the risk? If Trall lives, I can guarantee you that you will eventually be killed... *all* of you. I've seen firsthand what Trall is capable of, and it scared me."

"Do you know who you're talking too?" the father asked.

"No," Dah said, refusing to be baited.

"I *own* three casinos in the RLD. I have more resources than all of you combined. I appreciate your help, Captain Dah, but I'll take my chances."

"You'll take your chances with your son?" Dah asked angrily.

"Yes!" he snapped. "He... is... *my*... son! I know what's best for him, not *you*!"

"Is this what you want, son?" Dah asked the boy. "To be on the run for the rest of your life?"

"I want to be with my family," he said.

"Fine," Dah said. "Go. Be safe. I won't, and can't, keep you here."

"You're damn right, you can't!" the father growled, gathering his things and corralling his family. "Now, where can I buy a ship off this rock?"

"There's a ship dealer about five blocks from here. Tell him you know Joon and he'll give you a deal on good ship," Joon answered.

"Good."

He stormed out the door with his family in tail.

"No one else is required to stay," Dah pointed out.

Several more families packed up and left, following that fool's lead. Only one family remained... Kay's. Dah sauntered back into the recovery room where Kay and her family waited.

"They all left?"

"Yeah," Dah said, deflated.

"What now?" she asked.

"You said in a couple days we would have some more numbers, right?"

"Yes," Kay said with confidence. "And these Agents have no families to tie them down... well, at least that aren't in direct danger."

"Then at least we have that..."

Two days later, Dah was watching the Net'Vyyd when a breaking news story showed a witness's recording of a ship crashing into a casino in the RLD. The footage showed the ship rolling as if its hoverpads on the starboard side malfunctioned. The ship nosedived straight into the building prompting several explosions that soon engulfed the whole area in flames.

Dah watched sadly, knowing exactly what happened. The SCIIA most likely tracked the purchase, waited for a ship matching that description to come out of a black hole and opened fire, targeting the hoverpads so it looked like a malfunction to the general public. *Stupid bastards!* Dah seethed. He warned them—no, he had *promised* them—this would happen.

"So much death..." Kay whispered from her bed.

"Unnecessary death, at that," Dah added ruefully.

"Maybe the others saw this before making the trip home," Joon remarked, but with very little hope in her voice.

"We can only pray to the Founders that they did..." Dah murmured.

Chapter Nineteen

Khai awoke, his eyes lazily opening. He looked over to his left and found her right where he left her. Brindee'Lyyn Brook was indeed beautiful. It was now day five and they had spent almost every hour of the last three days together. He never thought in a million years that he could feel this away about anyone, much less after only three days *and* despite the fact that she was a Vyysarri. But she was indeed an intriguing woman. She was fifty years old, but didn't look a day past thirty.

Khai thought maybe the fact that she *was* a Vyysarri added to her allure. Physically, she was as strong as Khai and possessed comparable stamina, which he found out very quickly. But the connection they made in such a short time was uncanny. She was funny, attractive, strong, everything Khai could hope for in a woman. She stirred, rolling over to look at Khai, her curiously beautiful reds gazing at him.

"Good morning," Khai said, with a smile.

"Good morning, to you," she responded both in speech and smile. "How'd you sleep?"

"Like the dead. How about you?"

"It was the best night's sleep I've had in years."

"You must have been tired," she chided. "Did I wear you out?"

"A little," Khai admitted. "It's been even longer since I... you know."

"I could tell," she said warmly. "But it was still amazing."

"You're right. It's just..."

"What? What's wrong? Was it not good for you?" she asked, a hint of insecurity seeping into her voice.

"N-no... I mean, yes. It was amazing. I've never felt this way about anyone before. I'm just... I don't know..."

"Khai, talk to me. Something else you will learn about me, I am a good listener."

"You're a Vyysarri, and I... It's been *ingrained* into my head to hate you and your kind. And now that I'm here, now that I've met you and Sibrex, and several others, I-I..." He sighed sharply. "I can't hate you anymore."

"Sounds terrible," Brindee said sarcastically, almost hurt.

"I knew you wouldn't understand..." Khai said, sitting up and burying his face in his hands.

Brindee sat up and scooted to sit behind him. She wrapped her arms around him, laid her head on his back and played with his chest hair, their naked bodies touching. Her touch was surprisingly warm.

"I'm sorry," she said after a few moments. "I know this must be difficult for you."

"That's the understatement of the century!" Khai scoffed. "I mean, doesn't it bother you that I've killed literally *thousands* of your kind in my life?"

"Sure it does," she said honestly. "But I can also tell you that those who fight the Seryysans do not share my views of life—none of ours, for that matter. In this drifting colony, we were schooled in the truth and that we need to accept our Seryysan brothers and sisters. A good number of us desire peace between our people. What better way to start that than to fall in love with a Seryysan?"

"How can you know this is love?" Khai asked, hoping for the right answer.

"You said it yourself that you haven't felt this way about anyone, right?"

"Well yeah..."

"And you I can assure you that I would have never bedded anyone for whom I didn't care... *deeply.*"

"You're not just saying that?" Khai asked.

"Look at me." Khai turned to sit on the bed cross-legged and faced her. She sat there, unclothed. At no other point in someone's life were they ever that vulnerable, that exposed and she *was* beautiful. "I've never slept with *anyone* I didn't love," she reiterated. "What I gave you last night was something only a handful of people have experienced. And the last time was almost twenty years ago."

That struck Khai like a shuttle falling from orbit. She hadn't felt the warmth of another in her bed for twenty years. Well, technically it was *his* bed, but still, was it possible to fall in love in only three days? He had never felt true love as it applied here. He truly loved his dad, he loved Sergeant Moon as father and mentor, but the truth was, he never felt he had time to have a relationship. And when he got out of the military, he figured he was damaged goods. What woman would want a man who killed for a living, especially a man who exclusively killed her kind? Maybe she did love him. Maybe it was possible to fall in love in such a short time. Maybe it was possible to love someone from a race of people he was conditioned to hate.

"What are you thinking?" she asked at length.

"That I may have found something I've been looking for... for *years.*"

"Someone to love?"

"Something, well, *someone* to live for," he said. "And direction for the rest of my life."

"You discovered all that just now?" she asked.

"No," he said, looking straight into her eyes. "Over the last three days."

Tears welled up in Brindee's eyes. They embraced with a long kiss that led to Khai pulling her down onto the bed...

"I love you," Khai whispered into her ear.

"And I you..." she whispered back.

Dah sat at a bar in Joon's house, drowning his sorrow with a particularly strong drink from an unlabeled bottle he found in a locked cabinet under the bar. He picked the lock and had poured himself his third shot when Joon walked in.

She sat next to him and reached over the counter, producing another shot glass. She poured herself a shot and downed it, making a sour face.

"My late husband's homebrew," she remarked. "Thought I locked it up."

"You did," Dah said from his barstool.

"Hmph!" Joon nodded and poured herself another shot. "So, what brings you down here alone to kill brain cells with my husband's engine degreaser?"

Dah actually laughed a genuine laugh. "Really? This is engine degreaser?"

"It has... *many* applications. But don't change the subject."

"Yes, ma'am," he slurred with a mock salute. "Honestly, I wanted to be alone to feel sorry for myself."

"Why? What do you have to feel sorry about?"

"I tried so hard to save those families. I risked everything, my career, my life, my future... all for nothing. They still ran off and died."

"Listen here, youngling. You can't possibly control people's thoughts, right? If they chose to leave, they chose to put their own lives at risk."

"But I could've made them stay!" he snapped, slamming his shot glass down on the bar.

"Holding them prisoner wouldn't have made you any better than those who were trying to kill them. You know that. That's why you let them leave," Joon said downing another shot.

"Yeah, and now they're dead. And so will several others within the next day or so. So now what?"

"Actually, that's why I came here looking for you," Joon said.

Damn it! He knew the others would follow that arrogant asshole to their deaths. But he would play along for now. "What about them? Have they come back?" he asked sarcastically.

"Actually, yes."

"What?" Now he *was* surprised.

"Yeah. They must've seen the report on the Net'Vyyd and turned around. Two have already arrived and the others have asked for clearance to land."

"Really?" Dah breathed.

"Mm-hm, and the others will be here the day after tomorrow."

"How many, total?"

"Well, you saved seven families, six of them survived. Kay told me that she was able to recruit fifteen more Agents."

"So we have twenty-one Agents, sixteen officers—*if* they're willing, me, Puar, Brix and Naad."

"I spoke to one of the officers just before coming down here. He seemed encouraged by the fact that we have so many Agents on our side. It would appear that they're all in."

"Well, that's something. This might actually work."

"It should," Joon agreed. "You've got the element of surprise, good intel and some of the best fighters this system has to offer. I'd say your chances are better than average."

"I would have to agree with you."

"Now that was the most positive thing you've said since you got here. Did it hurt?"

Dah laughed again. "No. I suppose it didn't."

"Good. 'Cause I want to hear more of that."

"Yes, ma'am! Now, how about one more shot?"

"I'll drink to that," she smiled warmly.

"How did you know Khai?" Dah asked.

"I knew him when he was a little boy. His father was killed by a burglar hopped up on who-knows-what. He would come into the diner where I worked every now and then and I would buy him a piece of pie. That is, until the military picked him up and took him to Gor'Tsu Gorn Planet to be trained to kill."

"He was an orphan. All orphans become wards-"

"I know what happens!" she snapped. "He was a sweet boy. He wouldn't've been a killer, if it hadn't been for the man who 'recruited' him."

"Why didn't you take him in? The state surely would've given him to you, if you wanted him."

"I had several children of my own," Joon said with sorrow in her voice. "I couldn't afford another mouth to feed. I was single mom already."

"I thought you were married?"

"He was my second husband, my first died in the war."

"Oh, I'm sorry. I didn't mean to pry," Dah said.

"It's okay. Just... not something I really enjoy talking about."

"Then I'll drop it," Dah said, setting down his glass.

"Thanks," Joon replied, doing the same.

Joon put the brew away and locked it up, then followed Dah back upstairs to join the others.

Three more had arrived by the time they came back, the rest were landing.

"We can't go home," one of them said.

"I know," Dah said, not showing an ounce of smugness.

"We know you need our children," one mother said. "Just... please, bring them back."

"I would gladly give my life to save theirs," Dah sincerely stated.

"We know," she said back.

"Now, we have work to do, plans to make. We should start immediately..."

"You can't go!" Brindee cried.

"I have too, Brindee. You know that," Khai said calmly.

"What about all that talk about having someone to live for?"

"That is why I won't die," Khai responded, a roguish grin creeping across his face.

"That's not what I had in mind," Brindee retorted. "I meant not going at all."

"I have to help my people, and yours. I can't do that here."

"Do you have a death wish?" she snapped. "Because it sure appears that way!"

"No, I don't," Khai said softly. "Not anymore."

"I want to be with you!" she pleaded.

"I know that! And I want to be with you, but some things can't be stopped. My friends need me. If I save the Prime Minister's life, he may be willing to open negotiations with your people. Isn't *that* worth it? I mean, you *do* realize that we would never be accepted in either culture. We would be outcasts."

"I would forsake everything to be with you," she proclaimed.

"And I would for you, too. But I have to at least try. I can't let Trall destroy everything I've fought for my whole life."

"I know," Brindee said sadly. "How will you find us once you've finished?"

"I have your current coordinates and I've had my ship's computer calculate your current drifting speed and bearing. I can make a good guess on where to jump and then all I have to do is look for a giant, drifting station in the middle of nothing."

"I suppose that would work," she said, trying not to show her fear of losing him. "When will you depart?"

"Tomorrow morning," Khai answered, "once my ship is finished. I had them install a pop-hatch above the cockpit. The last-minute modification added a day to the repairs."

"What would you need that for on a ship designed for space travel?"

"You never know…"

"I see." She smiled mischievously. "What are your plans until you leave, then?"

"I don't know." He smiled back. "You have anything in mind?"

"I might," she said suggestively, leading him back to her quarters. "I hoped you did."

That night was the most amazing night of his life. They were connected on a level only achieved by those who were made for each other. The next morning came way too quickly. They remained intertwined the entire night, only stopping when the call came indicating that Khai's ship was complete, fueled up and ready to depart. He dressed in silence, Brindee was not happy with him leaving and it was obvious by her body language. She sat on the edge of the bed, arms folded, looking down at her feet.

"Must you leave so soon?" Brindee groaned.

"Yep. I have a world to save… *two* actually."

"Be safe," she pleaded, "and come back to me."

"I will," he assured her. "I have no choice."

"I love you. I know that's crazy, but it's true!" she revealed.

"I know," Khai responded. "I love you, too. I *will* be back for you… sooner rather than later, preferably."

"I will be waiting," she said.

"I know."

With that, he walked out. He stalked through the labyrinth of corridors and made his way to the Hub. There were thousands of people walking about, interacting with each other, laughing, loving. He envied them. He was most likely heading to his death, but he had to try. To do nothing made him no better than the evil that threatened to tear Seryys apart.

As he entered the hanger, Sibrex was waiting there for him.

"Seeing me off, are you?" he said casually.

"More or less," the old Vyysarri said with a shrug.

"What does that mean?" Khai was clearly confused.

"Is it not obvious?" Sibrex looked at Khai's bewildered face. "I am coming with you."

"Oh no you're not!" Khai chuckled.

"Yes, I am," Sibrex insisted. "If you don't like that, I'll just take your ship."

"Well, it's hard to argue with that. Welcome aboard the *Star Splitter*."

"Thank you, Colonel Khail." Sibrex strolled up the ramp into the ship. Khai followed him. "Not very comfortable, is it?"

"Well it's not a star cruiser, obviously, but she's got a lot of heart," Khai defended the ship. "And keep your voice down, she's kinda sensitive."

"I am not," Joon replied with righteous indignation.

"See?" Khai said ruefully. "Get your stuff stowed. We're leaving in five minutes. Joon, run pre-flight checklist."

"Running now, Khai."

Khai worked his way up to the cockpit; the pop-hatch was installed, the damage was repaired and the engines were warming up. He sunk into the chair and grabbed the controls. "You ready yet, Sibrex."

"I am," his deep voice rumbled behind him, prompting a slight jump.

"Whoa!" Khai shouted. "You can't sneak up on me like that."

"My apologies," he said. "Next time, I will announce my presence beforehand."

"You don't have to do that. Just... don't be all sneaky-like."

"As you wish," Sibrex complied.

Khai pulled back on the yoke and the ship lifted up on its hoverpads. The ship thrummed as he throttled it forward to exit the hanger and through the force field. The ship bucked lightly as they passed through and the ship's artificial gravity kicked in.

"Punch these coordinates into the navigational computer."

"These are not the coordinates for Seryys," Sibrex pointed out.

"I know. It's a small colony just outside the Seryys System. I don't want to come out of a black hole into the middle of the Seryys Combat Defense Fleet. This way we come out beforehand and flying in on thrusters. Sure, it'll take another two or three hours, but this will help us avoid a grand entrance. I'm saving that for later."

"A wise plan," Sibrex complimented. "The coordinates are set. Shall we the make the jump?"

"Let's get this over with," Khai growled.

The Eve'Zon Drive opened a micro-black hole and the console in front of Khai stretched out before his very eyes. The maw swallowed the ship like the waves of a turbulent sea. An instant later, they emerged on the other side. With one powerful burst from the thrusters, the ship sailed out toward a date with disaster.

Two hours into the trip, Khai was able to plot their trajectory and they would be arriving at Seryys within the hour. He called out to Sibrex, asking him to come to the cockpit and he heard obnoxious stomping coming back into the cockpit. Sibrex entered and sat down next to Khai.

"What was that about?"

"What?" Sibrex asked, genuinely confused.

"The stomping. What's with the stomping?"

"I was merely trying to adhere to your request, to be less 'sneaky-like.' Is that not what you wanted?"

Khai laughed so hard, his belly hurt. "That's perfect, Sibrex! Keep it up!"

"Was I amusing to you just then?"

"Actually, yeah. That was funny."

"That was not my intention."

"I know," Khai said, wiping tears from his eyes. "It's just... never mind. Can you take the controls for the remainder of the trip? I need a power nap."

"Yes."

"Thanks."

"You are welcome. Feel free to sneak up on me when you are ready to take over." Sibrex's voice rumbled through a full-bellied laugh. Khai just stared at him. "*That* was a joke."

"Oh," Khai said, forcing a smile and a strained chuckle. "Very funny."

Within the hour, Sibrex called Khai into the cockpit again. He yawned as he entered.

"That was quick," Khai grumbled. "It felt like two minutes."

"I assure you, it was just less than an hour," Sibrex told him.

"All right," Khai said. "First thing we need to do, is contact a friend of mine."

"Do you think it's wise to contact anyone this close to Seryys?"

"Relax, old man," Khai chided. "It's a secure unit dedicated to his. It won't be traced."

"Who is this friend?"

"His name is Dack'Tandy Dah. He's a captain in the Seryys City Police."

"And he will help?" Sibrex asked. "It seems unlikely that a police officer would aid you in such an illegal act."

"He's the one who helped me destroy the *Hammer Cannon*. I'm pretty sure we can count on him to help."

"Indeed."

"Joon," Khai called out. "Send a signal to Dack's com unit."

"As you wish."

A moment later Dah's voice came over the channel.

"Tell me I'm not dreaming!"

"Okay, you're not dreaming. That was easy. Anything else I can do for you?"

"I thought you were dead!"

"Well, for a while, I thought I was, too. But I was found and nursed back to health."

"Who do we have to thank for that?"

Sibrex looked at Khai with concern furrowing his snowy brow. "Uh... that's a little complicated. It would be easier to explain in person. Where are you?"

"I am at Joon's place on Seryys Four."

"What the hell you doing *there?*"

"Uh, it's a long story. Should we meet up somewhere?"

"Yeah. The Honorifical Office in twenty minutes. I'm about to make my grand entrance. Wouldn't want you to miss it."

"What're you planning, Khai?"

"Just meet me at the Honorifical Office in twenty minutes. Got it?"

"All right. Am I bringing backup?"

"If you got it," Khai admitted. "But if not, just you would be fine."

"I'll be there in twenty minutes."

"Good man. Khai out."

The channel closed and Sibrex looked at Khai. "Why is he worried about you? Should *I* be worried?"

"No," Khai laughed uncomfortable. "Why? Don't you trust me?"

"I did," Sibrex admitted. "But now, I'm not so sure."

Khai looked at him with righteous indignation, but there was twinkle in Sibrex's eye that gave it away. Together they laughed so hard, tears rolled down their faces. Then, instantly, Sibrex's jovial disposition vanished. "Seriously, what are you planning?"

"There are two parachutes in the back," Khai said, jabbing a thumb toward the rear compartment. "Grab them will you?"

"Why do we need parachutes?"

"Don't ask stupid questions! Just do it! I'll fill you in as we enter orbit."

Without another word, Sibrex stood and walked to the back. It took him a few minutes to find the parachutes, but Khai knew exactly when he found them because he promptly started stomping back to the cockpit.

"I have the parachutes," he stated.

"Good. Put one on and then take the controls while I put the other one on."

Once that was done, they were dropping into low orbit of Seryys.

"Khai?" Joon's voice called out.

"Yeah?"

"I have Captain Dah on the channel for you."

"Khai, we're here."

"Who's we?"

"Oh, just some new friends I've made while you were screwing around out there. I have to tell you, though. I have Puar's location. He's holed up in some presidential bunker."

"In Kal'Hoom Canyon?"

"Yeah! How did you know?"

"I've been there before, but I've never had to storm the castle."

"Thought you might want to know, that's all."

"That's *great* news! One less thing to beat out of Trall. So, if you feel inclined to help, I could use it when I land."

"Just tell me where!"

"You'll know where when you see it. Khai out." Khai looked over at Sibrex, took a deep breath and blew it out. "Uh, you might want to strap in... this is gonna get a little bumpy."

"Indeed."

Most ships, the *Star Splitter* included, came equipped with deceleration jets that slowed ships during reentry. Khai shut them off to become a harder target to hit and the ship began to rumble like the ground during a desert bull stampede. The canopy was awash with red fire as the Ti'tan'lium on the nose became super-heated. Their stomachs did handsprings indicative of a freefall. Khai fought the controls as sweat ran down his face, arms and back from the extreme heat.

With one final buck that jolted them both into their restraints, the *Star Splitter* dropped into the lower atmosphere and then it was smooth sailing for a while. The sun had just set a few minutes earlier, and they cut through the twilight sky like a bird of prey stalking its meal. Eventually, however, the atmospheric fliers caught up to him and opened fire with rapid-fire laser cannons that pelted the ship's shields. Khai banked hard to the right and then to the left, trying to shake the jets. They stuck to him like glue. Normally under these circumstances, he would have come to a complete stop and let them pass by and then give chase. But he needed to get to the Honorifical Office. Being the top room of the Hall of Justice, it was an easy target.

His destination became visible, his heart began to race. He was going to get that son of bitch and end his reign of terror and corruption. As they approached, the ship bucked as the jets kept scoring hits on the ship's hull. At this point, they were so close that Khai didn't care. They could blast the ship apart as long as it made to the Honorifical Office. The ship bucked again and an alarm sounded within the cockpit.

"The rear shields are gone," Sibrex announced. "Shall I divert power from the front shields compensate?"

"Do it." *Hold together, baby*

Khai pushed the ship to full throttle and they heard the faint *pop* of breaking the sound barrier. The blasted jets kept up with them. Another alarm sounded.

"What's wrong now?" Khai asked, his plan starting to unravel.

"They have a missile lock on us."

"Shit! What're the shields looking like?"

"The rear shields are at seventy percent. I do not believe they will withstand more than one or two impacts."

"That should be all we need. Go ahead and get unbuckled," Khai ordered, freeing himself from the restraints. Sibrex followed suit.

"Are you planning on crashing?"

"Yes," Khai said, his arms shaking while he piloted the ship. "Why? You getting too old for this shit?"

"No," Sibrex said, almost offended. "I am only a hundred and thirty-two years old!"

"*Only?*" Khai marveled. "How long do you people live?"

"Roughly two hundred to two hundred and twenty years. So you see, I am still young."

"Damn!" Khai growled. "Okay. Get ready to pop the hatch."

"The hatch?" Sibrex asked. Khai motioned upward with nod. "Ah! I see."

The ship rocked hard to the right and the shields failed. Another impact caused the ship to roll off course. Khai held fast and got the ship into position.

"Blow it!" Khai shouted.

Sibrex hit the button and the emergency hatch popped off and was whisked away by the wind rushing by. The cockpit roared. Joon was saying something angry as Khai held up three fingers. Sibrex nodded. Khai counted off and mouthed out the numbers. *One... two... THREE!* Together they jumped and were sucked out of the ship only seconds before it buried itself all the way into the building. Instantly, Sibrex and Khai pulled their chutes and drifted quickly over the Honorifical Office. Just over it, Khai cut his chute loose and dropped into the hole the ship made. He landed and rolled to his feet.

Trall sat on the floor, leaning against the wall near the back of the office. Blood flowed from a gash on his forehead deep enough to show skull. Ten Kyyl'Jah Assassins lay dead on the floor all around the office. Seconds later, Sibrex made his landing. Khai helped him to his feet and they approached the newly-appointed Prime Minister, Tran'Ri Trall.

"Please," he cried, raising his hands. "D-d-don't kill me. I-I beg you!"

"Oh, you're not going to live after today, Trall. So you should at least die with some fucking dignity."

Instantly the helpless facade dropped from his gaunt face and there was only anger and rage.

"Damn it, Khail! How is it that you are both still alive and thwarting my plans?"

"I'm the good guy," Khai joked.

"You'll never get anything out of me!" he hissed at the soldier. "Especially with *that* in my presence."

"Oh, you mean ol' Sibrex here?" Khai waved a dismissing hand. "Ah! He's harmless."

"Consorting with the enemy is punishable by death!" Trall yelled.

"Well, lucky for you, I already know the location of *Prime Minister* Puar. So I have nothing to ask you."

"Go to hell!" Trall spat.

"I was hoping you were gonna say that," Khai said with a diabolical grin. He picked Trall's frail body up by the collar of his shirt. The sheer terror in his eyes was enough to fill Khai's craving for revenge, but he was not nearly finished yet. "Not so tough without your guards, are you?"

"I have nothing left to say to you, *traitor*! So do what you're going to do!"

"That's fine. I'm not gonna kill you, you piece of shit," Khai growled, putting the man down.

Khai waiting just long enough for Trall to relax before grabbing him by the throat, lifting him off his feet. Trall had only two seconds to realize what had just happened and the fear in eyes was something Khai would remember with fondness for years to come. *Snap!* Khai broke his neck with a quick twist. Trall was dead and his reign with him. "Changed my mind." He dropped Trall's lifeless body and it flopped to the floor. Khai looked down at the body with an almost casual expression of boredom.

Suddenly, the doors swung open and armed guards rushed in, yelling commands.

Blasted Dack, where the hell are you?

"Khai!" a familiar voice called out.

Khai looked up and saw Dah leaning over the loading ramp of a ship. He had a rope knotted at increments dropping down to them at that moment. The guards, knowing the two were about to escape, advanced, guns drawn. Gunfire rained down on them from the ship above. Khai and Sibrex climbed as though their lives depended on it and reached the top in seconds. Before they could even climb up over the lip of the ramp, the pilot pulled away heading west.

They climbed aboard and crawled up the ramp. Dah was waiting for them, his arms crossed and a grin on his face. When they both stood, gasps filled the main hold. Dah drew his gun and pointed it at the Vyysarri as a chorus of clicks filled the hold for a few seconds as everyone followed suit.

"What the hell is this?" Dah shouted.

"Easy, Dack," Khai soothed. "His name is Sibrex. He's the one who saved me."

"Bull shit!" Dah shouted, pulling the hammer back on his gun. "That's a *Vyysarri!*"

"He's not going to hurt anyone here. He is my friend. I will *personally* vouch for him."

"What're you talking about? You *hate* Vyysarri!" Dah spat, not hiding his disdain.

"I have learned a lot while I was gone. Most of the Vyysarri are good people. Hell, even better than us. Here." Khai handed him the disk. "Watch this, it'll explain everything. Now, *please*. Lower your weapons, all of you."

"I'm sorry, Khai. But you're looking a lot like a traitor right now. I'm going to put the both of you in the brig for the time being."

"Like hell you are!" Khai growled. "You think I'm *stupid*? You think I didn't notice that you were rolling with Agents? Come on, Dack."

"They defected," Dah said plainly. "I've saved their families and in return they were able to show me where to find Puar. What has *he* done for you?"

"He mended my broken bones, fed, clothed and housed me while I recovered," Khai growled, taking a menacing step forward. "Sibrex here has shown me nothing but kindness and friendship since we met. He had more than *ten* opportunities to kill me, but he didn't."

"No!" Dah said sarcastically. "Why kill you when he could brainwash you and make you his puppet?"

"It didn't go down like that," Khai said, taking another step closer.

"Stop that!" Dah shouted, the gun in his hand beginning to tremble. "Don't come any closer!"

"Or what? Huh? You gonna shoot me, Dack? After I saved *your* life?"

"I just saved your life down there in the office. As I count it, we're even. Now, take them to the brig."

The Agents obeyed and one of them moved so fast, that Khai found himself disarmed before he even registered movement. Sibrex, however, was not taken by surprise. He moved just as fast as them and had two on their backs before they could disarm him. With the once-holstered gun of one of the Agents pointed at Dah, Khai intervened. He stepped in front of Sibrex.

"Khai, this man has betrayed you. Do you not wish retribution?" Sibrex asked.

"No," Khai said. "Put the gun down. Please, don't shoot my friend here."

"As you wish," Sibrex said, dropping the Agent's gun.

"There," Khai said, spinning to face Dah. "Are you satisfied?"

Dah looked at Khai, then past Khai at the Vyysarri. "For now," he said to Khai, then addressed Sibrex, "but if you slip even an inch, I'll fill you with lead. Get me?"

"It is a fair bargain," Sibrex said.

"Good. Now buckle up, we're heading to the bunker right now. So if this Vyysarri shithead doesn't fuck us on the way, or once we get there, then I'll trust him... and you."

"Fair enough," Khai agreed to his terms. "What's the plan?"

"Kay will explain it," Dah said, leading them to the cockpit, sitting down at the controls and taking over for Kay.

"We will be arriving at our destination within half an hour. Upon arrival, you will be dropped into the water. Several hundred feet down is where you will breach the facility. It won't be easy. You will have to cut through the hinges on the main access hatch above the airlock. You won't have to worry about pressure equalization as the entire shaft leading up to the facility is also filled with water. It will not be an easy ascent, either. There are depth charges attached to the shaft wall every twenty feet the whole way up. They are attached to pressure sensors that detect the water displacement of objects moving past them. What's worse is that once one goes off, all the others will follow."

"Okay, that's bad," Khai said. "So, how do we *avoid* meeting our deaths down there?"

"I have a suggestion," Sibrex spoke up. "You said that the sensors detect an increase in water pressure based on displacement, correct?"

"That's what she said," Dah retorted.

"Does it detect a decrease?"

"No," Kay said. Because-"

"Because the water drains out when the code is accepted," Sibrex finished her statement.

"Exactly," Kay agreed.

"I don't understand how that's helping us," Dah hissed impatiently.

"If we can find a way to drain the water from shaft, say... equal to our mass, we could enter and safely make our way to the top."

"Great!" Dah was being even less tolerant than ever. "So how do we get the water out of there?"

Sibrex looked at Kay, then said, "Can the main hold of this vessel be sealed off from the rest of the ship?"

"Yes," Kay answered.

"Does this vessel possess an umbilical?"

"Yes! Yes it does! Off the port-side airlock," Kay said, catching on to Sibrex's plan. "And it can withstand water pressure beyond two hundred feet!"

"What does this mean?" Dah asked, completely unimpressed with what they were devising.

"Come on, Dack!" Khai snapped, finally losing his temper with him. "Think! One man goes down into the water. He cuts the hatch and then the ship goes down. We hook up the umbilical and pop the airlock and we not only displace enough water to keep the bombs from going off, we can enter straight from the ship. That also gives us *two* escape routes. We go back down the shaft and meet Kay there, or we can call her and have her meet us at the platform. It's quicker than waiting for the airlock to let us in."

"That is not exactly how it will work," Sibrex said. "If the hatch is removed from the facility airlock, the water will flood in and set off the bombs. First, we must attach the umbilical, *then* remove the hatch. That will prevent reverse pressure. Be warned, Agent, the ship will be vulnerable. You cannot move while attached to the airlock."

"Understood," Kay said.

"Okay," Dah said. "So he came up with a good plan. Doesn't mean he's one of us yet."

Sibrex seemed unaffected, but Khai saw his jaw muscles twitch. He put his hand on the Vyysarri's shoulder and said, "But it's a good start."

"Whatever," Dah grumbled.

"We need to make a detour," Khai said.

"For what?" Dah demanded.

"What? Do *you* have breathing equipment for... oh, thirty people?"

"No," Dah growled.

"Then we need equipment. Fortunately, I know a guy who can help us out. Hell, he probably has it in stock. Let me make a call."

Khai stepped out for a moment and disappeared into the engineering section. A few minutes later, he emerged, a grin on his face.

"Can we make a quick trip up to Tanbarder? It shouldn't be more than ten minutes. The guy owes me a favor."

"I don't see a problem with that," Kay said. "It should only take us about fifteen minutes out of the way."

"Exactly. And what we get from it far outweighs any setback."

"I agree. Where am I to land once we have arrived at Tanbarder?"

"It's just outside the city limits. A small shack, you can't miss it." Khai came up to the navigational console and punched a few keys. "Here's the coordinates."

"Got them. I'm changing course. ETA in fifteen minutes."

"Thanks," Khai said, giving her shoulder a gentle squeeze. "Oh, uh... and sorry for shooting you in the stomach and... leaving you for dead."

"Sorry for almost cutting your guts out," she responded. "No hard feelings?"

"None whatsoever."

"Good."

It was a little less than fifteen minutes when they landed the ship twenty feet from an old rundown shack.

"We're getting what we need from *there*?" Dah asked incredulously.

"Yep. Stay here. I'll be right back."

As many as could fit, they crammed into the cockpit to watch Khai. A stout man strolled out from the shack and gave Khai a hardy handshake. They spoke to each other for a few minutes and then they both walked into the shack. Suddenly, the ground began to shake and tremor. A small fissure opened in the ground. Small amounts of dirt fell in as the small fissure became two heavy slabs of metal sliding apart. The slabs stopped and the hole was perfect square five-by-five feet. Khai and the man walked down into the hole, stayed about five minutes and emerged with several duffle bags. He helped Khai carry the bags to the ship, gave Khai another healthy handshake and walked back to the shack.

Sibrex came down the ramp to help him out and they brought all the bags up into the ship; the others just watched. Once they were all secured, Khai gave the order to take off. The ship hefted her bulk on her hoverpads and took off.

"Who was that?" Dah asked.

"Guy whose life I saved," Khai answered his friend. "Like I said. Owed me a favor."

"Who was it, though? He looked familiar," Dah insisted.

After a heavy sigh, Khai told them. "Ken'Neth Kreer."

"You mean, the Ken'Neth Kreer?" Dah asked.

"The same," Khai said with a shrug.

"How'd you save his life?"

"That's a story for another day. Let's get everything ready."

They spent the remainder of the trip to the canyon securing the main hold of the ship. All doors leading away from the hold were sealed. Every door in the ship produced an airtight seal. It was designed to be able to function with multiple hull breaches. Before they dove into the water, they made sure every single door was sealed. There were three doors that lead directly from the hold to the cockpit. They decided that if they needed to displace more water, they could open another door and take on another hundred cubic feet of water. Kay warned though that taking on too much water may result in the ship being too heavy to leave the river; though unlikely, it was still a possibility.

Chapter Twenty

They geared up for storming the castle. Each sported an underwater oxygen extractor, or a UOE, that literally filtered oxygen out of the water for them to breathe. They were all one piece that covered the eyes, mouth and nose to clear pressure from the goggles and allow speech. Off of the mouthpiece was the filter; it was approximately three inches long and cylindrical and housed the radio transceiver for communication and the actual filter. They were small, portable and effective, but only could be used for up to twenty minutes before the filtration system became overtaxed and quit. It was perfect for a covert operation such as this.

They were suited up and ready to ride. Aside from UOEs, Ken also supplied a high-power, ultra-fine cutting laser. All the officers who volunteered to go had their own weapons and armor, the Agents didn't need armor and, Brix, Puar and Naad had their own gear, too.

Kay, locked up in the cockpit, announced their arrival at the bunker. *"Hang on, everyone. We're going down."*

"Copy that," Khai said. "We're ready."

The ship shuddered as it plunged into the deep river of Kal'Hoom Karr Canyon. The *Bolt Bucket* groaned in protest as the pressure mounted on the hull. The lights dimmed as the ship pitched one way then the next.

"Brace yourselves, I'm turning on the artificial gravity."

"What for?" Dah asked.

"I have to stand the ship up on her port side so the umbilical will extend over the hatch and make a seal." Their stomachs turned as the AG kicked in and the ship rolled ninety degrees. A loud clank resonated through the hull of the ship. *"We are engaged to the hatch. You may cut it now. When the water fills the ship, I'll disengage the gravity so that you can move more easily. Just prepare for some disorientation."*

"We'll be fine, Kay. Just watch after the ship for us."

"Will do."

Khai walked to the airlock, the inner door rolled open and Khai stepped in with the cutting laser. With his UOE securely fastened to his face and his free hand anchoring him to the ship, he cut the hinges off the hatch and instantly, water rushed in.

"Hold on!" Khai shouted as the water threatened to suck him back into the main hold.

He heard grunting over the communication channel as the water filled more than fifty percent of the ship. The ship groaned and creaked again. *Just hold together,* Khai prayed. The AG was disengaged and Khai began to float freely.

"Whoa," Puar said. *"That's weird."*

"You'll get used to it," Dah said. *"Just give it a few seconds."*

Once they were able to regain their bearings, they swam from the ship into the lift shaft. They worked their way up, passing red light banks every ten feet. The shaft was otherwise dark and no one wanted to stop long enough to take a look around.

"How will we know if our plan worked?" Naad asked.

"We won't die," Khai responded.

"Oh, that's *reassuring,"* Puar grumbled.

"Quit your bellyaching," Khai ordered. "And cut the chatter. It's possible they're monitoring our frequencies."

"Not likely, Colonel," Kay interjected. *"The frequencies you're using are secured and reserved* exclusively *for Agents. In fact, they can't even be accessed without a voice print identification and clearance code."*

"Who is to say that there are no Agents in there right now," Sibrex asked the obvious question.

"I know where every Agent is located at this exact moment and have been monitoring their movements since we left Seryys Four."

"And how do you know you're not being fed false data?" Dah asked.

A legit question, Khai thought as they worked their way up the water-filled shaft.

"Not every Agent loyal to our cause is currently with us," Kay let them in on a little secret. *"There are a few operatives working on the inside."*

"Can they be trusted?" Khai had to ask, though he hated questioning the loyal of very useful help.

"Their families are in just as much danger as ours were. They will not *betray us, because that would mean betraying* their families *as well."* Kay stated with absolute certainty. The confidence in her voice was enough to convince Khai.

"Okay," Khai said, "let's get this over with. Kay, can you tell us how much further we need to go?"

"Yes, Colonel. It's-"

"Just... call me Khai. I'm retired, now."

"And yet you still serve your people," Sibrex pointed out. *"Would that not constitute still being active?"*

"I'm doing what I feel is right," Khai said. "This has nothing to do with my military actions. *Especially* since those actions were carried out for the wrong reasons."

"Okay, Khai. If that's what you want..."

"It is, Kay."

"As you wish," Kay continued. *"You have passed the point of detonation. You have approximately sixty feet of your ascent left."*

"How much time has gone by?"

"Ten minutes, fifteen seconds."

"Damn!" Khai snapped.

"What's wrong, Khai?" Dah asked.

"Too much time has elapsed," Sibrex filled in for Khai. *"These devices will not last for our return."*

"Meaning, there's only one way out."

"The landing platform." Brix finally said something. *"Well, Kay. Go ahead and detach, then. We're gonna need you topside."*

"No!" Sibrex shouted.

"Why not?" Dah Snapped.

"If she disconnects the umbilical now, the shaft will flood with water. Kay, wait for my signal. When we are safely within the compound, then disconnect. We will signal you when it is time for us to make our escape."

"Got it."

"Wait!" Dah shouted. *"You trust his judgment? Hell, for all we know, he could be setting us up for death."*

"What's your call, Khai?" Kay asked. *"You're in charge."*

Khai paused, as he ascended some more. "Wait for Sibrex's signal. He'll let you know when it's safe for you to unplug."

"Okay, Khai," Kay followed his command.

"I sure as shit hope you know what you're doing," Dah grumbled. *"Trusting a Vyysarri over your own friend."*

"Dack," Khai stopped his ascent and swam over to Dah. He grabbed the man by his tactical vest and jerked him closer. "If you don't like where this is going, or you don't like my command, get the *fuck* out of here. I *will not* have you questioning every decision I make. Is that understood?"

Through the visor of their UOEs, they locked eyes. Khai could see the hurt behind his friend's eyes, but knew full well that his overwhelming hate for Sibrex was clouding his judgment. Deep down, Khai knew that he knew, but some habits were harder to break than others and this particular habit was engrained into the minds of every single Seryysan alive for over hundreds of years.

The hurt turned very quickly to anger. *"Fine,"* was all Dah said. He went inverted and swam back down the shaft, letting gravity take him to ensure he didn't drown on the way back. *"But just remember that this was my plan from the beginning!"*

"Then stay and follow it through!"

"I won't go any further with that Vyysarri on our side."

"Then you're no good to us, Dack. You don't have to trust him, but I do and he's coming."

Dah kept on his descent without even looking back. *Damn it!* Khai thought.

With a heavy, sorrow-filled sigh, Khai continued on up the shaft. "Let's move out, everyone. We're almost out of time."

They swam the rest of the way up and emerged from the water. The water level was just below the lift doors. Khai hefted his bulk out of the water and pried the doors open with his bare hands. Making a quick visual sweep in both directions of the dark engineering level, he deemed it safe to bring the others up. First was Sibrex, followed by Brix, Puar and Naad. They quickly took up firing positions and covered the others as they emerged from the lift shaft. Once everyone was accounted for, they moved out.

Kay provided them with the schematics of the whole facility, so, following the map, they navigated their way through the engineering level. The next level up was hydroponics, according to the schematics. They didn't get very far. As they rounded the corner into the corridor that led to the lift they needed, they ran headlong into the two SPEARs. The Security Patrol Enforcement and Assault Robots were waiting for the party and planned on catching them flatfooted... it worked.

"Shit!" Khai shouted, firing once at the closer of the two SPEARs. The bullet lodged into the sensor package of the robot, but it returned fire anyway. The other swiveled on its treads and opened fire as well. Khai dove around the corner and took cover. The SPEARs picked the perfect place to lay an ambush. The hall was bare, nothing was usable as cover and the SPEARs were advancing.

"What do we do?" Puar asked.

"*You're* the demo expert, *do something!*" Naad shouted over the chain guns.

Puar moved to Khai's position and peered around the corner. They were only a few yards from them. Puar nodded, Khai covered his ears and so did the rest. Puar pulled the pin on a grenade and rolled it directly under the treads of the lead SPEAR. The grenade detonated, blowing the treads clean off. The SPEAR grinded to a halt, but was still firing.

"It's a start!" Khai admitted. Khai leaned out from the corner and squeezed off two shots. Both bullets lodged into the SPEAR's sensor package and the thing started firing wildly in every direction. With its back turned, they flooded the corridor and unleashed a barrage of fire that brought the SPEARs down slowly. They were successful at a loss of only three officers. Though Khai hated quantifying it that way, it was the truth. Three officers for two SPEARs when *one* SPEAR was far more superior than any *five* officers combined, was about as good an outcome as any.

The lift was empty when they slowly, cautiously approached it. But that wasn't the problem. The problem was that now the facility was on high alert and the lift had been shut down.

"Kay," Sibrex called into his throat mic, "You may proceed when ready."

"Got it!" Kay called back.

"Wait!" Khai snapped. "Has Dah returned to the ship yet?"

"Negative," Kay responded.

"Then wait 'til he gets there, *then* disconnect," Khai said, eying Sibrex suspiciously.

"Okay, Khai."

"Then let's get this over with," Naad growled.

They removed the emergency access hatch and climbed out onto the roof the lift car. There was a ladder that led all the way up to the top level and the command/panic room. Khai looked up the long lift shaft and cringed, remembering that his last trek through a lift shaft didn't exactly go well for him.

After a heavy sigh, Khai spoke. "Up we go."

"Great..." Puar grumbled.

They started climbing. It was all they could do. All the Agents present jumped from the ladder and grabbed onto the cable of the lift car. They started climbing up that way, faster than the others.

"See you at the top," one of them said playfully.

"Hey!" Khai shouted. "Conserve your strength! You'll need it for the fight that's coming."

"Trust us, Khai. We've been at this for while," one of the Agents said.

"And I've been doing this half my life! There's no glory-seeking in this mission. Got it?"

They all slowed their ascent, swung back to the ladder above Khai and started climbing at a normal rate. The engineering level was the equivalent of ten stories tall and hydroponics wasn't much better. In fact, only ten percent of the bunker was living space—two levels. The bottom residential level was the presidential suite; five thousand square feet of all the luxuries of home. The upper residential level housed the control/panic room, storage space for the maintenance robots, meeting rooms, additional staff quarters and the main hanger.

They finally reached the hydroponics level where they stopped for a breather.

"How much longer?" Puar practically whined.

"Hydroponics has six levels," Kay responded. *"Then the residential levels are next. That's where you'll find the Prime Minister. He'll be on one of the two levels. Unfortunately, the whole facility is shielded from external sensors, so I can't pinpoint his exact location."*

"Well, then we'll start there and go room-by-room 'til we find him," Khai said. "What kind of resistance are we looking at, Kay?"

"I honestly don't know. There could be ten or twenty SPEARs, it's impossible to say."

"Hazard a guess?" Naad asked.

"Given the number of SPEARs in the Hall of Justice, I would say roughly fifteen."

"Is that an educated guess, or a shot in the dark?" Brix asked.

"Shot in the dark."

"Great!" Khai scoffed. "Break's over. Get moving."

They climbed again. Khai was going over the maps and pictures of the facility in his head. The lift opened up into a large, ballroom-style foyer that connected lift cars on both ends of the facility. That was where their current lift ended; it was hidden from view as a security measure and a second form of escape should the facility be compromised. The other lift was the only way up to the top level. The foyer had high vaulted ceilings and grand pillars made of marble laced with gold and silver. To the right of the foyer was the cafeteria, kitchen and food storage. To the left of the foyer was the Prime Minister's suite; it consisted of six bedrooms, two living rooms, a private kitchen with bar and all the amenities of home. That would be the most likely place to find him on that level. Otherwise, the second most likely spot would be the control room on the top level.

The overwhelming amount of resistance that was inevitably going to meet them the moment they emerged from the lift confounded him. The complete lack of any intel was driving him mad. Even in the worst-case scenarios, Khai had a ballpark figure of the opposition's numbers. This was almost literally like going in blindfolded to the surprise birthday party from hell.

"Hey, Agents!" Khai called out. "Stop for a moment, would ya?"

"What is the problem, Khai?"

"We need a plan once we get to the foyer."

"We have been formulating a plan since hydroponics."

"Oh, good," Khai said. "So when were you going to let us in on that plan."

"When it was finished," the boy said plainly.

"Okay," Khai said. "Maybe we could help with that."

"I don't believe so," the boy responded.

"Listen, kid," Khai growled. "I was killing Vyysarri before you were a glimmer in your daddy's eye. I have a trick or two up my sleeve. Oh! Sorry Sibrex, I didn't mean that in the... uh, no offense."

"None taken, Khai. Your history is well known."

"Thanks, I guess. Anyway, what's your plan?"

"We were planning on being the first wave. Our reflex packages will make us harder targets on the move and we can draw their fire while you and the others escape the shaft."

"That's a damn good start," Khai said. "What comes next?"

"You guys open fire and we mow them down with overwhelming force."

"That's it?" Puar asked incredulously.

"I said we were still working on it," said the boy.

"Okay. You guys draw their fire; if you can, corral them into the center of the foyer and then we can use the pillars as cover and catch them in the crossfire."

"What would you suggest we do next?" the boy asked.

"I'm not sure," Khai admitted. "It's something we'll have to play by ear."

The boy shrugged then said, "Whatever you say, but you're not inspiring much confidence in us."

"Look here, kid," Khai growled. "Winning battles like this is ten percent inspiration and ninety percent getting your ass kicked! Just get up there and start jumping around or something. Get them corralled into the center and we'll all gun them down from our cover points. Got it?"

"You're in charge, boss," the boy said, sighing.

"Fucking kids..." Khai half growled, half whispered through a clenched jaw, shaking his head.

In short order, they made it to the bottom of the residential level. The lift doors were sealed—as was to be expected. What was not expected was that the doors were welded shut from *inside* the shaft.

"Shit!" Khai scoffed.

"What is the problem?" Sibrex asked.

"I don't think we're alone in this shaft," Khai said ominously. "These doors were sealed from this side."

"That's bad, right?" Puar asked.

"Right," Khai responded.

"So what do we do?" Naad asked, his low voice echoing down the shaft.

"Kay?"

"Yes, Khai?"

"You said this thing was completely self-sufficient, right?"

"Yes, right down to maintenance bots. Why?"

"I have an idea. I don't think we're alone, but I don't think we're in danger, either."

Khai pulled out the laser cutter and got to work on the door. Only moments later, the shaft echoed with whirring servos as two maintenance bots emerged from small alcoves on either side of the door. Using tiny magnets at the ends of their tiny legs, they crawled along the walls like spiders and began welding the spot on the door where Khai was cutting. His theory was right. They wouldn't let him cut through the door.

"Puar!"

"Sir?"

"Time for some fireworks," Khai said, moving farther up to let him in. "Blow the doors."

228

"With pleasure, sir," Puar moved up as the maintenance bots were still welding. As Puar started fastening the plastic explosives to the door, one of the bots stopped. Puar hesitated and the bot got back to work. "Sir?"

"They're not a threat," Khai assured him. "Keep going."

Puar nodded and stuck the igniters into the plastic mold. The bot chirped at him and took a more aggressive stance. The arc welder attachment angled and sent a good jolt through Puar's hand.

"Youch!" Puar yelped, letting go of the ladder to hold his hand. "Shit!"

Puar lost his balance and fell. Before he could get too far, and with reflexes honed from decades of fighting, Khai caught Puar buy his flak jacket. Using his superior strength, he lifted Puar back up to the ladder. "Thanks," he breathed.

"Don't mention it."

"Uh, Khai?" the boy called out.

"What?" Khai's voice betrayed a little bit of annoyance.

"We have incoming! *Lots* of them!"

Khai looked up and saw at least a hundred spider-like maintenance bots skittering down the shaft wall. "Puar!" He shouted, shooting the two bots on the doors.

"Sir?"

"I want that door in pieces ten seconds ago!"

"I'm on it!"

"Open fire!" Khai shouted.

They fired into the swarm of bots as they crawled down at them. The seemingly unlimited number of bots flooding the shaft were only held at bay for a few moments before the bots skittered into range of their arc welders and started sparking them. The shocks scalded hands and arms and faces. The Agents jumped from the ladder to the lift cable and out of range of the bots' welders. From there they were able to take them down by the hundreds.

Khai was shocked hundreds of times as the bots swarmed him. His high threshold for pain kept him in the fight, but some of the shocks were leaving severe burns. Sibrex also leapt from the ladder to the cable and aided in the cover fire. Brix was directly under Khai and above Puar, who was getting the charges set. Brix ran out of ammo and was taking too long to reload the dual magazines.

Too many shocks sent him falling, but again, Khai was there for the rescue. He grabbed hold of the man, still getting shocked tens of times every second. A bot shocked Khai's leg and he lost his footing on the step. He dropped his machine gun and grabbed the ladder. Everyone watched as Khai dangled, holding onto Brix with his left hand and the ladder with his right. The Agents couldn't kill them fast enough and officers below could only fend them off with hand-to-hand techniques at the risk of hitting their teammates with friendly fire.

Sibrex stopped shooting and started climbing.

"What the hell are you doing?" Khai practically screamed. Sibrex didn't respond. "Sibrex?" *Maybe Dah was right! How could I have been so stupid?*

Sibrex climbed about four yards up the cable past the Agents. He flipped a switch on his right gauntlet and a strong pressure filled the shaft making everyone's stomachs turn and ears pop for a brief moment. Only seconds later, the bots all shut down and fell into the dark depths of the lift shaft. Once the bots were gone, Sibrex leapt from the cable down to the ladder above Khai. He reached down and grabbed Khai's wrist and hefted both him and Brix up far enough for Khai to get his footing.

There was silence for almost a minute, only the sound of panting filled the shaft.

Suddenly, Naad broke the silence. "*Not a threat,* my black ass!"

Khai shrugged. "They didn't look like a threat."

"Charges set," Puar announced.

"What timing," Brix said, sarcasm saturating his tone.

"Everybody above the door—now," Khai ordered.

They complied quickly. Khai was pretty sure that everyone was about as ready to be out of the shaft as he was. The doors blew open and the Agents instantly leapt from the cable into the foyer and equally instant were the sounds of gunfire issuing from the SPEARs in the room. Khai was the first to respond by quickly and easily dropping himself down and helping the others up. He spared a look at the Agents and marveled at their speed. They almost moved too fast to track. He was impressed with their abilities and also a little jealous. He could only imagine what he would be capable of, had he been given one of those of reflex... hoop-a-joobs.

As the Agents did their job, Khai got to work. His intention was never to do the whole crossfire thing. He was going to show those kids how it was done. As the others scrambled to get themselves out of the shaft, Khai charged in with his trusted sidearm in hand. There were six SPEARs in the room, four of which were mostly in the center of the Foyer. He took four large bounds and leapt high into the air over the cluster of SPEARs, raining bullets on them as he flipped over them.

He landed in a dead run straight for one of those SPEARs that hadn't been corralled. Its chain gun tracked him with only the precision that a machine could, but it wasn't good enough to take down a man like Khai, a man on a mission, a man *without* a death wish. He kicked off the wall, during which he grabbed the knife from the boot that was momentarily planted on the wall, coming down on the robot and driving the knife straight down into its head.

The robot hadn't even hit the floor before Khai was making his way across the room to the other that hadn't fallen for Khai's plan. The SPEAR was ready, and Khai was counting on that. He darted to the right and rolled to the left, bullets ricocheting off the marble floor the whole way. He stopped right in front of the corralled SPEARs. He reared up and leapt backward into a back flip and let the center SPEARs get riddled with bullet holes.

The Agents, so stunned by Khai's performance, finally reacted and swarmed the remaining SPEAR. In short order, the threat was neutralized and they all took a deep breath. The acrid smell of singed wires and smoldering hydraulic fluid stung their noses, but they were alive. Doing a visual inventory of his men, Khai counted only four dead, one Agent and the rest were officers.

"Everyone okay?" Khai asked.

"We're fine," Puar spoke for Dah's old team. "But *I've* definitely been better." Puar took some shrapnel to the upper calf. The shrapnel was sticking out about two inches and blood was beginning to pool around his boot.

"I got it," Khai said, as others moved in to help. "This is gonna hurt, kid. You ready?"

"No," Puar said, his voice shaky.

Khai put a leather strap in Puar's mouth and used the pliers of a multi-tool to grip the shrapnel. "Bite down on that, it'll help." Puar nodded and bit down, squeezing his eyes shut. "On the count of three, you understand?" Puar nodded. Everyone watched it like it was a movie on the Net'Vyyd. Khai prepped his cauderizer. "One-"

"Wait!" Puar interrupted. "Is it going to be: one, two, three, *go*? Or one, two, *three?*"

"I don't care," Khai said curtly. "What do *you* want?"

"One, two, three, *go*."

"Fine. You ready now?"

Puar nodded, putting the leather strap back in his mouth.

"Okay. One..." Suddenly Khai ripped the shrapnel from Puar's leg. He cried out in pain through a clenched jaw, biting down hard on the leather strap as tears ran down his face. Only seconds later, Khai ran the cauterizer over the wound and stopped the bleeding.

For a few tense moments, everyone held their breath, waiting for Puar to say something as he finally relaxed. The strap fell from Puar's mouth as he took a couple deep breaths. He motioned for Khai to come closer and he did. He leaned in close to Puar. Without any notice, Puar struck Khai in the jaw. "What the hell happened to two, you asshole?"

Everyone let out a collective sigh of relief as they realized that he was going to be all right and that his charming personality was still intact. Khai grinned and chuckled as he packed up his medical kit.

"Brix," Khai said at length. "You stay here with Puar."

"You got it, sir," Brix said with a lazy salute.

"Me, Naad, Sibrex and *you*," he pointed at the boy, "will take the Kitchen. The rest of you search the apartment. Keep the channel open, I want to hear every word you're all saying, got it?" He got nods from everyone. "Good. Move out."

Chapter Twenty-One

Khai kicked the swinging door in leading into the kitchen. It was dark but the smell of food being cooked still hung in the air.

"*Someone* is living here," Sibrex pointed out.

"Got that right," Khai said, pointing his entry light at some used pans sitting in a sink. He turned to face the boy. "What's your name, kid?"

"Ten," he answered.

"How 'bout your real name, son?"

"Ed'Ward Eddarri. My parents called me Ed."

"All right, Ed, take point."

"Yes, sir."

They moved through the huge kitchen checking every nook and cranny.

"Khai?" Ed asked. "May I ask a question?"

"Sure."

"Was that your plan all along?"

"Yep," Khai said casually. "Thought I'd show you a thing or two about how to be a soldier."

"Your performance was quite impressive."

"Thanks," Khai said, beaming with pride. "Not as fast as I used to be. Lots of injuries have slowed me down."

"Still, your skills are remarkable."

"Thanks." Khai had to grin. "It took a long time of fighting. Fighting that I now realize was a waste of my life."

"I am truly sorry for that," Sibrex said, placing a gentle hand his shoulder.

"Well, now I have something—and *someone*—to live for," Khai said, trying to put a positive spin on it.

"Indeed," Sibrex agreed.

It occurred to him that everyone on that channel could hear what they were saying and no one had said word about it. That meant one of three things: they were too scared of him to speak up, they were in trouble or they were dead.

"Brix, you copy? Brix?"

"Agent Nineteen, respond," Ed called out.

"Hm. It is as I expected," Sibrex said.

"What're you talking about?" Naad asked.

"Your radios are dead. So is contact to Agent Thirteen."

"How? Why?" The tentacles of doubt and suspicion were weaving their way into Khai's heart and mind again. "How do you know that?"

"The device I set off was an EMP. That is what disabled the maintenance robots. I was hoping that the blast wouldn't affect our communications, but it did."

"And when were you going to tell us?" Khai demanded, taking a defensive step toward a cooling unit as cover.

"If I had said something beforehand, would you have used my idea?"

Khai thought about it for a moment. "I suppose not," he admitted, still not completely convinced of Sibrex's loyalty.

"I believe the kitchen is clear, Khai. Should we go back to the foyer to regroup with the others?"

"Yeah, let's go. There's nothing here we can use."

By the time they got back, the other search party had already finished with the apartment and was fixing to go into the kitchen area to look for Khai and the others.

"We lost radio contact," Brix said. "What the hell happened?"

"The trick Sibrex used to stop the maintenance bots also knocked out our radios," Khai said, not hiding the suspicion in his voice.

"What was it?" Brix asked.

"An EMP," Khai answered.

"What's that?" Brix asked again.

"An electromagnetic pulse," Sibrex explained. "It disables most electronic devices within its area of effect."

"Oh," Brix murmured.

"Right," Khai said impatiently. "Now, with the science lesson out of the way, let's finish our mission."

They moved to the lift opposite the foyer from the hidden lift and waited. Suddenly the floor beneath their feet rumbled like a ship being bombarded with its shields down. They all struggled to stay on their feet and the metal load-bearing beams groaned with protest. The floor bucked, sending them all crashing to their backsides.

"What the hell was *that?*" Puar asked.

"The depth charges," Sibrex said.

"You think Dah made it out?" Brix asked.

"He had to," Khai said. "At this point he would've drowned."

"A more likely scenario would that the *Bolt Bucket* detached from the airlock."

"So our only way out is the landing platform." Puar said.

"Uh-huh," Khai said.

"So, now what?" Puar asked.

"The bunker is still on lockdown, so we climb," Khai said, prying the doors open.

They all filed into the lift shaft and started climbing. With the control/panic room being the on the next level, it was a short a climb. Khai pried the doors open and took a step in. The whole floor was shrouded in a deep umbra, like looking into the event horizon of a black hole. He flipped on his entry light and shone it around the immediate area. The lift was located in a small utility room.

"Okay, it's clear," Khai said. They all filed out into the small room. "Me and my team will take point. Ed, you and your team will provide cover and the police team will watch our asses. Are we ready?"

"No, but we'll go anyway," Puar said.

"Good," Khai said. "On three."

"Are you sure it's not on *one*," Puar scoffed.

Khai ignored him. Mouthing the numbers and nodding, he counted. *One... two...* Three! Khai kicked the door clean off its hinges and rolled into the corridor. Sibrex followed right behind him and the others swiftly behind. Khai moved down the corridor sweeping his gun back and forth scanning for enemies. The layout etched into his memory, he knew exactly where to go. The power was still down and the corridor was dark, but the combined lighting from several entry lights was more than enough to illuminate most of the corridor through which they moved. It was too quiet.

Khai came to a stop, signaling the other to do the same.

"What's wrong?" Puar asked.

"This doesn't feel right," Khai whispered back. "They know we're here. They know there's only one way to get here. What're they waiting for?"

"I don't know," Puar admitted. "I just thought maybe they were so scared, they ran away."

"They're robots, idiot," Brix growled, slapping Puar up the back of his head.

"What? A guy can dream, can't he?" Puar whispered.

"So where are they?" Naad asked. "There must be a tactical reason they're not attacking."

"There were several times where they would've had a tactical advantage. Any one of those intersections we passed would have been the perfect place of an ambush," Khai insisted. "There has to be another reason."

"Khai," Sibrex spoke up. "Perhaps they are conserving their numbers for a final stand at the control room. There is only one way in or out of that room, and if memory serves me, there are even barricades to provide a degree of cover."

"That has to be the reason," Khai said thoughtfully.

"So, what do we do?" Brix asked.

"We find a way to circumvent their defenses and get in," Ed said.

"That won't work," Khai insisted.

"Why not?" Ed shot back, almost insulted.

"They're robots, right? They only think logically, right?"

"Where you going with this, Khai?" Puar asked.

"They don't have intuition, so they can only think logically," Khai pressed.

"I don't follow," Brix admitted.

"I do," Sibrex said. "If they think with pure logic, then any way to circumvent will be covered because that would be the logical thing to do."

"So, Brix's question still stands," Ed pointed out. "What do we do?"

"We do the most illogical thing we can think of," Khai said.

"And that is?" Ed asked.

Puar, Naad, Khai and Sibrex all looked back at Brix. "What?" he asked them.

"What would you do, Brix?" Puar asked.

Brix stared at them for a moment, his jaw muscles twitching, mulling over the question in his head. "Go in guns blazing?"

"Exactly!" Khai said.

"You can't be serious!" Ed snapped. "We don't even know how many are in there!"

I know," Khai sympathized, "but we need to get to the Prime Minister at all costs. That's our plan. They won't see a frontal assault coming."

"Essentially, taking them by surprise," Sibrex added.

"Well," Naad sighed. "I suppose we should get this show on the road."

"Everyone!" Khai whispered. They all looked at him intently. "Keep your heads down!" He got courageous nods from his soldiers and it filled him with pride. "Move out."

The control room was a relatively small room within an expansive hanger big enough to house two *Dron'Jawk*-Class Cargo Frigates named after hulking four-legged mammals with horns on their heads that had a unique ability to store large amounts of water within their bodies as they traversed the deserts of Seryys. The hanger door was an impenetrable force field disguised with a holoproj as the canyon wall. The corridor emptied out into the hanger on the opposite side of the control room. The retractable landing platform sat roughly four feet above the hanger floor on giant metal rails on which it slid in and out. The whole thing was supported on thick metal girders that also acted as the framework leaving the interior hollow to allow maintenance bots to enter.

There were ten SPEARs waiting in a defensive wedge formation in front of the door leading to the control room. Six of the ten were using the cover spots in front of the control room.

"So, what's the plan?" Puar asked as they surveyed the hanger.

"You're gonna shoot them with your grenade launcher and cause as much damage as you can. While they regroup, the rest of us charge in, guns blazing."

"Courageous," Brix said. "*Stupid*, but courageous."

"That's what makes it such a good plan," Khai countered.

"They will respond quickly," Sibrex's grave voice rumbled.

"Once Puar fires, just follow my lead. Give me ten seconds and then charge in. Got it?"

"Ten seconds," Naad echoed.

Khai took a deep breath and blew it out quickly. To Puar he asked, "Ready?" Puar nodded, tightening his grip on his RPG. "Do it."

Thoomp, thoomp, thoomp! Three grenades launched into the air and the SPEARs reacted instantly finding firing solutions and unleashing hell. The grenades impacted—*boom, boom, boom*—right into the center of the formation. Two of the SPEARs went down immediately as their treads were blown off. They were still able to fire, but they both fell behind the barriers.

Just as the SPEARs started firing, Khai started running. In the confusion, Khai was able to sprint almost the whole distance, firing his trusty sidearm the whole way. Most of the bullets ricocheted harmlessly off their armor, but some did find their marks. Bullets shattered the receptors of two more and they started firing wildly all over. Summoning his antean strength, Khai leapt high into the air, over the leading SPEAR and landed behind it. With a thunderous kick, he solidly connected with the leading spear in the back, sending it tumbling over the first barrier to the floor. Its treads spun helplessly, trying to right itself.

Running for another SPEAR, he pulled his final grenade, lodged it into a crevice between the torso and lower strut leading to the treads, planted two steps up its back and bounded off backward into a back flip. The grenade went off blasting the SPEAR into two pieces spouting fluids and sparks as they landed.

"Ten!" Puar shouted. "Move!"

They all charged in, bellowing war cries. Naad opened up with his twin SMGs, Puar was firing off with his pistol and Brix jogged in firing his heavy machine gun. The Agents bounded in doing their acrobatic thing, while the remaining officers followed up.

It was a massacre. The remaining four SPEARs picked off the officers before they could even fire off a shot and, despite their elusiveness, only two Agents remained; the others lay on the floor dead with several bullet wounds. At ten yards out, a SPEAR homed in on Naad and riddled him. He only had time to squeak out a short yelp before he tripped over his own feet and fell to the floor dead, a pool a blood collecting under him. Brix stopped dead in his tracks at the sight of his friend taking a dive.

"Naad!" he cried. "You ba-" he caught a bullet in the head and fell back motionless.

Puar dived for cover behind a forklift which was immediately blasted with holes. The two Agents tirelessly dodged bullets with twists and turns, flips and handsprings. An Agent came down on the one that flipped over the first barrier. He sliced with his Kit'Ra removing its head and it stopped struggling. He paused just long enough to get riddled with bullet holes, reducing him to a basically a pile of goo. The final Agent came to rest down in the pit under the landing platform.

Khai was in trouble. He took cover around the corner of the control room facing away from the hanger exit. He could hear the whirring of servos in the sudden silence that enveloped them. The silence meant one of two things: everyone else was dead, so there were no targets, or the remaining people had found cover, so there were no targets. Either way, Khai was in for a world of hurt. The whirring got louder and louder; Khai was certain that the SPEAR was going to turn the corner any minute.

Sibrex stood atop the control room, fixing his gaze on the SPEAR stalking Khai. Going all the way around the hanger to get to his current position was painstakingly slow and frustrating, especially when he saw Naad and then Brix go down. He pushed his misgivings aside as he stealthily crept to the edge of the control room and activated his EMP device again. The pulse hit all three of them but nothing happened. Instead, they all fixed on Sibrex's position. Sibrex sighed and jumped down on top of the one closest to Khai. As they both struggled, Sibrex lodged a knife into the separation between the plates on its back.

The other SPEARs fixed to open fire on Sibrex, Khai decided it was time to return his favor by drawing their fire. He sprinted out back toward the entrance from which he came, the SPEARs focused on him and opened fire. Sibrex lost sight of his friend to the darkness just before he worked the panel off. He then haphazardly reached in and started yanking out cords and wires that looked even remotely important. After four handfuls of circuitry, the SPEAR finally sputtered, coughed up some sparks and fell dead to the floor with a final twitch.

Khai finally found cover behind a stack of metal crates and immediately knew that his situation was dire. His heroism was rewarded with several bullets ripping their way through his flesh. Most had hit his flak jacket—knocking the wind out of him, but some of them found their mark somewhere on his body—one of which hit him in the right leg just below the knee, shattering the tibia. Blood was already pooling under him where he sat and a blurry haze was clouding his peripheral vision.

As the three SPEARs moved off in Khai's direction, Puar came out from his cover spot and fired the two remaining grenades in his launcher. Each one connected. One SPEAR flew apart spraying fluid everywhere. The other had its bottom half blown apart which showered the hanger with molten slag, circuitry and tread links.

Only one remained; and now it was severely outnumbered and outgunned. The remaining people (Sibrex, Puar, one Agent and Khai—who was crawling along the floor firing wildly at it) converged on the singled-out SPEAR. Bullets connected with vulnerable spots from head to tread. Eventually, the overwhelming fire caused a hydraulic line to rupture on the pivot point just above its treads and it sagged. Using one of its gun-mounted hands to brace itself up, it continued to fire; only now it was firing wildly in arcing sprays. The remaining Agent streaked forward and buried his Kit'Ra straight down through the head into the floor and left it there.

"Khai!" Sibrex breathed.

Khai was on his back, staring blankly up at the hanger ceiling, a bloody trail marked the gleaming floor from his hiding spot to his resting spot where more blood began to pool. The sight of that much blood caused Sibrex to reflexively salivate. He pushed his temptations deep down, despite the fact that he hadn't fed in days, and knelt down next to his new friend.

"Khai'Xander Khail, you are not permitted to die this day," he whispered. He looked up at Puar. "Get to the control room, free the Prime Minister and deactivate the hanger force field. We need immediate transport to the nearest medical facility!"

"Right!" he said.

Puar pushed past the Agent and sprinted for the sealed door to the control/panic room, placed small charges around the perimeter of the door and took cover as he blew them. The heavy door fell with an echoing thud. As the smoke cleared, Puar ran through the door with reckless abandon. His brother, the Prime Minister of Seryys stood, his fists bloodied and a SPEAR lying twitching and sparking on the floor.

"Damn!" Little Puar breathed. "Someone ate the wheat cereal this morning!"

"'Bout damn time, little brother!" he barked in his military voice. "Can we *please* get the hell out of here?"

"Yeah! We just need to lower the hanger force field and extend the platform. Do you have a communication console in here?"

Prime Minister Puar pointed. Officer Puar tapped the console and it lit up. "*Bolt Bucket!* This is Puar! Mission was successful; I have the Prime Minister and I'll have the platform extended in moments. Please-"

"*Shut up and forget the platform!*" Dah's strained voice came over the channel. "*We've been meeting heavy resistance here in the sky! Just get that force field-*NOW!"

"Copy," Officer Puar said, nodding at his brother to lower it.

Dah had already detached the umbilical and was purging the water from ship when Kay radioed him.

"*Dah, I've lost communication with the team!*"

Sibrex! Dah thought. *Fucker double-crossed them!* Dah stripped his gear and discarded the useless UOE. He had to finish the last twenty feet of the shaft without air after the UOE's filter died. After almost five minutes of holding his breath, the water level in the main hold had drained enough that he could finally gasp for air. He coughed and hacked between gasps, spitting water away from his mouth.

He was barely able to croak out, "Get us out of here! We'll find a way in and rescue them from topside!"

"You got it!"

Once again the ship groaned with protest as Kay brought her up out of the water into the sky where she belonged. Dah ran the short corridors of the *Bucket* for the cockpit and plopped down into the co-pilot's seat.

"That damn Sibrex is to blame for this, I can *feel* it!"

"Are you sure?" Kay asked. "He did nurse Khai back to health."

"Yeah! And now he's within *steps* of the Prime Minister. Small price to pay to completely collapse the entire Seryys Government, don't ya think?"

Kay only raised her eyebrows and nodded.

"Do you know where the hanger door is located?" Kay asked Dah.

"No," Dah admitted, but still carried a very determined voice. "But we'll find out soon enough."

"What do you propose?" Kay asked.

"Blast the walls 'til we find it!" Dah said with resolve, bringing the targeting computer online.

"We should start with areas along the wall that put out an energy signature more than just normal geothermal activity," Kay stated.

"Fine. Whatever. Just get me a target."

The first designation appeared on the HUD and Dah opened fire, reducing the rock wall to head-sized boulders that crashed to the water with a splash. "That's not it, next target!" Another area lit up on the HUD, Dah opened fire with the *Bucket's* cannons.

"Dah!" Kay shouted over the thrum of the cannons' fire. Dah ignored her. "*Dah!*"

"*What?*" he snapped.

"I have hostiles inbound. Five of them, coming in fast, too fast to be atmospheric fliers."

"Here come the cavalry," Dah grumbled. "Okay, move out. We'll keep'em busy 'til we hear from the team." If *we hear from the team,* he thought angrily.

"Got it!" Kay said, yanking back on the yoke and pushing the ship to full throttle, sending her into the gut-churning climb that pasted them into their seats. The *Shark*-Class Interceptors followed suit right behind them firing as they climbed. The *Bolt Bucket's* engines roared and their seats bucked as cannon fire ricocheted off the shields. Another volley found its mark, the *Bucket* jolted to the right sending the two into their crash restraints.

"We have to lose them!" Dah shouted.

"Tell me something I don't know!" Kay snapped as she fought the controls.

"I'm diverting power to the rear shields," Dah said. "That should hold them off long enough to lose them."

"You could try killing them, too, you know!" Kay shouted over the rumble of the ship's engines.

"What the hell does it look like I'm doing?" Dah snapped.

The HUD showed five ships in hot pursuit, pouring fire at them. Dah's stomach turned as Kay put the ship through some hair-raising maneuvers that Dah had never seen. He never realized that a ship of the *Bucket*'s size could barrel roll while banking to one side or the other. Dah opened fire on the pursuing ships. Their shields were obviously angled full forward because most of the shots connected and were shunted by them.

"Damn!" Dah growled with frustration. "They're fast!"

"That's why they're called interceptors, Dah! Keep at it!"

Dah locked onto the lead ship and fired; the cannons bashed through its shields and the remaining ships flew through its debris cloud.

"Ha ha!" Dah hooted.

Kay rolled the *Bucket* over and went inverted. She then pulled back on the yoke sending the ship into a nosedive toward the canyon; the interceptors followed. Only yards before hitting the water, Kay jerked back on the yoke and the ship leveled out spraying water to the sides. The hoverpads thrummed in their ears trying to keep the ship airborne. One of the interceptors didn't pull up in time and crashed into the river. The water spraying off the river from the *Bucket*'s hoverpads temporarily blinded the pursuing pilots and in the confusion, Kay sent the ship into a tight loop at full throttle. Their stomachs screamed during the maneuver, but the end result was exactly what Kay wanted: they came down right behind them.

"Fire!" Kay shouted.

The *Bucket*'s cannons lashed out at them from behind. Two of the ships went down in flames before the final remaining ship juked hard to the right and exited the canyon.

"Shit!" Kay spat out.

"What?"

"Three more coming in from the south!"

"Shit!" Dah echoed his pilot. "We're in trouble. How much longer can you hold them off?"

"I could do this all day, but I worry we may be sticking around for nothing."

"Don't say that!" Dah snapped. "If Khai is with them, they're alive."

"We *have to* consider the possibility, Dah," Kay pressed her point as well as her piloting abilities as the next wave of ships entered the fray.

"We need to hold them off just a little bit longer!" Dah insisted. "You don't know Khai like I do."

"He is a formidable warrior, but if he was betrayed by the Vyysarri, there's no telling what became of him."

"Just shut up and fly. You'll see."

Kay did just that. She jerked the ship hard to the right jamming them into their restraints. The *Shark*-Class Interceptors were designed for speed and maneuverability and were more than a match for the bulkiness of the *Bolt Bucket.* As fast as she was, the *Sharks* were faster. But what the *Bucket* lacked in speed and agility, she compensated for with sheer toughness... *and* a superb pilot. Kay was still doing things that Dah didn't know were possible. It was only when the ship bucked hard enough to give them whiplash that Dah started to feel the gravity of their situation.

"Kay," Dah said softly.

"A little busy, here..."

"Prepare for orbit," he ordered, confliction and grief filling his voice.

Kay took her eyes off the sky, looked straight at Dah and said "You sure?" Kay's voice bled surprise.

"Yeah..." he said, disengaging targeting HUD. "We're sitting ducks."

"All right..." Kay's voice betrayed hesitation. "Breaking for-"

"Bolt Bucket! This is Puar! Mission was successful; I have the Prime Minister and I'll have the platform extended in moments. Please-" Kay and Dah exchanged excited glances as the Demolitions Expert's stressed voice came over the airways. Kay smiled as she swung the ship back down toward the bunker entrance.

"Shut up and forget the platform!" Dah snapped back. "We've been meeting heavy resistance here in the sky! Just get that force field down-NOW!"

"Copy."

Just as they swooped down low into the canyon, the holographic rock wall fizzled away revealing the cavernous hanger beyond. Kay dropped the shields, diverted that power to the hoverpads, threaded the needle into the hanger, spun the ship a hundred and eighty degrees and used hoverpads to slow the ship. The force from the hoverpads sent smaller debris flying about and caused the people inside to brace themselves.

"Jeez!" Puar shouted over the roar of the overtaxed engines and hoverpads.

Before the ship could even settle on its landing struts, the loading ramp was down and Dah was running down it with a gun drawn. Dah instantly spotted Khai's motionless body lying on the floor in a pool of blood. He knelt down next to his friend and pushed the old Vyysarri out of the way, pointing the gun at him.

"Stay the *fuck* away from him, *Vyysarri.*" The words came out as a hiss.

"Whoa!" Little Puar said. "Easy, Cap'. He's a friendly!"

"Like hell!" Dah spat. "Why did we lose communication, then?"

"Sibrex activated an EMP that saved all our lives," the Agent said.

"He hasn't made any move to harm me, either," Prime Minister Puar also commented, though his tone suggested suspicion.

Sibrex raised his hands in surrender and backed up several steps. "I mean you no harm," he rumbled.

"Whatever," Dah grumbled. "Just stay where I can see you."

"As you wish," Sibrex said.

"Come on, Khai! Stay with me!" Nothing. "Khai!" Nothing. "KHAI!" Dah screamed, slapping him across the face.

Suddenly, life returned to Khai's eyes. His Adam's apple bobbed as he swallowed.

"Dah?" he asked so faintly only Dah heard it.

"Yeah!" he laughed. "It's me."

"Where... the hell... have *you* been?" he whispered.

"Dodging ships so you can leave this place."

"Then... what are... we waiting for?"

Suddenly alarms went off in Dah's head.

"Watch out!" the Prime Minster shouted.

Sibrex drew his weapon and fired it in nearly the same second. The bullet passed by Dah's head so close, he could feel the heat from it. The bullet hit something behind him and he spun to see a SPEAR, its bottom half missing and a bullet hole in its face fall to the floor.

He looked at the dead SPEAR, then at Sibrex, to his friends and back to the SPEAR, gasping the whole time. No words were exchanged. Sibrex silently holstered his weapon and stayed right where he was. There was silence for several minutes until...

"Told you!" Little Puar shouted.

Kay emerged from the ship, nursing her still-healing wounds. "Are we leaving or having a reunion?"

"Help me," Dah said, worming his arms through Khai's blood under his body. Sibrex was the next to help. Dah and Sibrex exchanged gazes for a fleeting second, then, together, they lifted Khai up. The Prime Minister jumped in to help as well. Little Puar followed close behind. As they made their way to the ship, Puar heard the faint groan. He stopped.

"What is it?" Dah asked.

"D'you hear that?" Khai asked faintly.

"Yes," Sibrex said. "But I thought it was my stomach."

"Was that... a joke?" Khai asked.

"An attempt," Sibrex admitted.

Khai wheezed out a light chuckle.

"But seriously, what *is* that?" Little Puar asked.

"It's coming from that direction," the Agent pointed in the direction.

Little Puar moved to investigate. The closer he got to the source the more it sounded like a person groaning for sure. Puar stopped and homed in on it. It was coming from his right where two bodies lay... the bodies of his colleagues, his friends, his brothers. Suddenly, movement. *What?* Puar thought. A hand lifting up, and more groaning.

Puar rushed over. Naad was dead, but Brix...

"Oh, my achin' head," he whined.

Puar laughed aloud. "I told you, you had nothing up there to damage!"

"Guess my thick skull came in handy, huh?"

"I guess so," Little Puar said. "Looks like it glanced off your forehead."

"Doesn't hurt any less," Brix groaned again, sitting up and wiping the blood out of his eyes. "Is the fight over?"

"Yeah, it's over. We're heading out now," Puar said, helping his friend up and leading him to the ship.

Khai didn't really know where he was; all he knew was that he heard Dah's voice, Sibrex cracked a bad joke and he was floating through a dark cavern. Next thing he knew, he saw some blurry lights shining in his face, people glowing in white running circles around him, and the faint, almost distant sound of urgent voices going back and forth. A long, droning beep was the last thing he heard and then, sweet darkness took him to a place where the pain stopped and where the woman with whom he fell in love waited with open arms. He thought that, before he went, he may have actually cracked a weak grin, but he couldn't be sure.

Epilogue

Broon'Kur Broor, known to his friends as Sibrex, still got gaping stares every single time he entered; and, as he had several times already, strolled down the corridor amongst the night staff. He rounded a corner and came to a halt at a door. The sign on the door indicated that visitors were not welcome, but in his case—being allergic to sunlight and all, an exception was made. He knocked and entered. Khai was sitting up, using his combat knife to scrape away the notches on his trusted pistol. Several tubes and wires were attached to him, and the droning beep of a heart monitor filled the room only slightly drowned out by the sound of the Net'Vyyd running.

"It is good to see you well, Khai," Sibrex said with a fanged smile. "I have brought you a gift."

The door swung open and the unmistakable curves of her body made him smile wide.

"Brindee!" Khai gasped, still reeling from his injuries.

She rushed up to his bedside and sat, giving him a long, passionate kiss. "I missed you!"

"You sure are a sight for sore eyes!" Khai said, his heart monitor beeping a little faster.

Sibrex nodded at Khai's scraped up 92-30:11-1 Assault Pistol. "What are you doing?"

"Erasing a mistake," Khai said soberly despite the jovial occasion. "I've spent a lifetime killing your kind; each notch on this gun represents a mistake I made."

"That is a lot of mistakes," Sibrex pointed out.

"I know," Khai said, scraping another notch off. "This is my first step towards redemption."

"No," Sibrex said, compassion filling his voice for once. "It is the second."

They all smiled at each other and a real moment took them. That moment was lost when Kay'Lah Kayword, Captain Dack'Tandy Dah, Officer Pual'Branen Puar, Bria'Nah Briar and Brix entered, noisily laughing.

"Hey, Khai! You're awake!" Puar said.

Dah went straight for Sibrex and gave him a hardy handshake.

"What're you all doing here?" Khai asked.

"Well," Dah said. "We were informed that you were awake and that we could come see you now since Sibrex and your lady friend here can't go out in the sun. So here we are!"

"It's good to see you all," Khai said. "And, I heard that Prime Minister Puar dissolved the Agent Program."

"Yes," Kay said with a big smile. She somehow looked different, healthier, happier, Khai couldn't tell exactly what had changed, though. "It was the wish that Prime Minister Puar granted me."

"I'm glad for you, and all the other Agents," Khai said sincerely.

"Yeah!" Dah laughed. "And Captain Byyner and Minister Puar let me keep the *Bucket*!"

"So we have a ship, now we just need a destination," Brindee said.

"Which reminds me," Puar cut in. "My brother's coming to see you tomorrow."

"Why?" Khai asked, truly puzzled. He had already granted Khai's wish, bringing Brindee to Seryys.

"I promised I wouldn't tell you, but I can't keep this in!"

"Surprise, surprise," Brix muttered under his breath.

"He's coming to offer you a job heading up a new government outfit, the DFC."

"DFC?"

"Department of First Contact. He wants you to be our liaison to the Vyysarri People and any other new race we encounter."

Everyone erupted in excited chatter of well wishes.

"That's wonderful!" Brindee exclaimed.

"Wow..." Khai said at length. "That's... that's huge." *Purpose,* was all he thought.

"So Khai-" Brix was about ask something when Puar cut him off.

"Shush!" Puar shouted. "My brother's about to speak."

They all turned their attention to the Net'Vyyd. The regular show was interrupted for a special bulletin that would broadcast to every corner of Seryys territory. It had already been released that the Prime Minister was alive and well, and back in office. His chiseled features filled the screen; his eyes were hard and resolute but his smile was filled with kindness and hope.

"My bro looks good up there!" Puar said and was quickly shushed for the speech.

"My fellow Seryysans. Throughout my time here in the Honorifical Office, you have grown accustomed to the way I do things. You know me to be a man of few words, but many actions. Tonight will be something a little new.

"I want to start by thanking everyone for their kind words of encouragement and praise pertaining to my days in captivity. I assure you, I am in perfect health. But I wanted to share a few things about my time as a hostage to a man whom I thought I could trust. Out of respect for his loved ones, I won't drag his name through the mud, but I will tell you that we, the Government of Seryys, have been keeping many things from you...

things that need to be brought out into the light for all to see... things that make me embarrassed to call myself a Seryysan.

"I will be as forthcoming as I can and simply say that I am calling for a truce with the Vyysarri people, an end to a war that has raged on for centuries comes to an end tonight. I have already ordered our entire fleet back to Seryys Space and have sent a message via subspace to the leader of the Vyysarri people requesting an audience with him and his council to sign a treaty that will end this destructive and costly war.

"The fleeting economy will recover as we will not be spending so much of our money on the war machine; taxes will decrease; the Seryys People will become the focus of our great nation once again and we will prosper; and, most importantly, hundreds of thousands of lives will be saved in the process. And hopefully, in time, the Vyysarri People will learn to forgive us and maybe one day, be our allies.

"I close the address with a piece of information that was brought to my attention by a Vyysarri who aided in saving my life. He had every opportunity to take advantage of my vulnerability and didn't. For that, Broon'Kur Broor, I, and the whole nation, owe you the deepest, utmost gratitude. You do your race a great justice with your kindness and courage. To put your life on the line for an enemy shows integrity beyond the boundaries of good and evil, right and wrong. You are a friend to Seryys and are welcome here anytime.

"Now, without further delay, I present the information that was brought to me... the information that changed the way I see the Vyysarri and changed my life forever. I must warn you, though. The images you are about to see are disturbing and I urge you to use discretion with your children. But amid the horror, keep in mind that they had this power, and they never used it..."

The screen blinked to a hauntingly familiar female scientist in a lab coat that Khai recognized immediately. The bruises, scrapes and cuts no less disturbing the umpteenth time around.

"I can't believe they're actually gonna show it," Khai murmured.

"At last..." Sibrex said, raising his chin and closing his eyes, basking in the radiant rays of glory and success.

"This is Doctor Tash'Door Tashar," she said, her voice strained, *"and I am the leading physicist of Operation: Bright Star. If you are viewing this, then the Vyysarri were successful in their mission. This is a warning to the Seryysan People..."*

The End

Author Biography

Raised in the beautiful mountain town of Breckenridge, Colorado, Joe Nicholson now lives with his beautiful California girl and bride, Bonnie, in Northern Colorado. In 2006, he graduated from Adams State College (a small university in Alamosa, Colorado) with a Bachelor's Degree in Music Composition. By day, he's a mild-mannered (yeah, right!) banker and by night, a father, a writer, a musician, a composer, an RPG gamer, a mean video game player and a masked vigilante (not really, but he does own several Superman shirts). He loves Sci-Fi and Fantasy, still reads comic books, has an impressive Star Wars book collection, an unmatched knowledge of Star Wars trivia, has been watching Star Trek since he was in diapers, loves going to the park to read with his wife, HATES sparkly vampires, LOVES Superman, and volunteers every year at StarFest, a Sci-Fi Convention in Denver, Colorado.

DEATH WISH

Acknowledgements

There are so many people that I would like to thank, I could fill ten pages! But I wouldn't get away with that, so I'll be as brief as possible.

First and foremost, my wife, Bonnie: For loving me unconditionally and fully supporting me in all of my passions, whether it be writing, drumming, role-playing or playing video games! My parents, David (1941-2001) and Cindy: For raising me right and always putting up with an ultra-nerdy kid whose imagination was in perpetual motion. My good friend, Linda Foster: For reminding me that hard work and perseverance do pay off and that you can achieve your dreams. My high school English teacher, Mrs. Denise Oaks-Moffett (1958 -2009): For seeing something in me that few teachers took the time to notice, introducing me to great works like, *The Hobbit*, *The Lord of the Rings*, *Beowulf*, *The Odyssey* and *The Iliad*. All of my role-playing buddies (you know who you are): For playing through all the adventures I'd write and always putting up with me when I would say, "Because I'm the DM and I say so!" Malachite Quills: For giving a no-name, fledgling author a time to shine and a chance to advance. And last, but certainly not least, my editor, Kristin Hamm: Who, because of me, now probably has a few grey hairs.

And to all my Readers everywhere: Without your support, I am nothing but a guy with a head full of nonsense!

Thanks,

-Joe

Clockwork Quills presents the sequel, *The Seryys Chronicles: Of Nightmares*:

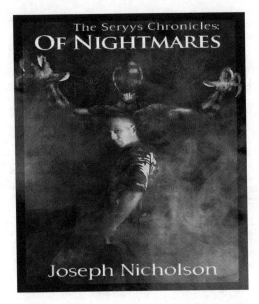

Thanks to the heroic efforts of Khai'Xander Khail and his comrades, a tentative peace now exists between the Seryysans and Vyysarri, with efforts to find the Vyysarri a new home underway. However a routine exploration mission ends in the destruction of a Seryysan ship boasting the first crew of both Vyysarri and Seryysans. Khai and company are forced to make a hasty escape and stumble upon a most intriguing and hugely significant discovery: a rogue planet beleaguered in the void of space.

Meanwhile, anti-integration resistance groups have surfaced that threaten to destroy the hard-won fragile peace between the two races. Things quickly come unraveled as the mysterious leaders of these resistance groups, with vast resources and operatives in every branch of both governments, begin to meddle in affairs.

The efforts of these dissidents set into motion events with catastrophic consequences; events that force Prime Minster Pual'Kin Puar to make the toughest decision any Prime Minister has made in a hundred years; events that force Khai to leave his comatose wife behind to lead a mission to the other side of the galaxy; events that lead to the destruction of an entire Seryysan fleet; events that are truly of nightmares become real...

Clockwork Quills presents the space opera best seller *First Admiral*:

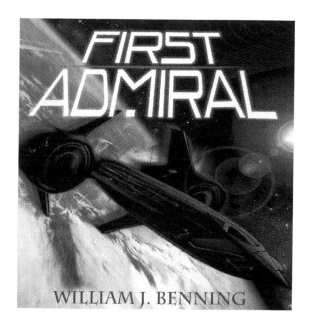

It's not easy being an ordinary teenager leading a hazardous and exciting double life. The Garmaurians, the most advanced species in the universe, wiped themselves out with a bio-weapon in a senseless civil war. And, in a desperate attempt to protect the secret of the potentially dangerous Trion technology - the ability to manipulate the fundamental particle of the universe - their leader sends one last covert mission to Earth. The mission goes horribly wrong, leaving Billy Caudwell; an overweight, acne-scarred 14 year old, with the Mind Profile of a military genius, a huge battle fleet and a mission to unite the intelligent species of the universe in a Universal Alliance. With people to rescue, space fleets to battle and villains to defeat, Billy has to overcome his own inhibitions, insecurities and a vicious bully before he can start saving the universe.

Made in the USA
San Bernardino, CA
14 May 2015